AS
MANY
SOULS
AS
STARS

NATASHA SIEGEL

AS MANY SOULS AS STARS

BLOOMSBURY ★ ARCHER

LONDON · OXFORD · NEW YORK · NEW DELHI · SYDNEY

BLOOMSBURY ARCHER
Bloomsbury Publishing Plc
50 Bedford Square, London, WC1B 3DP, UK
Bloomsbury Publishing Ireland Limited,
29 Earlsfort Terrace, Dublin 2, D02 AY28, Ireland

BLOOMSBURY, BLOOMSBURY ARCHER and the Archer logo
are trademarks of Bloomsbury Publishing Plc

First published in Great Britain 2025

A catalogue record for this book is available from the British Library

ISBN: HB: 978-1-5266-8462-2; TPB: 978-1-5266-8459-2;
EBOOK: 978-1-5266-8461-5

2 4 6 8 10 9 7 5 3 1

Typeset by Integra Software Services Pvt. Ltd.
Printed and bound in Great Britain by Clays Ltd, Elcograf S.p.A

To find out more about our authors and books visit www.bloomsbury.com
and sign up for our newsletters
For product safety related questions contact productsafety@bloomsbury.com

To my dear friends Evangeline, Hannah, and Susie,
for showing me how powerful women can be

Had I as many souls as there be stars,
I'd give them all for Mephistopheles.
—Christopher Marlowe, Doctor Faustus

PROLOGUE

She remembered little of her creation, save that it was painful for all those involved, and that she immediately punished those responsible for it. In hindsight, she had acted rashly, leaving herself with questions that would be forever unanswered—but still, she did not blame herself for it. As she plunged her bloody hands into the frigid waters of the Baltic, her only regret was that she had not taken the time to learn her own name.

Once her skin was clean, there she remained: naked and unflinching, despite the snow that fell listlessly onto her shoulders. The nascent night curled around her waist, curious at this new shadow that seemed somehow deeper, *darker* than the rest. She petted it idly as she stared across the sea, considering the wild chain mail of froth and foam, the glass shards of ice that spun from wave to wave. She was hardly ten minutes old, but she had all the knowledge and wisdom of an ancient evil. That was what her creators had believed her to be, after all. And thus, so it was.

What meagre memories she did have were hazy, indistinct: the ritual with its circle of bone-pale faces; the chanting in an invented language; the acrid scent of burning herbs. Her creators had offered themselves to the shadows, believing their pact would summon a demon—but the demon they had believed in did not exist. The shadows had to birth one for them instead. And so, this *new* shadow, this pact-made creature, had stepped forward and found herself pressing against an intangible barrier. Her feet burnt where they touched something fine and crystalline on the floor. A circle of salt.

One of the men had said, 'We would like to make a deal.'

She had looked at him and smiled with sharp teeth, reaching a hand towards him. Flinching, he had stumbled back. His foot skidded on the ground. Salt scattered, and the circle was broken. Suddenly the barrier between her and her creators was gone; the burning faded. She heard the blood running in their veins and saw the dimpled imperfections of their flesh. She hated them.

They had made her what she was, and she had killed them for it. Death for life. An exchange, just as all magic was, though not the trade they had wanted. And here, standing at the precipice of the ocean, she understood the defining principle of her existence: there was no one else like her. She was alone.

She would always be alone.

High above her, a crow flew, weaving through the air. Delighted by this new creature, and still uncertain of her corporeal form, she seized the shadows and pulled them around herself. Her arms became wings, her mouth a beak. She launched into the sky, flying beside the crow like a mirror image. Further inland unspooled the seething streets of a dying town, a labyrinth of dirt roads, squat stone houses, plague carts rolling from door to door. She soon heard the shrieking, the desperate voices of a thousand unquiet minds: hope and fear, desire and anger, sorrow and regret. She saw a starving woman at a street corner, clutching her child to her chest, desperately imagining deliverance. There was a faint ember glowing at the point the woman's heart would be, a light barely visible. It was her potential, her being, her *soul*.

That light was an absence in the shadow's own self that, once apparent, felt impossible to ignore. She felt the darkness within her as an emptiness, a hunger. And as she saw this stranger's soul, she knew that all she wanted—all she *needed*—was to take it for her own.

Still a crow, she alighted on the street corner and then took human form. She chose the shape of a woman, dark-haired and dark-eyed, a reflection of the person she was watching; but the shadow lacked the fragility of her victim's expression, and the vulnerable hunch of those slender shoulders. Instead, with instinctive curiosity, she sent the shadows forth to seep into the stranger's skull: they brought her back memories, each bright and sweet as berries. The shadow made herself as tall as the man she could see in the stranger's past, the one who had kissed her goodbye that morning before he went to beg for alms at the church gates. She gave herself his clothes, his gait, his heavy eyebrows—becoming an amalgam of the woman and the man whom she loved. In her newborn naivety, the shadow believed this would be pleasing.

The woman watched as she approached, wide-eyed and silent with astonishment. As the gap between them narrowed, the baby squalled.

She was so hungry. They both were. The shadow wished to tear the woman apart, crack her open and feast. But this mortal soul, enclosed within its fragile shell of skin and bone, would only flee if its cage were opened. The shadow instead turned to the principles of her creation; she was a creature of exchange, after all. Blood for blood. Magic for magic.

'Please,' the woman said. 'Do not hurt me.'

'Do not hurt me,' the shadow echoed, delighting in this first creation of sound, in the churning of muscle in her throat and the press of her tongue against her teeth.

'Who are you?' the woman asked.

'Who are you?' the shadow replied.

'Miriam Richter.'

'Miriam Richter.' The shadow liked the name, how it was soft, then sharp, a kiss before a grimace. It seemed another shadow she could slip into. She thought of the words her creators had spoken to her when she was born, and she felt the rightness of them, the potential. She smiled as she said, 'Would you like to make a deal?'

The woman said, 'A deal? What deal?'

And so, the shadow told her.

And so, the pact was made.

That woman was the first. She sold both her soul and her name to the shadow in exchange for relief from her hunger. Eventually, the human would still starve, of course—she had not specified otherwise, in the deal she had made—but that did not matter. She would not feel the emptiness of her belly, even as it hollowed her cheeks and carved furrows in her flesh. She would feel nothing, now her soul was gone.

The woman walked away, nameless and empty-eyed, as the shadow—the *new* Miriam Richter—watched the glowing mote of the mortal soul she had won dance along her fingertips. She placed it on her tongue, and she swallowed. It blazed a comet's trail down her throat, filling her with light. For the first time since she was born, Miriam felt satisfaction.

That woman was the first, but not the last.

Miriam Richter was hungry still.

Part I

Suffolk

1

Cybil Harding was born on Christmas Eve, 1576, under inauspicious stars. Her father had drawn the chart himself; it told him that his daughter was destined for an early death, that she would bring calamity to those she loved and those who loved her. But that was hardly surprising, after all. She was a First Daughter, and a First Daughter was always cursed.

It was clearly laid out in the family grimoire, passed down between generations of Harding witches and written in ink that was no longer blood but might once have been: the firstborn child of each Harding generation would be a witch. But if that witch was a girl, then the grimoire was very clear. No woman could bear the weight of such power. She would be tainted, her magic uncontrollable, bringing disaster to all those around her.

Some would call the Harding inheritance evil, even Satanic. The grimoire spoke of dealings with shadows, a dark bargain made in years forgotten that had traded pieces of each heir's soul for power. But Cybil's father, a witch himself, refused to believe his ancestors would have made such a pact. Christopher Harding, a man of the Renaissance, saw his unusual inheritance as an *angelic* blessing. What else could such magic be but a heavenly gift?

The Hardings were an ancient family—a line that may have once been truly venerable, before the rumours began that they dealt with the dark. They had owned their land since time immemorial, had built their great houses on the same Suffolk hill, over and over, through myriad cycles of destruction: walls of daub and lumber and stone falling to war, flood, and flame; the tenants of their village dying from invasion, plague, and famine; and yet, still, they persevered. Now their walls were brick, they had the favour of Queen Elizabeth, and the village prospered once more after decades of failed harvests.

Christopher Harding had been raised within the fervour of the Reformation. He knew the false idols of stained-glass windows and golden statues; he knew that God's plan, inevitable, ineffable, would never afford such power and prosperity to a family that dealt with the devil. Mayhap his misinformed ancestors had believed otherwise, but now *he* would lead the Hardings down a path of sanctity. With a touch, a chant, he could make lead into gold, sing a storm silent, cause the stars themselves to fade. All 'magic' was an exchange, paying with the light of a soul to command the dark—was this not a form of *conversion*? The spreading of miracles?

To him, the Hardings were nothing less than a line of saints. But if their blessings were biblical, it made sense that—just as Eve herself was tempted—so could little Cybil, squalling red-faced in his arms, someday squander the angels' blessing and tumble into sin. There was only one thing to do with a First Daughter, the act all Harding witches before him had performed when faced with the same problem. He would leave her in the woods for the wolves to take.

Cybil had often wondered why he had not done it. It may have been Christopher's first and final moment of fatherly affection, cradling his child in his arms. It may have been the tearstained and pleading face of her mother, begging him to spare her. It may have been the strength of his faith, that great commandment prohibiting murder. But truthfully—and Cybil knew this well, she spent her whole life knowing it—the only thing that saved the little girl-child was Christopher Harding's hubris. He had heard the wails of his baby and thought, *Here is the final puzzle, the final failing of our bloodline; I shall be the one to solve it.*

Christopher Harding did not leave his First Daughter in the forest. He took her to the ritual table instead, laying a salt circle around her. He lit candles and chanted an incantation, calling upon the Holy Ghost to release her from her sins innate, to rebirth her pure.

4

And—as he did so—Cybil began to glow with a light that Christopher could not consider anything less than holy. Her cries ceased, and she looked at him with eyes lucid and burning.

Once the light had faded, once Cybil slept and the candles had burnt out, he proclaimed the curse cured. It did not matter that he had no proof, that the shadows had swarmed around the edges of the circle and pressed against it, eager and hungry. There was only one thing Christopher Harding feared more than his daughter, and it was the prospect of his own failure. It was the possibility that he was not a saint. It was the realisation that God did not favour him, that the Hardings were witches and their souls damned.

Cybil sometimes wished he had accepted the inevitable and left her to the wolves, after all.

Cybil grew. Cybil learnt to walk, to speak, to fear the darkness that waited for her in the shadowed corners of Harding Hall.

She knew from an early age that her father did not love her. How could he? To acknowledge her, to accept her, would be to accept responsibility for whatever disaster she might cause. He would much rather pretend she did not exist.

Cybil did not seem to have magic, not in the manner he did, but there was something unearthly about her, something alienating. Sometimes, she had more shadows than she should; sometimes, she had none at all. The flames of candles bowed to her. Once, at church, the water in the font began to boil without reason. They stopped going after that. Once she had the words to do so, Cybil told her parents that she saw visions of violence, that she felt phantom pains as if pieces of her were being carved away. Her father told her she was mad. Her father told her not to speak of it, or else she would make her visions reality.

Cybil's only real parent, then, was her mother. Bess Harding loved her daughter. She combed her hair out every night, called her 'my dove', taught Cybil her letters, and read her Aesop's Fables. Together they explored every nook and cranny of the Hall, which had so many rooms and corridors, Cybil felt she could never see them all. With its vaulted ceilings, its pale brick, its sprawling gardens—the Hall was a monument, not a home. It exposed its innards to the surrounding countryside through windows so wide and tall that if Cybil stood before them she would get vertigo, feeling herself falling, tumbling over the edge of the glass to impale herself on the rosebushes below. Bess tried to make it feel friendly, feel familiar: she sang little songs as she carried Cybil from room to room. 'Harding Hall, more glass than wall. Harding Hall, wonders all.'

But meanwhile, outside the safety of the walls, whispers of the cursed girl began to spread through the village.

The Hardings employed only a dozen servants, not quite enough to keep the entire place clean. Solitude was Christopher's preference, and as many rooms in the building were shut up as were used. *His* father had built the Hall to entertain, as a home magnificent enough for a Royal Progress. But Christopher Harding was not a man who wished to entertain. He had a holy calling, and he would not be distracted from it.

Only a dozen servants, then, but enough to notice the child's strangeness. Cybil was too intelligent for a girl, too brazen for a lady, and there were further oddities about her, too: she would sometimes whisper words to people who were not there, pluck and swipe at the air as if fighting something off. When she was only four, one nurse-maid claimed she had seen little Cybil leaking light in her sleep, a glowing substance running down her cheeks like tears. But then she had been dismissed, and the servants spoke of it no more.

By the age of nine, Cybil was fluent in four languages and had yet to make a single friend; at twelve, she had read all of Machiavelli and had found him to be very reasonable; and at thirteen, she was interrupted by her mother in the midst of a virginal recital—performed to an audience of empty chairs—to be told that she ought to be betrothed. When she heard this, all the chairs began to tremble, as if fearing her reaction. Bess smiled tightly and said, 'No fear, my dove. All will be well.'

The next week, Cybil was introduced to the son of a local lord, sixteen and pimpled, with one tooth already rotted from a diet of sweetmeats. The boy's father had come too, and he had taken a lock of Cybil's hair in his hand and grunted in approval, for Cybil had the queen's hair, flaming red, and this was considered beautiful enough to make up for her low forehead and squarish jaw.

The boy spent the entirety of his visit bullying her and trying to peek down her bodice. As the sun set that day, he had shoved her into the garden pond. Cybil, silent and sodden and furious, had stared and stared at him as he laughed and wished that he would *die*. A bough from the oak tree above them cracked and fell on top of him, breaking his neck. Shocked, Cybil stood in the water, skirts pooled around her, hands balled into fists. She did not know whether to laugh or to cry.

'A terrible accident,' Bess had said. 'Oh, how terrible, my dove. Trouble yourself not over it.'

But Cybil's father did not believe it was an accident. He believed it was magic. Not the wild, uncontrolled power of a curse—of course not; to admit as much would be admitting defeat—but perchance something more useful. Perchance Cybil *did* have the powers he and his forefathers laid claim to: not doomed and uncontrollable, but the sort that could be honed and applied—the stuff of miracles, the blessings of a saint. So, for one extraordinary year, Christopher Harding had cared for his daughter. He had permitted her to read from the grimoire. He provided her incantations and elixirs, and showed her strange dances to do around ritual circles, teaching her an alphabet of angel letters that squirmed upon the page like leeches. Then he had taken her to the gardens, standing her before the apple trees in the orchard. 'Break the bough, Cybil,' he would say, watching her with wads of parchment notes crumpled in his fists. 'Break the bough.'

But nothing ever occurred. When Cybil saw the darkness begin to surge beneath her feet like floodwaters swelling across a plain, when she felt the furious, hungry tug of those shadows reaching within her, eager to swallow her whole—Cybil had feared the power too much to allow it purchase. She felt the burning of magic within her, and she made herself douse it. The pain was too much, as if a wound deep within her were being opened anew—and even more so, the *possibility* was too much, the sense that if she gave the darkness what it wanted, she would set the world itself aflame. She closed her eyes and pulled her light within her until it was smothered. She was not a saint—she was a First Daughter. Cybil had seen the grimoire, and she knew the legacy she carried.

Cybil felt the hunger of the shadows; she heard the voices in the dark.

Her father may have believed the curse was gone, but Cybil knew that he was wrong.

Once it was clear his daughter had no talent for magic—or, at least, none that she could control—Christopher ignored her once more.

No more local lords sent their sons for courting. Cybil told herself she did not mind. She had never liked the manner in which young men observed her, as if she were ripe fruit on the turn, as if they wanted to both eat her and throw her away to rot. Better for her to be alone, surrounded by her books and her mother's love, without any distractions within the walls of Harding Hall.

That winter, the winter of her fourteenth year, Cybil's mother bought her a marchpane-and-jam dollhouse for her birthday. It was a reproduction of the Hall: a perfect confection of quince-paste brick, blown-sugar windows, oozing black-red raspberries from its foundations and almond-studded roof. There was even the orchard in miniature, the marchpane trees growing comfits for leaves and fruit: sugar-glazed seeds of fennel and caraway, stained red and orange with beet and turmeric.

Cybil did not like sweet things; she never had. Bess continued to hope she would, for loving sugar was that most basic of childhood traits, a last hope of Cybil's normalcy. So, she pretended to like it, pretended she would eat it later, but then she brought the entire thing down to the servants in the hopes it might make them like her better.

It turned out the jam was tainted. Many fell sick, and one man died—Cybil would never forget his limp face, the manner in which his body had spasmed. 'Terrible,' Bess had said, pale and weeping. Christopher Harding examined the corpse before returning to his study, silent.

The servants had been wary before, but now they were frightened. Although Cybil had never been close with them—she was a lady, it would not have been right—these were among the few faces who were familiar: Mrs Verney, the ruddy three-toothed laundress with a cloud of grey hair, who on occasion had taken pity on her, and listened to her play the virginal; Mr Stapleton, the gardener, who hummed tunes as he trimmed the hedges; even Jane Lennard, a young housemaid the same age as Cybil, who had once smiled at her and complimented her hair. All of them now blanched to see her, turning away after stuttered bows to busy themselves with chores. Jane did not smile at her anymore. Once, she dropped a glass in the same room as Cybil, and apologised so profusely, so fearfully, that she began to cry and had to flee to another room.

Afterwards, Cybil went to her mother.

'She despises me,' Cybil said to her. 'Mother, Jane despises me. What should I do?'

Bess's face collapsed in sympathy and regret.

'My dove,' she replied, 'there is nothing to be done. There is a Great Chain of Being that determines how each of us is born and lives and dies. Jane stands below us on the chain; your father stands higher. We must not worry ourselves with those who live on a different link than ours.'

'What if I wish not to be chained?' Cybil asked.

'You must be,' Bess said.

And Cybil imagined this chain, the Great Chain of Being, wrapping tighter and tighter around her, until her flesh was bruised and she could not breathe.

When Cybil was fourteen, Bess became pregnant once more. A miracle at her age, past forty, with no sign of another child since Cybil. Every morning, the two of them prayed at their private chapel, and every night, Cybil washed her mother's swollen feet and rubbed soothing tinctures into her shoulders, then pressed her ear to Bess's belly to hear the baby move.

'Your little brother,' Bess told her. 'I cannot wait for you to meet him, my dove.'

Cybil told herself, *He will be perfect. We will be happy.*

He was born a week before Cybil's fifteenth birthday. He was born silent and unbreathing, with an extra finger on both hands, and gold-brown eyes the same colour as Cybil's own.

The last time Bess Harding ever left the Hall was to stand over her son's grave as he was buried. After that, she became a different woman. Whenever she tried to pass the threshold, she trembled in fear and turned back. She stopped brushing Cybil's hair, stopped reading to her. She began to have screaming nightmares and fits of terrible, overwhelming grief. After one night when she went to the roof and stood on its edge, Cybil's father had had enough. He brewed a tincture of mandrake and forced it down his wife's throat. Cybil would never forget the manner in which her mother's eyes had gone matt and dark the moment the tincture hit her stomach, a beatific smile spreading across her face.

Bess soon started taking mandrake every day, and Cybil—alongside everything else—was forgotten.

Cybil soon grew accustomed to solitude: her own link on the Chain, iron, unmoving. Each morning, she checked the accounts for her father and brought her mother her mandrake and pottage. Upon her own initiative, Cybil siphoned funds to purchase more books, taught herself Greek and Latin and the basics of mathematics. She even arranged for singing lessons with a music master who was too intimidated by her to tell her she was awful at it. She knew she was awful—she had ears—and sometimes she sang badly on purpose, to see if he would complain, if someone, *anyone* would be honest with her. But still, he never did. And after their lessons were done, she would return to her mother's room to play her the virginal. Sometimes, Bess would even smile when the song was finished.

But on the worst days, the days when her mother refused to even wake up, Cybil could feel the burning again. She would feel a grief that was as much anger as sadness, and as she swallowed her tears and her fury, she could sometimes see a curious light that leaked out of the tips of her fingers and the corners of her eyes. And around her, the darkness would deepen in response, just as the sun at noon casts the starkest shadows: her light made it stronger. The shadows would follow her, form strange shapes on the walls, mime curious plays of grinning devils and screaming women. They would stretch out their hands to her, and, in a trance, Cybil would follow. They would lead her to the orchard, to the stillness of the Suffolk night.

Break the bough, Cybil, they would whisper to her. *Break the bough.* A familiar pain, bright and searing, would build—until Cybil broke from her trance, and realised where she was. She would close her eyes and tell herself, *Enough, enough, douse the flame, enough.*

And so, the bough never broke, except just once: on the evening of her eighteenth birthday. On that day, Cybil stood there for hours in the silence and the rain, and she realised that she had not seen her father for ten days; that her mother had said nothing to her for just as long; and, with a sudden shriek of anger, she lunged at a tree and tugged and clawed and strained until a branch came away in her hands.

The next week, her singing master tried to kiss her. She pushed him away, screaming curses at him. As he scrambled away, he slipped at the top of the stairs and cracked his skull open. The corpse skidded halfway down and laid there sprawled out, feet pointing to the sky. She stood there for too long, watching the blood drip down, down the lower steps, looking into his vacant eyes.

Cybil went to her father to tell him what had happened. Christopher Harding's response was to instruct her—while he was elbow deep in a bowl of powdered antimony—to return the next day, he was busy now, Cybil, couldn't she see he was busy? But it didn't matter in the end; when she returned to the staircase, the body was gone. All that remained was a flickering shadow in the shape of a dead man, twisting its head to look at her and raising its hand to wave.

She received a letter from the singing master's family the next week: he had gone missing on the way back from their last lesson. They knew bandits frequented the path—would the Hardings, in their wisdom and mercy, be willing to make a donation to aid the search?

Cybil made the donation, but there was little doubt after that. Her father's ritual hadn't worked; Cybil was a First Daughter, and Cybil was cursed. The realisation didn't *change* anything, of course. The seasons continued to turn, and Harding Hall—as eternal and stoic as a Saxon rune stone—remained silent upon its hill.

Cybil was alone.

Cybil would always be alone.

2

Three months before Cybil's twenty-third birthday, she was pressing herself against a window on the first floor, watching the fog of her breath stretch across the glass. It was evening, and the sun was setting. In the orchard below, a sparrow flitted from tree to tree. The apples were coming in, despite the unseasonable chill of this year's autumn. Cybil amused herself by pinching her fingers together around each fruit, imagining that she could pluck them in miniature from the branches.

'*Greensleeves was my heart of joy,*' Cybil sang to herself, voice sharper than a knife. She always sang loudly, to see if someone would come and complain; no one ever did. She drew a jagged line in the condensation left on the glass by her breath. '*And who but my Lady Greensleeves?*'

There was movement in the garden. Lifting herself onto her toes, Cybil saw a procession of horses marching down the gravel path.

Visitors. Cybil was so astonished she almost laughed. It had been years since anyone of consequence had stopped at Harding Hall. Her parents had not told her anyone was coming, but then again, why should they? She hadn't seen either of them in days; they ate at different times, in different rooms, and the Hall was large enough that their paths rarely crossed. When she would press her ear to the door of her father's study, she could hear him mumbling in languages she did not understand, and there was an awful smell that seeped from the gap over the threshold: burnt hair and vinegar and salty sea air, as if Christopher had bottled up the ocean then spilled it upon the floor.

One of the horses in the garden whickered. It had heraldry on its saddle: the Harding three-headed hawk, black-eyed, wings outstretched. It was as familiar to Cybil as her own face, a symbol that was carved into every mantel and stained into every window. *Three heads, for past, present, and future,* her mother had once told her. *The Hardings persevere.* Was this a relative, then? She knew there were more members of the family, scattered through England, although few bothered to come to the Hall.

Cybil went back to her chambers, where she painted her lips red with cochineal and put powder on her eyelids. She wrapped her neck in pearls, and studded her fingers with rings. After pulling a few strands of red hair from their pins to frame her lead-white face, she dripped belladonna into her eyes to dilate her pupils. They blew so wide she could hardly see the gold-brown of her irises—could hardly see anything but the pupils themselves, staring back at her, wide and dark as the bottom of a well. The belladonna made her vision cloudy and uncertain. The walls trembled, the glass of the mirror distorting her reflection.

She used two more drops, just in case. When she stood from the mirror, and turned to the door, there was a human-shaped shadow on the wall watching her, cocking its head at an impossible angle.

'Leave,' Cybil snarled. 'I do not want you here.'

It turned its head to the other side.

'Leave,' she said again. She took a pot of cochineal from the dressing table and threw it at the shadow. The pot shattered against the wall, flinging red paint across the tapestry there: a peaceful garden scene of a lady riding a unicorn. The lady now appeared to have suffered a terrible accident.

The shadow, with a distinct petulance, faded away. Shuddering, Cybil left the room.

She had to fetch her mother, had to prepare her for the visitor. But when she knocked on Lady Harding's door, no response came. This was typical. Cybil had had the lock of the door removed years ago, and so it was no trouble to enter the room.

Bess was sitting up on the bed, staring out of the window, the virginal on the mattress in front of her. She was dressed—unusual—and she had even applied paint to her face: a thick layer of white lead, cracking in the creases of her forehead like the impasto of a painting.

'Mother,' Cybil said, 'someone has come calling.'

Bess plucked a discordant note on the virginal.

'Mother,' Cybil said again.

'Yes, I am coming,' Bess told her, pushing the virginal away. She slipped off the mattress—Cybil lurched forward to steady her—and together, they left the room and descended the steps to the foyer.

Her father was standing by the front door, already in conversation with their visitor. He was a tall man, pinch-faced, with dark, greasy hair, and deep lines carved into his forehead—somewhat younger, mayhap, than Cybil's parents. There was something vaguely familiar in his countenance; Cybil had the impression they might have met when she was young.

The stranger paused in his speaking to watch them as they approached. 'Ah. Bess. It has been years, has it not?'

Bess gave him the same distant sort of smile she always used—as if he were standing very far away, a dot on the horizon. 'Gilbert.'

The man's gaze then fixed on Cybil. He had the same gold-brown eyes as her and her father.

He said, 'This is the girl.'

'Yes,' her father replied. 'Cybil, this is Sir Gilbert Harding, your uncle.'

Cybil dropped into a curtsey to hide her confusion. She had known that her father had a younger brother who had taken a position at Court; but she could not recall Gilbert ever visiting the Hall or taking an interest in their affairs.

Sir Gilbert swept her a stiff bow. Afterwards, there was an awkward, expectant silence, which was interrupted only by the bell ringing for supper.

That night, for the first time in years, Cybil ate at the same table as her parents. The cook had reacted to the prospect of visitors with excitement, and there was a vast array of dishes, far more than the four of them could eat: chicken stewed with plums and caraway seeds; red wine spiced with cinnamon; candied roses, so delicate they crumbled to powder when pressed with the blade of a knife. Her parents had known, clearly, that Gilbert was coming. And yet Cybil had not been informed. She did not know if that was a result of ignorance or malice.

Once the plates were cleared and the servants gone, Gilbert said, 'There has been a witch trial in Ipswich.'

Cybil's father looked mildly betrayed. 'This is the reason you came?'

'A witchfinder came to investigate the accusations and found them credible. Four women have been accused of maleficium.'

Maleficium: the legal term for witchcraft. Cybil knew, now, why Gilbert had come. For all his insistence on an angelic origin for his gifts, her father's work often resembled the satanic. Cybil had seen Christopher break the neck of a rabbit then bring it back to life, had watched him stir water and whisper over it until it thickened and reddened into blood. When he had tried to teach Cybil the same, she had felt the darkness reach for her and pushed it away. The rabbit remained dead, and the water remained water.

'These are peasants,' her father said to Gilbert. 'Women, as you say.'

Gilbert replied, 'They had formed a coven. I heard they killed almost an entire herd of cattle. The cows grew great buboes on their feet and could not walk.'

'What a pointless curse,' Cybil said. 'For what cause would anyone bother?'

Bess flinched at the word *curse*, crushing her napkin in her fist.

Gilbert looked at her archly, his face that of a stranger's still, but his familiar eyes as cold as her father's. He replied, 'According to the prosecution, merely for mischief. The farmer said he saw them digging in the field, laying down charms for their magic.'

'So they were judged guilty?'

'Yes. All four are to be hanged.'

Bess crossed herself and whispered, quietly, 'God save their souls.'

'Surely, if they are capable of killing a cattle herd, they could find some manner to escape the execution,' Cybil said. 'If they go to the gallows, would that not prove their innocence?'

Her father clicked his tongue. 'That is not how the authorities see it, Cybil.'

'How *do* they see it, Father?'

He scowled at her, clearly considering the question impertinent.

'Regardless,' Gilbert said, 'none of these women were actually witches; that much is obvious. But they were scolds and gossips. The village wanted to remove them. If not through the courts, it would be done by some other method, and no doubt more cruelly.'

Cybil pictured the women's dangling feet as they hanged. 'More cruel?' she asked. 'How could that be possible?'

Gilbert shrugged. 'At least they had the privilege of a trial.'

Cybil said, 'From what I have heard, once someone is accused of witchcraft, they are as good as dead. In that case, is a trial a privilege, or a pointless delay?'

'That is not something for you to decide,' her father snapped at her. 'Nor discuss, Cybil, in civilised company.'

It was Gilbert who had brought it up; but Cybil fell silent regardless, plucking at the tablecloth.

'The issue remains,' Gilbert said. He steepled his fingers beneath his chin, leaning with both elbows upon the table. There was a sudden earnestness to his expression, perhaps calculated, perhaps not. 'Suspicions are rising, Christopher. We live in a time of fear: Papists at home and abroad; the Crown's succession uncertain. I hardly foresee things will improve. Already I have been questioned in regards to your activities. With our family's reputation…'

Christopher snapped, 'The queen herself granted me funds for my research. We are richer, more protected, than we have ever been.'

'You believe that will save us? Considering what you have done?' Gilbert laughed, coldly and cruelly. He glanced quickly to Cybil, and that glance was an indictment: there was a First Daughter sitting at the table, and he was clearly no more convinced of her father's 'cure' than she was. 'Among the first imprisoned for witchcraft in England was a *duchess*. Merely two years ago, an earl in Scotland was convicted.'

'We are not *witches*, brother. Our family carries a heavenly gift.'

'That has always been your opinion, but that does not mean it is that of others. You have been living in denial for so long, you refuse to see the danger within your very home.' Gilbert did not look again at Cybil; he did not need to. His steepled fingers rippled back and forth in vexation. 'If you had done what I had suggested, we might not be in this position. The curse—'

'Not here,' Christopher barked, and stood up from the table. 'Come. We will speak in private.'

Cybil rose, also. 'But—'

'No,' her father told her, voice thunderous. 'Sit down, girl, and be thankful your insolence has for so long gone unpunished.'

She sat back down.

Her uncle followed Christopher out of the room.

Bess watched them quit the dining hall without comment, then looked back to Cybil. The white paint she had applied to her face, combined with the ashen colour of her hair, made her mother look skeletal and sickly.

Cybil said, 'What does Gilbert suggest Father do? Why has he never before come to Harding Hall?'

There was a glimmer of *something* in her mother's expression— was it fear?—and she said, 'I must rest, Cybil.'

'It is only just past sundown,' Cybil replied. 'Mother, I beg of you. He mentioned the curse. Surely he is referring to me?'

Bess shook her head and laid a bone-coloured hand across her chest. 'I am very tired,' she murmured, voice nearly too faint to hear. 'I will go to bed.'

Bess stood up, then paused.

'Your father cares for us, Cybil,' she said in quiet resignation, her head bowing. 'In his own manner. We are women, and thus we cannot know the burdens of such a man. But we might support him as he carries them himself.'

'You believe love is submission,' Cybil replied. 'If that is so, then how can he ever love you back?'

Bess did not reply. Instead, she turned, head held high, and left the room. Cybil watched her go without protest; it would be futile to press her any further. It was already the longest conversation they had shared in years.

Once she was certain her mother had reached her rooms, Cybil left the dining hall and ascended the main steps. She had climbed this staircase so many times; she had seen a man die here. She knew with great familiarity the echo of her steps upon the marble, the smooth chill of the oak balustrades beneath her hands. The walls of the upstairs corridors were painted blue to resemble the sky, an illusion broken by numerous portraits and tapestries that floated in mismatched scatterings of faces, frames, and fabrics. These portraits, shrouded in the gloom, regarded Cybil with detachment and dismissal, their pale skin and gold eyes mockeries of her own.

A servant had lit the lamps, casting formless patterns of shadow and light across the floor. There was a suit of armour on display at the top of the steps, worn by an ancestor at Bosworth, its helmet plumed with green feathers, its breastplate showing the three-headed hawk in gold. As Cybil reached it, the suit's shadow shuddered, then moved: pointing right, towards Christopher's study.

Cybil took an instinctive step back. 'That way?'

The shadow pointed again, more insistent.

She was wary, but she did as she was bid.

Instead of returning to her chambers, she stopped outside her father's study. The door was closed—it was always closed—but she could hear voices within. The wood of the door was carved with angel markings, the strange, spiralled letters her father used in his rituals. Cybil ignored these, pressing her ear against the door to listen.

'… had listened,' Gilbert was saying.

'It was not an option. I lifted the curse.'

'You *truly* believe that? Christopher, you must see sense. Every time there has been a First Daughter, the house has seen terrible consequences. The last time—'

'That was centuries ago.'

'We nearly went extinct. The pestilence took all but the very woman who had caused their deaths.'

'All England suffered then.'

'And who is to say she did not cause their suffering, too? Our father told us the stories, how shadows followed her and suffering came in their wake.' Gilbert sighed, loudly enough Cybil could hear it through the door. 'I reminded you when she was born what was necessary, and you had not the strength to do it. No—you had not the *humility*. You were so convinced you could resolve it in another manner.'

'I did what I could.'

'You know your measures did not work. If all is well, then why is Cybil not at Court? Why is she not betrothed? It is known that Christopher Harding has a daughter—who, I remind you, is heir to this estate—'

'The queen's law prioritises children over siblings, Gilbert. You know that as well as I. If she has no children, your son will inherit—'

'God's *teeth*, Christopher,' Gilbert spat. 'That is not the issue. You have kept her here her entire life. Of course there are suspicions. People say she must be mad, or diseased. And we both know why she cannot be seen. Now is the time to admit—to yourself, to me, to her—that you did not save her. That you did not save *us*.'

There was a long moment of silence. Cybil heard her own heartbeat, loud and insistent as a war drum.

'You think I know not my own folly?' Christopher said. He sounded defeated. 'After all these years? You think I do not look at her, every day, and know that I failed? She is a *shade*, a shell. She has been since she was a child. The shadows follow her, and her magic manifests only in cruelty. I will always remember... when she was six, she fell into a bramble patch, and her legs were covered in scratches. But still, she did not cry. She just stared at the wounds as the blood dripped onto the ground. And where that blood pooled at her feet, days later, I found a sprig of deadly nightshade—grown from the soil as if it had been there for months.'

Gilbert muttered an oath.

Cybil's father continued. 'I tried to fix her, to transmute her into something purer, but it did not work. I accept, now, that it has not worked. I accept that God has forsaken our family, and we are cursed as you say. And so, I must turn to other solutions.'

'Other solutions?'

'Yes.'

Gilbert's horror was hushed, the words only barely audible. 'You cannot mean…'

'I am using a greater quantity of henbane, and more repetitions of the incantations; it is certain to work.'

'When?' Gilbert asked.

Cybil had never heard such determination in her father's voice. 'Next week. The equinox.'

'I will have returned to Court by then.'

'I know.'

'It is ill-advised,' came Gilbert's answer, his tone sceptical. 'It has been largely accepted such a summoning would require too dear a price.'

'Too dear for some, certainly. But I will pay it. I have no choice.'

'The girl—'

'If this attempt fails,' Christopher said, 'then I shall do what must be done.'

Cybil bit her lip so savagely it bled. Her hand pressed more firmly against the door, the tips of her fingers whitening. The grooves of the angel markings dug furrows into the skin of her palm.

Christopher continued. 'To end the curse, I must become greater than my forefathers, greater than all those who lay claim to magic. I require assistance. The only path to surpassing Faust…'

Cybil stepped back from the door. There was something hot and furious burning in her chest; it grew brighter and brighter, as if she could bring the walls of Harding Hall down with the heat of her anger, and beneath her feet, darkness gathered, the candles on the wall beside her flickering.

I shall do what must be done.

She imagined her father within the study, stooped over his ritual circle—regretting Cybil's birth, regretting her life, regretting he had not killed her while she was too young to fight back. In an instant, she saw all the little cruelties she had endured beneath him: the callousness and dismissal; the disappointment and anger; staring at the tree as he screamed; watching him pour mandrake down her mother's throat. Cybil imagined sending the shadow of the suit of armour into that room, commanding it to swallow him whole, to break his neck, to suck the life from him like marrow from a bone. She felt the fire within her intensify—it was painful; it was glorious, burning and sharp and *alive*. It was almost wonderful enough to bear. Almost.

Desperate, fearful, Cybil reached for the shards of her self-control. She breathed a deep, shuddering breath. She told herself, *Enough, Cybil, enough*. She took that ember of fury in her fist and encased it in ice, layer upon layer of it, making it colder and colder and harder and harder, until her anger was dimmed and the shadows had retreated.

She turned around and walked in a measured pace back to her rooms. At the basin, she scrubbed the paint from her face. The shadow at which she had thrown her cochineal had returned; it had taken a form to mimic the shape of the lady on the tapestry, albeit with a neck long enough to curve like a snake. It watched her as she wiped the water away.

'You wished to warn me,' she said to it. 'You wished me to know what my father was planning.'

The shadow did not react.

Cybil went to the window. Breathing on the glass, she began to draw a symbol in the fog with the tip of her finger, thinking of her father saying, *I shall do what must be done.*

'*Ah, Greensleeves, now farewell, adieu,*' she sang again, not minding that her voice was not beautiful, that it was as distorted as the shadows on the wall. '*To God I pray to prosper thee; for I am still thy lover true…*'

She finished the drawing on the window: it was a noose around her own neck.

Cybil's finger dropped. '*Come once again and love me.*'

3

Miriam heard the call on the equinox.

She was in Constantinople. That morning, a drunk and amorous man had offered her his heart and soul in exchange for a smile. He may have meant it as metaphor—Miriam could never really tell—but she honoured the deal as it was made. Once she had swallowed the soul and sated her hunger, Miriam had not known what to do with the heart, so she had flung it to a stray dog outside. It had gulped it down in two bites and then followed her down the street with a reverent expression, its tongue lolling out of its mouth. Animals typically disliked her, and Miriam had not known how to react. Eventually, she had become irked by its attention, and she had pulled the shadows around her and flown away.

She existed, as she always had, in solitude; a spider makes no conversation with the flies in its web. Miriam could engage in human pleasures such as food and drink and flesh, but temptation was rare, and indulgence rarer still. The centuries grew tedious, but she did not count the years as a person would. She noticed time passing only with conscious effort. Otherwise, there was no difference between a decade and an hour. On occasion she blinked, and weeks would pass.

Miriam measured her existence in deals instead. She was always hungry, and her greatest pleasure remained the fullness consuming a soul gave her: the brighter it burnt, the more intense the satisfaction. And there were always exchanges to be made, because humanity was as hungry as she was, even if that hunger was for other things. She was asked for money, power, magic. Miriam gave her petitioners what they wanted, and she took her rewards happily. She needed them as much as they needed her, after all. All magic was give and take, light for dark. With no light of her own, Miriam needed to take it from others.

Once, utterly overwhelmed by her own inertia, she decided to see how long she could go without consuming a soul. She had lasted three weeks before that howling emptiness howled too loudly and it became difficult to keep corporeal form. When she had finally indulged, she had torn the man apart afterwards, seeking some further shred of soul within him that she could eat. If she were capable of shame, she might have felt shame for it, but she did not. Her experiment had been successful. She knew her limitations now.

And so came the equinox. That evening, the streets of Constantinople were awash with rain and crowded with bodies: spice merchants, printers, prostitutes, carpet sellers—all the rabble were there. The air was thick with the scents of sewage, incense, the cool mist from the Bosphorus. Miriam could sense a thousand deals to be made. She wandered between the people and ignored their curious eyes, accustomed to the scrutiny. She was out of place almost everywhere, having retained the same human form for centuries: a woman taller than most men, with wild dark hair and ink-spill eyes, strolling with all the thoughtless confidence of a lord.

A drunkard stumbled into her. She shoved him into the gutter. Then, as she scrubbed her hand on her sleeve, she suddenly heard a man's voice, as loudly and as clearly as if he were speaking next to her. It was an ardent drone in ill-accented Latin: *Propitiam vos, ut appareat et surgat Mephistophilis, quod tumeraris…*

Miriam paused and cocked her head to listen. It was an attempt at spell work, that much was clear. A call—a hand reaching through the void to offer itself to her. She was impressed. In the past few centuries, many had attempted to find her, but few had actually managed to do so. Other shadows feared her, and they were reluctant to contact her, for fear of her ire; it was rare that someone had enough to offer the darkness in exchange for the task.

She allowed the man to continue for some time, amused by the spell. Despite his efforts, he was failing to actually bring her to him, instead only calling out to her as one might shout for a servant. Miriam was under no obligation to answer. Still, by the time he reached the end of his incantation, her curiosity had moved her. She took a step forward, into the shadows, offering them a scrap of her most recent meal. At the step's beginning, she was in Constantinople; at its end, she was in a darkened room.

It was a study of some sort. The place had a strange, unpleasant smell, like vinegar and incense and burnt hair. To the left of Miriam, a crack in the curtains permitted a stripe of dim, sunset-tinted light, bleeding red on the floor like an injured animal. The room was furnished with a desk, a pair of lit candelabra, bookshelves, and a vast cabinet full of jars; piles of pamphlets and bound manuscripts littered the floor, half covering an ancient rug that had at some point been burnt at its edges. The scent was of sweat and sweet oils, salt water and the faint iron of old blood. The air carried the static crackle of power, both lingering from previous rituals and arising from the current one. There was a man standing over the desk, his hands pressed against the wood, muttering to himself. Miriam had appeared behind him, so she could see only his back.

'*Surgat nobis dicatus, Mephistophilis!*' he cried, with sudden fury. The flames in the candelabra blazed higher, although he did not seem to notice; the bottles on the shelves rattled. He was clearly experienced with magic, but despite the offerings he must have made, his soul remained powerful—one of the brightest Miriam had seen, roaring in his chest like a bonfire. The shadows behind her stretched forward in curiosity, drawn hungrily to his light, and she raised a silent hand to admonish them. They retreated.

There was an extended pause as the man waited for the result of his incantation; then he stooped further, pressing his forehead against the desk. He groaned in defeat.

Miriam stepped forward and made to tap him on the shoulder— but her hand rebounded inches from him, as if hitting an invisible barrier. She glanced down to see a thick line of salt surrounding her feet, and she sneered.

At the sound of her footstep, the man spun around. Seeing Miriam's face, he cried out, flinching away from her with such violence that he fell to the ground.

'Well?' she said, looking down at him.

He crossed himself, which looked rather ridiculous; he had used charcoal, for some reason, to paint the shape of eyes on the backs of his hands. He stuttered, 'I— What— Who are you?'

She raised a brow. 'Who do you think?'

'You are a woman.'

'Not particularly,' Miriam replied. 'But close enough.'

His eyes widened, and he barked in laughter. 'Of course. Of course. The Seed of Eve. Just as the curse... I should have known.'

'The curse?'

'If the first seed is that of Eve, ruin shall take root,' the man babbled. 'The branches of the House of Harding shall wither and fall.'

The man's pupils were pinpoints, and his fingers trembled and twitched as he spoke, clawing at the air. A half-empty bottle was standing on the table. He had taken something, clearly. Miriam stared at him, frowning, as he continued to mutter to himself, scrambling to stand. He was slightly built, fair-haired, mayhap attractive by human standards, quite ugly by hers: desperation and rancour seeped from his face as ichor stains a bandage.

The man cleared his throat, interrupting his own mutterings. 'I— if—I—' He ceased speaking, and he wrung his hands, as if to cleanse himself of the stutter. 'You are Mephistopheles, yes?' he asked, finally. 'The demon of legend?'

Miriam grinned, amused. She had been called many names, and she could not remember all of them; she was as likely to be Mephistopheles, she supposed, as anyone else.

The man took her smile as agreement. 'I wish to make a deal,' he said. 'I require a familiar. You must lend your power to mine.'

Miriam sighed. How *dull*. 'You already have power.'

'Not enough to accomplish what I desire. But were I to use *your* magic...'

'And in exchange? I traffic not in pieces. I would want your soul entirely.'

The man squared his shoulders; he raised his head high upon his neck. There was a new righteousness to his expression, a blazing sort of certainty. 'I am a Harding, chosen and blessed by God. I have tamed you, foul demon, and entrapped you in my circle. If you ever wish for freedom, you must follow my command.'

Miriam glanced down at the salt circle once more. She was trapped, but hubris of this calibre made men gullible. And his zealotry, amusingly, seemed entirely without foundation: his soul was somewhat exceptional, yes, but it had no touch of the divine.

She was not particularly hungry—she had just eaten, after all—but a meal was a meal. And Miriam could amuse herself, could she not? What use was immortality without a little fun?

She widened her eyes, affected awe. 'God and all His saints,' she whispered. 'I see it now—their heavenly presence.'

His answering smile was triumphant. He was obviously deranged. 'I shall not be conquered.'

'Indeed, your soul cannot be mine to reap,' Miriam said, 'as long as the angels enfold you within their arms. Even my Lord, Lucifer, could not defeat such power.'

'You are mine, then? To command as I wish?'

'I swear it,' Miriam replied. 'I shall not take your soul, as long as God protects you. While that is so, I am your servant, sir. These are the laws by which I am bound. Is this amenable to you?'

'It is,' he said. It was enough that Miriam felt the deal slide into place, slither down her spine, and hiss expectantly for its fulfilment. It was curious that people made pacts on such uncertain terms, but they did so constantly.

She stretched out a hand to him. Above her palm, the shadows formed a quill, its tip sharp as a blade.

'You must break the circle to release me,' she said. 'Otherwise, you cannot sign.'

He hesitated for only a moment. The contract was before him, his dream in reach: Miriam knew well the power of pageantry.

Trembling with excitement, the man kicked a section of the salt away. Miriam felt the pressure around her release, and she swallowed a smile.

He took the quill. 'Where?'

'My hand.'

The man seemed uncertain—they usually did—but, obliging, he dug the tip of the quill into Miriam's palm, carving his signature: *Christopher Harding*. Shadows seeped from the open wound and ran down her arm, dripping onto the floor. Miriam watched him, unblinking. She did not feel pain.

He finished his signature. The quill disappeared.

'It is done,' she said. 'The pact is made. I shall take it now.'

'Take what?'

'Your soul,' Miriam said.

'But God protects me.'

She sighed. 'What a pity,' she said, 'that you seem to have misunderstood. If there is a God, Christopher Harding, He cares little for you. And even if He did—I do not answer to Him, now or ever.'

His eyes widened. 'I—'

She reached forward and tore his soul from his body. A meteor trail of light bloomed from his chest before it collapsed into a mote in her palm. The man's gaze became empty, and he swayed on his feet. The deal was complete.

She lifted up the soul to inspect it: an impressive specimen, truly, nearly too bright to look at. Clearly, magic ran in his blood. That was likely the result of another deal, one almost as ancient as that which had made Miriam herself. The shadows recognised the light, and they swarmed around Miriam's hand with an almost tender familiarity.

A shame the man's intelligence had not matched his aptitude for spells. Miriam would have usually left him as he was, to live the rest of his life semi-catatonic, unfeeling and uncaring. But she had been impressed by his efforts, and she was feeling unusually benevolent. With her free hand, she reached forward to break his neck. Dead, he slumped forward against the desk, skull rebounding on the wood.

His soul remained in her hands, and she pressed it to her tongue. When she swallowed, she could feel the fire of it course down her throat, sink into her belly, then radiate outwards to her fingertips; she sighed in satisfaction and swatted irritably at the darkness around her, which was tugging eagerly at her shoulders in hopes of a share of the meal.

Someone knocked on the door. 'Father, it is Cybil,' came a voice.

Stepping back from the desk, Miriam slipped into the shadows, making herself insubstantial. After a moment's pause, the impatient visitor wandered into the room.

The newcomer was a young lady. She was porcelain-skinned, with long hair the startling orange-red of a polished carnelian. She wore a grey gown with an unstarched ruff that draped languidly over her collarbones. Her nose was small and upturned, her eyes large and heavy-lidded, but the remaining architecture of her face had an almost Gothic severity: her jaw cast a shadow over her neck with lines so dark and clean it almost severed her skull from her spine.

But all that paled in comparison to her soul—her *extraordinary* soul—which, even through the prison-bar occlusion of her ribcage, even through the semi-opaque gauze of her skin, glowed so brightly and so intensely, it pressed a bruise onto Miriam's vision. When she glanced away, Miriam could still see the burn of it: the shifting blue-black stain of a self so furious, so powerful, that it could feed her for decades. The soul was so bright that it was leaking light onto the floor; no wonder the shadows followed the young lady so lovingly. On her very heels, the darkness sipped from her magic, whispering, offering itself to her, desperate to trade for more—but she was deaf to its pleas. No one had taught her how to listen.

Some had such souls innately; some had them forged through adversity. Some, like the one she had just eaten, had been enhanced through generational magic. This girl—Cybil—might have been the product of all these things in tandem: a rare and potent brew. Thrumming with excitement, Miriam reached into Cybil's mind, seeking something she could offer to her in a deal. But it was difficult to distinguish anything of clarity there. Her thoughts were freezing to the touch, hard and unforgiving as granite. Miriam could find nothing there, no crack to hook her fingers in and pry apart.

'Father,' Cybil said, 'we have a letter from the Crown. They are demanding their dues, with interest. Did you not pay them this last year?'

The corpse, of course, did not respond.

'Father,' she repeated, this time with an edge of annoyance. 'I did the calculations for you, as I always do. I left the ledger on your desk. What—what are you doing?'

She approached the body and laid a hand on its shoulder. When she was met with only silence, she shook it. The head lolled grotesquely against the desk.

'Oh.' With sudden urgency, Cybil stooped over to listen for breathing, pressing her fingers against the body's neck. But it was a futile endeavour. The corpse's eyes were still open and empty, its swollen tongue protruding from its mouth.

'Oh,' she repeated. She had a high voice that dropped low at the end of each word, like petals wilting. 'Oh, God.'

She released the body and stood up straight. Behind her, one of the candles flickered, and her hair seemed to glow with it. Her father's corpse lay unmoving before her. In the heavy droop of its skull, disconnected from its spine, the body seemed less human, more a ruin: an ancient statue toppled, reduced to rubble.

Cybil's breathing sped up in panic. Her eyes fluttered, and Miriam wondered at the marvellous delicacy of that movement, the tender skin of her lids and the paleness of her lashes. And the light, that *incomparable* light, somehow grew brighter with her distress, seeping from her skin as blood from a wound. And—just as the moon glows only at night—that light seemed to have a tidal pull on the darkness around it. The shadows swarmed, wailed, desperate, ecstatic. They gathered at her feet, draped around her shoulders, drinking from that light like leeches. Miriam felt the pull too, found herself taking a half step forward. She wondered if Cybil's soul was somehow too powerful for her body—if it would detach itself from her of its own volition, shuck off the shackles of mortality, and join Miriam in eternal existence.

And then Cybil closed her eyes. She balled her fists. She pressed her lips thin and measured her breathing, light leaking from her eyes like tears.

'Enough, Cybil,' she whispered. 'Enough.'

And—as a wave pulling back from shore—her soul returned to her body, light fading.

The darkness shuddered in disappointment. Miriam felt a moment of loss, of grief, that was so alien, so powerful, that she nearly forgot her own shape; she plunged halfway into the floor as a pool of shadows, before recalling the necessity of limbs with a feeling approaching shock.

Cybil considered her father for a moment in silence. She glanced briefly at the bottle on the desk; lifted it; sniffed it tentatively. 'Henbane. But—your neck… Did you fall against the desk?'

Reaching forward to shake the body again—assuring herself that he was dead—she bowed her head as she stepped away.

She said, in a whisper, 'You should have left me in the woods when you had the chance.'

Miriam shifted a little closer. Cybil paused, cocking her head, and turned to the corner where Miriam stood.

Miriam herself was in her shadow form: immaterial, invisible, threaded through the darkness. Still, the woman had clearly sensed her presence. She stepped closer to the shadows, eyes narrowing in concentration. Another step. Miriam could see her pulse thrumming beneath the delicate skin of her collarbone.

'Is someone there?' she said.

Miriam wanted to touch her. Cybil's soul may have been trapped, still, but it remained bright—as she approached, it became almost painful to look at. Miriam's eyes prickled, a scaring ache building in her temples. She wanted it. She wanted her. If Cybil had come near enough, Miriam would have put her mouth against that lovely neck and bitten down, such was the desire that overcame her: she would consume every part of her, flesh and skin and bone and soul together. Miriam would lay her down against the floor of this study and plunge her hand into her chest, find the heart beneath her ribs. She wanted to hold it in her fist, feel it pump. She wanted to press her bloody fingers to her parted lips and paint them red as roses.

Cybil took another step forward, so that she stood at the edge of the shadows. She was so close that Miriam could hear her stuttered breaths, could smell the heady incense scent of her perfume and see the flush of her cheeks. Another step—that was all Miriam required—and Cybil would be entirely enveloped in Miriam's embrace.

Miriam could not help herself; she reached out towards Cybil. With her, the shadows extended, and one of the candles snuffed itself out.

Cybil's eyes widened. She stumbled backwards.

'Wait,' Miriam said, forgetting she was still a shadow. The word emerged as a whisper, almost as quiet as the shifting of the air.

Cybil did not wait. Gasping, she took her skirts in her hands, and she fled the room. The door slammed shut behind her. Miriam let out a hiss of frustration; every candle went out, and the henbane bottle on the desk burst into shards of glass.

The shadows swirled slowly in the newfound darkness. Miriam perceived, in their mulish movements, an element of disappointment—an element of recrimination—and she clawed at them, furious, until they were still.

4

They buried her father on the thirtieth of September. An overdose of henbane, an unfortunate fall. That is what Cybil told people—that is what, at first, she told herself. But she knew, as she watched the first cloud of dirt hit the coffin, that her father had died because she had killed him. She had stood before his study and imagined his death, and in doing so she had murdered him, her curse had murdered him; as it had murdered her brother in the womb, and that servant with the jam, and that boy who had come courting. Because Cybil was a First Daughter, and all she could do was destroy.

When Cybil had told her mother, Bess's only response had been to turn away, silent, go into her room, and shut the door. She did not come to the funeral, and so Cybil alone wore the white mourner's hood. Mayhap Bess Harding fully understood that her husband was dead; mayhap she did not. When Cybil brought her mother meals, Bess would not speak. Once, she laid a palm on Cybil's cheek, as if in quiet apology. Somehow that was worse than not being acknowledged at all.

There was a heraldic tapestry in the corridor by the great hall, depicting the family's three-headed hawk; since her father's death, Cybil had slowly been unpicking it, thread by thread, with a helpless sort of obsession—she could not walk past it without pausing to unravel a corner. After that moment, after feeling her mother's hand on her cheek, Cybil had tugged at the threads so long and so viciously that her fingers bled. Were they to grieve this man, who had loved

Cybil enough to spare her, who had hated her enough to regret that mercy? Who had made his wife a hollow shell and called it kindness?

Afterwards, Cybil rinsed the blood away and returned to work, ignoring the press of her wounds against the quill. There was much to be done: the Hall was now Cybil's, and under her father's tenure the building had fallen into much disrepair. There were glaziers and weavers to pay, servants to hire, gardens to tend. There was Christopher's study, the tome-lined shelves, the tinctures and rituals.

There was her mother, sipping her mandrake each morning.

In the days after her father's death, Cybil had often recalled his last conversation with Gilbert. Her uncle had not come to the funeral; mayhap he feared meeting his brother's fate. But when he had been at the Hall, he had asked why Christopher had never sent Cybil to Court. Now, for the first time—as though waking from a dream—Cybil had begun to wonder this herself. If she brought ruin to those she loved, then to Cybil it made sense that she ought to leave her mother and the Hall behind, so they could be safe from the curse. She could break free of this place, with its seething shadows and its empty corridors; she could pretend, if only for a little while, that she was the woman she wanted to be, a wealthy heiress with land and power. She could prove—or perchance pretend—to all of England that she was not mad.

But whenever she imagined this escape, she would then see— more vividly, for it was a memory, not a fantasy—her mother shaking beneath her sheets, and that hand upon her cheek, cold and trembling. For the moment, Cybil could not leave Bess behind, not while she was so swallowed by her grief, while she was insensate with her tinctures and regrets. If Cybil could do right by her, right by the Hall—if she could bring the House of Harding back into repute, wean her mother off her medicine and make her well again—*then* she might be permitted to leave. She would be able to carve a new life for herself, somewhere new, and know that Bess was safe. Until that day, she would read her father's books, and study his rituals, in the hope of finding something that he had missed.

Hope. Sometimes, she woke up in the middle of the night, and she fancied she could see it in the darkness—a glimmer of movement, a pair of eyes watching her. She would reach out for it, desperate, seeking. And sometimes, rarely, it was almost as if it reached back.

The village near Harding Hall was still given to old superstitions and rituals, the most persistent of which was the Hallowtide Dance: a gathering around the old grass mounds that stood between the estate and the village itself. The Harding family had always made an appearance—many of the villagers were their tenants, after all—and this year would be the first time Cybil would go without a chaperone. She had buried her father, and her mother, of course, was refusing to come. Cybil would have preferred to abscond, too; there would be too many eyes there, too many suspicious gazes. But she was mistress of the Hall now. Her presence was required.

It was only a short ride, and Cybil left as the sun was setting. The mounds were to the east. They quickly rose into view once she emerged from the forest, jutting awkwardly upwards on the horizon, like buboes on a plague patient. Cybil knew from her reading that the mounds were actually graves, centuries-old bones resting within their bowels: several of the barrows had already been dug into, gutted of whatever Saxon treasure their trespassers could find. In Henry's time, robbers had dug too deep into one of the mounds, and it had collapsed entirely, burying the thieves alongside their victims. But tradition still considered the mounds faerie work, grass altars erected by inhuman hands. On All Hallows' Eve, a great bonfire was burnt atop the biggest grave. The people of the village danced in a circle around its base, trading stories of hungry spirits. Cybil thought it was ridiculous, but they all seemed to enjoy it well enough.

The dance was an occasion attended by peasant and alderman alike, and Cybil was hardly the only one present with jewels on her fingers. Still, when she dismounted her horse, it was clear she was overdressed. She had declined to wear her mourning hood: she had no need of such displays, and she felt it would merely remind others of the Hardings' misfortune. Instead, she had pinned chips of amber to her hair, and she was wearing a gold gown and a high ruff, pearls stitched into the collar like a collection of polished teeth. Her face was powdered skull-white, her lips bloody with rouge. She looked like a moth with its wings wrapped around itself, or a spool of precious thread. People watched her with as much hostility as fascination; Cybil's family had always had a fearsome reputation, considering her father's occultism. They were never going to adore their landlords, of course, and Cybil could hardly resent them for that—but they had little respect for them, either, and that was due to Christopher's callous mismanagement of the estate, which had led to rising rents and little investment in the land. The village's dislike of Cybil's family had never felt quite so clear as it did now, with the cursed daughter the only Harding present. Despite their higher place on the Great Chain of Being, those below the Hardings had no compunction about craning their necks to sneer at her.

Cybil went to hitch her mount, then returned to the bonfire. She hovered around the edges of the dancers, uncertain what to do. Her father had always handled the conversation, the last few times she had been present.

After a few moments, she was greeted by John Pike and his wife, Nancy, some of the wealthiest people in the village. On occasion, they had come to the Hall as petitioners, although they had always left empty-handed. Cybil recognised them only by the badge on John Pike's hat: the sheep of the local weaver's guild.

Nancy Pike said, frowning, 'Where is your mother, Lady Cybil? Your servants?'

'My mother is indisposed,' Cybil replied, 'and I had no need for servants.'

'We are deeply regretful that Sir Christopher could not be here, my lady. He is sorely missed.'

'Yes. My thanks.'

Her gaze drifted past the Pikes' ruddy faces to watch the children dancing their ring around the barrow base. With the light from the bonfire between them, it was as if two chains of beings were surrounding the mound: some made of light and some of shadow, silhouettes emerging behind their makers to join them in the dance. Their only accompaniment was a stuttered tambourine beat from a grizzled man sitting beneath a nearby tree. His slapdash rhythm was largely ignored by the revellers.

'I heard,' said John Pike, who was always an eager gossip, 'that some churchmen from the town found out about the ritual this evening, and they were calling it popery. They even demanded the dance be done away with. But our Father Lowrey set them right.'

'We are blessed to have such a shepherd in our village,' Nancy said.

They both looked at Cybil expectantly, clearly presuming she would agree.

'Yes,' Cybil replied. 'He... shepherds us. Very much.'

Nancy, lips twitching with opportunistic malice, continued. 'I suppose it has been so long, Lady Cybil, since we saw you and yours at church... Mayhap you cannot recall?'

Cybil snapped her head around to look at them. 'I recall,' she said, voice tight.

'Truly? I believe the last time I saw you for services, you were still a girl.'

'We have a chapel at the Hall.'

'Of course. Strange, still, to even have Christmas services there, and the Holy Week also, away from your tenants.'

'We worship as we will,' Cybil replied. 'As is our right, by the queen's settlement.'

'There is a limit, surely? I fear only for your *soul*, my lady, now you are alone. Your father was always an unorthodox sort—'

'It is *unorthodox* to insult the lady of the manor, when she owns the land you live on,' Cybil returned. She closed her eyes, took a deep breath. 'Forgive me, I... I must attend to—I see a petitioner.'

'Where?'

'In the bonfire.'

'*In* the bonfire?'

'The other side,' she corrected herself, face growing hot. Leaving the gobsmacked Pikes behind, Cybil marched to the other side of the bonfire. By the time she had found another place to stand, she was biting her lip in self-recrimination, hard enough to break skin. *Thicken the ice, Cybil,* she told herself. *Lose not your temper. You are mistress of Harding Hall now.*

By the time she had regained her composure, the dance had ended, and the revellers had broken apart. Some were wandering around the edges of the mound in search of a new partner. Cybil noticed a boy watching her from a few feet away—when her eyes met his, he did not drop his gaze. He was tall, and the heat from the fire made his features shimmer and warp; unlike most of the congregation, who had looked at her with both fear and disdain, his was an expression of bashful awe. He was her age, cherubic, with hair the colour of straw. His cheeks were a little flushed and his eyes wide. When he realised she was looking back, he went even pinker.

Disquieted, Cybil turned her face away. She could still feel the boy's eyes on her.

Unbidden, she was reminded of the lord's son, the manner in which he had leered and laughed. She did not understand why he had done so, nor did she understand this new boy looking at her with such fascination. When Cybil was very young, her mother had sometimes looked at her father like that—back when Bess was well enough to desire something other than mandrake. What was there in him that had made him so compelling, that made Bess so willing to sacrifice her body for his children, her life at Court for Harding Hall? Cybil had never felt attraction to anyone; to her, it seemed attraction was a form of obligation, and she had no interest in accruing a debt.

Shouts rose from some of the villagers further afield, and Cybil saw that a group of riders were approaching the mound. As the group pulled their mounts to a halt, Cybil could see the reason the others had been so unsettled. There were ten men, all mounted and dressed in military cassocks, with swords at their hips. At their head was an older man with thinning grey hair and jaundiced skin. His bloodless, spherical face bore an expression of such intense scorn that Cybil took a reflexive step back. The crowd fell into a tense silence.

'Good evening,' said the man, his voice loud and low. 'My name is Henry Martingale, and I have been sent here by the council at Ipswich. There has been an inquiry launched into the spread of heathenism and witchery within the counties. It is the council's command that this gathering cease at once, and—'

Immediately, the crowd fell to booing and yelling at the man, their anger drowning out the rest of his sentence. He raised his hand to silence them, to little avail; then one of his men drew the sword at his hip. The glint of its blade in the firelight sliced through the noise, leaving everyone in a sudden, contemptuous silence.

A witchfinder. Cybil felt ice slide down her spine. Had Gilbert not warned them of this? That questions were already being asked? Now the hunters were here, dogs sniffing at their doorstep. And Cybil, complacent, uncaring, had been busying herself with books and dances. She ought to have known better. Was she not mistress of Harding Hall now? Had she buried her sense with her father?

'As I was *saying*,' Martingale snapped, 'it is the command of the council, and through the council, the Crown itself. These superstitions are doors for devilry and popery, which our good land should soon cast out.'

At this there was another great hubbub of discontentment. *This man is a fool*, Cybil thought, with a little relief. Such arguments may have succeeded in London, or even Ipswich—but this was an ancient village, and its traditions, passed down through generations, were held dear by those who lived there. To suggest that the dance was connected to witchcraft or popery would be seen as slander at best; at worst, it was an attempt by a stranger, a town dweller, to undermine the very fabric of the community.

Martingale swatted the villagers' complaints away, as if they were flies buzzing about his ears. 'I am a witchfinder, and I know well what such things lead to. In the town, I saw a man struck dead by witchery; I saw his limbs go black like burnt tinder, his tongue fall away, his eyes rot in his skull. Would you, good people, invite the same?'

There was a pause, then, as the crowd fell silent. Cybil felt as if some of the villagers were now staring at her, and she thought briefly of her father's corpse, how his tongue had jutted out of his lips in death as an oyster slips from its shell. She recalled how the shadows had seemed to reach for her after, as if they wished to swallow her whole; and she wondered how the witchfinder would have reacted if he had seen that, also.

'Good,' Martingale said. 'I am glad we are in accord. Now, then, if we return orderly to our homes—'

Someone threw a rock at him. It was but a small pebble, but as it glanced across his shoulder, he reared back as if shot. The crowd fell deathly silent.

'Who threw that?!' Martingale cawed, his voice rising dramatically in pitch.

Laughter erupted in response. Red with fury, he raised his hand again, gesturing to his men; more swords were drawn. 'Disperse at once!' he cried. 'I have the council's authority!'

The crowd seemed little inclined to disperse. Cybil cast them a wary glance, and then looked back at Martingale. If something was not done, the scene would soon turn into a riot. She did not wish to draw attention to herself, but it was likely the witchfinder already knew who she was, by name if not by face. And it was her obligation, as lady of the manor, to respond. If she did not show fear, then perchance it would demonstrate to Martingale her innocence—or, at least, her strength.

She stepped forward and started walking towards the men. The villagers parted for her, murmuring uncertainly among themselves, creating a path so that she could approach the lead horse. Martingale looked at her, and as she neared him, some of his confidence began to fade; he could now see the richness of her clothing, the pearls at her neck, the sternness of her expression.

'Good evening, mistress,' he said, shifting uncomfortably in his saddle.

'My lady,' she corrected him. 'I am Cybil Harding, lady of Harding Hall. You said you are a witchfinder?'

'I—I am.'

'And what authority does that title grant you?' she asked. 'Are you sheriff? May you make arrests without evidence?'

'The council in Ipswich—'

'Does the council ride with you?' she demanded, gesturing to the men behind him. 'Have you any *proof*, sir? Do you carry their seal?'

He spluttered. 'N-not on this occasion, no.'

There were mutterings from the crowd at this. Invigorated, Cybil continued. 'My father was once alchemist to the queen herself. Shall I write to Court, perchance, and tell them that at the first festival I have attended since my mourning was ended, after I spent weeks praying for my father's soul, a *witchfinder* from Ipswich ordered me to *go home*?'

It was an absurd and empty threat, but Cybil spoke with such certainty that Martingale blanched, and even his guards looked a little nervous. 'My lady, I meant no offence,' he replied.

'And yet, I am offended.'

He bowed his head. 'I beg your pardon,' he said, through gritted teeth. 'But it remains that this gathering—as benign as it may seem— could be repurposed with mal-intent. This is a pagan ritual, disguised as a godly one, and I am obliged to—'

Another rock was thrown. This time, the perpetrator was clear: it was the old man whose drum had accompanied the dancers. He held his tambourine in one hand, and the other was raised in the aftermath of the stone's throw. He implicated himself further by yelling a garbled stream of local dialect at the witchfinder, including a number of colourful curses, all accompanied by a gesture so obscene Cybil could not help but giggle. She tried to hide her laughter behind her palm; she failed, and Martingale gave her a disgusted look. He turned back to his guards, gesturing toward the old man. The guards slipped off their horses and reached for their swords.

Martingale might have thought this would cow the villagers into submission, but most of them were drunk, and those who were not had been buoyed by the old man's defiance. The crowd quickly became a rabble, shouting curses at the witchfinder. Someone threw another stone, and soon pebbles and rocks were flying in a tempest through the air. Cybil made to the side of the crowd, covering her head with her arms.

She thought, *They are going to get themselves killed.*

She looked back at Martingale, still sitting on his horse. He had dropped the reins, his arms flung up to cover his face and shield it from the pebbles. The solution to the problem seemed clear enough. Cybil wove around the edge of the crowd and gave his horse a sharp tap on the rump. It was already skittish from the stones, and it squealed loudly before taking off.

Martingale made a desperate grab for the reins, and he narrowly avoided being flung from his mount as it swerved away from the mound. Still, he was so shocked that he shrieked like a child. This alerted his guards, who dove for their own horses, fearful that they might bolt, also. Those who were fast enough leapt onto their mounts and chased after Martingale. Cybil felt triumph burning in her throat and fingers; she had not realised that she could feel this way, feel powerful, feel *useful*—

But the rabble were throwing dirt and stones after the horses and their riders. Cybil—who was now standing in the place where Martingale had just been—was hit in the face by a large clod of mud, intended for the now-absent witchfinder.

All was suddenly and terribly silent. Cybil could feel mud dripping from her cheek and running in rivulets down her neck. It pooled in the folds of her ruff and clung to her pinned-up hair. She went to wipe some away. There was a small pebble embedded in the dirt, and it scraped against her skin, scratching it. She winced in pain.

They were all watching her, none speaking.

There was no acknowledgement of what she had done, driving the guards and Martingale away. Cybil was standing there in her silks and her pearls, dirty and humiliated. What a fool she must have looked. She rubbed again at her face, her palm going brown with mud as she did so.

The silent shock of the crowd was somehow worse than if they had laughed. Many seemed more contemptuous than pitying. One woman, sneering, made a sign to ward away evil; Cybil did not know if it was in response to Martingale or to her.

'Lady Cybil...' a woman said, stepping out from the crowd. She was dark-haired, her face gentle if slightly afraid—Jane Lennard, the housemaid. Of course she would be here: they all would, all the servants—Cybil had released them for the festival. And this realisation, somehow, was the most awful of all.

Cybil felt her eyes prickle. She understood, with shame and astonishment, that she was near to tears.

Shoving her way through the crowd, she walked away from the mound. They all turned to watch her leave. She dragged her fingers through her hair, scooping away mud and detritus, flinging it to the ground. A single, traitorous tear managed to escape before she was able to control herself. It carved a canyon through the dirt and lead paint on her face, a burning trail in contrast to the coolness of the air.

It does not matter, it does not matter, it does not matter, she thought. *It does not—it does not—it does not—*

In her wake, the crowd remained silent.

Cybil ignored them. She kept walking until she reached the hitching post; then she paused and cursed beneath her breath, another set of tears welling. Her horse was gone.

Clearly, she had not tied the hitch securely enough. But Charmeuse was Cybil's favourite palfrey, and usually as loyal as any horse could be. She would not have gone far. Cybil swallowed the scream building in her throat and tramped into the woods. *Once I find her,* she thought, *I shall unlace my stays and ride like a man back to the Hall, and never come to one of these thrice-damned dances again.*

5

Cybil's horse had been utterly terrified of Miriam—as most animals were—and so, once Miriam had untied the rope, the beast had bolted into the trees. She followed its trail languidly, shifting between shadows; when she had found a suitable clearing, she stopped, and melded with the darkness.

For weeks, Miriam had followed Cybil with great interest. She had watched her as shadows in corridors, as a crow in the shade of an apple tree, as a distant silhouette in the October mist. If Cybil knew she was present, she never acknowledged it, although sometimes—in her furtive movements as she drew the curtains of her windows closed, or in the determined slamming of a front door—it had seemed that some part of Cybil realised, somehow, that she was being observed. There had been a *single* moment—only a moment— in which Cybil had sat before the dark wood panelling of the Harding chapel as the sun set. Dust motes had danced in the air before her, tinted a faint pink by the stained-glass window behind her, which depicted a saint bleeding from his neck. But Cybil had ignored this performance. Staring straight ahead, almost unblinking, Miriam had seen in the wide-pupiled vacancy of her eyes a sort of isolation Miriam had found uncannily familiar.

Then the shadows had swarmed beneath Cybil's feet, hissing and hungry. Cybil had bared her teeth like a wild animal, nearing a snarl. And Miriam had marvelled at this creature: this frightened, furious girl, who was too human to embrace the shadows, but not quite human enough to push them away.

She is alone in this world, Miriam had realised. *Unique. Near as much, mayhap, as I am.*

Although loneliness was not a notion Miriam was particularly intimate with, she still was familiar with the human desire for companionship. Love had given her just as many souls as greed had. For every supplicant seeking their fortune, there was another who wished to mend their heartbreak. And now, on this night—that night of all nights, All Hallows' Eve—it seemed as good a time as any for her to offer Cybil respite. It was a moment of vulnerability: Miriam had seen the horror and shame and grief in Cybil's expression as the crowd had stared at her. This was a woman desperate for acceptance, and desperate for connection.

The power Miriam could trade would offer Cybil so many things: it could make her loved, more than anyone else on earth, adored and respected and admired; it could remove her loneliness entirely, excise the emotion from her as one would an abscess, and make that veneer of callousness a reality; or Miriam *herself* could even provide the company Cybil craved. Christopher Harding had desired a servant, after all. Miriam could be that servant to his daughter instead: spend the decades watching that searing soul burn until it had almost snuffed itself out. It had been so long since she had truly savoured a meal. Miriam's hunger howled just to think of it.

The shadows, impatient, curled around her fingers. She held them close. *Soon,* she told them. *Soon.*

Cybil entered the clearing. She had scrubbed her face clean of paint and dirt; her skin was bare and blotchy from friction. The moonlight cast a grey pall over her. The only colours visible were the violent blaze of her red hair and the white-gold glow of her soul in her chest. The metallic threads in her bodice and the pins in her hair glinted faintly as she moved. Her step was not graceful, Miriam noted—more a stomp than anything else—but the manner in which her long, slim fingers trailed at her sides had a certain ethereal elegance, as did the faint tinge of blood at her thumbs, mayhap the result of a nervous picking at the skin.

'Charmeuse!' Cybil called. And then again, 'Charmeuse!'

She took another step forward, stumbling over an upturned log. She cursed. 'Hell's bells, this night is *abominable...*'

Miriam sank further into the darkness, shuddering with anticipation. Soon, she would make herself known, but something was lacking. She dredged up a piece of some long-swallowed soul and offered it to the shadows. 'Clouds,' she whispered to them. 'Pull them near. A *storm*, we must have a storm.'

Cybil would look magnificent, Miriam thought, in the furious wind, with her hair flying and terror in her eyes. But the shadows did not understand the significance of the moment, or the artistry behind Miriam's request. They were reluctant to distance themselves from Cybil, ravenous as they were. They writhed in complaint, even as they took Miriam's offering from her. Furious at their insolence, Miriam snarled at them with animal fury. In the clearing, Cybil heard the noise. She gasped and froze in shock.

The shadows trembled in fear and contrition. Miriam hissed, 'A *storm*,' once more, and within moments the bright coin of the moon had been tarnished by clouds.

The wind whipped through the clearing, tearing the pins from Cybil's hair, sending them glinting through the air like fireflies. She curled her arms around herself, face twisting with fear.

Oh, poor darling, Miriam thought.

'Is someone there?' Cybil called, and Miriam laughed. Her laughter echoed through the trees, multiplying itself. Cybil gasped again and made the sign of the cross.

Miriam stepped forward.

Across the clearing, a figure stood between two trees. The light was dim enough that Cybil could see very little, except that the silhouette was feminine: it was wearing a gown of some sort, and a ruff that stretched high above its head.

She had heard the howling of a wolf—had she not? And where were the moon and stars? It was so dark. It had been a clear night before, but now she was half blind.

'Hello?' Cybil said, but the wind stole her voice from her and tossed it away.

The figure came closer. It was a woman, tall and imposing. Despite the darkness, the shadows somehow failed to obscure her, and her features were clear. She had a handsome, fierce face, with an aquiline nose, square chin, and high cheekbones. Her thick tangle of dark hair shivered in the wind. There was a mole on her right cheek, and another on the left side of her jaw: a pair of pins keeping her skin taut, stretching it like canvas over her skull.

When their eyes met, the woman smiled at Cybil. Then her features rearranged into something more aggressive, mayhap even predatory. Behind her, thunder cried out, and a fork of lightning sliced through the sky. Something instinctive and terrified took root in Cybil's chest. She wished to turn, to flee, but she found herself unable to move.

'The storm suits you,' the woman said. 'Like this, my dear—without all that paint on your face, battered and bruised—you burn brightly enough to set this forest alight.'

Her voice was low, accented with some foreign, rolling tone that Cybil did not recognise; although her voice was not loud, it was clearly audible. Cybil had never encountered speech so tangible, speech that seemed to reach out and press against her in its demand to be heard.

Cybil took a small step back. Wind shook her skirts and rustled the autumn leaves on the ground, crisp with frost. As Cybil stepped on them, they snapped like breaking bones.

'Who are you?' she asked.

'My name is Richter,' she said. 'Miriam Richter.'

'Did you steal my horse?' Cybil asked, trying to keep her voice level. 'If you return her now, I shall not tell.'

Richter chuckled and swooped forward, taking a lunging, open-armed step that felt distinctly animalistic in character. Cybil recoiled.

'You need not fear me, Cybil,' Richter said. 'Others have been cruel to you, I know, but I am not like them. I am different. I can aid you.'

'I do not require your aid,' Cybil replied.

Richter's lips twitched—either with amusement or irritation. 'Oh?'

Cybil took another step back, and Richter followed.

'Leave me alone,' Cybil said.

Thunder crashed again, but still, there was no rain.

'Is that truly what you desire?' Richter asked. 'To return to your constant solitude? Another night in that echoing house, with only the dark for company?'

'It is no business of yours what company I keep.'

'And yet you wear your loneliness as clearly as a scar.'

Cybil drew a shuddering breath. 'What is it you require from me? There must be some cause for this ambush.'

Richter raised a brow. 'I thought to handle you delicately. Mayhap that was misguided.'

Then, suddenly, she was close, too close: only an arm's length away. Her fingers, long and slender and sharp-nailed, reached out to draw a line down Cybil's jaw. Her touch was cool and firm—it did not hurt, but Cybil felt as if it would leave bruises, all the same—and her breath, as it ghosted between them, smelt curiously of petrichor and autumn air.

Cybil should have pulled away, but it was as if she were frozen in place. There was magic here, that was certain. 'You are a witch.'

'A witch?' Richter's voice was coolly amused, but she wound her hand into Cybil's hair with a vindictive strength, moving too quickly for Cybil to shy away. Richter tightened her grip just enough for it to sting, and Cybil felt a spark of fear and traitorous pleasure trail down her spine. 'Is that what you think?'

Cybil asked, pulse thundering, 'What else could you possibly be?'

'Hm.' Richter tugged her hair so that Cybil's head tipped back, and their eyes met. 'I am better described by what I am *not*, than what I am. A shadow is nothing but an absence of light; I deal in desire, and desire only happens when there is something someone lacks.'

'What is it you think I lack?'

She leaned in close to her, their lips brushing, and whispered, 'Acceptance. Understanding. *Love*. I can give all you those things.'

Cybil pushed her away. Richter allowed it, releasing her hair from her grip.

'I do not *require* your *love*,' Cybil said. 'And I am not so foolish as to entertain someone—*something*—like you.'

The wind roared, the trees shook; lightning cracked the sky in half. For a moment, Richter somehow blurred, becoming only an impression of darkness—then, abruptly, she was human again.

'You are stubborn,' she said. 'I ought to have expected that. I saw you picking that tapestry apart, blood dripping like garnets from your fingers, eyes filling with tears—but still, you continued, until the blood had dried and you were numb to the pain.'

'Have you been *watching* me?'

She gave her a pitying look. 'Oh, darling. Of course I have.'

Cybil, attempting to hide her trembling, turned around and began to walk away.

'Your mother will never thank you for your love of her, you know,' Richter called. Cybil paused. 'Just as your father never thanked you, either. To them you were and always will be a burden, one who must atone for her very existence. And the villagers, too—what you did for them, scaring Martingale away. Why do you give so much to these people, when they offer you nothing in return?'

Cybil spun back to her, eyes blazing. 'What else do I have?' she demanded. 'What else has the world given me? I might be as lonely as you say, Mistress Richter—I know not how long you have watched me for, but I am certain it was evident. Still, I will not quit this place until I am certain I am not needed. I must know that I have tried. That I have *reached* for something, even if it has remained out of my grasp.'

Richter stared at her, and Cybil stared back. The air between them writhed like a trapped animal.

'It is extraordinary,' Richter said. 'Your light.'

'Pardon?'

'Your *light*,' she repeated, and there was something hungry in her voice, a fevered sort of excitement. 'It is like nothing I have ever seen. And that is a blessing, Cybil. The more beautiful something is, the more beautiful its ruin.' Richter was suddenly in front of her, somehow, even though it seemed she had not moved. When she spoke this time, her voice was coaxing, seductive. 'Such a rare thing should be treasured. I ought to have been more... gentle. I can offer you a deal—'

'There is nothing on God's earth you could offer me, Mistress Richter, that would compel me to deal with you.'

Richter shook her head. 'There is nothing of God here. You know that as well as I do. You have seen how the darkness follows you. You are *leaking* power, feeding the shadows parts of yourself without even knowing. And these people around you, who are so cruel and so frightened—they sense this, and they shy away. Do you not desire freedom from that? Freedom from their fear?'

'I...' Disarmed, Cybil shook her head. 'I would not call it power.'

'You deny your own magic?'

'It is not magic, it is—it is a curse. It *kills* people.' Cybil hissed a breath through her teeth. 'No matter. I know not who you are, *what* you are, but I will not listen to more of this. I shall find Charmeuse, and then shall return to the Hall.'

Cybil made to shove past her. Richter caught her at the waist and tugged her back with an iron grip. Cybil found herself trapped in the circle of her arms, back pressed against Richter's chest, a mouth hovering over her neck.

'A curse?' Richter murmured, her breath cool against Cybil's skin. 'How fascinating.'

'Release me.' Cybil squirmed against her grip.

'If I could remove this... curse—would you consider my offer?'

Cybil stopped moving. 'I am a First Daughter, the Seed of Eve. My family has been cursed for centuries. You could end it?'

Richter inclined her head.

'... What would you want from me, in exchange?'

'*You,*' Richter said, and Cybil shuddered at the naked desire in her voice. 'I want you, Cybil. I have from the moment I first saw you. I wish to consume you, piece by piece; and I will give you anything you desire, anything you can imagine, in order to do so.'

'You could truly remove the curse? From *me*, not only my bloodline?'

'I am made of darkness itself. If there is a curse, I can end it.'

For a moment—a brief, agonising moment—Cybil imagined it: imagined living without fear of loving, without fear of *being* loved. She thought of her mother running the comb through her hair when she was a little girl, humming songs beneath her breath—before her brother's death, when Cybil began to understand that her curse could not only summon shadows but end lives. There were times when Cybil wished for nothing more than to return to that childhood peace: when the world's monsters were in stories and shadows, not the mirror on the wall.

But those moments were gone now, and there was no reclaiming them. Her father was dead, her baby brother the same, her mother a shell of herself. Cybil would spend her life picking up the pieces of the things she had broken. That was her obligation, her repentance. If her father could not absolve her, why would this stranger be able to?

'Release me,' Cybil said once more.

Richter's arms tightened around her. She ghosted her mouth across Cybil's jaw, drawing teeth against her skin—it felt like the kiss of a blade, nearly sharp enough to cut. 'Know this, Cybil Harding: you might try to hide from me, you might try to deny me, but we are light and darkness, you and I. There is no choice. Eventually, one of us must destroy the other.'

'I will never permit you to destroy me,' Cybil said.

Richter laughed, low and deep. 'You shall,' she replied. 'One day, you shall beg me to.'

She released her. Cybil stumbled forwards.

'Think upon my offer,' Richter said. 'I shall await you.'

Cybil turned around to refuse her—to scream at her, to curse at her, to tell her to leave—but such protests were unnecessary.

Richter was already gone.

6

Cybil found Charmeuse nearby, trembling at the storm, eyes rolling wildly with confusion; she had to lead her back by the reins, knowing that if she tried to mount her, the horse was likely to bolt.

At Harding Hall, Cybil went to her bedchamber and undressed, shucking her silks and pearls from her body, discarding them on the ground like peeled potato skins. Then she changed into her night-shift and wandered the Hall: attempting to take comfort, perchance, in its familiarity. But this night, the corridors and yawning windows of her childhood seemed cruel, not kind. In the Long Gallery, eight enormous windows greeted partly faded tapestries with a starlit gloom—the faces of Troilus and Criseyde changed from lovers to ghouls, grinning at each other with drooping woollen mouths. The windows looked out onto the gardens. Cybil peered into the dark at the empty aviary, its gates open and shuddering in the wind.

When Cybil had been small, she and her mother had often visited the aviary to see the brightly coloured birds her grandparents had purchased from abroad. Bess had even talked of purchasing a peacock from the East Indies, a bird she had described to a delighted younger Cybil as a mythical beast: a purple swan with a fan of eyes, the emperor of all creatures, God's own hand upon the earth. But then Bess had become unwell, and the peacock was abandoned, and Cybil's father had emptied the aviary of its songbirds to use them in his rituals.

She went to the aviary now, clutching a lantern. Behind the bars of the half-open gate, there was only darkness, the stink of rotting

rushes and stagnant water. Then there was a flutter—a movement—
and Cybil thought there might have been a bird within, after all. Then
a great rush of shadows burst out, a half-shapeless mass of wings and
whispering voices she could not understand. Cybil cowered, covering
her head with her arms, dropping her lantern to the ground. The light
went out. She waited there until she was certain the shadows were
gone, and then, gasping and half blind, she stumbled back into the
Hall.

Cybil went to bed. In her dreams, there was a woman reaching
out to her. She had uncertain features, a shadow of a shadow—Cybil
reached out to take her hand, but she could never quite stretch far
enough, could never quite grasp it.

'*For I am now thy lover true,*' the woman sang, and her voice echoed
in a chorus: '*Come once again and love me.*'

Cybil woke up bathed in sweat, lying on top of the covers. The dawn
sun laid a gentle hand over her thighs. She turned her head toward
the window to find that she had left the curtains open. A crow was sat
on the sill outside, staring at her through the glass.

She stood. The crow flew away.

Unnerved, Cybil splashed her face in the basin, then scrubbed the
rest of herself with cold water until she felt new and raw. Once she
was dressed, she ventured into the Hall.

Cybil went to Bess's door. Knocking, she called, 'Mother?' quite
gently, and then more loudly when there was no response.

There was only silence. 'Mother,' Cybil repeated, 'will you not come
to the dining hall for breakfast?'

After a long pause, Bess replied, with a reedy, thin voice, hardly
audible through the door, 'I am tired, Cybil.'

'Then I shall bring you your bowl as always.'

No response came.

Cybil stepped away. Something swelled in her throat, something
aching and bitter. She swallowed it down.

She ate in solitude at the dining table, with only the great portrait
hung above the table for companionship. It depicted an ancestral
Sir Harding who had led armies at Bosworth. Cybil imagined him

emerging from the painting and sitting across the table from her, and then she imagined him another man entirely: a vague visage of curling hair and dark eyes, who called her 'dear wife' and danced with her at Court. Cybil took a curious delight in this image. She had never much considered marriage before, but then she had never met such a man as she pictured now, so different from her father or the gardener or the villagers. She knew little of Court, save that it was grand and rich and full of people; that they had extraordinary feasts and pageants and hunts. Mayhap it had been a lie, but Bess had once told her that the queen had called for a tiger all the way from Cathay, and had it released near her lodge so that she could hunt it down. Cybil imagined now riding beside all the ladies of the Court, the wind whipping through her hair; the freedom of it and the joy, hearing the tiger roar in the distance and knowing that such a beast could be conquered. She and her husband would peel away from the others, find a clearing somewhere, and speak words of love beneath the sun. He would take her in his arms and press his mouth to her neck. *I want you*, he would say. *I have wanted you from the moment I first saw you—*

Cybil pushed the image from her mind, horrified. She finished her breakfast, stomach churning, and then made her way to the study.

She always prepared her mother's pottage herself, and served her, also—the mandrake tincture was too dangerous to leave in the hands of a servant. On occasion, she found that Jane or another housemaid had attempted to bring Bess food on their own initiative. Cybil would reprimand them until she was certain they would not do so again, despite her guilt at the fear upon their faces. They did not understand—to give Bess food without the tincture, to cut off her supply that immediately, was very likely to kill her. Her father had made that clear enough to Cybil each time she had asked him to stop drugging Bess; and she believed it, seeing how sick Bess had become whenever doses were delayed.

Since Christopher had died, Cybil had been using the tincture he had left behind. Each time she added it to the food, she lessened the dosage, just enough that her mother might not notice the change. Eventually, she might wean her off it entirely, bring Bess back to sanity, and thus make her dreams of leaving for Court a reality.

Apart from Cybil's occasional visits, the study had remained untouched since Christopher's death. The books on his shelves were beautiful: all gilt pages and tooled-leather bindings. Before, Cybil had not been permitted to look at them, but there was no one to stop her now. She had time before her mother required feeding, so she idly flipped through instructions on alchemy, how to call on angels and summon demons. Circles of salt, pacts of blood. Cybil had attempted some of these rituals before, but they had always failed. The shadows had gathered, that burning pain had begun, and she had been too cowardly to continue.

Cybil retrieved the family grimoire from a locked drawer of the desk. It was bound in black leather, the cover embossed with the omnipresent Harding three-headed hawk. Early pages were written in a curious, primitive form of English, almost impossible for her to parse, all vowels and unfamiliar letters—but some passages had more modern translations scribbled in the margins or pasted in on additional scraps of parchment. One page was particularly well thumbed. It had a translation pasted beside it in her father's handwriting.

If the first seed is that of Eve, ruin shall take root, the translation read. *The branches of the House of Harding shall wither and fall. Let not her grow, lest the Inheritance be corrupted by her weakness, and that corruption spread—*

Cybil snapped the grimoire shut. She put it back in the drawer, fingers white with the force of her grip, and she went instead to the alchemy cupboard to retrieve her mother's tincture. Unlocking the doors with a key she kept chained around her waist, she held her breath instinctively as the glass vials greeted her—even stoppered, the stink of them was acrid, somehow malevolent.

The vial of mandrake tincture was almost empty. Cybil lifted it to the half-light coming through the curtains to inspect it, chewing her lip. She could brew more herself—her father's instructions were in the grimoire, and she had seen them a handful of times: low heat applied to water that has reflected the full moon, the mandrake carved with angel letters and sliced lengthwise. She could not bring herself to do magic, but such potions did not require the gift.

The issue would be retrieving more mandrake in the first place. It was an expensive ingredient because it was difficult to handle; the story went that the root screamed when it was pulled from the ground and killed those who heard it. Cybil knew that her father had sourced it from an apothecary in Ipswich, but she had neglected to make an order after his death. She was furious with herself for that now.

To Ipswich, then. Why not? It was hardly as if she had much else to do. She would give her mother her pottage and then take Charmeuse to town. It was barely an hour's ride, if that. Her father was not there to forbid it; the servants were not brave enough to call out the impropriety. Cybil could do what she wanted.

That realisation was enough, for a brief moment, to make her smile.

It was a cold day. Cybil wore her silver riding habit lined with white fur, sleeves puffed so wide they resembled pauldrons, her red hair pinned up and tucked into a feathered black cap. She did not whiten her face—the cold would freeze the paint, make it flake away. But she reddened her lips, and dripped belladonna into her eyes, and she told herself she looked the picture of a respectable lady. She told herself no one would see any darkness where they should not.

She took the path through the woods. The earth was wet and spongy, carpeted with decaying leaves, beneath Charmeuse's thundering hooves. The sun leaked watery beams of gold light through the gaps in the clouds. There was an autumnal rot in the air, and an owl hooted softly from overhead. Every autumn Cybil had ever lived had looked and sounded and smelt exactly as this one did, and for a moment, she wondered if her encounter with Richter the previous night had simply been another nightmare. Cybil had never seen the woman before, even though everyone knew everyone in the village, and the forest then had seemed hostile and alien; a different place entirely from this familiar wood, with its burnished trees and dappled sunshine.

Then the road—a road she had previously only ever travelled with her parents as a small child; it looked just as it did in her memories—and the gates of the town, glinting grey and metal, rising as an unhammered nail from the earth.

Cybil paid to stable Charmeuse with the inn outside Ipswich. Then she went to stare at the gates. They were open for the day's trade, but there was a host of corpses swinging from the tops of the bars, the sunlight casting them into sharp relief. Cybil did not know why they had been hanged; it could have been anything from murder to treason. One of the corpses was a woman, bloated ankles peeking out beneath rain-rotted skirts. Cybil found she could not look away from her—she felt, for some reason, as if she owed it to her to stare.

Cybil was hardly one to feel pity for corpses, to mourn for them, but seeing the dead woman made her feel flayed. It made her feel as if anyone passing her by would turn to look at her and say, *Should you not be swinging there, too? For all those you have killed, all those you will burden?* And the moment that thought occurred to Cybil, she could not help but envision herself up there, too, swinging in the wind, the flesh sloughing off her, her eyes open and unseeing. She felt a presence at her feet, and when she looked down, the shadow of the hanged woman had detached itself from its place and was floating slowly towards her, reaching out its arms. Cybil squeezed her eyes shut and attempted to calm herself. *Leave me*, she thought, desperately, *before anyone sees. No one may see—*

There was an exclamation of shock behind her. Cybil opened her eyes just as the shadow darted away from her, like a fish frightened by movement. She turned to see a young man staring at her through the open gate. For a moment, she feared that he had exclaimed because he had seen the shadow, but then she realised that she recognised him from the dance the previous night; he had been staring at her then, too. He was more handsome in the daylight, fair and doe-eyed, with a strong jaw and broad shoulders. There was a brace of rabbits dangling from one hand, and it was obvious he had come for market day.

'You are Lady Cybil,' the man said. 'I saw you at the dance.'

Cybil flushed; it would not do if he told the village she was wandering about the town alone. 'And *you* are?' she said, as imperiously as she could, as if there were nothing amiss with her presence.

He kicked the cobbles beneath his boot, glancing between Cybil and the corpses. 'Peter Oswyn,' he said, very slowly. 'I… Since you are here, I wished to thank you.'

Cybil blinked, surprised. 'Thank me? For what reason?'

'Last night. When you told the witchfinder to quit the village. It was brave. And I am sorry that you got muddy.'

'Oh.' Mollified, Cybil cleared her throat. 'Well—I—it did not matter to me. It was only mud.'

'You looked very upset.'

'I was not.'

Emboldened, Peter took a step forward. Cybil shrank back instinctively; he did not seem to notice. Behind him, the noise of the town—the tread of feet and the cries of the market sellers—faded to a low hum.

He said, 'You ought to be treated with respect. You are a *lady*, after all.'

He said *lady* with such awe that Cybil felt she ought to sprout wings and fly. 'I… I suppose so.'

'I never believed the rumours, you know. 'Bout you being cursed.'

'I am not cursed,' she said, keeping her face expressionless.

He glanced over her shoulder, towards the road. 'What is it like up there?' he asked her. 'In Harding Hall? My cousin works the gardens. He says 'tis very grand.'

Recalling her solitary breakfast; her mother's weak, piping voice through the door; the empty echo of her footsteps through the silent corridors, she replied, 'It is fine enough.'

''Tis true the *queen* sometimes visits?'

'She has not in a long time.'

'Will she?'

'I would not know.' Cybil was disarmed by his earnestness, by the wide, adoring eagerness of his gaze. She took a faltering step back. 'Listen, I—Master Oswyn—'

'Peter,' he said.

'Master Oswyn. I have business here, in Ipswich. Business that is not with you. Because it is with someone else. Who, as I said, is not you.' She cursed herself silently for her awkwardness. 'I— No matter. I appreciate your greeting me.'

'Oh.' He glanced down at his rabbits, then back to her. His expression was pleading. ''Haps I could aid you? Do you know your way around the town, my lady?'

No one had ever *asked* to spend time with her, let alone with such desperation. Propriety and logic dictated it would be best to dissuade him—but there was something so compelling about being wanted, especially when it happened so rarely. Without wishing to, Cybil thought of Richter whispering in her ear: *she* had wanted her, also. She had wanted her so much that Cybil must have dreamed it, because no woman in existence would hold another like that and tell her unashamedly how much she desired her.

Cybil looked at Peter, fair and sweet, smiling hopefully at her. Comparing him to Richter was akin to comparing a raindrop to a tempest. He was real, and normal, and *safe*. And considering her curse, perchance it endangered him for her to agree—in that manner, she was being cruel. But she did not have the strength to deny herself this. Surely, for one day, Cybil could allow herself the simple pleasure of a friend.

'Very well,' she told him. 'I am seeking an apothecary. Could you take me there?'

There was a crow on the roofs of Ipswich, watching incredulously as Cybil simpered at a mortal boy with a soul no brighter than a firefly.

Miriam was frustrated, and the shadows echoed that frustration. Diminished as they were by the daylight, they fluttered down Miriam's throat, twisted themselves in her feathers, hungry and insistent; they desired Cybil as much as she did. *Patience*, she told them, as she followed Cybil and Peter Oswyn toward the market square.

But she did not feel patient. After Miriam's first meeting with Cybil, she had taken an oak tree by its trunk and torn it out of the earth, flinging it with a great groan to the forest floor. She had never offered a deal that wasn't then immediately taken, so in tune was she with the desperation of her victims. Now to encounter this—this *capriciousness*, this *arrogance*? Miriam considered her interest a privilege, and yet Cybil seemed entirely unimpressed.

But then, Cybil was special—a rare delicacy, the sort of prize worth a chase. In centuries, Miriam had never seen such a soul. To consume it would likely be the greatest pleasure of her existence. It was her conviction in that which now led her to such frustration. No one could burn with such light unless they had some fire within them, some stubbornness. It was to be expected that Cybil would put up some resistance. It would be disappointing if she did not.

But this? *This* was an insult. To reject Miriam and take up with this man instead—it was akin to declining a banquet for a hunk of bread. As they walked, Oswyn said something to her, gesticulating wildly with his dead rabbits, and Cybil actually afforded him a glimmer of a smile. Truly, what was the appeal? In his colouration, Miriam thought Oswyn had something of unbaked dough in him, and it was hardly as if a woman as beautiful as Cybil needed to stoop so low. But that was the thing about beauty, *real* beauty, which was sharp and distant and isolating. Humans were so frightened of it. Mayhap this man was even commendable for his obvious infatuation.

Miriam had spent the morning in Ipswich, in fact—it was a stroke of luck that Cybil had come here also. A mere moment before Cybil had arrived at the gates, Miriam had taken her last meal: a man who had traded his soul for vengeance against a merchant guild that had wronged him. He had forgotten, of course, that he was still a member of the guild also, and so she had slaughtered him along- side his enemies. The guildhall had displayed a large portrait of some ginger-haired woman with a white face and too many pearls; Miriam had amused herself by washing the painting red with their blood. Then she had left, licking the gore from her fingers. There was still a crimson streak on the inside of her wrist. The guildhall was only a few streets away from here, where Cybil and Peter Oswyn were now avoiding puddles as they navigated the cobbles. The scene would be found, sometime soon, and the mortals would make their excuses— one of the merchants went mad, perchance, or a wild animal had attacked, or a local witch had laid a hex. They always found a method of dismissal, a method to tell themselves it could be prevented from happening again.

As Cybil and Peter neared the market, the air became heavy with the stink of horse dung and humanity. The space was thronging with people. Miriam landed upon the roof of a stall to watch Cybil as she wove through the crowd while staring nervously at Peter Oswyn's back. She was unaccustomed to this, clearly, the bustle and the noise; a blacksmith struck a horseshoe nearby, and Cybil cowered as if the sound had run her through. In the distance, a fruit seller was singing to entice customers, warbling about apples red and pears so green— Cybil clearly found this grating, as she kept glancing in the seller's direction, forehead creasing. The echoing silence of Harding Hall must have felt as distant now to Cybil as Miriam's birthplace did to her—across the sea, across centuries.

Cybil stopped, curious, at a stall selling fresh fish. An eel had been hooked and hung from the stall's front, glass-eyed in death. Below it, the fishmonger was busy gutting a pike. He gave Cybil a wary look, but he did not shoo her away. She watched as he pulled a ribbon of entrails from the animal, pale and thin, like the strings of a fiddle.

The eel on the hook suddenly spasmed and twitched. Cybil startled, jumping halfway in the air; the fishmonger laughed. 'They do that, sometimes,' he said. 'Last spark of life in 'em. They think they can get off the hook and splash right back into the sea.'

'Does it feel pain?' Cybil asked.

'I would not know, mistress. What is an eel's pain to a man?'

She smiled wryly, glancing back in the direction of the gate. The movement made a lock of red hair fall from her cap, catching the light like a strand of fire. 'Men are strung up sometimes, also.'

'We are all God's creatures,' he said. 'But there is a manner of things—a Chain of Being. The queen above men, and men above eels.'

'And God above us all,' Cybil said. 'Observing us squirming on our hooks.'

Peter Oswyn then appeared at Cybil's elbow. His expression was hopeful, and in his hand he held a fruit of some sort: round and orange, its skin glazed with honey, top cored and oozing with jam.

''Tis a stuffed medlar,' he said proudly, presenting it to her. 'With rose hip jam.'

Cybil plucked it from his hand uncertainly, and pinched it between two fingers as if it were a dirty rag. '... My thanks.'

They stared at each other for a long moment.

'Will you not try it?' Oswyn asked her, face crumpling.

'It is only that—I am not fond of sweetmeats,' she said, and she handed it back to him.

He was aghast. 'But you *must* like them.'

'Why?'

'Well—everyone does. 'Sides, my da says sweet things are good for women. Keeps them biddable.'

Cybil appeared vaguely disgusted. 'You ought to be cautious, Master Oswyn. Too much sugar and your teeth shall rot.' She turned her head away from him, towards the buildings at the other side of the market. 'Which way was the apothecary?'

Oswyn sighed. 'This way, my lady.'

'Then lead on,' Cybil said—still clearly irritated, to Miriam's delight—and she followed Oswyn into the crowd.

Their progress was not quick. Every second stall, Cybil would stop to inspect the sunlight glinting off knives, to peer at glass baubles and weigh pewter plates in her hands. The sellers could sense her wealth; they tried to lull her into conversation, making claims about the quality of their wares that were patently absurd. ''Tis an Indian bowl, from Roanoke,' one man claimed of a misshapen lump of half-fired clay. Cybil snorted, said, 'Oh, *indeed*,' and turned away. Then she looked up, her eyes meeting Miriam's where she sat on the canvas roof of a fur trader's stall.

Cybil looked at her for far longer than any human would stare at an ordinary crow. Miriam knew Cybil could sense the darkness in her, even if she did not know exactly its origin—and it brought Miriam pleasure to be *seen* in a manner she so rarely was. She spread her wings, letting the sunlight slip into the folds of her coal-black feathers and disappear. In the back of her throat, she mimicked a crack of thunder.

Cybil's eyes widened at the mimicry, and then she laughed, delighted. 'What an extraordinary creature,' she said, stepping forward towards her—and then Peter Oswyn returned again, looking beleaguered.

'Mistress, the apothecary shall soon close.'

'That crow made the sound of a storm!'

Oswyn glanced at Miriam, crossing himself. 'Ill omens, crows. My ma says they carry curses.'

Cybil's expression twitched, then went stoic. 'The apothecary, then.'

The apothecary was not a stall but a building at the edge of the square, bearing a sign with a crude drawing of a mortar and pestle. Cybil instructed Oswyn to wait outside—her patience with him had clearly grown thin—and as she entered, he leaned against the wall to stare up at the sky, chewing his lip.

Miriam opened her beak again and mimicked the sound of a man's scream. Oswyn hopped three feet in the air, face going wan, and then he noticed the crow. He crossed himself once more, glowering.

Miriam sensed an opportunity, and she would not allow it to slip away. If Cybil found this man interesting, so be it.

The heavy clouds meant the shadows were thin, but Miriam still found refuge in the darkness cast by the apothecary's sign, melding into its shadows. She was fortunate to have been so gluttonous the past few days; she had more than enough power to trade. As the sign swung back and forth in the breeze—the shadow swinging with it—Miriam waited for Oswyn's shadow and hers to make contact. He sighed and shuffled. Just another inch to the left, and she would have it. His soul was a dying star, hardly visible: that was good, because her plan would have been difficult otherwise. This trick required someone suggestible.

Peter Oswyn, still flushed from his interactions with Cybil, took a deep, joyful breath of Ipswich air, and leaned sideways—and the shadows slipped down his throat, wrapping themselves around the light in his chest. He panicked, but the panic was a distant thrum: he was in darkness—he *was* the darkness. When Miriam released him, he would feel as if he were waking from an uncertain and unpleasant dream. For now, he was trapped in a nightmare.

Mine now, Miriam thought, lifting Peter's hand to inspect it in the light. *Come along, puppet. You might prove useful, after all.*

7

The apothecary had raised his brow at the amount of mandrake Cybil requested, but the brow had lowered precipitously once her coins hit the counter. As he packaged the root, Cybil stared at the shelves behind him—they were covered in misted glass jars of pickled herbs and bone-coloured powders. The lowest shelf had a cage with a hedgehog in it, poking its tiny blackcurrant nose through the bars. Cybil stooped to observe the creature: it sniffed curiously at her fingers, then gave her a brief nip that stung like a nettle. Cybil smiled at its fury, its wild, dark gaze. It was pleasant to encounter something that was not frightened of her.

The apothecary was broad and tall; his forearms were thickened with hours at the mortar and pestle. There was a sharpness behind his eyes, a cold intelligence that reminded Cybil of her father. As he handed her the package, he told her, 'Careful with that, now. That witchfinder's been poking around these parts.'

Cybil bristled. 'What are you implying?'

'Only that folk see shadows where there are none, mistress. They look at shops like mine and think of spells instead of medicine. Last week, Master Martingale—that is the witchfinder—asked me for a list of all the women in Ipswich who had bought henbane from me.'

'And you gave it to him?'

The apothecary spread his hands in surrender. 'What was I to do? Put myself to the noose instead?'

Cybil swallowed the bile in her throat and put the package in her pocket. There would be no use in argument; she could not truly say she would have done different. 'How much for the hedgehog?'

He glanced at the cage. 'That depends. You want the whole thing, or just the quills?'

'The whole thing,' she said, in smothered horror. '*Living*, preferably—unless, for some reason, keeping a pet will alert the witchfinder, too?'

Outside, the sun had been obscured by clouds dark and discoloured as a bruise. The change from the morning's sunshine was so sudden and so stark, it felt portentous; Cybil pulled her cloak tighter around herself as she approached Peter, the hedgehog's little cage swinging from her hand.

He blinked at her. 'What is that?'

'Hm? Oh, it is a hedgehog.'

'... Is it for eating?'

'Her name is Aurelia,' Cybil told him haughtily, 'and no, she is not for *eating*. I must return to the Hall. My horse is stabled outside the gates. My thanks, for... for your company.'

'You wish to leave?'

'Yes.'

'I shall accompany you, then.' He offered her an arm, and she took it hesitantly—there was a new intensity to his expression that she found somewhat unsettling. 'This way.'

She allowed him to lead her away from the market square, winding through the back alleys to avoid the worst of the crowd.

'Surely it is lonely,' Peter said, as they walked. 'Up there in the Hall, all alone. Is it not?'

'I have my mother,' Cybil replied, but that felt like a lie.

'Still. You have much responsibility, as lady of the manor. Is it not difficult?'

She took a delicate step over a puddle glazed with grease. 'Not particularly.'

'Your father,' Peter said, striding thoughtlessly through the puddle. 'Surely you miss him?'

Cybil heard Christopher's voice once more, muffled by his office door: *I will do what must be done.*

'Not overmuch,' she said.

'You are angry with him,' Peter observed, and his voice was... deeper and yet also softer; it had a strange resonance that felt almost comforting.

Cybil leaned a little closer to him, gripping his arm more tightly. 'Yes.'

'Why?'

Usually, Cybil would have declined to reply at all, let alone reply honestly; but there was something curiously compelling about Peter in that moment, the way his fingers had come to rest lightly on her own, the half-lidded, inviting look he was giving her from the corners of his eyes. Cybil had never felt desire for any man—this was, perchance, the first time she had even come close to doing so. That realisation disarmed her utterly.

I want to talk to him, she thought. *To unburden myself, if only this once.*

She said, words hushed as if speaking a secret: 'He hated me. He hated me because I am—wrong.'

Peter stopped and turned to look at her. They were by the gate now; the light was so dimmed from the clouds that torches had been lit, and the flickering light made Peter look different: more angular, more ethereal. 'Wrong?'

'I...' Her throat closed up, and she swallowed, suddenly hesitant. A raindrop fell on her cheek. She swiped it away. 'Sometimes, I look at the shadows,' she said, 'and it is as if they are looking back at me.'

Peter cocked his head.

'What if they are?' he asked.

Cybil was trembling. She opened her mouth to respond—to deflect, as she always had; to deny, as she always had—but something stopped her from speaking.

In the brief moment of silence her hesitancy created, the rain whispered its disapproval against the thatched roofs of Ipswich. Cybil became distinctly aware of the emptiness of the woods outside the gate, and the vastness of the country surrounding them, and the solitude of the Hall's grand rooms awaiting her: the untrodden carpets, the unoccupied chairs. That place was a dollhouse. She had spent her life inside playing make-believe, hoping that someone would reach their hand within and pull her out.

Cybil turned and crouched at the edge of the gate, where the grass had grown long. She opened the door of the hedgehog's cage, and it was gone in a streak of brown and black. Cybil never could have kept such a creature as a pet, regardless of a passing fancy: her curse would have led it, no doubt, to some cruel end. Still, she allowed herself a moment of sorrow for her loss before she turned back to Peter.

'I have made you sad,' he said, frowning slightly.

'I am not sad,' she replied. 'Or—I am. But I think I am angry, also.'

'Why?'

'I grow angry when I feel sorrow,' she said. 'I grow angry with myself, because I feel as if I do not deserve sadness. Is that lunacy, do you think?'

He approached her until they were face-to-face, her skirts brushing his boots. He raised a trembling hand and pressed it against her cheek. His thumb caught the corner of her mouth; it was cold and damp from the rain. Cybil was so startled by this that she did not react, but stared at him blankly.

'You deserve all of it,' he said. 'Sorrow and fury. The beginning and end of all things.'

His palm against her face was like ice, and his eyes were dark and wide. Cybil opened her mouth to reply—then she paused. His eyes had been blue before, had they not? And had his accent not been broader, his smile more innocent?

There were a dozen explanations that would have made more sense, a thousand ways that Cybil could have rationalised it to herself; but once she recognised the resemblance, it felt impossible to ignore. It was as if his was a face that had fractured, and now all she could see was the crack.

'Richter?' she said.

Peter froze. His hand dropped away. The affected openness of his expression loosened, his features becoming crueller and colder.

'It *is* you,' Cybil said, horrified, and in response, Peter's jaw unhinged. Shadows began to pour out of his mouth and pool on the ground; the darkness bled from his eyes, blue irises swivelling wildly in their sockets. Cybil was too scared even to scream; she scrambled backwards, stumbling over an uneven paving, and scrabbled to standing just as Peter's mouth shut again.

His eyes rolled back into his head, and he fell to the ground, unconscious. Meanwhile, the darkness at Cybil's feet began to pool and swirl, coalescing into something tangible. She could hear a sound muddied by rain, but there all the same—the shouting of people from the way they had just come, all of Ipswich witness to the shadows that were reaching for her.

Cybil turned and fled.

The forest, once familiar, was made another world entirely by the rain: gnarled trunks shimmering sideways in the haze of water; the earth pulling at Charmeuse's hoofs as if to consume her and Cybil both. Cybil hadn't seen Richter since she had run to retrieve her horse, since she had galloped down the path home, swallowing her screams—but she swore she could hear footsteps behind her, could hear the crowing of a bird above her. And yet, each time she glanced over her shoulder, there was no one there.

It was some sort of dream, Cybil told herself, *a nightmare*—but it did not help. It did not loosen the terror that had closed its fist around her heart, did not slow her pace or her breathing. She raced through the forest like a stag with hounds nipping at its heels, until the Hall rose above her, cruel and familiar, the rain beating against its leaden roof.

Cybil dismounted. It was almost dark now, and the downpour had soaked her entirely. Her hair stuck to her face, and water sprung from her eyelashes when she blinked. She could still feel the imprint of Peter's—Richter's—hand on her cheek. Her stomach churned.

She dropped Charmeuse at the stables, from which the most direct route into the main building was through the orchard. Cybil stumbled her way over roots and decomposing leaves, gripping her wet skirts. Many of the trees still bore fruit, the last of the autumn's apples, but more still carpeted the ground in various stages of decay. In her haste, Cybil stepped on one, and it burst beneath her boot. She slipped, arms flailing—and someone caught her.

It was Richter, smiling down at her. This time, Cybil did scream, trying to bat her away. Richter disappeared. In the space of a blink, she was gone; disoriented, Cybil veered around—trying to find her—and then she heard a voice at her ear, saying, 'Good evening.'

Cybil lurched away from the source of the noise, spinning around. Richter was watching her, hands linked behind her back, head cocked at an unnatural angle.

For a moment, they stared at each other without speaking. Then Richter said, 'When all else is ashes, my dear, yours may be the only face that I remember.'

Cybil had no idea how to respond to that. Her cheeks heated, and she took a deep breath, ignoring the hammering of her heart. 'You were controlling Peter.'

'Yes.'

'How? What *are* you?'

Richter didn't respond. Instead, she stepped forward and seized Cybil's arm, pulling her closer.

Cybil was furious to find that Richter was just as handsome now, in the dim grey of dusk, as she had been beneath the moon. She was square-jawed, heavy-browed. There was something about the bluntness of her features that felt familiar, in the manner that a flame was familiar to burnt skin.

'Release me,' Cybil said. 'How might you convince me to do anything, acting like this? I know not who you are—*what* you are. If you are a witch, you are not as my father was. And if you are something else…'

'I told you; I am Miriam Richter,' she said. 'And I know who you are, Cybil Harding, now more than ever. I have found so many memories here in this orchard, buried beneath the leaves and mud. *Break the bough, Cybil*—is that not what your father wanted? Did you ever manage it?'

Cybil pulled away, taking a shaky step backwards. 'How—how do you know of that?'

Richter hummed in thought. 'He was clever enough, I suppose, to see the light in you, but still too foolish to understand its worth. How tragic. Would you have preferred if I had kept him alive? It would have been foolish. Who knows what else he might have summoned, if I hadn't gotten here first?'

For a moment, Cybil didn't understand. Then she remembered Sir Gilbert telling her father that *such a summoning would cost too dear a price*—and her father's confident response: *I will pay it. I have no choice.*

Cybil took another step back, and she tripped over a root. Richter lunged forward to catch her as she fell, one arm looping around her waist, bending her in a dance step beneath an apple tree's heavy branches. Ripe red fruit dangled like viscera above Richter's head. Cybil squirmed, trying to escape her grip. Richter grinned and tightened her hold.

'What to do, what to do?' she asked her. 'Are you frightened of me, Cybil?'

She was playing with her, as a cat with a mouse. 'Let me go,' Cybil gasped.

'You should allow me to help you,' Richter replied. 'It seems sweetness does not move you, nor does deception; perchance cruelty shall instead. If I took you apart, my dear, how much would you give to be put back together?'

'Let me go!'

'Stubborn girl. Ask me nicely, and I shall consider it.'

Cybil spat in her face and clawed at her hands. It did not work. Richter was as cold and unmoving as marble; Cybil bowed her back further, arching upwards, thinking to slide out of Richter's grip. But it was futile. All that happened was that her viewing angle changed, so that she was staring directly above them: at the clouded sky, and her captor's dark-eyed smile, and the tree branch looming over Richter's shoulder.

Cybil focused on the branch. Richter followed her gaze, turning her head. 'Ah, I see. Would you like my encouragement?'

'If you do not release me, I shall...'

'You shall what?' Her grin widened. 'It is when you are at your most furious, your most distraught, that the true light of your soul breaks loose. It is so beautiful to witness. Why fight it, my dear? The shadows wish to feed—you do not feel their presence? Give them what they desire, and they shall do anything you ask of them.'

Cybil squirmed again. Richter leaned in closer. For a brief, absurd moment, Cybil thought she was going to kiss her—she drew in a breath, lips parting, uncertain how to respond—but then Richter brought her mouth to Cybil's ear instead.

'Break the bough, Cybil,' she murmured.

'Hasten to hell, you—you *bitch*—'

Richter laughed, and she brushed her lips over Cybil's hairline; the touch felt molten, searing, as if it would leave a burn scar behind it. 'Break the bough,' she said again.

'I cannot.'

'Perchance not, but the shadows will. You could hear the whispers of the darkness if you allowed yourself. Give yourself to them, and they shall serve you in exchange.'

Whispers in the darkness.

The moment Richter said it, Cybil knew they were there: a noise she had always heard but learnt to ignore, as one can fall asleep to the sound of the rain, although it grows no quieter. The low hum of something hateful and hungry. She had always assumed it was her own hunger, her own loneliness and frustration that she'd heard—as a sort of pull that rose and fell within her, ever since she had learnt of her curse—but no. It was suddenly so clear. The darkness did not just follow her: it *spoke* to her, also.

'What does it want from me?' Cybil asked, half a gasp, trembling in Richter's arms.

'The same as I do. Your soul.' Richter reached to tuck a lock of hair behind Cybil's ear. 'At some point, my dear, your family made a deal with the darkness, just as my creators did. A mutually beneficial arrangement: the ability to hear the shadows, to make further bargains whenever they wished.'

'What sort of bargains?'

'Power,' Richter said.

'And they received the curse in exchange,' Cybil said, with dawning realisation.

Richter hummed. 'Mayhap. Darkness usually desires light more than anything else. All magic is a balance, as much offered as gained. You have light, my dear, an extraordinary amount of it; more than I have ever seen. It would be a shame to waste it all on other shadows, but for something as trifling as a tree, they will require only a tiny piece of yourself—little more than a spark.'

'Is that what *you* desire from me? A spark?'

She smiled. 'I am no petty shadow, my dear. I will have all of you, and nothing less.'

Cybil closed her eyes. The shadows hissed to her, in a language she knew but did not know: the language of hunger, of desperation. And, for a moment, she was tempted. She wanted to surrender to them, to allow them to find purchase in the fissures of her soul, to consume her and make every furious imagining of hers a reality.

But she did not. She could not. Instead, she opened her eyes, and her gaze met Richter's. She said, quietly, 'Let me go.'

Richter did not move.

'You say I have light,' Cybil said. 'My soul is mine alone to give. My terms, my choice—and I choose to keep it as it is. I will not change my mind through fear alone.'

For a moment, Cybil was certain Richter would drop her—or dash her brains out against the tree trunk—but then, mute and frowning, Richter pulled her back up to standing and tugged her away from the tree. 'You are stubborn,' she said, not without admiration. She reached out her hand, in a movement as coy as a blown kiss: the bough groaned as if in pain, then snapped cleanly at its base, falling heavily to the orchard floor. 'That is natural, with such fire within you. But you need not deny your own power. It is a shame to do so.'

Cybil said, 'The world is such an ugly place, Mistress Richter. I am not prepared to make it uglier.'

Richter clicked her tongue. 'Ugliness is a *human* concern, Cybil. You needn't debase yourself. With my aid, your beauty would only become clearer.' She reached forward to press her hand against Cybil's sternum, giving her a look that seemed almost fond. 'You have never truly *seen* yourself before, I suppose. I shall show you.'

Cybil looked down at Richter's hand, and a light began to bloom between them. For a moment, Cybil flinched, fearing that she was somehow catching on fire. Then she realised that the light was coming from within her own chest. Soon, it was bright enough that it began to hurt her eyes, and when she looked away, it left dark spots in her vision, as if she had been staring directly at the sun.

'Is that… part of me?' she asked Richter.

'It is your soul, Cybil. Every person has one, but *yours*—I have never seen anything like it.'

Cybil stared at Richter, trying to see the same thing in her, but there was nothing. Only a strange, shifting darkness behind the woman's eyes and within her chest, which seemed to grow darker and darker and bigger and bigger the longer she looked at it.

'You do not have one,' Cybil said. 'At least—not one like mine.'

'That is because I am not a person.'

'What *are* you, then?'

She shrugged. 'Whatever it was my makers made me.'

'You said you were summoned. A demon? An angel?'

'Either, neither. I was a shadow, once—perchance I still am.'

'And you wish to make a deal with me.'

'Yes.'

'Because my soul is strong? Because my family made some sort of deal themselves?'

Richter reached out and drew a finger down the centre of Cybil's chest. Cybil's breath stuttered, and she felt her cheeks heat. 'Yes.'

'What will you do with it?'

'Consume it,' she said. 'I have never wanted anything more. To have such a soul would be the greatest pleasure I have ever known. It would provide me with power for centuries.'

'I would never agree to such a thing.'

'Why not?' Richter asked, with genuine confusion. 'There is little need to rush. I can give you anything you want, Cybil. I find you fascinating enough to watch you for years; your anger, your sorrow, your beauty. I could break your curse, serve you, grant you your every desire, and eventually…'

74

'Eventually you will *eat* me? You will *kill* me?' she said, incredulously. 'Just as you killed my father?'

'You were always going to die regardless. This simply allows for more certainty. Tell me how much time you require, and I am certain we can negotiate.' Richter offered Cybil her hand. 'You need not be alone anymore.'

Cybil looked at her palm. It seemed, at first glance, an ordinary human hand. Its nails were a little too sharp, mayhap, the skin too smooth. She knew that Richter's touch was cold, but not so cold as to be alarming. She knew that her mouth was soft, from when it had touched her forehead. Even now—even half breathless with fear and confusion—Cybil's heart sped to think of that touch, to think of touching her once more. Miriam Richter could certainly pass for human, if she wished to, if no one knew any better.

But it was her eyes. It was always her eyes. When their gazes met, Cybil looked into that darkness, and she saw nothing human there. If Richter had pupils, they were the same colour as her irises, or else they were blown so wide that even belladonna could not have accomplished it. And Cybil wondered how she had never noticed it before: this woman did not have a woman's face, but the expectation of one. She was an abyss that promised a person at its end.

Cybil shook her head. 'I know better than to make deals with the devil,' she said. 'I want you to leave my property, Miriam Richter, and never return.'

Richter sighed. 'If you really *wanted* that, my dear, your magic would have kept me away.' Stepping backwards, she lifted the felled bough from the ground with one hand, and she held it in front of her. It was at least as thick as her torso, but she wielded it like a Myrmidon with a spear, raising it upright without effort. 'It is a shame,' she continued, 'that you refuse to learn the wonders you could work.'

The gnarled bark of the bough shuddered and began to unfurl, stripping itself away from the pale heartwood. That wood paled and thinned and hardened until Richter held a long, thin bone, sharp-tipped and slightly curved. A whale's rib, or else the talon of some indescribable leviathan. The bone was already beginning to yellow and crack with age the longer Richter gripped it between her hands. Cybil watched in horror and fascination as it darkened and went brittle, browned as if buried for fathomless years, and then—with hardly a whisper of sound—dissolved into dust.

Cybil felt something within her quail at this show of power. She wondered if Richter would reach her hand out once more, close it around her own wrist, and consign her to ashes, also. But Cybil allowed her fear presence for only a moment. Then she bound it up again, tied it in ropes too tight to unknot.

Lifting her chin, Cybil said, 'I wish to never see you again.'

Richter's eyes glittered. She did not respond.

Cybil turned and walked away. Behind her, a crow cawed; but when she turned instinctively towards the noise, she saw nothing but the waiting dark.

8

Miriam left the orchard furious, delighted, *hungry*.

She had exhausted herself. Her magic was always more difficult to call on beneath clouds—the darkness was weaker, more nebulous. Now she had spent so much of her strength, she would need to trade for more power, or else she would start to fade.

Miriam was growing sick of Ipswich, but it was the largest settlement in the area, and thus the greatest store of souls. Making her way toward the town, she flew into a murmuration of starlings to scatter them, taking vindictive pleasure in their shrieks of fear. She remembered Cybil trembling in her arms, recalled her scream as Miriam had appeared before her. The girl wore fear so prettily, but she was even more lovely when she was angry; it would almost be a shame to rob the world of something so beautiful.

Almost.

Miriam was immortal, but that did not mean she was patient. She was accustomed to getting what she wanted. Cybil would not come to her willingly; this was a novel problem to Miriam, in centuries of hunts, but not one that was insurmountable. Miriam would have to find a method of forcing her. It could never be as simple as taking control of her body and signing the contract in her stead: a soul had to be given willingly. It was one of the few limitations Miriam had discovered over the course of her existence. Besides, Cybil's soul was too strong for such tricks. She would simply spit the shadows out.

Miriam would have to attempt something new. For now, she required a meal, especially after that display of power with the apple-tree branch. She alighted atop the town gates, scattering another group of crows who were picking at the corpses dangling there.

As she peered down at the path, she saw a man with a black hat—a man she recognised. The witchfinder, Henry Martingale. Curious, she took flight to follow him.

Although it was late, the streets remained crowded. And people clearly recognised Martingale; they were either staying well out of his way or swarming about him like flies on a dish of blood, begging for help or offering him tips. 'My wife's mother is a witch,' said one man. 'I swear it—she cursed me, and a blister formed—' But Martingale ignored him entirely, walking further into the town.

Then a familiar voice came. 'Master Martingale! Master Martingale!'

It was poor Peter Oswyn, elbowing his way through the crowd. His eyes were small, with dark bags beneath them, skin sallow with exhaustion. He was not yet recovered, clearly, from his ordeal.

Martingale made to push him aside.

'Please, sir,' Oswyn whimpered. 'I've been bewitched.'

Martingale snarled, 'As has half of Ipswich, boy. Now move along.'

'But—'

'Move.'

''Twas Cybil Harding,' Oswyn blurted. 'She's a witch. I know it to be true, sir. I had heard the rumours that she was cursed, but I was a fool, blinded by lust. And I met with her here today, but then… I had no control of myself, I was her puppet. Others saw it—I was possessed. I cannot remember it clearly, but when I woke up, she was gone, and—and—I had *this*.'

He pointed to his right eye. Its pupil was swollen wide, double the size of his left, shadows drowning out the blue.

Martingale paused. 'Cybil Harding,' he said, and his lips thinned. 'I know of her. I have heard much of her family.'

Miriam searched his mind, and she found embarrassment, resentment: a flicker of Cybil's face, her supercilious expression as she ridiculed him on All Hallows' Eve.

Miriam had not experienced enough of this place to know what they did to witches, but she could guess. Rope or fire, water or blood: it did not matter. Either way, it was a fate any woman would be desperate to escape. Desperate enough, in fact, to trade anything for their liberty.

Grinning, Miriam returned to the shadows.

Cybil could not sleep.

Six days had passed since Ipswich, since she had seen Richter in the orchard. Since then, each time she closed her eyes, she smelt rotting apples and heard the thrum of the rain. An incomprehensible panic seized her without trigger, and her dreams were shockingly vivid. The previous evening, she had even taken a drop of her mother's mandrake tincture to try to find some respite—but her sleep that night had been so deep and consuming that when she woke up, she felt curiously convinced that, for a moment, she had been dead.

But without the tincture, it now seemed she could not sleep at all. Over the course of the week, winter had continued its slow invasion of Suffolk: at night, the windows rattled with frozen wind; the rooms remained cold despite Cybil lighting every fire and wrapping herself in furs. On Sunday, the chill was such that she gave up on rest entirely, and so she wandered the Hall, attempting to busy herself by taking note of any minute flaw she could find: here, a hairline crack in a windowpane, illuminated like a scar by her candle; here, some paint upon a hunting mural, flecked and faded; and here, a mysterious stain on a rug mayhap left by one of her father's more adventurous rituals, rust-coloured and shaped like a Hebrew letter. Cybil noted all of these on a list in her meticulous hand, taking comfort in the procession of words and predicted costs for resolution. The better the records she kept now, the easier it would be for her to hand the reins of the Hall to her mother and leave for Court.

In one room, long enough shut up that the door shrieked like a hawk when it opened, Cybil found—differentiated by the moonlight—a trio of person-shaped shadows sitting about a dust-covered table, gesticulating to one another as if playing cards. As she entered, one of them motioned for her to sit with them.

79

She was too exhausted even to fear them. Eyes stinging, the flame of her candle blurred, she said, 'Shoo,' and flapped her hand about.

They did not move.

'Shoo,' she repeated. 'This is my home, and you are not welcome here. You must leave. If you do not, I shall...' She recalled something she had read in her father's grimoire. 'Salt. I shall salt you like slugs, quite happily.'

The shadows shifted nervously in their chairs. Then, slowly— reluctantly—they faded away, leaving only the thin grey moonlight behind.

Triumphant, Cybil returned smiling to her rooms. But once she was in bed, the pleasure of this victory soon passed. Sleep continued to elude her, and she was left with familiar frustration.

After hours of restlessness, her thoughts turned, inevitably, to the orchard: Cybil recalled Richter's gaze on her throat, on her face, the manner in which she had called her lovely and bared her teeth as if she would bite her. And despite the lingering fear, the anxiety, Cybil found herself overcome with an almost painful rush of arousal.

Attraction of this intensity was alien to her. Cybil felt ashamed of herself, disgusted, even—but for a moment, she allowed herself to imagine that Richter *had* kissed her, after all. She pictured her biting her lip hard enough to make it bleed, pulling her hair until Cybil was gasping, pushing her against the trunk of the tree. Cybil felt as if her blood had gone molten, and her hand drifted between her legs. She pressed her fingers against herself, trembling, imagining Richter's hand instead of her own. The fantasy was so clear in her mind she could almost hear that dark voice saying, *My dear, if* this *was what you wanted, you need only have asked—*

Cybil pulled her hand away and sat up, horrified. There was movement on the windowsill outside; as she turned to look, a bird took off and flew away.

Admonishing herself, Cybil got up from the bed and pulled on a robe. There was little use in trying to sleep now. She went to relight her candle, and then she cradled it in her palms, leaning her face towards the flame, feeling the heat dance across her cheeks.

Someone knocked three times on her bedroom door. Her fingers tightened around the candle.

'Hello?' she called. The only response was another threefold knock. It was slow, almost teasing, with the same precise rhythm of a ticking clock.

Aggravated, Cybil crossed to the door, pulling it violently open.

But there was no one there. The hallway was empty. She turned back to her room, stretching out her candle to illuminate the space. There was something scarlet on her pillow: a red carnation, petals unfurled.

'Absolutely *not*,' Cybil said. 'Go away.'

The knocking came again, this time more distant. Cybil returned to the corridor, and she followed the sound towards the far staircase, the one that led up to the roof. Her candle gilded her face with light. As she ascended the steps, the flame dimmed and brightened with her movements like a heartbeat.

She stopped at the hatch. It led to the roof, which was flat and balustraded, to allow people to walk it and enjoy the view. She and her mother had oft taken the air there when she was small and it was summer, the green carpet of the Suffolk countryside unrolling before them—but Cybil was not small now, and it was no longer summer, and it was not her mother waiting for her on the other side.

'Richter,' Cybil said. 'I know you are here. I asked you to leave this place.'

There was a pause—then another, deliberate knock against the hatch.

Cybil hissed a breath through her teeth, caught between annoyance and fear. She shoved the hatch open and emerged into the night air.

The sky was clear of clouds, the stars glorying in their freedom. Up here, the wind was biting, the cold unerring. Cybil shivered in her nightgown as she stepped shoeless toward the balustrade. There was no one here—at least no one whom she could see—and she cursed herself for her naivety. It'd serve her right if Richter appeared behind her and shoved her over the railing.

Her father had performed experiments up here: rituals beneath the stars, with salt circles and half-shouted incantations. 'What are you doing, Father?' she had once asked, when she was still a child and had not understood the sheer depths of his disdain, or his delusion.

'Calling the angels,' he had said. 'Now leave me, Cybil. There is much work to be done.'

Calling the angels. Sometimes, Cybil wished she could have the same faith that Christopher had in their family's holiness, in the purity of his powers; she might have still been cursed, the Seed of Eve, but at least then she would resent him less.

Cybil shut her eyes and opened her arms to the night. She pictured shucking the curse off, like chaff from wheat, the darkness being pulled apart by the wind. She would be left clean, normal, with the shadows sent away, and the fear in her heart carved out. Perchance, if she wished it enough, she could make it so.

The wind blustered, her white nightgown drawn against her by the breeze. There were whispers, plaintive, seeking; Cybil responded instinctively and *listened.*

A sudden heat flared across her palms and wrists, crawled up her arms and concentrated in pockets of flame. It hurt, but in a manner that was satisfying, glorifying, an anointment of pain. The fire seared lines into her flesh and burst it open. And although her lids were closed, she saw—she *saw*—dozens of eyes dotted her skin, open and shining, staring up into the sky. Across her arms, her collarbones, on her open palms, each the golden brown of those on her face, each with pupils blown belladonna-wide, each glowing with their own inner fire, embers of the light that burnt sun-bright within her chest—

'Cybil,' a voice came, and Cybil's eyes flew open.

She was still on the rooftop. The night air was still and indifferent. She looked desperately to her hands, her arms, but there was nothing unusual there. A waking dream?

Miriam Richter was standing atop the balustrade, unconcerned by the danger of falling. She cocked her head, smiling darkly. 'You should not feed them without asking for something in return.'

'Feed... the shadows, you mean?'

Richter stepped onto the roof. Cybil shrank back from her. 'They will grow attached to you,' Richter said. 'Although... I suppose they already are. Have they been doing you favours, Cybil, in hopes of a meal?'

'I thought *you* were a shadow.'

'I am,' she purred. 'Of a kind. But you have yet to feed me anything at all.'

'And yet, you are still attached,' Cybil said, her voice shaking a little. *Hide your fear,* she told herself. *She enjoys it when you are afraid.*

Richter sighed a breath—it felt odd to witness, Cybil realised, because she had never seemed to breathe before—and then gave Cybil a tender look. 'I am *fond* of you, Cybil Harding. You charm me. It is a shame I shall know you so briefly.'

'What do you mean?'

Richter shrugged a shoulder. 'Once the witchfinder has you...'

Cybil froze. 'The witchfinder?'

'You did not know? Henry Martingale is starting an inquisition. It seems poor Peter Oswyn was bewitched.'

'But—but—it was *you* that...'

'Was it?' Richter laid a hand across her chest in faux surprise. 'And now you shall take the blame? Tragic.'

Cybil snarled in fury, running a hand through her hair, tugging hard in her frustration. It hurt, but the pain helped: it focused her, allowed her to tamp down the burning panic growing in her gut. 'I thought you wanted a deal. Is this really intended to endear me to you?'

'Fear is the greatest motivator of all, is it not? You will require my help if you wish to escape the noose. You know not how to deal with darkness; you are powerful, but that power is raw—unformed. It is not enough to save your life.'

Cybil swallowed, clenching her fists. 'I am a Harding. I do not need you to save me.'

Richter chuckled. 'Shall we test that theory?'

'What?'

'Let us see together,' she said, 'whether *you* can save yourself.'

Richter took a step forward, and suddenly she was standing behind her. Then she shoved Cybil, so that she stumbled forwards, over the balustrade and the edge of the roof.

Cybil fell.

The fall itself must have lasted only a moment, but it felt like eons. Wind sharpened with frost battered her as she tumbled; above her, the light of the stars streaked and bloomed as her vision was warped by her speed. The moon melted into a haze of indistinct silver, like the liquid mercury her father had once used at his ritual table. Possessed by some futile instinct, Cybil raised her arms above her head, feeling her sleeves fluttering, imagining she would take flight. But she did not. She kept falling, and the cold grew colder, and she thought, *I am going to die.*

Arms caught her in a bridal carry.

'There,' Richter said, tone satisfied.

The impact had dragged all the air out of Cybil's lungs. She slumped, limp, her back arched over Richter's forearms, hair falling in a red curtain towards the ground. She was too stunned to speak or struggle. Richter's fingers pressed into her waist, and for a moment both of them were silent.

'Put me down,' Cybil said.

With uncharacteristic gentleness, Richter lowered her to the ground. Cybil stood on shaking legs, ears still ringing.

Richter said her name, and Cybil turned to look at her. She did not look ashamed, or regretful; but there was concern, perchance, in the way she sighed, reached out a hand, then allowed it to drop to her side.

Cybil wished to scream; she wished to cry. 'Why did you do that?'

'To show you.'

'Show me what?'

'Your weakness,' she said. 'Your magic is not advanced enough to save you, from yourself or from others. Without my help, you will die just as all the others have done. For now, you remain a woman, and a woman merely.'

'Of course I am a woman. What else could I possibly be?'

'Much more than that, my dear, if you allowed me to show you.'

'You—you are confounding, and absurd, and— You *threw* me from the roof. Would my soul still be yours to take, I wonder, were I flattened into an oatcake beforehand?' Richter's lips twitched, and Cybil gave a cry of fury. 'You—are you *laughing* at me?'

'I cannot help it.'

'You find joy in your cruelty.'

'I find joy in your reaction to it,' Richter corrected. 'It is quite marvellous—the more distressed you are, the more amusing I find it.'

Cybil turned away from her.

'Are you angry at me?' Richter said, sounding pleased.

'Of course.'

'*Good*,' she said. 'Your fear is beautiful, but your anger is even more so.'

Cybil closed her eyes. She was so exhausted that it hurt to do so, lids prickling, tears welling; opening them again felt like ripping open a wound.

'This is not a stage play, Mistress Richter,' she said, quietly. 'This is my only life, my only home, and I must live in it, tragedy or no.'

'What home? *This* place?' Richter gestured to Harding Hall. 'This empty palace you wander alone, without hope, waiting to die?'

'I loved this Hall once, you know,' Cybil said. 'Years ago, when I was young. When still I had my mother and I was not so alone. There was beauty in it; the flowers bloomed every spring and the forest grew green. They still do so, but at some point, it all became ugly to me. The seasons turned and all I felt was fear for the coming of winter. And now winter has come—*you* have come, Miriam Richter— and I think I have lost all hope of loving it again.'

Richter shook her head, dark hair swimming about her as if she were underwater; it looked to Cybil as if she almost had no weight at all, as if she would float up into the sky. 'I mean not to *take* your hope, Cybil. I mean to give it to you.' Richter reached for her hand. Cybil shrank away.

'Still afraid, I see,' Richter said. 'Good.'

'I have the notion,' Cybil said, 'that the only reason you would ever leave me alone would be if you saw me dead.'

'Perchance not even then,' Richter replied, as much a threat as a promise.

'Light chases away shadows. Is that not the case for you?'

'Light *creates* shadows,' she corrected Cybil. 'No absence without presence. But if it would be a comfort to you, to pretend you are blind to the dark—then I will allow you that comfort, if only tonight.' She took a step back. 'I believe I have made my point. The witchfinder will be here soon. When he is, I will call upon you, my dear, and see how desperation changes your tune.'

Cybil did not reply. She watched Richter fade away, just as the shadows around the table had—a blurred silhouette, losing form and clarity, until nothing remained.

Cybil pressed her hands against the wood of her mother's door, imagining entering the room and screaming at Bess to *wake up, wake up, please, Mother, wake up*—but she did not.

The witchfinder was coming; Cybil needed to prepare.

She could not leave for Court, not yet, not even to ask for succour. She could not convince Bess to come with her—Bess who could not leave her own chambers, let alone the building. Left alone here, her mother would succumb to her madness entirely. She would take all her mandrake tincture in a single swallow and welcome her end; the witchfinder would take her; or else she would die of the withdrawal, slowly, painfully. Cybil could not do it. She could not leave the one person she had ever loved to rot.

So, she could not leave; she would instead do all she could to ensure their survival.

Christopher Harding had spent a lifetime making this place an altar to his own ambitions: marking it with rituals and spells, filling its shelves with potions and grimoires. There was more than enough evidence to convict her, and her mother.

Cybil had to destroy it all.

She was not frightened: she was angry. She was poking her head through the bars of her cage and biting those who came near. If this place was to be the mechanism of her downfall, she would bring it down with her. She went first to the hawk-head tapestry, half-unpicked and marked with her own blood. She pulled it down—Troilus and Criseyde, too, which was pagan and thus tainted, and she tossed them into the fire. The scent of the tapestries burning, rich dyes and ancient wool, was indescribably awful. Cybil ran to the window, choking on the smoke, and cleansed her lungs with the frozen night air.

Then she went to her office, with its endless ledgers of numbers, accounts marking the purchase of henbane and mandrake and phosphorus: to the fire she fed those, too. Other documents—letters from mystics on the Continent, recipes for tinctures and powders—she tore into pieces before burning, throwing the scraps of parchment around her like snowflakes, watching them flutter to the floor. In the hallway, she smashed three windowpanes in the east gallery that had been painted with ritual grids. Then to her father's study: the codices and potion bottles. The bottles she smashed in the garden—all but the mandrake tincture—flooding the soil with noxious liquid that made her head swim. She could not bring herself to destroy the books, precious as they were, beautiful as they were. She left them there on the shelves, keeping silent vigil over the dust and the darkness, telling herself she would deal with them later.

At first, the destruction felt rational, sensible; these things, these artefacts and pages, were the shovels with which the witchfinder would dig her grave. But as she continued to smash and tear and burn, she became less discriminatory, consigning almost anything her father had touched, anything his magic had made or affected. As the sun slowly began to rise, clay cauldrons were thrown from windows, poisonous plants pulled up by the root, Cybil's own virginal, her childhood instrument, smashed to wooden shards and loose catgut strings by the blade of an axe. *She used music for her rituals*, Cybil thought, delirious with fear and anger and exhaustion, imagining Jane Lennard giving testimony at a courthouse: *Lady Harding oft played for empty chairs, sirrah, for the chairs were laid out for the devil, and she was awaiting His arrival.*

The servants thought her mad already—what difference would this carnage make? Accepting this, destroying the trappings of her childhood, Cybil found she was almost relieved. She found, by the time she was through with it all, that she was almost giddy. She felt freer than she ever had. She was the hedgehog in her cage, prying the bars apart.

Cybil went through Harding Hall and destroyed it like an animal at a carcass: pulling it to pieces, scooping out the innards. And once she was finished, once the Hall had suffered sufficiently at her hands—she sat at her mirror and smiled.

9

Miriam had left Cybil alone for long enough. It had been three nights since they had met on the rooftop; since then, she had been in Ipswich, passing the time with deals. Now she bid the town farewell, soaring through a flurry of snow.

As she flew, Miriam passed over the village next to the Hall. It was exactly the same as all English villages were, as far as she was concerned: squat hovels, a Norman church, and a square at the centre that sometimes contained a market or maypole. Typically, the square was empty at this time of year; Miriam was surprised to see that, this evening, it was populated. A small group of men had gathered, some on horses, some not. They had torches and dogs and weapons, as if they were going to hunt. It was clear enough what their prey would be. Henry Martingale stood at the centre of them. Beside him was a nervous-looking Peter Oswyn, twisting the hem of his tunic in his fists, expression pale and reluctant.

Miriam swooped in closer, alighting on the roof of a nearby cottage.

'... northwards,' Martingale was saying. 'We must be cautious. We are given permission to search, nothing more.'

'And if you find something?' Peter asked him.

'Then she shall be arrested.'

Peter looked queasy. 'I see.'

Miriam made herself intangible, slipping into shadows. She slid to the ground and edged closer.

'Men, to me!' Martingale said, and the hunting party turned to look at him. He had his head lifted, imperious, lip half-raised like a dog about to snarl. 'Listen and listen well. We seek a witch, and thus we must harden our hearts and our resolve. If she is innocent, let her come quietly and prove herself so; and if she is not, we must prepare ourselves for resistance. For although we see a face of a woman, it is not a woman who we fight on this day. It is the devil, and we must cast him out.'

As the men cheered, flailing their torches, a triumphant Miriam pulled the shadows around her and returned to the air. How thankful she was for the cruelties of men; they often outstripped her own. Few of her deals would come to fruition if her victims had not before suffered at humanity's hands.

She flew north, until Harding Hall rose up in the distance: a vast cage of lead and brick, the lines of dead bushes in its gardens making a spiderweb-pattern of dark over the pale frosted grass. It was an impressive edifice, but in the night it lacked grace, finesse—its bulk, its symmetry and harsh angles, seemed in contention with the nature around it. It occurred to Miriam now that its presence, in its sombre squareness, recalled nothing so much as a tombstone: a memorial for some unnamed tragedy. Mayhap it was fitting for such a family, doomed as they were.

The weather had remained clear the past few days, and the night was silent and still. The moon had been made into a multitude, reflected dozens of times over by the glass panes of the building's enormous windows. Most of the Hall's interior was dark, save a few rooms on the upper floors.

There was a light on in Cybil's bedroom. As a crow, Miriam landed on the windowsill outside and peered within. Cybil was sitting at the mirror, combing her hair. It fell down to her elbows, and there was something suddenly violent about the vividness of its colour; it was bloody, woundlike, as if each stroke of the comb was slicing into flesh. She was singing as she worked at the tangles, terribly out of tune as always, some ballad about lovers and false promises. Her voice was muffled by the glass of the window. She was only half dressed, in a white chemise and scarlet kirtle. As she sang, her chemise sleeve slipped partly down her shoulder, and Miriam felt a hunger that was different in character to any she had felt before. It was softer this time, a whisper rather than a howl.

Miriam hopped closer to the glass. She wanted to be nearer to Cybil, to *feel* the light of her, rather than consume it. It was an unnerving impulse, largely alien to her, and she knew not how to resist it. The shadows that had gathered to form her feathers were reverent and afraid; they shivered as if they could somehow feel the winter cold.

Miriam melded into the darkness, slipped through the window, and stood, invisible, behind Cybil. The room smelt of the sweet oils she had applied to the comb. Miriam could see a droplet of the tincture beading at her hairline where she had swept the locks aside. It trailed downwards and then paused, caught in the short, downy hairs at the nape of her neck.

For a moment, Miriam watched. Then, a woman once more, she allowed her image to appear in the mirror's reflection. It took a few moments before Cybil noticed her; as she went to put her comb down, her eyes met Miriam's within the glass, and she shrieked.

'Forgive me,' Miriam said. 'I frightened you.'

Cybil was clutching the comb with both hands as if it were a weapon. Trembling slightly, she dropped it into her lap. 'Are you truly there?' she asked. 'Or merely an illusion?'

Miriam stepped forward and laid a hand on her bare shoulder. Her reflection did the same. Cybil could clearly feel the touch, because her head whipped around to look behind her, but Miriam was still invisible outside of the glass; there was nothing there for Cybil to see except darkness.

Her skin was warm and soft beneath Miriam's hand. Miriam could feel Cybil trembling beneath her touch—muscles tensing as she prepared to bolt away—and so she released her, dropping her arm.

'I came here to warn you,' Miriam said.

'... Warn me? You already told me that Martingale—'

'He is coming now,' Miriam said. 'Tonight. To search the Hall for evidence.'

Cybil shook her head. 'Now? But—I received no notice of the charges.'

'Why would he forewarn a witch?'

Cybil laughed bitterly, throwing the comb aside. 'Yes, why would he?' she said, standing. She pulled up the sleeve of her chemise so it covered her shoulder. 'You had better not be deceiving me.'

'Why would I?'

'To convince me to make a deal with you.'

'Well, I *do* intend to do that,' Miriam admitted, 'but no need for deceit, not when Martingale and his men are so near. Wait, if you wish, until they arrive; we can negotiate then.'

Cybil gave her a long, searching look, brown eyes flickering in the dim light of the candles. She said nothing.

Miriam sighed. 'You know as well as I do, my dear, that this house is teeming with evidence. Unless you intend to raze it to the ground…'

Cybil pushed past her and left the room. Miriam followed.

'I suppose I cannot convince you to leave,' Cybil said, as they walked.

'No,' Miriam replied.

Harding Hall was in disarray, furniture knocked over, paintings pulled from their hooks. Several of the windows were smashed, but Cybil seemed neither to care nor notice.

Miriam was impressed. 'You have been taking this place apart.'

'My father left much evidence,' Cybil said.

'You will not flee, then?'

'I cannot.'

'Why?'

'My mother. I will not leave her. But'—she squared her shoulders—'I will do all I can to save us. I will hide the grimoires and return to them once this matter with Martingale is finished.'

'You believe he will show you mercy?' Miriam asked her with derision, voice lilting. 'That you can survive Oswyn's accusations?'

'I could not say,' she said. 'If I die because of him—because of *you*—then so be it. Many women better than I have done the same.'

'And what of the curse?'

'What of it?' Cybil snapped. 'It will not matter if I am dead.'

'I saw the way you reacted when I promised to remove it. I know how desperately you wish that you might someday be free.'

'That wish was foolish. I see that now.'

'I do not believe you,' Miriam said. 'I have watched you, Cybil Harding, since the moment your father died. I have seen you study his books and mix his potions.'

'That was mandrake tincture, for my mother.'

'The fact remains, my dear. You have *hope*, still—and how beautiful that is. How tragic.'

Cybil sneered at her and turned away.

They stopped in front of a door. It was Christopher Harding's study, where Miriam had first seen her, weeks ago. Cybil touched the wood. It was carved with markings: a grid of strange, curling letters, clearly designed to keep demons at bay. With their creator dead, the markings had lost all their power, but it was still with some irony that Miriam crossed the threshold.

'You may leave,' Cybil said, as she began to scan the study's shelves, selecting books and making a pile of them in the centre of the room. 'I will never make a deal with you, Miriam Richter. If my hope is foolish, yours is even more so.'

Ignoring this, Miriam peered more closely at the books. They were mostly grimoires and alchemist tomes. She opened one to find a ritual inscribed on the very first page, incantations and a circle already drawn. 'What will you do?' she asked, dropping the book dismissively back onto the pile. The curiosity in her expression was clinical, disinterested—a physician observing a wound. 'Burn them?'

'Some of them. But most are too valuable.' Finished, Cybil went over to the books she had selected. She hefted a stack of them into her arms, and looked down, grimacing, at the substantial pile that remained. For a moment, she pondered in silence, and then she sighed. 'If I cannot be rid of you, you might as well help. Take the rest.'

Miriam had never been ordered to do anything before—not without the parameters of a deal—and she smiled at the novelty as she took the rest of the books, tucking them under one arm.

'Not that one,' Cybil said, sharply, and she took one grimoire back: it was a smaller book, with a black leather cover embossed with a three-headed bird. She laid it carefully at the top of her stack, tucking it beneath her chin. Miriam eyed it curiously, but she had no reason to protest.

They went down the corridor, where Cybil stopped in front of a closed door. She used her foot to thump on it, as her hands were full. 'Mother?' she called. 'Are you awake?'

No response came. Cybil shifted, trying to distribute the weight of the books.

'Mother,' she repeated. 'Listen to me. A witchfinder is coming from the town to investigate us. If you have any of Father's things in there—anything that might incriminate us—please burn them. Or hide them if you must. I will do my best to keep him away from you. And I shall—I shall return for you. I swear it.'

She did not wait for a reply, and she marched down the corridor without glancing back.

They slipped through the dark house in hurried silence, the only noise Cybil's staccato breathing. They came through the kitchen, into a servant's passage, and out into the gardens. Cybil fetched a cloak on the way, but the cold was clearly quite severe—the moment they came outside, her teeth began to chatter, and her cheeks flushed. In the far distance, Miriam could hear dogs barking. It would not be long before Cybil would hear them too, and she would grasp the true urgency of the situation. Would she respond with fear, Miriam wondered, or determination? A fox leaping for its den, or a wolf flashing its teeth?

Leaving her stack of tomes on the gravel, Cybil went to the shed, returning with a spade, another cloak, and a sack for the books. She tossed the cloak at Miriam, who stared at the fabric in her hands in confusion.

'I thought you would be cold,' Cybil said.

'You thought *I* would be cold?'

'I need you to aid me with the books,' she snapped. 'And you can hardly do that if you are—well—I know not if you *can* be cold, actually, so—no matter.'

She put her books into the sack and slung it over her shoulder. Then she spun around and tramped toward the exit of the gardens. Amused, Miriam followed her, obliging to pull the cloak around her shoulders.

94

The forest swallowed them whole, plunging them into black. Miriam could see without trouble, but Cybil clearly could not, as she quickly stumbled over a branch. Miriam caught her.

'Release me,' Cybil said, tugging at Miriam's hands. There *was* fear in her voice; fear and anger both—how lovely it was to hear, the music of her desperation. But then Cybil froze; she was looking into the distance, where the glimmer of torches was edging the horizon. Miriam could hear the dogs louder now, and the men shouting, the horses shattering the frozen leaves beneath their hooves.

Shuddering with cold and terror, Cybil pulled away from Miriam. They walked a little longer before they found a suitable clearing. Beside a wizened oak, Cybil attempted to break the earth with her shovel, only to find it frozen solid. She swore and bit savagely at her bottom lip.

'Fool that I am,' she muttered to herself. 'Of *course* I cannot bury them, not in November. I am acting without sense. I shall have to burn them, after all.'

Miriam, tempted by the novelty of benevolence, took the spade from her and began digging, tossing clods of icy earth behind her shoulder. Cybil watched her silently with widened eyes, clutching the cloak around her shoulders.

'Stop,' she said, eventually. 'It is deep enough now.'

They laid the sack of books within the hole. At the last minute, Cybil said, 'Wait,' and stooped to reach into the sack. She withdrew the book with the black embossed cover, tucking it beneath her arm.

Miriam covered the hole with dirt; then Cybil covered the dirt with fallen leaves. There was something funereal about the whole process, as if they had dug and filled a grave. The way Cybil bowed her head after was a mourner's movement, strands of red hair falling to veil her face.

'Why are you aiding me?' Cybil asked her. 'Because you still believe I will bargain with you? Because you take amusement from my presence?'

Miriam smiled at her. 'Perchance both.'

'You laugh at my misery.'

'I marvel at your destruction,' Miriam corrected. 'Do men not do the same? Gasp in delight when a great tree is felled?'

'You are so insistent I will be destroyed—'

Miriam's patience was beginning to thin, and she interrupted. 'Because you *shall* be, Cybil. We both know that. The grimoires may be gone, but Martingale will find something else. That house stinks of witchcraft.'

Cybil's face remained hard, her eyes cold. 'I know. And you are the one that led them here.'

'What difference does that make? I have paid you a favour.'

'A *favour*?'

Miriam pitched her voice low, gentle. 'Sweet Cybil. You are not made for this world. Someone had to take you out of it.'

'What do you mean?'

'How hollow is the heart of a mortal,' Miriam said. 'How starving the soul. Your kind has spent thousands of years crawling out of the dirt, and yet still to the dirt you return. A curse, a gift—whatever your power is, you deserve *better*, my dear.'

'Deserve better? I have *killed* people, Mistress Richter. My curse has killed people.'

'Mayhap that is so. But if you permit your life to finish here, at the witchfinder's hands, that shall be the only legacy you ever leave behind. Make a deal with me, and your existence shall mean something more; its ending will mean something more.'

That resonated with Cybil—Miriam could see it upon her face. Scenting blood in the water, she stepped slightly closer.

'I could give you all you desire,' she continued. 'I could find you a place without loneliness, without fear. Without the weight of your guilt upon your shoulders. I could bring you there.'

Cybil said, 'The curse—you could truly lift it?'

'Certainly.'

'But it would cost me my soul.'

'Eventually. Still, we could come to an arrangement. You would have years before then. Decades, even.'

Her expression wavered. Miriam took another step closer, and their skirts brushed.

'How much time would you like?' she asked her. 'I am your willing servant. As long as you want me, I will be yours; I will follow your every command. Simply promise me, Cybil, that you will be mine, also.'

Cybil tilted her head up towards her, in a movement that seemed more unconscious than deliberate. Miriam cupped her cheek, and Cybil's breath sped up, blood rushing to her face.

Miriam said, 'I see the desire in your eyes,' and looped an arm around her waist, tugging her closer. Cybil stumbled forward, and when Miriam pressed her mouth against her neck, nipping at the soft skin there, she whimpered.

'You…' Cybil whispered. 'You *cannot*—I…'

'Just say it, darling. Say your soul is mine, and I'll give you what you need.' Miriam brushed her lips against the underside of her jaw, the skin beneath her ear, the crest of her cheekbone. She touched her mouth with hers—promising a kiss, withholding it at the last moment—and asked, 'You *do* want it, do you not? All you need to do is ask.'

Cybil's pupils were blown wide. 'Yes,' she said. 'Yes, I—'

In the distance, someone screamed.

Both women froze; then Cybil said, confused, 'Mother?' and shoved Miriam away.

The shriek sounded again. Cybil turned to Miriam, eyes flickering back and forth like flames, hands reflexively plucking at her skirts; the wildness in her face, the panic, was utterly breathtaking. 'What is happening?' she demanded. 'Did you do this?'

Miriam shrugged. 'It must be something to do with the witch-finder. Does it matter?'

Cybil looked aghast. Then, taking her skirts in her hands, she turned and ran towards the Hall.

Miriam groaned in frustration. 'Cybil!' she cried, exasperated. 'Cybil, wait!'

But Cybil was not listening. She continued to run. Her mother's screams were a constant wail now—almost musical in pitch, a melismatic song.

Miriam picked up the spade and followed her. As they ran, Harding Hall rose before them: its hill a grave-mound beneath it, and its windows laid out like an epitaph.

10

Cybil could hear Bess wailing, could hear the baying of dogs and the shouts of strangers. As she approached Harding Hall, she saw a throng of people outside the front door: men with pikes and chest plates and gravelly voices. Some were entering the building, and some were exiting it, bearing books and bottles, one even carrying her father's desk. Peter, Martingale, and all of Martingale's men were there, as well as the servants, who huddled in the corner, hissing to one another in urgent tones.

And on the rooftop, a gargoyle balanced on the balustrade—Bess Harding.

Cybil's heart stuttered. She whispered, 'Mother,' to herself, dropping the grimoire to the ground. But as she was about to rush forward, and reveal herself to everyone, someone placed a hand on her shoulder. Cybil gasped in fright, spinning around to shove them away. It was Richter, still holding the spade; Cybil's shove met her sternum, but it did nothing more to her than it might have done to a tombstone.

'Cybil,' Richter said, urgently, 'if they see you, they will—'

Cybil wrenched the spade from her hands. 'I care not what they do. My mother is up there, and if I do not act—'

'You are endangering yourself,' Richter interrupted. 'You need my help.'

'I do not *want* your help. I do not belong to you. My life is my own.'

Richter made a snarl of frustration, a sound so removed from humanity in its bared-teeth viciousness that Cybil almost flinched. 'A mere moment ago, you were prepared to agree to a deal.'

'And that would have been a mistake; we both know that. You bring nothing but destruction, Miriam Richter. I do not need you. I never shall.'

Richter's expression went cold and slack, and she took a step back. In her expression, Cybil suddenly saw a great, yawning emptiness, a darkness as vast as all the skies and all the seas the world had ever known. It made the hairs on her arms stand on end, her chest constrict.

'Go, then,' Richter said. 'Bury yourself with your pride. I will not give aid until you are willing to surrender.'

Terrified, furious, Cybil turned and ran towards the Hall. Richter did not call after her. Cybil peered back over her shoulder to see her still lingering by a tree, shadows gathering around her.

Approaching the crowd in front of the door, Cybil wielded the spade in two hands like a polearm. Peter was the first to notice her. When he saw the fury on her face, he stumbled backwards into Martingale, his mouth hanging slack in dismay.

Martingale pushed him aside and took a step forwards, clearing his throat. 'Lady Harding,' he said. 'I am Henry Martingale.'

'Yes, I recall.'

'Good. I have come upon the authority of the Council to arrest you upon suspicion of—'

Cybil ignored him, craning her neck to look at Bess on the roof. She was pressed against the balustrade, fingers curled over its stone edge; Bess was a tall woman, and the barrier hardly reached her hips. Harding Hall, three-storeyed and stoic, stood between Cybil and her mother with the silent grimness of a gaoler. Cybil pressed her hand against one of the Doric columns that framed the front steps, as if she might somehow push the house away.

'Mother, I am here!' she shouted. 'Come down, I beg you, before you hurt yourself!'

Bess swayed in the wind, a dandelion tuft in her white nightdress. Her red hair, the same vibrant shade as Cybil's own, swarmed around her shoulders; she was lit solely by the torches below, and ghoulish shadows seeped around her brows and jaw.

'It is finished!' she shrieked, clawing at her arms. 'It is *all* finished!'

'Mother, please—!'

'He said he would fix it,' she wailed. 'That we would no longer be cursed. But oh, oh, Cybil, my love is dead, and there is no escape for us. There never shall be.'

'I can help you, if only you would come down—'

Bess laughed, a laugh as much a scream. 'I will meet them. My husband, my son. Away from the curse—somewhere better. Somewhere new.'

'Mother, *do not*—!'

Bess stepped off the rooftop.

Cybil did not look. She could not look. She turned away, squeezed her eyes shut. She heard the thump against the ground, like a pheasant shot down; she heard the men shouting in horror. In the darkness behind her lids, she saw flickers of red light from the torches surrounding her, and the network of her own veins, tree roots spreading wider and wider. The spade was heavy in her hands, the wood made warm from her touch. It felt like a living thing, a loving thing, ready to obey her command.

Behind her, Martingale's voice came, unshaken by what he had seen. 'Come with me, Lady Cybil. If you are cooperative, the courts shall be merciful.'

Cybil opened her eyes. She turned to look at him. She could feel the heat she had felt on the roof rising once more, a prickling burn across her skin; and she could hear the shadows whispering, too, as familiar to her as the sound of the music she had once played on her virginal, or the threads of the tapestry she had once unpicked. Their whispers gathered in the tips of her fingers, in the base of her belly, in every bone and sinew of her limbs. They were hungry, so *hungry*. All she needed to do was feed them.

All she needed to do was make a trade.

'I do not require your mercy,' she said. 'If you believe me a witch, then a witch I shall be.'

Then she allowed every ember that had collected within her hollow heart, every ounce of loneliness and regret, every frustrated desire and fragile hope, to release itself from her—rising, meteoric—and she fed them, grinning, to the shadows.

The pain was indescribable: something being rent from her, torn and seared, a new emptiness where she had not known a presence had even existed. But the pain was beautiful, also. It was a new colour she had never seen; a language she had not known she spoke. The shadows welcomed her, consumed her—and as a slice of her soul was lost, she knew the darkness would do anything she wanted.

A trade, she told it. *My fire for yours.*

The shadows spun about her, joyous, grateful, a whirlpool of darkness, singing their thanks in incomprehensible hisses. Then they flew towards Harding Hall.

It took only a moment. With a great groan, the roof of the Hall collapsed upon itself, as the entire building burst into flame.

The fall of the roof sent a shower of sparks into the air. It made an echoing boom that shook the ground beneath their feet. The heat that arrived in its wake was so shocking in its intensity, so dry and furious, that most of the men cried out in alarm and began to run into the shelter of the woods. Cybil did not flinch. She looked up at the burning shell of her childhood home, and as she watched, several of the windows burst, unable to survive the sudden rise in temperature. Lead began to melt in great drips from the sections of the roof that had survived. An acrid scent filled the air.

A deep, fearful silence fell upon those who remained. Both Martingale and Peter had become insubstantial with terror, shivering like sheets in the wind. Cybil's home was gone, her mother dead, but she did not feel sadness, or even fear. She took a deep breath of ashen air and then began to laugh.

No evidence now, witchfinder, she thought. *There is nothing left. Nothing.*

For a moment, no one reacted. Then Martingale cried to those men still present, voice shaking, 'Well? Arrest her!'

None of the men moved. Peter sat on the ground and covered his face with his hands.

Martingale cursed and ran towards Cybil, clutching his hat with one hand to keep it on his head. Cybil swallowed her laughter, then turned and fled back towards the gardens; he gave chase. Despite the fact that the spade was slowing her, unwieldy and almost too heavy to lift, she could not abandon it. She had no other weapon, save the power that had set the Hall alight.

But the shadows had now gone silent. Cybil felt suddenly and profoundly exhausted, and when she tried to summon the spark, it doused itself before it could catch. The exhaustion only worsened as she ran, feet skidding over frost-limned stone and half-melted snow. When she reached the flower beds, she tripped, falling to her knees. Her elbows skimmed across the ground, ripping twin tears in the silk of her sleeves. Her skin burnt from the scrape. In front of her, endless rows of soil lay orderly in the darkness, scarred with frost, crowned by barren trellises.

For a moment, Cybil could hear only her breathing, and the creaking sounds of Harding Hall as it burnt. Then footsteps approached on the path. As they slowed, she turned her head to see the worn leather of Martingale's boots.

'Stand up,' he said. 'Surrender willingly, and you may still survive this night.'

Howling in anger, Cybil spun around and slashed at his stomach with the edge of the spade.

The tool was not sharp enough to cut through his clothes, but it was a good blow all the same. Martingale fell like a sack of stones before her. Groaning in pain, he reached for the spade and attempted to wrestle it from her; they became entangled, rolling together across the ground, four hands on the handle and legs flailing wildly.

Cybil was more furious, more desperate, but she could not match Martingale's strength. Eventually, he managed to shove her down, so that she was flat on her back against the ground. He wrenched the spade from her grip. Brandishing it triumphantly, he loomed over her, flushed with exertion.

'Enough now,' he said to her. 'You are mine.'

Cybil spat at him. 'You will burn in Hell. When you see the flames, know that I sent them.'

'Silence,' he hissed. 'You will see Hell yourself, soon enough.'

'Oh, yes, all glory to you, Master Martingale: killing women with another man's rope. That is how you shall be remembered, as a murderer too cowardly to use his own hands.'

'I am not a murderer.'

'No? Then what do you call your trials, your accusations?'

'Righteousness,' he replied. 'And it shall be righteousness to hang you, also. You are a witch, Cybil Harding. I am certain of that.'

'Perchance so, but the crimes you have killed others for are imaginary,' she told Martingale. 'You have led innocents to the gallows.'

'They were *not* innocent—'

Cybil sneered at him. 'They were victims of your ambition.'

'I have no ambition. This is a calling.'

'Your calling is nothing but a fantasy. God will punish you for it one day.'

His eyes widened with fury. 'No,' he said.

'Yes,' she replied. 'You are not cleansing the land, Master Martingale. *You* are the one corrupting it. *You* are the witch.'

Martingale, purple with rage, lifted the spade in both hands. Something feral flashed in his eyes; he brought it down towards Cybil's throat.

And perhaps Cybil ought to have realised sooner: she took after her father more than she had ever wished to accept. They shared the same hubris, after all. He had believed he could save Cybil. And for a brief, foolish moment, Cybil had believed she could save herself.

How wrong they both had been.

Cybil gasped and said, 'Richter,' in both a plea and an accusation. Then metal met skin.

Her windpipe collapsed upon itself, with the same inwards groan as the roof of Harding Hall.

As if shocked by his own actions, Martingale stared down, horrified, at the spade in his hands.

With a gurgling, guttural noise, Cybil began to die.

Miriam was standing by the burial site of Christopher Harding's grimoires. Her stillness was unearthly: such was the absence of movement that a winter moth had taken her for a statue, and it crawled leisurely across her face, one foot stepping on her unblinking eye.

Why had Cybil rejected her once again? Why had she looked at Miriam from within the circle of her arms and told her no, even while her desire was so evident? Cybil was like a reflection in the glass of a window, a pair of images at once—self superimposed upon self. Outside, inside, it was impossible to tell which parts of her were real, and which were those Miriam had constructed in her own mind.

But it did not matter. In her frustration, in her cold and ferocious anger, Miriam had half a mind to shatter the glass. She wanted to make Cybil *pay* for denying Miriam that day. Certainly, she would come to regret her fickleness in time, when a noose was looped around her neck, or a hungry fire set burning at her feet; but even before then, there were infinite possibilities for retribution. Miriam would start, perchance, with the mother that Cybil seemed to hold so dear—

Then Miriam heard Cybil's voice in her head, saying, *Richter.*

Breaking the silence of the clearing, Miriam breathed once more. Her sigh caused the moth to flutter away in alarm. Cybil wanted her back. She had not rejected her, after all.

Miriam stepped forward, paying a mote of light to the shadows, and then she was in the garden. She saw Martingale standing hunched over, with the spade clutched in his hands. She also saw the prone figure of Cybil lying on the ground, wearing a necklace of bruised and bloody flesh. In her chest, her soul flickered, a dying light. Seeing it fade, Miriam felt a shock and a significance of grief so intense, so *human*, that she trembled at the wrongness of it. What was more significant, she wondered—the loss of the meal? The loss of the woman, the first mortal with whom Miriam had felt some sort of kinship, as fleeting as it had been? That it was even a question felt absurd. It was rare that Miriam recognised some of herself, some of her isolation and her power, in someone else. But that rarity seemed not to merit the sadness she now felt. It seemed a weakness, and an unwelcome one.

Martingale turned around and saw her, jumping slightly in surprise. 'Who are you?'

Richter stared down at Cybil's body. 'You have killed her,' she said.

'I did what I had to—'

'You have *killed* her,' Richter snarled. The darkness coalesced behind her, creeping along the soil towards him. Martingale dropped the spade to the ground in shock.

'I—' He took a step backwards. 'Stay back. Get away from me.'

Miriam lurched forward and shoved the man to the ground. He had only a moment to make a noise of protest—an interrupted squeal, like a piglet being squeezed—before she had her foot on his stomach, her hands around his neck. 'You were supposed to *wait*,' she hissed. 'Why did you not wait?'

'I—I—do not understand.'

Miriam's fury was so powerful, it writhed around her, sent the shadows shuddering and twisting like snakes. She flayed the humanity from her face, leaving only a swarming darkness where her features should have been; she was too angry to remember the arrangement of eyes and skin that comprised a person. 'Tell me, Master Martingale,' she said, as he struggled against her hold, 'how many women have you brought to their deaths?'

Her voice was many voices, each a scream, each a whisper. Martingale whimpered. 'Please, I—I know not.'

'You do know. *Tell me.*'

He tried to shake his head. She tightened her grip, warningly; hissing in pain, he spat, 'Fifteen.'

'Including Cybil?'

'Sixteen.'

'I see.' Miriam hummed in thought. 'It is a shame I cannot give you a death for each of them. I suppose the one shall have to do.'

Martingale began to reply, but he did not finish. Miriam had pulled his skull from his spine as if she were uncorking a bottle of wine.

She tossed his head over her shoulder. It fell into a patch of ice and skidded along the path. Meanwhile, a great gush of blood fountained from the torso's torn neck, falling in a rainbow across the hedgerows. Miriam kicked away the body and went to Cybil, crouching beside her.

Her eyes were fluttering sightlessly, mouth twisted in a grimace; she was not breathing, and if her heart was beating, it would soon stop.

Death would suit her less than life, although she would make the prettiest corpse Miriam had ever seen. Miriam brushed some hair out of her face and glanced at her chest. The light there was barely visible now, but the soul was present still, faint yet persistent. Relieved, Miriam made herself into shadows and slipped within Cybil, reached for that remaining glimmer of existence. She found it soon enough, ephemeral and fading, falling through her fingers like sand. Cupping her hands, Miriam said Cybil's name once more, and allowed the light to engulf her.

There was nothing here, no sky or ground or air to breathe. But there was Miriam Richter, and there was Cybil herself.

Richter was standing in front of her, present and yet absent. When Cybil tried to look down—to perceive herself, to see her own body— her flesh was flickering, light and dark, like a dying candle flame.

Her voice an echo in the void, Cybil said, 'Where am I?'

Richter replied, 'Half departed, my dear, much is the pity.'

'I am dead.'

'Near enough.'

Cybil's hands flew to her neck. 'Oh, God,' she croaked, voice trembling. 'I am *dead*.'

Richter sighed. Her hair floated behind her in an amorphous storm cloud of shadow, making only the faintest impression of materiality. 'That is hardly a surprise,' she said. 'Death is inevitable. Thousands of fools have suffered it, and thousands more will do so.'

Inevitable. Cybil saw, in the awful and infinite clarity of hindsight, every moment of the life that had now ended: the ceaseless days of isolation, the echoing corridors of Harding Hall, the empty eyes of her parents, the slow drag of a finger against a windowpane. The shallow existence Cybil Harding had lived had hardly been worth the effort of her breathing. She had never cured her mother. She had never gone to Court. She had failed to make anything of herself, to *do* anything with herself, except suffer her curse and resent herself for it.

'It is a tragedy,' Richter continued, heedless of Cybil's distress, a frown stitching new lines into her forehead. 'You were my favourite, I think, of all those I ever tried to consume. And now I am denied my meal.'

Is this it? Cybil asked herself. *Is this really it? Is this all that I am worth?*

'Could I return?' she demanded. Richter raised an ink-stroke brow. 'Could I live again?'

'Anything is possible if you are willing to pay the darkness a price. That is the sole law by which magic is governed.'

'I want it,' Cybil said. 'This cannot be it; this cannot be all I shall ever have, all I shall ever be. I must do it again. Another chance.'

Richter thought on this, and then she smirked. Cybil had a sudden, powerful sense that she had made a mistake.

'A resurrection,' Richter mused. 'Powerful magic indeed. For a new life, nothing less than your entire soul would suffice. Most shadows would not have the patience to wait for such a meal.'

Cybil said, with grim acceptance, 'But you would?'

'I would,' Richter said. 'If you promise your soul to me—I can assure you, my dear, you will live once more.'

Cybil did not reply. The silence of the void they stood within was all-consuming. The darkness was a living thing, sinking its teeth into the empty space between their words.

Richter continued. 'A new life. A happy life. One free of loneliness. I can offer that to you—I can re-form you in a place, a time, where you are guaranteed companionship. You could be free of the curse, even: a second daughter, or a third—someone part of a large family, with people who love you. And with a second soul, merged to your first, you would be twice as powerful as you are. Would that not please you? Would you not be glad?'

'But you would still take all of my soul, in the end,' Cybil said.

'Yes.'

'How long would I have?'

'As long as the life you have already lived—that seems fair to me.'

'Twenty-three years?' Cybil asked, and in the emptiness, her anger echoed endlessly, a chorus of voices. 'That is not enough!'

Richter grinned at her, an animalistic grin, teeth pulling back to the gums. 'It is more than nothing,' she said. 'Which is what you will have otherwise.'

Cybil shuddered at her expression, which was so cruel in its aspect, so alien, that she wondered how she could have ever felt attracted to her—but then their gazes met, Miriam's eyes liquid and dark, and she remembered.

Mayhap Cybil's desire for her was some convoluted attempt at self-destruction. She had always known she was destined for an early death—the curse made it a moral imperative—and now Miriam offered a death more perfect than any other. Because that was what this offer was, in the end: a second death, later than the first, but an ending still. Twenty-three more years, but those years lived while indebted to a higher power. Was that not another curse? Another obligation, another destined misfortune?

And, oh, while Cybil found herself a new life, and played at normalcy, another First Daughter would eventually be born. There were other branches of the Harding family, more magicians to be made; someday, some poor girl would be left to the wolves again, or thrown to the sea, or locked away to live her life alone. Perchance Miriam Richter would find her too, and offer her this same deal with a smile and an open palm. And she would take it, because she would be desperate, and afraid.

Cybil was desperate, and afraid.

But Cybil wanted more.

'You told me all magic is balance,' Cybil said. 'A trade: light for shadow. Does that extend to wagers, also?'

Richter paused. She frowned. 'Wagers… ?'

'The next time there is a First Daughter—the next time a Harding girl is born cursed. Make that daughter me.'

Richter laughed so harshly, so incredulously, it emerged as half a shout—a wolf's snarl, teeth gnashing. 'You *wish* to be cursed again?'

'I have seen my power now. I can break it myself this time. I am certain I can. The family grimoire has rituals my father designed. He tried it himself when I was born, but clearly, he was not strong enough. If *I* am reborn, you said I will have two souls, and twice the power. Twenty-three years to break the curse. If I succeed, the shadows leave me alone, and allow me to live my full life in peace.'

'And if you fail?'

'If I fail,' Cybil said, 'my soul will be yours.'

Richter replied, sharply, 'My deals are never conditional.'

'But the souls you take are never so powerful—you said so your-self. Surely that balances the scales.'

'Twenty-three years to break the curse,' Richter murmured to herself, considering. 'Hm.'

Cybil began to reply, but then her view of Richter dimmed momentarily, and she felt a strange coldness begin to grip her. Richter's expression transitioned into one of alarm.

'What is happening?' Cybil said.

'We must work fast. You are fading.' Richter moved forward to take Cybil's hand, cradling it in her own with surprising tenderness. Darkness coalesced within Cybil's grip, making the form of a quill. 'Very well,' Richter said. 'As you suggested: twenty-three years to break the curse. If you succeed, I will leave you to your mortality. If you fail, your soul is mine.'

Cybil looked at the quill. She thought of the curse in the grimoire, the three-headed hawk on its cover.

Past, present, future.

Cybil adjusted her grip on the quill. Richter, smiling hungrily, flipped her own hand over and presented her palm. 'Here—sign.'

Cybil signed her name.

She felt something click into place—a latch sliding shut—and as it did so, Richter gave a triumphant laugh and pulled her closer, sealing her mouth over hers. It was less a kiss than a claim, with a hand closing around the back of Cybil's neck, fingers pressing bruises into her skin. Richter's palm was still bleeding—was it blood? It felt too cold—and the liquid ran in freezing trails down Cybil's back. When Richter released her, she felt lightheaded. She looked down at her own arm, still outstretched from where it had fallen around Richter's waist, and she could barely distinguish it from the darkness.

'You are mine now,' Richter said. 'In this life, and the next.'

The shadows surged, the darkness coming to greet them. They slipped beneath it, submerged themselves into the nothing. With that, all light was doused—and Cybil Harding, finally, was gone.

Intermission

Manila, 1762

'Do you believe, Don Miguel,' Miriam said, blood running in rivulets down her extended forearm, 'that there is a difference between love and hatred?'

Don Miguel de Valdez, prone and trembling upon the floor before her, made no reply but to continue his fervent muttering of the Lord's Prayer.

Outside, there was the sound of cannon fire—that of the Spanish or the British, Miriam didn't know; it made no difference to her—and the muffled screaming of dying soldiers. The Englishman who had traded her his soul an hour earlier was likely dead by now, so he would never see the fruits of his labour. Those fruits were the dozens of corpses that draped themselves across the wooden furniture of the garrison house, the iron tang of their blood thick in the air. The heat was oppressive—Miriam could not feel it, but through the window she could see the way the air shimmered on the distant, tree-lined horizon—and the flies were already beginning to swarm.

Before her, the Spanish man had been reduced to tears and entreaties for deliverance. This really had been a pointless deal, in the end—helping one conqueror displace another—but perhaps the people here, those who had been forced to suffer such brutality, could take some comfort in Miriam's having delivered their oppressors brutality in turn. Miriam had watched as blood had run through the streets of Manila, had seen the tears and the fury of those who had for so long called it home. This was nothing less than what was deserved.

'Love and hatred,' she repeated, advancing nearer. 'It is all desire, in the end. No doubt many men have thought the same. *If she thinks of me, she is mine; whether or not it is with affection.* A fair assumption, no? I've been considering it for some time.'

Don Miguel shook his head mutely and skittered back from her. There was a severed leg on the table above him, dripping blood, and his hands slipped in the puddle that had formed. He fell onto his back, whimpering.

'You do not agree?' Miriam asked, curiously. 'Well, there is a counter-argument. Perhaps we should prefer to be forgotten than resented. At least that allows the possibility of future acceptance.'

He clasped his hands in a prayer position. 'Spare me,' he said. 'I beg you.'

Miriam clicked her tongue. 'You have been a dull conversation partner,' she replied, in the tone of a long-suffering parent speaking to a child. 'It isn't that I am *lonely*, mind, but rather that I am bored. You are responsible for so many atrocities, I thought that at least you would be interesting—but you are not.'

'B-bored?'

'*Bored*,' she repeated, shooting the word from her mouth like a bullet. 'I have been waiting centuries for a First Daughter, and I must admit'—here she bent over and plunged her hand into the man's chest—'I am growing'—she closed her palm around his heart, admired the speed of its beating, and then pulled it out—'*impatient*.'

Don Miguel did not respond.

Miriam put the organ in one of the trenchers on the table, next to a hunk of stale bread. The blood saturated the flesh of the loaf immediately, turning it from white to scarlet. Idly, she pressed her finger into the bread, listening to it squelch. As she did so, she felt the insistent pull of the deal she had made with the English soldier that morning disappear.

Miriam took the form of a crow and flew out of the garrison house window. Outside, the South China Sea glowed cerulean, pockmarked with galleons and plumes of smoke from cannon fire. Souls glimmered within the whitewashed walls of the Intramuros, and—further, shining along the winding dirt roads of the town's outskirts—there were souls brighter still, inflamed with conviction and fury. Miriam smiled to see them. Revolt would soon be coming to Manila, and with it a feast of desire, of hope and dread and ambition. Miriam would stay there for the next few decades and gorge herself.

Love, hatred—Miriam didn't see much need for the distinction. Both were simply hunger, in the end. And that was all her existence was: hunger and consumption, in an endless cycle. Past, present, future. No matter how full she became, she would always be hollow again.

You ought to hurry, my dear, she thought, recalling Cybil's face. *I grow so weary of a world without you in it.*

Part II

London

11

Esther Harding was born on Christmas Eve, 1790, under inauspicious stars.

Not that anyone cared they were inauspicious—her father had never been interested in that sort of superstitious nonsense. But Esther's dim uncle, who had always had a fascination with the family lineage, solemnly informed his brother that his daughter would be cursed.

'Balderdash,' Reginald Harding said, sucking on his cigar. His fair hair curled insouciantly over his forehead; his gold-brown eyes were the same shade as his child's. 'My daughter is perfectly normal, thank you.'

Esther found out when she was six. On one of his visits, her cousin Thomas had let it slip that his father called her the cursed girl, the misfortunate one, a *witch*. Thomas said that she was a 'bad seed of Eve, like the apple but worser,' and would kill them all if they weren't careful. He said this with the same little vindictive smirk he always said everything with—Thomas was like that. He was younger than Esther, but he had always treated her like she was a baby.

For some reason, Esther did not find this knowledge surprising—but she found it upsetting, all the same. She felt the truth of it in the same instinctive way she felt pain when the darkness was near, or when she was made to eat sprouts. She was cursed. Of course she was. Her mother had died of consumption when she was only one; her father had chosen to abandon England rather than remarry. Now he was on an East India Company appointment far away, leaving Esther in the hands of the help: eight servants housed in the base of their townhouse in Brunswick Square, replaced so often by her uncle that Esther hardly ever learnt their names. She was surrounded by lovely things: frosted-glass chandeliers and paintings of insipid courtesans; silk gowns and gold-framed mirrors; a lavender-coloured rocking horse she had named Charmeuse. But every joy she had seemed coupled with sorrow. Consider the little songbird she'd received as her fifth birthday present from her father: she'd found it dead at the bottom of its cage the next day. Think of the shadows that swarmed around her when she was angry, the way she heard whispers in the dark.

She was a First Daughter, and she was cursed. That was simply how it was.

After that, after she knew about the curse, it only seemed to get worse. Her governess, Harriet, took her out on an excursion on the lake in Hampstead Heath that summer; upon seeing shadows dancing on the water, she had taken such fright that she had fallen into the lake and drowned. Her successor had apoplexy. By the time Reginald returned from his appointment—another squirming baby in his arms, the product of an affair in Penang—Esther was feared by everyone in the household.

'She *is* cursed,' her uncle said. 'Our father told us the stories—what happened the last time there was a First Daughter. Shadows followed her, and suffering came in their wake.'

'Nonsense,' Reginald Harding said again. He had always been stubborn, carving his opinions upon himself like words carved into stone—he had neither the twitching paranoia of his younger brother nor, perhaps, his foresight.

Esther didn't tell *her* brother, Isaac, about the curse, not even once he grew old enough to understand it. Her father had given him a room near the servants' quarters for shame of his bastardry, and yet—despite this—Isaac seemed to approach the world with great vigour and optimism; it was often commented that his personality was the opposite of his curt, callous sister's. When Esther walked down a hall, he would spring from behind doors and leap to grasp her skirts; he would babble and laugh with all the joy of a piping flute; he was sweet and kind and gullible, craning his neck when Esther told him she saw a pig flying through the sky, gasping in delight when she somehow removed her thumb from its socket.

Eventually, though, as the shadows grew more familiar, their darkness more insistent, Esther learnt to keep the pigs upon the ground, her thumb attached. She did not want to ruin him. She did not want to love him overmuch, or else the curse might take him, also. Instead, she made herself alone.

And so, Esther Harding grew from girl to woman. She ignored her doddering father and her earnest brother, who always tried so hard to get her attention, and whom she pushed away. They stayed in the London townhouse all year, regardless of season, as the family estate belonged to her uncle's line; and although that was terribly out of fashion, Esther didn't mind it. To her, London was not only the Ton, with its pastel dreams and white-marble houses, its gilded carriages and manicured lawns. It was all the filth, too: the horse dung on the cobbles, the thin film of soot that coated everything, the stench of the summer and the bitter cold of the winter. It was oily puddles and coal smoke, street vendors shouting, butchers lugging sweating cuts of meat. It was the constant rain, the darkness of the clouds, the way that thunder sometimes shook the chandeliers in their red-papered dining room and made the crystals clatter. On occasion, Esther would dream of other places—faraway houses, with empty halls and shadowy hills—and it was always with relief that she awakened, remembering she was in London still. London was so *human*, so *real*. It kept her grounded.

The town offered opportunity, too. There were bookshops in the town, those run by secret societies, full of shelves of esoterica and occult scribblings. Esther would sneak out at night and explore dark alleyways with closed doors that only opened to the correct pattern of knocks; she would seek ancient manuscripts in labyrinthine libraries that claimed to hold the secrets of the universe.

At seventeen, the night before Esther's first day out in the marriage market, she went to one such library and held a book in her hands that was bound with human skin. Bringing it home, she followed the ritual inside to the letter, sourcing each ingredient, muttering each incantation with solemn precision: but nothing seemed to happen. Nothing *ever* seemed to happen, no matter how many attempts she made.

Esther groaned and tipped her head back, rolling her neck. It was late, very late, the only illumination in the room the candles she'd lit for the ritual circle. She remained in the gown she'd worn to tea that afternoon, a pale-blue capped-sleeve dress with bluebells stitched on its hem. Its incongruity with the pentagrams inked on the back of her hands was almost amusing.

Something tapped on the window. Esther turned to look at it, and she smiled, going to open the sash. The crow on the sill cawed in approval, outstretching its wings as if to imply an embrace. Something glinted in its claws.

'You brought me something?' she asked it, and in reply it thrust a curled talon towards her. It dropped something small and red and bloody onto the windowsill: a tiny sparrow's heart, dead and unbeating, a vivid stain on the white-painted wood.

'Oh.' Esther reached forward to take the heart in her hands. A droplet of blood welled between her clasped palms, trailing down her wrist. It tumbled down to the hem of her skirts, where it bloomed red against the cerulean petals of an embroidered bluebell.

'Thank you,' she said, and the crow bowed its head.

The crow had been visiting Esther at the townhouse for as long as she could remember. Perhaps, as a young girl, she had given it something to eat, and so ensured its loyalty; she couldn't remember. If so, Esther declined to question how the crow had lived so long, or why it continued to visit with little reward. As with all things in her life, it was largely inexplicable.

She went to her dressing table, laid out an old silk kerchief, and placed the heart upon it. She knew she would have to throw it away soon, but she wanted to appreciate the gift while it lasted. She stared down at the tiny, fingernail-size organ, noting its silence and stillness, and she cocked her head.

The darkness had been whispering to her for years. It was only natural that, sometimes, she had listened.

Their interactions had started as tiny trades: she would ask for something small of it, like setting the logs alight when the fire failed. In exchange, Esther would feel a brief moment of burning within her, like searing a finger upon a candle flame, and a brief moment of emptiness. It had become second nature to her, now, to make these miniature deals. The wonders they created were always worth the pain.

Slowly, gently, she held her hands out to the shadows, welcoming them to her. They knew her well enough to understand she wanted an exchange. Immediately, she felt a heat prickle in her chest, and—being careful not to let the pain overwhelm her—she reached forward, placing a trembling finger on the sparrow heart.

Make it beat, she thought. And with that thought, the shadows stretched forward like fingers, curling themselves around the organ. The heart quivered, inflated, and slowly, steadily, began to pulse in time with her own.

Esther's shoulders slumped as the pain faded. She had this, at least. Her power had made her isolated, but perhaps, someday, it would bear the key to her freedom. She simply had to find the correct ritual, the correct set of spells, and it wouldn't matter anymore that the other women in the Ton found her off-putting, or that her dreams were full of fire; it wouldn't matter that sometimes—in the most silent moments of dark between sleeping and waking, when the mind is half present, half dreaming—she heard someone saying a name that was her own, but not her own. An oracle's name, just as Esther was, and one that seemed as familiar to her as Esther did.

The crow on the windowsill cawed. Esther felt the sparrow's heartbeat for a moment longer, then lifted her finger. *Thank you*, she told the shadows.

The organ fluttered, shuddered, and was still.

Esther's father died when she was twenty-two.

It had happened while he was sleeping. No one knew why. 'His spirit left him,' the doctor said, as if spirits were prone to spontaneous flight; but either way—he was gone.

Esther felt grief, but very little of it. He had been an absent father, not cruel, but not kind; sometimes it seemed he almost had an aversion to her, that he avoided her gaze and her conversation. She had never grown to love him.

At the funeral, as they laid their father to rest, there was much commentary on the tragedy of the Harding bloodline. They were a scandalous family, after all—seventeen-year-old Isaac was illegitimate; Esther had been out in the marriage market for several Seasons but had yet to make a match; and this was the third Harding death in as many years. The first had been her uncle, of distemper; the second her cousin's poor little wife, Lily, upon the childbed—and now Reginald had followed them. Left without a guardian, Esther and Isaac had nowhere to go but to their cousin's household. The three of them were the only Hardings left in London, the other branches of the family huddled away in country estates, resolutely pretending their scandalous town relatives didn't exist.

Esther met the curious stares of the funeralgoers with open defiance, while Isaac simply ignored them. No doubt they were ill-matched, the two of them, standing beside the casket in their mourners' clothes: Esther pale and flame-haired, face impassive, swaddled in her black pelisse, while her brother—brown-skinned, brunet, expressive to a fault—grimaced and winced at the belaboured droning of the vicar. Their eyes caught; Isaac's lips twitched. Esther did not quite allow herself a smile.

Afterwards, walking out of the church, with the stares of dozens beating on their backs, he said, 'A bloody relief it's over.'

Esther wasn't certain whether he was speaking of the funeral or their father's life. She had considered, many times, that she might have been Reginald's killer; but that was his fault, she supposed. Their uncle had tried to warn him several times about her curse, and he'd never listened.

'We could go see a play,' Isaac continued, hopefully. 'We have time to catch the matinee.'

'We ought to return home and pack our things,' she said.

'Come, Esther, it's our last day of freedom. Surely we ought to do something *fun*.'

'We are supposed to be grieving,' she snapped, and then tried to ignore the way his expression shuttered.

They approached their carriage. The lamppost beside it, bent slightly sideways from some historic storm, had a crow sitting at its top. Esther gave the bird a secret smile. It cawed and took flight, its shadow passing over them like a mourning veil.

'Cousin Esther,' Thomas Harding said. 'And little Isaac—how you've grown. Welcome. Watch the steps, they are Italian marble.'

Thomas's townhouse was larger than theirs had been, much larger. As they'd finished packing their things the previous day, Esther hadn't shed tears, although part of her had wanted to; she'd been leaving the only home she'd ever known. She'd chosen the sage-green carpet in the tearoom, the India-wood furnishings. She had painted the walls of her bedroom the silver-grey of a storm cloud, had carved ritual circles on the inside of her closet. Now it was all lost to her, buried alongside her father.

Despite being younger than Esther, Thomas was now head of the Harding family—as his father was dead, also, and he was the eldest son. As Isaac and Esther were ushered inside, it became clear his townhouse was much like him: pale and tall and overdressed. Thomas had poured the family wealth over the place like sudsy water from a wash bucket: each lamp and curtain had a gold tassel, each wall a pastel-toned painting, each chair leg a curlicued accent. The air smelt of dried roses and damp, the small windows emitting only the barest hint of light.

They stopped in the parlour to admire an enormous oil portrait of a dour-faced man with a high ruff, glaring at his viewers as if to admonish them for daring to raise their eyes. There was something in his face Esther felt she recognised.

'Christopher Harding,' Thomas said, proudly. 'My father made it his mission to recover all the family artefacts that had survived the fire at Harding Hall; this was the only portrait saved. You have heard of him, I presume? Christopher, I mean.'

Isaac replied, 'Oh, yes, assuredly, assuredly,' in his driest tone.

'An alchemist and a scholar, of the greatest degree,' Thomas told them, as if Isaac hadn't replied. 'One of our most venerable ancestors. This way—I simply *must* show you the music room.'

Esther knew very little about Thomas. There had been talk of them marrying, when they were younger, but nothing had come of it, as he had married Lily instead. Now it had been years since they'd carried on a conversation. Thomas bore little resemblance to either Isaac or Esther; the three of them shared only a surname and a pair of arrestingly large, leaf-shaped eyes, a trait that was considered either beautiful or unsettling depending upon the disposition of the viewer. Otherwise, Thomas was unfortunately woeful in appearance. He had an excessive amount of hair that was both too light and too dark to suit his sallow complexion, eyes that were either grey or blue, and a bone-thin, hawkish face that could have been used to chisel stone. It was not a handsome face, or a welcoming one. Esther supposed she would become accustomed to it.

They continued their tour. The townhouse was so cramped and silent, it felt closer to a coffin than a home. The dining room was painted the colour of Madeira wine, a grotesque Hogarth of ruddy-faced drunk-ards watching over the empty table; the hallway beside it had a still life of a dead lobster, its vibrant shell the same shade as Esther's hair. The music room smelt of mothballs, and it was so dark within that Thomas was obliged to light the sconces. The pianoforte was beautiful, a deep mahogany nearly the shade of blood. Thomas explained at great length about its ivory keys and imported casing, but it was difficult for Esther to pay attention. The room felt so stuffy that his words sounded muffled, like cotton wool was being pushed into her ears.

Isaac was given a good room on the second floor, well positioned, albeit a little small. It had apparently once been furnished for a child; now an adult-size bed was shoved awkwardly in the corner, incon-gruous with the beribboned curtains and a tiny chest of drawers. Isaac didn't bother to protest, but he closed the door in their faces with a dramatic sigh.

Esther inferred the room had been intended for the baby Thomas and his wife had been expecting. Lily and the baby had passed a few months ago.

'Forgive Isaac,' Esther said, as they descended the steps to the first floor. She so rarely apologised that it felt somehow cruel to do so, as if this false courtesy was ruder than if she hadn't said anything at all. 'He is... young, still.'

Thomas nodded curtly. He was staring at her, considering, his jaw tense. He had one protruding vein high on his forehead, pulsing a faint blue against his sallow skin. It seemed as if he intended to say something; but then he did not, and they moved on.

They came past a door with roses painted in oils along the frame. The art was subtle, the work of a talented hand. Esther said, 'What is that?'

Thomas gave the door a brief glance. His lips tightened. 'That was Lily's room,' he said, and then he continued to walk.

That made sense—the flowers recalled what little Esther had known of his wife before she had died: a quiet, delicate girl who had grown flowers in her garden and spoken hardly a word. Esther chased after Thomas and made some attempt at solidarity. 'I know it must be... odd, to have us here, after all that has happened.'

Thomas shook his head. 'Lily always liked you. She would have— she would have insisted you stay with us.'

'I...' Esther cleared her throat, looked down at the floor. She sought desperately for another topic of conversation. 'The Cheswicks are hosting a fete tomorrow. Will you be attending?'

'Unfortunately not,' Thomas said. 'I did receive an invitation, but I can't come.'

'Oh. Why?'

'Well—' He cleared his throat, clearly disarmed by her direct manner. Esther quickly cast her eyes back down to the floor. 'I have a meeting here with my lawyer. I am finalising the sale of your father's townhouse.'

Esther knew that Thomas had hardly left his own home since Lily's death; it had been the subject of much Ton gossip, the reclusive Harding driven half mad with grief. She felt foolish for asking. 'I understand.'

'The money shall be yours, as his will stipulates,' Thomas said. 'I shall put it toward your dowry.'

'Thank you.'

They stopped in front of a door. 'This shall be your room,' he told her, with some pride. Then his voice became hushed, as if he were imparting a secret. 'Esther...'

'Yes?'

'We are family. The Harding bloodline: that is all that matters.' He reached forward then, and placed his own hands over hers; his fingers pressed against the fabric of her gloves in a proprietary, searching sort of way.

Esther gently extracted her hands. Something about the way he'd touched her had made the hair on her arms stand on end. She told herself that was an instinct borne of the curse. She couldn't let herself grow too close to Thomas, couldn't allow him any sort of intimacy, or else she would lead him to disaster. At least this offer of friendship, as futile as it was, showed he had offered his guardianship in good faith. 'Thank you.'

'I sincerely hope you will be happy here.'

Her throat tightened. 'As do I,' she said, and suddenly she was utterly overwhelmed. 'Excuse me, I must rest before supper.'

She entered the bedroom and shut the door in his face before he could reply.

Her room was lime green: lime-green wallpaper, lime-green furnishings, lime-green sheets and curtains. It made her feel queasy. The servants had laid out her cases, and she went to open one, removing one of her books—the first volume of Machiavelli's *The Art of War*. It was familiar to her, comforting. She sat on the bed to read. On the opening page, an ex libris had been pasted in, with the three-headed hawk of their family crest.

'Past, present, future,' Esther murmured, and then she turned the page.

Something moved on the wall opposite her. She knew she shouldn't look, that granting it attention would only encourage it—darkness was childlike, in that way, poking and whining at her to elicit a reaction. Still, Esther glanced upwards. Two shadows were engaged in a curious play upon the wall. One had taken the form of an odd sort of beast—feminine and humanoid in shape, but with the feet and wings of a bird. The other was a smaller woman in a wide-skirted gown. These silhouettes performed a fluid dance about each other, spinning up and down the walls, until the bird-woman suddenly widened her wings, grew a long beak, and swallowed her partner whole.

Esther felt her heart speed up with anxiety, but she was accustomed enough to the shadows that—although she feared them—she didn't flee. Since she had first understood her curse, and first understood her father's refusal to either acknowledge or aid her, she had learnt to make use of the dark; to bear the pain of her powers, albeit in small doses, so that she could make her miniature miracles. She tolerated its presence as best she could, and she told herself that one day, she would be rid of it entirely.

The shadow-figure paused. The bird-woman unhinged her jaw, and the woman in the gown crawled out of it, miraculously whole. She raised her hands to her throat as if in pain. In response, Esther felt her own throat close, a strange, burning ache growing at the skin there, as if it was bruised—she gasped, and then gasped more, horrified at how the air caught in her throat, as if she were suffocating.

'Go away,' she pleaded to the shadows on the wall, her voice hoarse, panicked. 'Shoo now. Please. I do not know what—what is happening, but it hurts. It *hurts*.'

The darkness hesitated—and then, chagrined, faded away.

The pain disappeared. Esther took a deep breath, relieved at the ease of it, and she put Machiavelli aside. She closed her eyes. *All is well*, she told herself. *You are well. The shadows can't touch you. Not unless you allow them to.*

Once she had calmed, she opened her eyes again. Staring up at her ceiling, she found—curiously—that she had a melody stuck in her head.

'*For I am still thy lover true*,' she murmured, half singing, half whispering. '*Come once again and love me*.'

12

It wasn't that Miriam had expected to gain much from her repeated visits to Esther Harding; in fact, she knew there was nothing to gain from them at all. There was only one thing that was required of her, and that was to wait until Esther's time was up. Miriam wasn't concerned that Esther would find a way to break the curse. That had never even been a consideration.

It would have been amusing, perhaps, to speak to her in human form—but Miriam was wary of reminding Esther of her past lives, of accidentally removing whatever mortal obstruction had prevented Cybil's memories from resurfacing. By the time of her death, Cybil had been extremely powerful; now Esther was even more so. Once she realised that attempting to break the curse was futile, who knew what havoc she could wreak in search of an escape from the deal? No. Miriam had all she needed this way, watching her as a crow from the windowsill. She saw Esther's pleasure, her pain, her confusion and regret. The deal had done its work well: Cybil and Esther were physically indistinguishable, save for the absence and presence of a few scars, and a slight gain in height that a more varied diet had afforded the latter. Now Esther was grown to the same age as Cybil had been, they were the same woman entirely. Perhaps Esther was somehow now even *more* herself than she had been as Cybil, her soul reaffirmed with a second light, glowing even brighter than it had before. The shadows rejoiced in her presence, swarming to sip from the power that leaked through her skin.

With her father's death—and wasn't that fascinating? Esther's life a dark mirror to Cybil's, like a clock, hands pointing to the same number at two different times of day—Esther had quit the home of her childhood and found herself replanted within her cousin's townhouse.

It hardly made much of a difference to Miriam, of course; one windowsill was much the same as any other. But on the first night of her residence there, Esther herself had seemed disquieted, tossing and turning in her sleep, fingers carving canyons into the sheets.

Miriam wanted to take pleasure in her distress, in the beauty of it, the sheer sensuality—but she knew what it forewarned. With each passing year, the weight of Cybil's memories grew stronger, and Miriam was no longer confident that Esther would live and die without knowledge of her previous life. If it did not risk invalidating the deal, and starting the cycle anew, Miriam would kill her at this very moment: preserve the sleeping elegance of her lashes falling softly against her cheeks, her back arching as she bucked against the dream. But Miriam was confident another rebirth would only lead to disaster. One life was difficult enough to forget, let alone two.

The knob of Esther's bedroom door turned—so slowly, so gently, that even Miriam almost did not notice someone was entering. But then a knife of flickering light sliced across the threshold. A shined-leather shoe pressed forward, then another; the man that followed had a bright soul, as bright as Christopher Harding's once had been, although it was no match for Esther's. He was brown-blond, and hawkish. The candle he held made his face a skull, light eyes lit golden. Miriam concentrated, and a soft touch upon his psyche revealed his name—Thomas Harding—as well as his purpose. Hatred, bitter bright, made his fingers twitch against the candlestick, his brows furrow, his steps stutter. He hated the woman in the bed with such intensity, such passion, that he *desired* her, too—he wanted to conquer her and ruin her. He blamed her for every disaster his life had ever had: the failed Company appointments; the death of his father; the death of his wife. One week had separated them at birth. Because of that week, the family gift had become hers, magic denied to him forever. And that gift had not only been given to Esther, but twisted by her, corrupted ineffably. She was a First Daughter, and she was cursed. The Hardings were cursed.

Thomas crept forward and stood over Esther, watching her as she slept. His face was grim and furious. The candle wobbled in his shaking hand. Grimacing, he took care to right it.

Miriam fed upon the basest elements of humanity: regret, desperation, sadness, lust. For this reason, she had always recognised the darker emotions that had infected her creators. She felt satisfaction at others' pain, fury at a lost cause, desire and hunger, as much as any person would. And now she saw something familiar in Thomas Harding's expression, something she imagined was often in hers, in the moment before making a deal. He was uncertain—this was not a calculated visit, merely an impulse of obsession—but still, he remained as capable of destruction as Miriam was. He was capable of touching the candle to the sheet and setting it alight, or lunging forward to throttle Esther as she slept.

Miriam could not allow it. She shifted partly into shadows, making herself intangible, and went to step through the glass—then bounced back, feeling a stinging pain skitter across her feathers.

There was salt laid on the windowsill. Only a line of it, grain by grain, thin enough to be undetectable. But it was enough to forbid her entry. Enough to save Thomas Harding's life for now.

Was this how it felt to be mortal, to be trapped and impotent, to see disaster approach and accept it as inevitable? Furious, Miriam pecked at the window with her beak, making a loud clunking sound. Inside, Thomas froze. Esther muttered to herself and shifted in her sleep.

Miriam cawed and pecked again at the window. A hairline crack appeared in the glass, and Thomas stepped back, candle shaking wildly in his hands. Miriam was tempted to continue and see the window shatter, but doing so wouldn't remove the line of salt, or permit her entry. Instead, she focused on making as much noise as possible, cawing and shrieking, clawing at the window with her talons. The glass squealed as if in pain.

Thomas, eyes wide, spun away and ran out of the room. The door slammed shut behind him. Esther bolted up in the bed, gasping in shock, holding the sheet to her chest. She looked at the window.

'Little shadow,' she said, loudly enough that Miriam could hear her through the glass. 'What are you *doing*?'

She slid off the bed. Her nightdress, semi-sheer in the moonlight, clung invitingly to the round of her stomach, the lines of her thighs. But Miriam could hardly indulge herself—particularly not with a line of salt between them, and the cousin threatening his return.

Instead, she tapped her beak once more against the window, expanding the crack in the glass, just to see Esther flinch in response. The rush of possessiveness Miriam felt was dizzying.

No one else should ever make you feel fear, darling, she thought. *No one but me.*

Then she turned away and took off into the night.

Miriam was walking a tightrope, that much was clear. Esther was on the precipice of remembering her previous life—any event too jarring, a moment of shock or anger, could tip her over the edge. Meanwhile, Thomas Harding had ensconced himself in his salt-rimmed house, defended from Miriam's intervention by the safety of his walls. He would have to leave eventually, she knew, but he seemed stubbornly resistant to the world outside; he spent the entirety of the next day in his library, flipping through old books and taking notes in a ledger. Miriam saw something of Cybil's father in the man, in the wild twitch of his fingers as he turned the pages, in the minute pinpricks of his pupils as they caught the light of the sun outside. It was a bloodline, clearly, that was prone to obsession, prone to ambition. It was both the Hardings' greatness and their ruin.

The afternoon came, and Esther bid Thomas farewell: she was going to some sort of society event. Miriam was torn between following her and watching Thomas for longer. Eventually, she settled on Esther—there was nothing more entertaining than watching her try to navigate high society—and she was about to fly away from the windowsill when Thomas stood from his seat, went over to the lefthand wall, and crouched down to pull up a floorboard.

Miriam watched, fascinated, as he lifted a book out of a hiding place. Thomas stayed there for a while, crouched, staring at it—perhaps considering whether to open it—before he squared his shoulders and stood up.

The book had a black leather cover. Even from this distance, Miriam recognised it immediately. The three-headed hawk pressed to the cover stared back at her, beaks open. *Past, present, future.*

Thomas gripped the grimoire with white knuckles.

'Lily,' he said to himself. 'For you, Lily.'

He left the room.

Miriam slumped, pressing her head to the window, beak clinking softly against the glass. If she had been human in that moment, she might have groaned. But she had no choice. If the deal was to complete, Esther had to live her twenty-three years. Miriam had to warn her.

Isaac hadn't wanted to accompany Esther to the Cheswick fete. Frankly, she hadn't wanted him to accompany her—she avoided him as much as possible, as the curse demanded—but she still required a chaperone. Still, his dramatic sighs as they stepped into the carriage made her wish she could have asked someone else.

Esther understood her brother's reluctance to attend society events, and she tried not to blame him for it. She knew firsthand how awkward these things could become for him, considering his parentage: the side glances, the sniggers behind palms. Once, at a ball, a man had tried to trip him over for sport, and Esther had borne the pain and bid the shadows to set the hem of his jacket on fire. It had been blamed on an errant candle, thankfully, but since then she had made a greater effort to keep her temper under control.

Afterwards, Isaac seemed to have known that she was the one to blame. 'Thanks,' he'd said, wide-eyed with appreciation. And she'd replied—chest constricting—'You must learn to take care of yourself.'

If Isaac had ever blamed her for her iciness towards him, he never acted as if he did; sometimes Esther wondered if he had sensed, somehow, that she was maintaining distance for his own good. He didn't know about the curse, of course, but he knew that Esther was different. He knew that she was incapable of closeness to anyone, family or not. Once, at a ball, she'd overheard him defend her notorious callousness to a group of friends. 'It isn't that she is rude, or cruel,' he'd told them. 'She is simply... honest about what she wants. People don't like it, but I think it quite admirable.'

This morning, he was sitting across from her in the carriage, reading Byron. He loved poetry, even fancied himself a writer; Esther had never told him so, but he had real talent. He was in full mourning attire, with a black jacket and gloves. Esther had dared to dress in half mourning, despite the funeral being only a week ago. She despised wearing black, and besides, it wasn't as if she had a reputation to salvage. Her dress was a deep, dark plum, and she was wearing a coral necklace the same shade as her hair.

'God willing,' Isaac muttered, as he turned a page, 'this is the last of these things we have to go to.'

'We have the Carroway Ball next month,' she reminded him.

He groaned and pressed his head into the book. 'Kill me.'

Esther rolled her eyes. 'I'll keep that solution in mind, in case all else fails.'

Isaac sniggered, eyes crinkling. Esther felt her own lips twitch, and she turned her head back to the carriage window, admonishing herself. When it came to her brother, kindness was cruelty, she knew that. But sometimes it was so difficult to pretend she didn't love him. Esther often imagined putting her arms around him, burying her head into his shoulder, and telling him, *Forgive me. Forgive me for all of it.* But she knew better than that, and so here they were—the inch of carriage space between them vaster than an ocean.

They passed the remainder of the journey in silence.

The fete was being held in honour of an orphanage of some sort, and the Ton swarmed the green in front of Cheswick House like a collection of pastel-coloured gnats. White tables studded the grass, the strains of a string quartet floating through the air. As Esther exited the carriage, dusting off her dress, the other visitors suddenly all paused, and turned to look at her. Esther watched in silent shock as they each linked hands, forming a chain, and began to move in a slow dance around her; the sky darkened, and their shadows extended behind them like watercolours bleeding through paper.

'Esther,' someone said, grasping her arm. Esther shrieked, and the vision fell away.

It was Isaac, staring at her with abject concern. Many other members of the Ton were staring, too—the shriek had alarmed them—and Esther flushed.

'Forgive me,' she said to him, under her breath.

'What's the matter?'

'I...' Esther shook her head. 'It is nothing.'

The Langwith family passed by them, perfectly matching in their peach-coloured gowns and neatly pressed collars. Their youngest, Elizabeth, gave Esther a smirk, leaning towards her brother to make a comment obscured by her fan.

'Prigs,' Esther muttered, scowling. She stalked ahead into the crowd, and Isaac followed at her heels.

They both accepted glasses of cherry-flavoured ratafia from a waiter and stood awkwardly by the veranda. Isaac said, 'I still don't know why you insist we come to these things.'

Events like this were Esther's only real chance to see other people, cruel as they were, snide as they were. Besides—'It is important for you to be *seen*, Isaac, if you're to advance in society. If you could secure a position at a company, that would help. Perhaps you could even make a match.'

'Shouldn't *you* be the one looking for a match?'

'We both know there's little chance of that, not after so many Seasons out.' Taking a sip of the ratafia, Esther grimaced—it was far too sweet for her tastes; she should have expected as much—and then she disguised her disgust with a cough. 'Go mingle. I will sit down.'

'I could sit with you?' he asked her, frowning in concern. 'Aren't I supposed to be your chaperone?'

'It is fine. Enjoy yourself.'

She left him there before he could protest further, sitting at one of the tables set up by the fountain. She was immediately presented with a plate of finger sandwiches by an enterprising server. Esther tried to ignore the stares of the Ton, the muffled giggling of some of the children staring at her from the other side of the water. She watched as in the distance Isaac fell in with a group of other young men, who were swigging port and who welcomed him with friendly jeers. Despite his illegitimacy, he was well-liked by the more accepting members of the Ton for his perceptiveness, his confidence, his sharp wit.

Esther took a large bite of a sandwich—too large, crumbs falling from her lips, prompting giggles from a nearby young couple who had evidently been watching her. Cheeks burning, Esther put down the sandwich and busied herself with fraying the edge of the tablecloth, concentrating on the rasp of the fabric between her fingertips. She couldn't get too upset, too nervous, or else she might lose control—making the shadows swarm around her. Recently, it had felt more and more difficult to prevent such accidents. It was as if part of her was rebelling against everything she had been working towards these past few years; as if it wanted her to *use* the curse, release it, and watch with glee as it destroyed everyone around her.

There was a sudden clap of thunder. Esther flinched, then looked upwards. The shadow of a cloud suddenly passed over her, obscuring the sun. In a matter of moments, the entire sky had gone grey. The colour was so dark it was almost black, as if the blue had been painted over with soot. It was utterly extraordinary: there had been no sign of rain all afternoon.

Those across the green had also noticed the change, and hundreds of guests were now staring up in shock. A cold wind gusted over the congregation, and a few women shrieked as their shawls and hairpins were torn from them.

For a few minutes, most people were uncertain how to react, and some continued to wander around the fete as if the clouds would blow away. But the clouds didn't change, and soon a streak of lightning flashed across the sky. A new crash of thunder came immediately after, loud enough to rattle the crockery on the table. The lightning had been so bright, it left a fissure across the clouds; it was as if the earth was an egg being cracked open. There was no rain, but the wind picked up its pace, and more ladies shrieked.

Esther, strangely entranced by the storm, made no reaction except to stare.

A third crash of thunder came, and with it, the exodus finally began. A sea of pale gowns and coattails surged away from the tables and towards Cheswick House. Esther didn't follow. The clouds swirling above her seemed to have an unbearable loveliness about them. She wanted to reach toward them, fly away with the wind. She'd always liked storms; when she was a child, she would press her face to the window and feel it rattle with a gale. There was something satisfying, something raw, about each crash of thunder, how it vibrated against her sternum. It reminded her of music, the way the floor of a concert hall trembled along with the symphony. Almost familiar, somehow— almost comforting. Another one of those strange half memories she couldn't explain.

It had yet to rain, but soon Esther was the only one left on the lawn. She was considering this—trying to remember whether she had ever experienced a dry storm—when an unfamiliar figure stopped at her table.

'I thought you might desire some company,' said the stranger. Her voice was low and accented with something Esther couldn't recognise, with lilting vowels and rolling consonants. 'You shouldn't be sitting alone.'

Esther looked up at the woman. She was around her own age, early twenties, tall, dark-haired, and harsh-featured; there was a foreignness to her face, an intensity to her gaze, that was utterly alien amongst the society sort who were usually at these events. Esther was so arrested by her presence that she felt unable to reply.

The woman gestured to the empty seat. 'May I?'

'I... I'd rather you didn't.'

She sat. Another crash of thunder came; the woman didn't react. Esther frowned at her, wondering if they had met before. There was something recognisable, perhaps, in the subtle blade of her smile; the paint-like sweep of her eyebrows; the pair of moles upon her chin and cheek. Their eyes met, and the force of her familiarity hit Esther like cannon fire.

She took a gulp of her ratafia to hide her nervousness.

'Forgive me my insolence,' the woman said.

137

There had, on occasion, been other people like this stranger—those who pitied Esther, who thought to befriend her as an act of charity. But there was nothing that Esther despised more than pity. 'You are not forgiven,' she said. 'I was enjoying my solitude.'

'I was surprised to see someone else willing to brave the storm, so I thought we should acquaint ourselves.'

'And now we are acquainted; you may leave.'

The woman chuckled. 'I don't even know your *name*, my dear.'

Esther sighed. 'Esther Harding.'

'Esther,' she echoed. She gave Esther a conspiratorial smile. 'Named after a great beauty. How appropriate.'

She leaned over the table, took up Esther's hand from her side, and brought it to her lips, brushing a kiss over her knuckles. Esther was so astonished by this she could do nothing but laugh, and she pulled sharply away. 'Have we met before?'

'Perhaps,' the woman replied, with a flippant wave of her hand.

'I don't believe I've seen you at any events this Season,' Esther said.

'I was born on the Continent,' she replied. That explained the accent. 'Since I came to England, I haven't taken much part in society. I find it distasteful.'

'Distasteful?'

She gave an elegant shrug. 'One English dance is much like any other dance, and one Englishman, much like any other man; I find myself quite exasperated by them all.'

There was an unmistakable significance to her tone. Esther felt herself beginning to flush, and she cleared her throat. 'What was your name?'

The woman paused, considering. Her fingers drummed a rhythm against the table; the strike of her thumb coincided with another crash of thunder.

'Miriam Richter,' she said.

Esther swallowed, her stomach squirming. She had a sudden and inexplicable sense of danger.

'Miss Richter,' Esther said, 'I am flattered by your interest. But there are many other ladies at this event, no doubt, who are far more fascinating than I am.'

Richter smiled at her. 'I doubt that. You are a bloom among weeds, my dear. But tell me—why are you sitting in this storm, all alone? Where is your chaperone?'

'I presume my brother is inside with everyone else.'

'He is a fool to leave such a gem unguarded.'

'Do I require guarding?' she asked.

'From whom?'

'You,' Esther said. 'I don't know what your intentions are.'

'You needn't be frightened of me.'

'Perhaps,' Esther replied. 'Still, something about you is… strange.'

'Oh?'

'I…' She paused to consider her explanation. Richter watched her with dark eyes half lidded, chin resting on the heel of her hand. Esther said, softly, 'Have you ever had a dream so beautiful that when you woke, you wept?'

Richter's smile widened. 'Do I feel like a dream?'

'No,' Esther said. 'You feel like the moment I wake up.'

The thunder rumbled once more.

Esther might have expected Richter to be offended by this comment, or else confused; but the other woman made no reaction except to cock her head and narrow her eyes, as if calculating something.

'You are living with your cousin,' Richter said. 'Thomas Harding.'

'So you *do* know who I am. If this is some sort of trick—'

'Do you trust him?' Richter interjected.

'Pardon?'

'Your cousin. Do you trust him?'

'That is an impertinent question, don't you think?'

'So, you do not.'

Esther huffed. 'Of course I trust him. He is family. He gave Isaac and me a home.'

'Is it a home, my dear? Or simply another snare?'

'What do you—who *are* you, really? What is this?'

Richter blinked at her, in a slow, deliberate manner, as if blinking wasn't an unconscious movement for her, as if she had to decide to do it. Otherwise, she didn't respond.

Esther stood from the table, suddenly disturbed. There seemed a new darkness to Richter's expression that she hadn't noticed before—a coiled-snake sort of impatience.

'I should leave,' Esther said. 'All the other guests are inside.'

'Ah. I have offended you.'

'Yes, Miss Richter, you have.'

'Call me Miriam,' she said.

'I will not call you Miriam,' Esther replied, and then she heard a scream. She gasped and turned to look at the house behind them. 'Did you hear that?'

'Hear what?'

'I swear—a woman screaming. I thought…'

'I didn't hear anything,' Richter said. 'I think you ought to sit down.'

'But what about the fire?'

'What fire?'

What fire? Esther had no idea. There was not a fire, and she didn't know why she'd thought there was. A searing, migraine-like pain began to build behind her eyebrows, and she hissed, stooping over as she clung to the back of the chair.

Richter stood. 'Are you well?'

'My head hurts.'

Cold, strong hands took hold of Esther's arms and guided her back down into the chair. 'There, now,' came a voice in her ear, 'calm yourself. No memories, no fear. All is well.'

At these words, a curious numbness spread through Esther's mind, dousing the heat of the migraine, leaving her feeling dozy and disoriented. She gripped the sides of the table—momentarily dizzy—and waited for the strange sensation to subside.

Esther had never had one of her episodes so effectively dispelled. When she looked back to Richter, she was sat opposite her, smiling genially, as if nothing odd had happened at all.

'How did you do that?' Esther asked.

'Do what?'

'Fix the… You helped me.'

'A drop of magic, that is all,' Miriam said. 'To soothe an unsettled heart.'

Magic.

Esther regarded her warily. She was scared, but also delighted—she'd never met anyone who had a similar gift to hers. No wonder she'd felt such a curious sense of familiarity when they'd first met; like recognises like, after all. But still, without certainty...

'Prove it,' Esther said.

'Prove what?'

'You say you can use magic? Prove it.'

Richter sighed, as if she were placating a child. Then she raised a languid arm, wrist limp. A fork of lightning speared the sky and struck her open palm, pooling there in a twisting rope of light; it lasted only a moment before it was gone. It left a sharp ozone scent and a crackling static in the air. Esther could feel her hair lifting from her shoulders.

'Jesus Christ,' Esther said.

Miriam dropped her hand. 'I am like you. Our power is the same.'

'You knew what I was when you came to speak with me.'

'Yes. I wanted to warn you.'

'Warn me of what?'

'He knows,' Richter said. 'Thomas. He knows of your curse, your power. He blames you for his every misfortune, and he intends to enact revenge.'

'He blames me,' Esther echoed, feeling the blood drain from her face.

'Yes.'

'How do *you* know about that? About Thomas?'

'I... I cannot tell you.'

Esther spluttered. 'Then why in God's name should I believe you?'

Richter reached over the table and cupped Esther's cheek. Esther froze, a deer before the rifle, and their eyes met. The other woman wore a strange expression: something between joy and concern. Although her skin was cold, her touch had a curious warmth, and Esther could feel it radiating across her chin and down her neck.

'Because,' said Miriam, 'no one else shall ever care about you as much as I do, darling. You could live a thousand years, a thousand lives, and no one will. I promise you that.'

Esther wanted to say something to deny her, but she couldn't. This woman was a stranger still, appearing as suddenly and as violently as the storm itself. She was asking Esther to cast aside all of Thomas's kindness, refuse herself the one refuge fate had offered her; and she couldn't. Of course she couldn't.

So why did she want to?

Esther felt her gaze drift to Richter's lips. *She is handsome,* she thought, *so handsome for a woman, so striking in aspect, so strong of feature.* She found herself imagining what it would be like to touch the harsh line of the other woman's jaw, to lean forward and taste those lips herself. And then, quite unbidden, came a succession of images: a darkened room, a bed—her bed—sheets rumpled, twin bodies, a sharp-nailed hand pressing hollows into her thighs, fingers wound into red hair, a tongue tracing the jut of her hip. Esther shuddered with the intensity of them, with the sudden ache she felt.

Richter's eyes darkened. Another clap of thunder: with it howled the wind, streaming against Esther with such fury, it was an animal leaping at her, clawing at her face. Her hair flew back, pins tearing away in pricks of fleeting pain. Esther scrambled after them, tried to catch them in midair, but they were lost. She looked back to Richter, flushed, her hair falling in a wild tangle across her shoulders.

Richter did not seem to mind her sudden disarray. If anything, the desire in her eyes reflected Esther's own.

'I know what you are thinking of, my dear,' she said. 'I would be amenable, if you are.'

'I—I wasn't...' Esther groaned. It hardly even felt worth denying. 'Well—that's not—if you know about the curse, then you shouldn't wish to associate with me, regardless.'

'I needn't worry about *that*, my dear. I'm much too powerful for such a thing to affect me.'

Esther paused. 'What? Is—is that really true?'

'Naturally,' Richter replied, tone placid.

Esther swallowed. The thought that there might be someone she could spend time with, without fear or guilt—she couldn't even dare to consider it. If it proved untrue, it would crush her.

But hadn't this woman held lightning in her palm? Hadn't she soothed the terrors of Esther's visions, and put her own visions in their place? That sort of power was beyond anything Esther had accomplished. It was the sort of power she'd never imagined. The sort that could break a curse.

'I still believe you may be a lunatic,' Esther said. 'And I don't believe you about Thomas.'

Richter's mouth curled downward in displeasure. 'I see.'

'But… if you are willing to teach me how to use my magic, as you can use yours? If you can help me break my curse? Then I might give your warning more consideration.'

Esther had expected immediate agreement—Richter *wanted* her, after all; that had been made clear enough—but Richter hummed in thought, leaning back in her chair. There was a new distance to her gaze, as if she were remembering something from very long ago; when they'd met, Esther had been certain they were the same age, but now there seemed something older about her, something almost weary.

I am like you.

Esther wondered if Richter was lonely, too.

'You wish to break your curse,' Richter said.

'Of course. Why wouldn't I?' Esther sighed, folding her hands in her lap. It discomfited her to speak of it in public, even as isolated as they were, with all the Ton inside. 'Call on me later, if you are willing to speak more on the matter. Explain what you know, and how you know it. Otherwise, I will consider our acquaintance at an end.'

Miriam held out a hand to her. 'Tomorrow, then.'

Esther slowly, reluctantly, placed her hand in hers.

'Tomorrow,' she echoed, ignoring the instinct to pull away.

13

Miriam went to watch Thomas Harding again that night. The first thing he did, once the rest of the household was sleeping, was to carefully apply salt on every window and threshold; his paranoia would have amused her if it hadn't been so justified. He even put down lines of glue to keep the salt in place, painted on with a brush with the careful precision of an old master. Perhaps he thought it kept Esther's curse at bay. Either way, the measures had saved his life, even if he didn't know it.

After the salt, he went through his other rituals. He was practising magic in his study, using the grimoire—but he didn't know how to speak to the shadows, couldn't make offerings to them. Without this ability, his ritual circles were simply circles, his chants simply the ravings of a man teetering on the precipice of sanity.

When he was finished, he left the study and disappeared into the house. He entered a room on the top floor with its curtains drawn, the only indication of his presence there the faint light of his lamp peeking out through the glass. There was clearly something in *particular* that he was attempting; but Miriam herself had no need for spells and incantations, and she hadn't the knowledge to recognise what it was he was doing. His visit to Esther the night before had clearly been an anomaly, a sign of weakness. He had something much larger in store.

So, then—despite the risk of her memories returning—Miriam would need to see Esther again. Even if she couldn't convince her of the danger, at least when Miriam was present, she would be safer. Preserving her life meant preserving the deal. Preserving the deal meant that Miriam would have her soul—and she had waited long enough for it, hadn't she, pining after Harding for centuries? She had asked Don Miguel if there was a difference between love and hatred, but perhaps she should have asked about love and *hunger*. She was starting to believe they were the same thing. When humans wanted each other, they were all mouths and teeth, desire and satisfaction. Miriam wanted Esther in that way, also. She didn't see the need to distinguish between lust and love, consumption and devotion. Miriam loved her. She wanted her life and her death and each bloody beat of her heart in between.

So, Miriam called on Esther twice the next day: first in the morning, as a crow, to watch her dress and to indulge in the fleeting pleasure of her fingers trailing down her wing; then in the early evening, as a woman.

Esther herself opened the door. When she saw Miriam, she seemed shocked. 'I did not think you would come,' she said.

'Why?'

'Because no one does.'

Miriam arranged her expression into what she hoped was a friendly smile. 'It is a beautiful evening. Shall we go for a walk?'

'No,' Esther replied. 'What on earth are you wearing?'

Miriam glanced down at her attire. 'Clothes.'

'*Men's* clothes.'

'Oh. I hadn't realised.'

Esther made an exasperated sound—although Miriam could tell, from the lingering heat of her stare, that she found the outfit attractive—and she closed the door a little further, so that she was wedged between it and the frame. 'You must change. You can't look like that in here.'

'Why not?'

'My cousin will have a *fit.*'

'Well—I needn't come inside,' Miriam said. She *couldn't* come inside, but that was another matter. 'I thought we could go somewhere else. I can't teach you magic in your home, where your family might see.'

Esther's shoulders slumped. 'I suppose that's true. But we can't just wander the streets; we are ladies. Let's go to Vauxhall.'

'... Vauxhall?'

Esther sighed at Miriam's blank expression. 'The gardens? How long have you been living in London, anyway?'

Miriam gestured to the street. 'Lead the way.'

Esther still looked reticent, glaring at Miriam's coat collar. In the corridor behind her, an extravagant chandelier swung slightly with the breeze from outside, scattering shards of rainbowed light across Esther's pale shoulders, the bright fire of her hair.

Miriam said, 'If you are still concerned about my dress—I won't be noticed unless I wish to be. That is the nature of my magic.'

Esther bit her lip, considering. Then she turned away. 'Very well. Wait here.'

She shut the door in her face, and Miriam had to wait on the step for a few more minutes before it opened again. Esther was now wearing a pair of long gloves, and a lace shawl had been tied over her mint-green gown. She had rouged her lips and cheeks, also, and it occurred to Miriam that she looked beautiful.

'We'll have to take a hackney.' Esther turned back inside, and hollered, '*Isaac!*'

Her brother's face appeared around the corner of the hallway. He was in a state of some disarray, waistcoat unbuttoned, dark hair flopping foppishly into his eyes. Miriam had never seen him otherwise, not once, after years of spying through their windows.

'Ah, hello,' he said cheerily. This was unusual. Most men found Miriam immediately disturbing; Isaac Harding was either extraordinarily brave or entirely lacking in survival instincts. 'Esther's friend, are we? What a distinctive cravat. I didn't know knots could be tied in such a fashion.'

'They can't,' Miriam replied.

Esther said, 'Ignore her—she's mad. We're out today. I'll be gone until late.'

Isaac nodded. 'Righto. Vauxhall, is it?'

'Yes.'

He eyed Miriam again. 'You'll make a splash. Bring me back a Shrewsbury, would you?'

'Fine. Can you tell Thomas? Where is he?'

'In his study, probably, crying about his dead wife or frigging himself over a venerable ancestor.'

Esther didn't even blink at his crudeness. 'He is the only reason we have a roof over our heads,' she said, 'so mind you don't talk like that to his face.'

Isaac huffed as Esther tugged Miriam away from the door.

Esther hadn't asked Thomas if she could use the carriage—Miriam wondered if she was embarrassed by her company?—so they had to hail a hackney coach on the street, which Esther clearly found demeaning; she was flushed with shame the entire time. Once they were inside the hackney, however, she seemed to calm down. She sat opposite Miriam and gave her a sceptical, narrow-eyed look.

'Don't try anything,' Esther said.

'Like what?'

'The magic you used yesterday. Who knows what you could do to me, if you were so inclined.'

Miriam smirked. 'What sort of things would you like me to do?'

'Not *that*,' Esther replied curtly. She flexed her hands fretfully in her lap, stretching the fabric of her gloves. 'I still can't trust you.'

'That much is evident. But I am not the one you should be afraid of, Esther.'

'You mean Thomas.' Miriam nodded. 'You haven't even *met* him. None of your accusations make any sense. Yesterday, you wouldn't explain—'

'I can explain now, if you wish.'

This surprised her. She untangled her fingers on her lap. 'Go on, then.'

Miriam had spent some time considering the lie, and so it was with practised smoothness she replied, 'I have long been a scholar of the occult. I have been tracking the whereabouts of a book: a grimoire of Christopher Harding's. It outlines several important rituals.'

Esther frowned. 'A grimoire? There was a big fire at the old estate, in the Elizabethan period—you're saying it survived?'

'Yes.'

'Thomas's father collected old family relics,' Esther murmured to herself. 'If he found it, then Thomas...'

'Exactly. Your cousin has obtained this book.'

'And you want it from him, I presume. That's why you talked to me.'

Miriam *did* want it. Holding an object once so important to Cybil could be the last thing needed to make Esther's memories return— and besides, even though Miriam couldn't use the spells inside, Esther might be able to. Miriam still wasn't particularly concerned about the curse, but there was no way she could risk Esther's wriggling out of the deal.

Miriam said, 'If the grimoire were all I wanted, I wouldn't be in this carriage in the first place. No—I watched Thomas, trying to divine the location of the grimoire, and I discovered he knew of your powers, your curse. Now he is preparing some sort of ritual. He must be dealt with, before he attempts to complete it.'

Esther seemed sceptical. 'What sort of ritual?'

'Well—I'm not sure, yet.'

'He has powers, too?'

'No. I doubt he's managed to work any magic successfully.'

'So what issue is there?'

'Even without real power, many rituals involve violence, or even murder. He is *unhinged*, Esther. I have no doubt he's willing to kill you if he deems it necessary.'

Esther said, 'We've known each other since we were children. He wouldn't hurt me.'

'How can you be so certain?'

'Because—because I have to be.' She rubbed her forehead with the heel of her hand, suddenly weary. 'Isaac and I have nowhere else to go. My brother and my cousin are my only true family remaining. And if Thomas is angry at me, because of my curse—if he blames me for what happened to Lily, then... perhaps I deserve his anger.'

Miriam resisted the urge to gnash her teeth, to tear the carriage door from its hinges. 'You can't possibly believe you deserve *death*.'

'I don't want to die, Miss Richter, but I've long been resigned to the possibility. It's odd, I...' Esther turned her face to the carriage window. The light of the setting sun gilded the tip of her nose; then they passed by a tree, and it was brushed away by the shadows. 'I have often felt as if I am living on borrowed time.'

'You don't understand.'

Their eyes met. 'What don't I understand?'

That your life is mine *to take. Your death is* mine *to give.*

Miriam said nothing.

Esther sighed. 'How did you watch him?'

'What?'

'Thomas. You said you "watched" him. How?'

'In shadows,' Miriam said. 'With the use of magic it is possible to make yourself immaterial—invisible to others.'

Invigorated, Esther leaned forward. 'Truly? Can you teach me how to do that? And other magic, too, like what you did at the fete. Calling the lightning.'

Miriam wavered. It was a dangerous proposition: the more powerful Esther became, the more likely she was to remember her time as Cybil.

'I do not know what Thomas is planning,' Esther said, 'but surely, if I could use my magic better, I'd be better placed to defend myself from it.'

Miriam shook her head. 'You don't truly need me to teach you. Magic is a simple trade: light for darkness.'

'What? What does that mean?'

'If you offer the shadows enough of your soul, they will do anything you wish them to.'

'That's what the pain was?' Esther asked incredulously. 'I've been *feeding* myself to them?'

Miriam shrugged. 'Your soul is strong enough to withstand a good number of deals, Esther. These tiny miracles you make—it would take a thousand, a *hundred* thousand of these to deplete your power entirely. For most people, however, even one such pact could kill them.'

'But we are not most people,' Esther clarified. 'You and I.'

It was Miriam's opinion that she herself *had* no soul, inhuman as she was. Her materiality was entirely the result of the intention of her creators. They had signed a pact designed to create a demon, and Miriam was the demon they had envisaged. That was why she was subject to ludicrous laws like salt circles and dealmaking; she was the moon, reflecting others' light. She had no spark of her own, and to control other shadows, she had to consume souls, then trade them what she had consumed.

'You and I,' Miriam said, delicately, 'are different from the others. And if you are to work wonders, my dear, you must stop affecting normalcy.'

Esther frowned. 'If that's what I've been doing, I don't think I've been doing it very well.'

The cab halted then, and Esther reached for the door.

As Esther went to the front and paid the driver, Miriam inspected the entrance of Vauxhall Gardens: an enormous redbrick gatehouse, rooved in sky-blue tiles, men in sanguine livery standing to attention and greeting visitors. The sky above them was blushing with the sunset, the park beyond the house lit with a dazzling array of dangling lanterns. A bronze placard by the entrance informed visitors that entry would cost four shillings.

Miriam said, 'Four shillings. Is that a lot?'

'It is extortionate,' Esther replied, as they joined the queue. 'I thought it was less.'

'Did you bring enough money?'

She huffed, insulted, but it was clear from the discomfort on her face that the price was more than she wanted it to be. 'We're here now, so...'

Miriam took her arm and pulled her from the queue. 'Let's find another way in.'

'It's walled all the way round,' Esther said, galled, as Miriam dragged her away. 'And now we've lost our place.'

Miriam ignored this. She kept walking around the perimeter of the gardens until they reached a quiet spot away from the crowd, where the road was paved with shadows.

The trick would be to teach Esther something inane, something superficially impressive, to prevent her from reaching for higher powers. Miriam said, 'Your first lesson: the darkness is drawn to your light. It speaks to you, even if you cannot hear it. Listen and reply.'

'Is that how you do it?'

Miriam's interactions with other shadows were less conversations than sets of orders; they feared her enough that she didn't need to bother with much else. But Esther didn't need to know that. This was just a diversion until Miriam was paid her due. 'Yes,' she said. 'Now— watch me.' She reached towards the darkness cast by the wall. *Come to me*, she told it.

The shadows shuddered and began to crawl slowly towards her. Esther wasn't particularly impressed, watching in silence until the darkness had cloaked Miriam entirely; then, finally, she allowed herself some surprise. 'You've disappeared,' she said. 'Or... not entirely. You're still there, aren't you? I feel as if I can see you, if only from the corner of my eye.'

Miriam moved behind her and drew her finger down the nape of her neck. 'Still here,' she murmured, her words wisping between them like smoke.

Esther shivered at her touch. Miriam withdrew and turned to walk through the wall. She released the shadows once she was on the other side.

Here, obscured from the streetlamps, the darkness was more entire. The trees were of the same sort England had always grown, children of centuries, just as Miriam was—pale-flowered linden, sharp-leafed holly. If she could not see the distant lights of the lanterns, Miriam could almost believe she had returned to the forest near Harding Hall.

Miriam called, 'Your turn.'

'My turn!' came the muffled reply. 'You didn't show me how to do it!'

'I told you—just ask the darkness.'

'Just *ask* it? "Make me invisible, if you'd be so kind"? That seems ridiculous.'

Miriam felt a stab of impatience. 'Make a deal. Offer them a taste of your soul while picturing the outcome you desire. It is a simple transaction.'

There was a long pause—a period of minutes, during which Miriam began to wonder if Esther had simply left—and then a small, muffled, 'Ow.'

To her own surprise, Miriam laughed. 'Did you walk into the wall, my dear?'

'No!' came the reply, although it was unconvincing. 'I almost have it. Be quiet.'

Miriam lapsed into silence, amusement lingering.

The wall in front of Miriam shimmered, and Esther stepped through it, a hazy figure as immaterial as mist. The moment she was entirely inside the park, the shadows dissipated.

In the gloom, Esther's pale gown had faded to a colourless ash. The necklace of pearls she wore glinted dully at her throat, pooling in the hollow between her collarbones; Miriam wondered what would happen if she reached out, wrapped her hand around the necklace, and tugged—whether Esther would lurch forward to save them, or permit the strand to snap.

Esther gasped as if she had been underwater. 'That felt strange.'

'Well done.'

She didn't acknowledge the praise, although a brief, small smile betrayed her sense of accomplishment. Then she surveyed the surroundings and frowned. 'This is the Dark Walk. We ought to leave.'

Miriam didn't know what the Dark Walk was, but she could guess from the name's connotations. The trees surrounding them scored lines of shadow across the lilac sky. The path beneath their feet was a meandering ribbon of uneven paving stones, punctuated every so often by a steadfast weed sprouting through the cracks.

'I find it quite pleasant here,' Miriam said.

'It isn't proper.'

'Why not?'

'People come here to...' Esther made a sound of frustration. 'A lady ought not to be seen here. She could be ruined.'

It was obvious enough what she meant. Miriam chuckled and reached for the shadows once more; they rose and curled languidly around her forearm. 'Sex, magic, it is all the same,' she told Esther.

'Desire and its fulfilment; this is a good enough place for either. Shall we continue?'

'Continue?'

Miriam stepped in front of her and laid her hands lightly on Esther's shoulders. Esther's breath hitched.

Bending to whisper in her ear, Miriam said, 'Close your eyes.'

'Why?'

'You wanted me to teach you, didn't you?'

Esther still looked displeased, but she sighed and closed her lids. She was pale enough that Miriam could see the lavender web of her veins through the skin, a fisherman's net that trembled with the movement of her eyes beneath; there was a curious beauty to the way humans sought to see even in darkness.

Do you hear me? Miriam asked, within Esther's mind.

'Yes,' Esther gasped. 'How did you do that?'

Reply to me like this. Consider the thought—shape it, give it form— then bid the shadows to send it to me.

Esther's brow furrowed, and then something pressed tentatively against the edges of Miriam's consciousness, feathered and fluttering. Esther had made her thought a bird and sent it flying; how sweet. Miriam caught it in the air and split it open.

Hello?

You are a quick learner, Miriam returned. *Now, if you—*

I want to leave this place.

Why is that?

It is too dark here, Esther said, *eyes open or closed. I am afraid.*

Why are you afraid?

Because sometimes, in the darkness, I see things. I see terrible things.

Murky images emerged: a man's face, indistinct, hovering over her; the roar of a great fire; a dark corridor, tall windows, a great and ceaseless silence.

Miriam let her hands fall along Esther's arms, until she was circling Esther's wrists. *You aren't there anymore*, she told her. *You are here, with me. You are Esther Harding. The year is 1813. We are in the Dark Walk.*

'I am Esther Harding,' Esther murmured to herself. 'We are in the Dark Walk.' But around them, the trees seemed to grow taller, more ancient, and the pavement beneath their feet was softening to soil. Clouds rolled over the twilit sky like a cavalry charge. It was an illusion only—a vision made by memory—but still one far greater than Miriam had ever seen a mortal accomplish. She tightened her grip on Esther's wrists and pulled her closer. Esther was too lost in her reverie to notice.

I often hear a woman screaming, Esther whispered in her mind, and then aloud—'I hear her screaming now, Miriam; do you hear it?'

Miriam felt something not unlike fear—not fear *itself*, of course, that would be ludicrous, but… trepidation. Esther must not remember her past. Not now, when things between them seemed so fragile, when so much of the bitterness in Cybil's eyes had been forgotten.

'It is an illusion, my dear,' Miriam said. 'Your magic reacting to your fears.'

Esther did not seem to hear her. 'The woman is screaming. Who is she? I think it is my mother, but I've never heard my mother scream.'

'Open your eyes,' Miriam said, sharply. 'Enough of this now. We will go elsewhere.'

But Esther didn't open her eyes. One of the trees bowed towards them: its branches bore enormous apples, or so Miriam thought. As it neared, she saw their red colour was just a glaze of blood. The tree wasn't growing fruit, but instead hearts in clusters of three or four; they pumped into veins that wrapped around the branches like sprawling fingers.

Miriam was enchanted by the vision—touched by it, even, touched to be offered a heart—but when she looked down to tell Esther so, she was gone. Around Miriam, the Dark Walk was now transformed into a warped visage of Harding Hall's orchard. Other trees gathered around her, each bearing hearts or lungs or dangling, bean-shaped kidneys; the air was metallic, suffocatingly powerful. Beneath her feet, the soil was damp with blood, rising up to meet the pressure of her shoes.

'Esther?' she called, and then she heard a sharp laugh.

Miriam turned again to see a figure standing between two heart-trees. It was a flame-haired woman in a white dress and high ruff, embroidered with gold filaments that seemed to glow in the darkness.

'*Greensleeves was my heart of joy,*' the woman sang, mockingly. '*And who but my Lady Greensleeves?*'

'Cybil,' Miriam said.

She stepped closer, and as she did so, Miriam could see her forearms and hands were dotted with eyes, each blinking and moving in tandem with those on her face. Miriam, startled, almost took a step back. *Only a vision*, she told herself, squaring her shoulders. Cybil had taken control of Esther, was commanding the darkness to create this illusion—but the vision would end, eventually. It would have to.

'You could not keep away, could you?' Cybil reached up to the tree and plucked a heart from the branch, with the grotesque sound of tearing flesh. 'Could not wait for me to die in peace?'

'I thought you were gone.'

'Simply because I am forgotten does not mean I am not here,' she replied. 'I am Esther; Esther is me. Our souls are joined. I do not remember now, but I shall. Your presence ensures that.'

Miriam said, 'Your soul is mine regardless. It doesn't matter if you remember me.'

'Doesn't it?' Cybil lifted the heart to her lips and took a bite, staining her mouth scarlet. Once she had chewed and swallowed, she continued. 'Do you know the tale of the scorpion and the frog?'

'The what?'

'Of course. Why should you?' Cybil dropped the half-eaten organ to the ground and advanced slowly towards Miriam. Once they were close enough to touch, she pressed her bloodied hand to Miriam's chest, looking up at her through her lashes with an expression that could only be described as inviting. Miriam found herself leaning closer, and Cybil tapped her finger against her sternum, tutting. 'Do not become distracted,' she said. 'The scorpion and the frog, remember? It is a story. A fable, by Aesop. My mother once read it to me.'

'I haven't heard of it.'

'I shall enlighten you, then. The scorpion asks the frog to take it across the river. The frog is frightened, as it believes the scorpion will sting it while they cross. The scorpion points out that if it did so, they would both drown. The frog sees that as guarantee enough, and thus it agrees.' Cybil paused then, and Miriam raised a brow, inviting her to continue. 'Well—as you might imagine, the scorpion stings the frog regardless, and they both drown.'

'Are you the frog in this parable, my dear?' Miriam asked. 'Or the scorpion?'

'That is not the significance,' Cybil murmured, lifting herself up onto the balls of her feet so that she could whisper into Miriam's ear. 'The significance is that it does not matter. Scorpion or frog, Miriam Richter: either way, *both* of us shall drown.'

Then Cybil pressed her bloodied mouth against hers.

Miriam had only a moment to chase the kiss, to feel the nip of her teeth and the heat of her tongue, before she felt hands pushing her backwards. Miriam allowed herself to be moved away, blinking in confusion—and they were in the Dark Walk again.

Esther stood in front of her in her mint-green gown. Her cheeks were flushed, eyes wide.

'What are you doing?' Esther demanded.

'I…' Miriam was confused; it was an unpleasant feeling, alien, and she was irritated by it. 'You kissed me.'

'I did not.'

'You did,' Miriam replied—it was both the truth and a lie.

Esther seemed uncertain. 'I feel odd. I… Perhaps I did. I don't know. I can't recall.'

Miriam offered her an arm. 'All this magic was perhaps too much for you,' she said, soothingly. 'Let's go somewhere brighter, hm? And we can continue our practice tomorrow.'

Hesitantly, Esther looped her arm around hers. 'Yes. I think—I think that would be best.'

They walked slowly toward the distant light of the lanterns. The scent of blood faded; the trees that surrounded them bore no fruit, only nascent blossoms and sharp green leaves. As they continued, Esther's breathing slowed, and her shoulders dropped.

They reached a fork in the road. Miriam turned to stare at her. Esther stared back.

'Why is it, really, that you are so interested in me?' Esther asked. 'Is it attraction? Kinship? Both?'

'I could ask you the same thing.'

Esther chewed her lip. 'All these warnings about Thomas, and yet you won't be honest with me. Not entirely. Why?'

'You think I am lying?'

'There is more to this, certainly, than what you have said.'

Miriam didn't reply. She watched her, patiently, half a smile on her lips.

'You want me to hurt him,' Esther said, in dawning realisation. 'Thomas. You haven't told me to run away from him. All you've done is make me suspicious, make me afraid. You want me to use my power to do something unforgivable.'

'Yes.'

'Because you want the grimoire? Why not do it yourself?'

'I can't while he's in the house. He's warded it.'

Esther shook her head. 'That isn't everything, though. You want *me* to do it. You want my hands to be the ones that hurt him. Why?'

Perceptive girl. Miriam herself hadn't realised how much she'd wanted that, until Esther had pointed it out. She considered the question, imagined the outcome Esther described: Esther, shrouded in darkness, calling the shadows to enact her bidding, tearing Thomas's soul from his chest and consuming it as she watched. Violence was a beautiful thing, a powerful thing. Miriam had always thought so; it was an acceptance that humanity no longer mattered. In some small way, perhaps it would be an acceptance of Miriam herself.

'I think it would be beautiful,' Miriam breathed, letting all her desire, all her hunger lace her voice; Esther gave a trembling sort of gasp in response, as if the words had caressed her. 'Oh, *darling*. I see it, now. All I want in the world is to see you covered in blood.'

Esther turned away. Miriam couldn't tell if the expression on her face was nausea or arousal.

'You are mad,' Esther said.

'Does that scare you?'

'No,' she replied. 'In a way, it is a relief. Madness has long been a solitary art for me. It will be a comfort to share it.'

14

Miriam's reaction to the lanterns in the gardens was one of scathing disinterest—'Do people in this town truly pay to see these? They're only lights'—which Esther really should have found aggravating. But Esther could think of nothing except the pounding of her heart, the trembling of her hands at Miriam's nearness—and Miriam's voice saying, *It would be beautiful,* over and over in her mind. Esther felt as if she were ripe fruit, about to burst its skin, a cloud about to rain, and she was so undone, so confused, so *exhausted* of feeling constantly on the edge of something without actually reaching it.

The hour grew late enough that they had to depart. Esther didn't know whether she felt disappointed or relieved. They hailed another cab, both clambering inside. Then they stared at each other from opposite seats in a heavy, significant silence. Esther could hear her own heartbeat in her ears, thudding in a syncopated rhythm between each judder of the coach. Miriam wore her typical small, self-satisfied smile as she watched her.

'I can get you the grimoire,' Esther said. 'I needn't kill Thomas for it. Tell me where it is, and I'll find it.'

Miriam shook her head. 'He keeps it with him always.'

'I know you said he may be violent, but I am more powerful than him. If he can't truly use magic, I don't see how he could be a threat.'

'Your fa— Christopher Harding,' Miriam said, 'was, for all his faults, a capable ritualist. There may be something in that grimoire that presents a genuine danger, regardless of your cousin's abilities.

And he knows the truth of your powers, your curse. Surely, he could ruin you, if he were so inclined?'

'He is a wealthy man, and I am a woman; he could always do that, regardless.' Esther turned her head away, staring resolutely out the window. 'I am capable of many things, Miss Richter, but I cannot kill willingly. I have lived my life this far with relative liberty because I am willing to play by society's rules, as much as they chafe, and I expect you to do the same. Otherwise, this brief acquaintance will be at an end.'

'He shall live, then, until you set this stubbornness aside,' Miriam said. 'But you *must* set it aside eventually, Esther. Your life depends on it.'

Esther looked back at her. Miriam's eyes were so dark, her features so dramatic—a face unearthly enough that Esther felt she would never grow used to looking at it, even if they knew each other for the rest of their lives.

She cleared her throat. 'If you continue to teach me magic, I will see what I can do about the grimoire.'

Miriam bared her teeth at her derisively. It felt shockingly crude. 'You still believe you can break your curse?'

'Why shouldn't I be able to, eventually? It is all magic, ultimately.'

'Such hope; it feels incongruous with your nature.'

'All the hope I have goes towards the curse's end,' Esther replied, sharply. 'I have no other optimism left to me.'

Miriam had been hunched over, leaning forwards; she pulled back, shoulders lowering minutely. 'I have been harsh,' she conceded, although there was little apology in her voice. 'Of course you would wish to free yourself.'

Esther swallowed. 'It—it is a burden. I do not know the exact details, only what my uncle and my cousin have spoken about when they thought I wasn't listening, but… only the firstborn of each generation is supposed to have magic, and when that firstborn is a woman—the Seed of Eve—that magic becomes corrupted. I may have power, like yours, but I also bring misfortune to those around me. Those who love me, and those whom I love.'

'What sort of misfortune?'

'Death, usually. Grief, and injury. I can list to you now those who have died because of me—unhappy accidents too common to be accidental: my mother, when I was born; my nursemaids, as I grew; my uncle; my father; even Thomas's wife, Lily. They were only married a year, you know, before she died on the childbed. She and their baby both. If I were him—' Esther's voice wavered, and she cleared her throat. 'If I were him, I would hate me, too.'

The cab came to a standstill. They exited, and Esther paid the driver. Miriam walked her up to the front door.

'Esther,' Miriam said.

'Yes?'

'Regardless of this curse, you deserve to be loved,' she told her. 'Not hated. Not in the way you think.'

It was a sweet sentiment, but her tone made it sound like a warning, not consolation.

'What sort of love?' Esther asked.

'Eternal,' Miriam replied. 'Eternal, and undying.'

Esther had a nightmare that night.

She was standing in a hallway she'd never seen before, picking a fraying tapestry apart with her bare hands. She pulled and pulled at the threads until her fingers were bleeding and raw, staining the fabric scarlet.

'Esther,' a voice said. 'Esther, Esther.' But when she turned around, she saw—herself, and yet not herself; this not-Esther had a necklace of bruised flesh around her neck, and she wore an old-fashioned gown covered in blood.

Then again, a voice came from behind her: 'Esther.' And when she turned around, she saw herself again, but this self was not injured. Her neck was clean, and her hair was cut shockingly short, up to her chin. She wore a curious slip of silver silk, covered in shimmering beads.

As Esther turned back and forth between her two selves, they began to multiply in endless lines—it was like standing between two mirrors, surrounded by infinite reflections.

'Weave us back together,' the short-haired Esther told her. 'Those before, those after; you can weave us all together again.'

Esther turned back to the tapestry and scrambled to twist the threads back into place. But she didn't know what she was doing; there seemed to be no way to undo the damage she had done. The fabric slipped between her bloody fingers, as intangible as spider silk.

'Weave,' commanded the bloody Esther.

'Weave,' commanded the other.

Esther felt a tear slip down her cheek. 'I can't,' she told them.

'Weave,' short-haired Esther repeated. 'You have to kill me to do so. Remake history, so I'll never exist.'

And then Esther saw that she was offering her a knife.

She took a step back. 'I can't,' she said. 'I can't, I—'

'Do it,' bloodied Esther told her. Esther spun around to look at her. 'It is the only way.'

Short-haired Esther said, 'Kill me, and our souls can be mended.' Then she stretched her arm out further, to display the weapon. It was an oyster knife, snub-bladed and hooked. 'Cut me like she did.'

Esther took a small, hesitant step forward. Then someone screamed, and the scream was painful, white-hot and burning. Esther shrieked, scrabbled at her own skin, writhed and gasped as the dream burst its seams—and she was in her room. It was dark. Something was moving outside her window, cawing furiously, raking at the glass, filling the room with high-pitched squeals.

Esther groaned and rolled off the bed, stumbling toward the window. She saw the bird outside and realised, betrayed, that it was her Little Shadow. 'Stop,' she cried, as she opened the window. 'Stop, please.'

The crow cawed and shuffled in place, seeming almost contrite. A cool breeze flowed across the room, Esther's skin puckering with the chill.

'You wanted to wake me,' she said to the crow. It cocked its head at her.

Now that Esther thought about it, there was something newly familiar in her Little Shadow. Its eyes, featureless pools of black, seemed to betray a flash of human intelligence.

The crow hopped nervously from foot to foot. Esther reached out a hand—usually, it let her pet it—but this time, it turned and launched itself into the night sky. Esther opened her mouth to call out for it, but it was no use; the crow had disappeared.

Her eyes prickled with exhaustion. Esther closed the window, and then she went to pull the covers back on the bed. She was surprised to find the tips of her fingers raw and oversensitive, dragging against the fabric with a painful rasp. Hissing, she withdrew her hand to look at it. There were specks of blood and dark filaments beneath her fingernails, as if she had been pulling a tapestry apart.

Esther spent most of the next day practising what Miriam had taught her, making her hand immaterial, over and over, putting it through tables and walls. Then she did it with her entire body, becoming as insubstantial as air; she stood in the cavity between two rooms, feeling the shadows curl around her. She usually didn't like the dark, but it was almost comforting to be part of it, to disappear entirely. No curse, no Thomas, no Miriam Richter. Just Esther and the shadows, twins in the black.

It was an unpleasant feeling, the faint pain of the shadows taking power from her; but the joy of the outcome seemed to allay the cost. Miriam had said, hadn't she, that her soul was strong enough to sustain such magic? Everything worth doing required sacrifice— Esther knew that intimately. Her life had been full of the sacrifices she had made in the name of her curse: her relationship with her brother; her chances of marriage; her ability to live without regret or fear. In the face of those things, *this* seemed so inconsequential. She would feed herself to the shadows with a smile, knowing that this time, at least, she was guaranteed her reward.

At one point—her hand halfway into the wall—Isaac emerged from his own room into the same corridor. He had a top hat on that appeared a little large, halfway falling off his head, and a gold-topped cane that Esther suspected he had stolen from Thomas.

'I'm off to my club,' he said. 'Daniel Hawthorne got his ear cut off in a duel, and he's put it in a jar to be displayed. We're doing a ceremony for it.'

'I am very happy for you,' Esther replied.

Isaac glanced at her outstretched arm. 'Your hand is in the wall.'

'Yes.'

They stared at each other in silence.

'Righto,' he said. 'Bully for you, I suppose. I'll see you this evening.'

'Have a good day,' Esther said, and he tipped his hat to her.

Once he was gone, Esther grew bold enough to experiment further, offering more and more of herself to the shadows. The more she did it, the more instinctive the process seemed to become—the darkness started to intuit her requests before she could even form the thoughts fully. In exchange for a mote of her soul, it formed a series of shapes on the wall: silhouettes of ships on roiling seas, spinning snowflakes, a bent-over apple tree. It felt like offering a dog bites of food for tricks—if the food were herself, she supposed, as macabre a thought as that was.

As Esther made one of the shadow-apples fall to the floor, she noticed a light patter, and looked outside to see that it was raining.

Esther crept down to the kitchen, out the back door, and into the garden. She took her coat with her, expecting to cover her hair from the rain—but once she was outside, she found the sensation of it pleasant, and she let the water drip into her eyes. It wasn't a cold day—likely the warmest day of the year so far—and the rain was soothing as it drummed softly against her skin. Esther discarded her jacket onto a bench and reached her hands outwards.

She wasn't certain it would work. It was midday, and the clouds prevented many visible shadows. Little to command, then, but they would be enough; they had to be.

Esther closed her eyes, and she offered herself to the darkness. She imagined that this spring rain was a storm, that the clouds were seething and furious. She pictured lightning dancing dragon-like above her, weaving its way toward the ground; that when it touched her, it would not hurt her, but instead embrace her as a lover; and then there was pain as the shadows took their due, a searing sharpness that was both awful and exquisite. Through her lids, she saw a furious light, and the air filled with the scent of char. When she opened her eyes again, her hair was floating with static around her face. A crackling brightness was pooling in her palm: lightning squirming like a living thing, fluttering between her fingers.

'Esther,' came a voice, and the lightning skittered away, shooting back into the sky.

Esther turned around. Thomas was in the doorway, watching her with his face blank, as she stood, soaking wet, in the middle of the rain.

He didn't look surprised. He didn't look frightened. He didn't even look angry.

Esther thought that somewhere—in the minute fissure of his pressed-thin lips—there was the beginnings of a smile.

Isaac was at his club for dinner, so it was just her and Thomas left at the townhouse. They ate in the dining room, a space dominated by a large oak table so tall Esther's elbows had to raise awkwardly high so she could eat. Despite there still being some waning daylight, Thomas had the curtains closed and the candles lit. It could have been much later than it was; there was no clock here, unusually, and so the passage of time was uncertain. The stuffiness of the room, with its heavy Persian carpets and its dark-green walls, was oppressive. The air smelt more of damp and candle smoke than it did of food.

Thomas had yet to comment on what Esther had done with the lightning. He had only told her it was time for dinner, and then walked inside. She had followed him, dripping water onto the floor, and traipsed upstairs to change. When she'd returned to the dining room, he'd been sitting at the table, waiting for her.

It was a luxurious spread: red wine, quince jelly, cheeses and sliced meats to start, as well as a gold tureen of hazelnut soup. In their blue china bowls, the soup formed a thin skin as it cooled, wrinkling at its edges like old paper. Thomas's nose wrinkled as he took his first spoonful.

'You don't like it?' Esther asked him. She had dried off as best she could, but her hair was still hanging limp, and when she'd changed her dress, she'd noticed that the water had made it quite transparent. The embarrassment had been overwhelming. Now that she was confronted by him sitting opposite her, she felt a sort of fear, too; fear of some sort of retaliation for the crime of revealing her body to him—or worse, some sort of reward.

Richter's warnings rang in her mind, also, as clearly as the bell Thomas used to call the servers over when his wine glass was empty. In his eyes, Esther saw only a resigned discomfort, rather than the virulent hatred Richter had implied. But she knew better than to take that for granted. Deceitfulness was a family trait.

'Not particularly,' Thomas replied, in reference to the soup.

'Then why did you have it made?'

'I always do. It was Lily's favourite.'

'Oh.' Esther took another spoonful, warm and thick as blood. 'I see.'

She didn't remember much of Thomas's wife, having only met her a few times before her death. Esther recalled that she had been quite lovely. She'd had large eyes, but everything else was tiny—a waist like a needle's eye. She'd been shy too, quiet, trying to sink into the wallpaper at events. But it had always been an imperative for Esther to try to make her laugh. Esther remembered Lily's extraordinary laugh most of all, high and clear and sweet as music. When she did laugh, you always had to smile back at her. Even Thomas would smile back at her; that was why he had married her. It had been a love match, everyone had known that. He'd loved her so much that he hadn't left his house since she'd passed.

And Esther had killed her.

She ate another spoonful of soup.

'We were going to name him Christopher,' Thomas said. 'Our son.'

'I am so sorry.'

'As am I.'

They didn't speak again until the main course. It was roast quail, a bird for each of them: honey-glazed legs folded demurely against each other, comically tiny in contrast to their bulging bodies. The meat was tender and savoury, the accompanying carrots swimming in butter. Esther found it difficult to swallow.

Thomas took a sip of wine. 'Do you believe in the soul, Esther?'

She paused. 'The soul?'

'Yes. All creatures who think, who feel, have souls. Religion, of course, would have that the soul releases itself after the body's death, and disappears into the aether; but the teachings of many occultists would hold that it is recoverable, that it can linger even once the body is gone.'

Esther took a slow, careful bite of her quail. 'A fascinating idea.'

'Isn't it? I find it brings me much comfort. That the body is only a vessel, and that souls can be removed and returned.'

'Or swapped,' Esther said.

'Oh?'

'Well—it is only logical.' Uncomfortable in her high-backed chair, she rolled her shoulders. 'If one can remove a soul, or return it, surely it could also be replaced.'

Thomas's lips pulled into a tiny smile.

'Yes,' he said. 'How insightful.'

They stared at each other across the table. Esther felt the distinct sensation that, for the first time, someone else's perception of her entirely matched her own: in Thomas's eyes, she saw the anger, the regret, the burden of every death she had witnessed, every person who had left her. Their shared responsibility, this Harding legacy. Their inheritance, through no fault of their own. In some ways, it was as much Thomas's curse as hers. *We are family. The Harding bloodline: that is all that matters.*

'When our forefathers sought power,' Thomas said, 'however many generations ago that was—that power came conditionally. They made a deal with the darkness, and that deal came with a price. Our ancestors accepted that some must suffer, for the good of the rest. So, whenever a First Daughter comes…'

He didn't finish the thought. Esther didn't prompt him to do so.

Thomas drained his glass. He stood up from the table.

'Come with me,' Thomas said, taking one of the candlesticks from the table.

Esther didn't move.

'Do you mean to kill me?' she asked him, unable to dance this dance anymore, to hide from the horror of it like a lady demure behind her fan. 'As revenge, for Lily and all the rest?'

'No,' he replied.

'Then what? Don't tell me again you invited me here out of the goodness of your heart. I know about the rituals, Thomas. About the grimoire.'

A flash of anger in his eyes, quick as a striking blade; then it was gone. 'I should've known better than to keep secrets from a witch, I suppose,' he said. 'No matter. Follow me, cousin, and I will explain everything.'

Against her better judgement, Esther stood and followed him out of the dining room.

They went to the second floor, to a door painted with roses: Lily's old room. Thomas unlocked the door with a key from his pocket, and they entered.

In the dim illumination from the candle, the room's colours were grey and black, although a corner of the bedspread revealed by the light seemed a pale yellow tone. The main piece of furniture, as was to be expected, was the bed: a large double, generous enough for two, its headboard carved with flowers.

And on the bed itself—Esther was convinced, for a moment, that she was imagining it.

'What is this?' Esther asked, in half a whisper.

'Your redemption,' Thomas replied.

It was a coffin, a handsome dark wood coffin, lying heavy on the covers, dipping the mattress with its weight. It only just fit on the bed—but it was a tiny coffin, too, Esther thought. For someone unusually small.

'Thomas,' Esther said, slowly, 'is Lily in there?'

'Yes.'

Her stomach rolled. 'But—I *saw* her buried, last year—'

'A separate coffin, full of stones. I had this one stored here, at some expense.'

'*Why?*'

'For the ritual,' Thomas said, blandly. 'Her soul is still in there, you see. My father always said salt kept spirits away. The moment she died, I lined the house with it—the coffin, too. Her body is dead, but Lily remains. All she requires is a vessel.'

'A vessel,' Esther said, and she took a trembling step back. 'A vessel like me.'

Thomas turned to her. In the darkness, lit only by the guttering candle, his movements seemed jerky and sporadic: a monstruous marionette, strings pulled by the shadows.

'Don't you see?' He smiled at her. 'All the guilt, Esther, all the cruelty you have inflicted—I am giving you a chance to undo the damage you've caused. Release your soul, end the curse. It is the only way.'

'You want me to die.'

'The others died,' he said. 'And more still will. You love Isaac, don't you? You want him to live a long, happy life? I loved Lily, too. But you took her from me. I can't blame you for it—that is your nature. The First Daughter. My father always warned me, but it took me so long to finally understand.'

Esther took another step back, toward the doorway. Thomas's hand closed around her arm.

'Let me go,' she said.

With his free hand, Thomas reached into his coat pocket. Esther flinched, expecting a weapon—but instead, he pulled out a book, its cover black leather, pressed with their family's crest. The three-headed hawk. Past, present, future. Seeing it now, Esther had an intangible moment of recognition, as if she had seen this grimoire before, long ago; as if it were something from a dream, now made reality.

'I tried so desperately to do it myself,' he said. 'But it was no use. And I know, now, that it never will be. You are the only one with the power to do this, Esther. To remove your soul and put another in its place.'

'You want me to replace my soul with Lily's,' she whispered.

'Yes. It must be your sacrifice. Your absolution.'

Esther reached forward, shaking, and took the book from him. Thomas released his grip on her arm.

'There,' he said, satisfied. 'You finally see—'

Esther pulled the shadows around herself and began to run.

15

The night had brought stars with it, clear and indifferent. They watched Esther's flight as she weaved through London's streets; the cobblestones made hazy mirrors with the afternoon's rain. Moving through shadows was different than moving when tangible—faster, lighter, more difficult to control—and Esther made her journey without a destination in mind, thinking only *Get away, away,* away *from there*. She could feel the phantom pressure of Thomas's grip on her arm, still, see the white flash of his teeth in the darkness as he smiled. Part of her felt as if she was still in poor Lily's bedroom, staring at the coffin on the bed as Thomas explained—pleaded—demanded... And part of her, even now, thought that perhaps she should turn around and return to the townhouse, return to his offer of redemption. *Your sacrifice. Your absolution.*

Esther was still running when she reached the riverbank, the grimoire gripped in both hands. But she remained half a shadow, mostly immaterial, and she failed to judge her momentum; unable to stop moving, she tumbled over the edge of the quay and floated toward the water like a falling feather.

The Thames itself was still and silent, reflecting Richmond Bridge in a haze of grey brick and purple sky. Esther's impact made no splash, not even a ripple—she didn't break the surface of the water. Instead, she landed on two feet, the river lapping gently at the soles of her shoes. She was so surprised by this that she laughed, despite the horror of the evening so far.

Esther fed another mote of her soul to the shadows, to ensure their compliance. Then she tucked the grimoire beneath one arm and pushed herself forward, as a skater would on ice. She turned a wide loop, feeling the gentle hand of a breeze.

Where would she go now?

What would she do?

Isaac would soon return to the townhouse. *Thomas* was still at the townhouse. The curse remained, her guilt remained, and all she was doing to deal with these things was spinning around on the river. Esther wanted to slap herself. She wanted to release the shadows and fall into the water, sink like a stone until she drowned.

She paused. In the distance, a figure was approaching. It was Miriam, walking across the water with messianic confidence, arms linked behind her back.

'What are you doing here?' Esther demanded, as she came nearer. 'Did you follow me?'

Miriam's lips quirked. 'Would you believe me if I said no?'

'Of course not.'

'Then why ask the question in the first place?'

Esther kicked at the water, frustrated when her shadow-leg failed to create a splash. 'I am not in the mood for your games, Richter.'

'After all this, you still won't call me Miriam?'

'*Miriam*,' Esther snarled. 'I hope you are pleased to know that you were correct. My cousin is a madman. He wishes me to swap my soul with his wife's.'

'I thought his wife was dead?'

'She is. He's kept her soul inside the house with salt.'

Miriam snorted. 'Poor fool. Hope springs eternal, after all.'

'So it isn't possible, then?'

'To swap souls? I presume it must be, although it would take an exceptional amount of power. But salt does not contain souls. Your cousin's wife is long gone.'

'Well, then. That's that, I suppose.' Esther gave a small, bitter laugh, and turned another circle on the water.

Miriam watched her with an arched brow. 'You've been practising.'

'Yes.'

'You should be careful. If your concentration breaks, and you release the darkness from your service, you'll sink.'

'Hm.' Esther bit her lip, regarding Miriam cautiously. She felt the same, instinctive hostility towards her she had since they'd met—and the same attraction, too—but she couldn't help but feel a little grateful, also; Miriam's warnings had been correct, after all. She really *had* been trying to save her.

Miriam saw the book beneath her arm. 'You have the grimoire.'

'This is what you've been looking for, isn't it?'

'Yes.'

She looked so hungry, staring at Esther in that moment; it made Esther's blood run hot, her cheeks flush. She wanted Miriam to look at her like that for longer. She wanted to forget Thomas and the curse and the coffin, just for a moment, and lose herself in the darkness of those eyes.

'Come and get it, then,' Esther said—and she turned and skated further into the river.

When she glanced back over her shoulder, Miriam was giving chase, grinning savagely.

Esther gained momentum, pressed by some joyous and fearful instinct, as they skated past the weeping willows at the bank, toward the towering arches of the bridge. They picked up speed until London was a blur around them, until Esther could hear nothing but the sound of her breathing, the roaring of the air. When they reached the bridge, however, Esther failed to move in time, and she gasped as her body connected with one of the columns that pierced the water—but she was shadow still, and she simply travelled through it, emerging on the other side.

To her right, Miriam was avoiding the columns easily, winding past them on a single foot. *Show-off*, Esther thought, with a begrudging admiration. Miriam moved through darkness as if she were made of it.

Ahead, light and music spilled across the Thames. It was a pleasure barge making its way west. Esther could have simply passed through it again, as she had done the bridge, but her instinct to move away was too strong. She dove for the riverbank to avoid it, and in so doing lost her balance—and her concentration on the shadows. She flickered, then gained substance again, plunging into the water.

It was cold, so cold. The river was murky and dark, duckweed and algae creating a thick slurry that clung to her face and eyes. As the barge passed above them, an uncaring behemoth, water entered Esther's nose, her throat, her lungs. She should have been panicking, but instead she felt a curious sort of peace. Perhaps this was meant to happen. Perhaps she was supposed to die here, in the Thames with the grimoire in her hands. Who knew how many other First Daughters had died the same way, thrown as babies into the river?

A hand clamped around her wrist and pulled. Esther was dragged through weeds and water, passing through the detritus dumped near the bank: pewter pilgrim-badges, broken stopwatches, disintegrated newspapers, sodden clothes. And then there was air in her lungs and mud beneath her. She stooped over, coughing up river water, scrubbing silt from her arms.

When she opened her eyes, Miriam was across from her, also wet—and her expression was furious.

'You cannot *swim*?' she demanded.

'Of course I cannot swim. Who would teach a lady to swim?'

Miriam swore again, and tugged fretfully at her hair. 'Are you suicidal?'

'I do not know,' Esther admitted. 'I told you already, I don't want to die. I just… Sometimes, I have a curious sense I already have.'

Miriam lunged forward and gathered Esther into her arms, pressing her face into the crook of her neck. Esther was so shocked, she went limp. 'Don't,' Esther said. 'I'm filthy, I—'

Miriam bit her neck, hard enough to bruise. Esther gave a startled sort of moan and slapped ineffectually at Miriam's shoulder. Miriam's tongue soothed the bite. Esther whimpered.

Miriam pulled back to look at her, winding a hand into Esther's sodden hair. She tugged, with enough force it felt like punishment. 'When you die in my arms, darling, it will be on *my* terms, not yours.'

Esther should have found that terrifying. She didn't. She was so shamefully aroused, she might have done anything Miriam asked of her, if she'd asked it in that moment—but Miriam didn't ask her anything at all. Instead, she released her, and turned partially away, as if to compose herself.

Esther shuddered with the cold. 'I need to go back and bathe. I…'

'Back? To that house? To *him*?'

'My brother is there. All my possessions.'

'Thomas hurt you!'

Esther stood, legs trembling. 'I am a witch. He is only a man.'

'You must sleep eventually. All he needs is one moment, to catch you off guard.'

'I won't hurt him, Miss Richter,' Esther said sharply. 'Enough.'

Miriam folded her arms. For a moment, the darkness in her eyes seemed to swallow them entirely—pupil and sclera—and Esther shuddered.

'If you will not take action,' Miriam said, 'then, at least, you must do me a favour—in payment for the warnings I gave you, the lessons I have taught.'

'What favour?'

'Remove the salt from your windowsill tonight.'

'Why?'

'So you can tell Thomas you have done so. If he believes his wife's soul is gone, he will be unable to proceed with his plan.'

'That is… a good idea,' Esther admitted. 'Thank you.'

Miriam stretched out her hand. 'Now. The grimoire.'

Esther hesitated. She'd been holding the book when she'd been underwater—she would've expected it to be waterlogged—but in her hands, it looked as pristine as if it had been bound yesterday. Some charm, she supposed, imbued in it by its creator.

Perhaps she'd been underestimating the grimoire's value. Was this not the sum of all her family's work, all their secrets? She knew it held information about the curse; it might hold information about its breaking, too.

'Why do you want this?' she asked Miriam. 'What will you use it for?'

'You needn't concern yourself with that.'

Esther took a step away from her, the marshy ground sinking beneath her feet. 'I could use it too, you know. To break the curse.'

Miriam's eyes somehow, impossibly, grew darker, and her face hardened to stone. Esther felt the hair on her arms stand on end.

'Esther,' Miriam said, warningly. 'Give it to me.'

'I don't—'

'*Give it to me!*' she snarled, and it sounded less like a shout than a clap of thunder, her hair rising around her face as if blown back by wind, her features half consumed by shadows. And Esther saw, in the centre of her chest, a curious, swirling blackness—a void that seemed without end.

'What—what are you?' Esther asked in horror, the hairs on her arms standing on end. 'What is that in your chest?'

'My chest?' Miriam asked. 'Oh. That is my soul—or lack of it, I suppose.'

But you must have a soul, Esther thought, recalling Thomas's words. *All creatures have souls.*

It was not the time to argue the point. Instead, she said, 'You are no witch, Miriam Richter. I ought to have realised that earlier.'

Miriam gave her a pitying look.

'It doesn't matter what I am, my dear,' she said. 'Your last hope; your greatest regret. It doesn't matter, because I am all you have.'

I am all you have.

Esther felt the truth of that in the marrow of her bones. How often had she wished to find someone like the monster standing before her? Someone immune to the cruelties of the curse, the cruelties of Esther's own heart, her hostility and her regrets. No one had ever accepted her as Miriam had. No one else ever would.

That realisation felt miraculous and terrible. It was a cauterisation, a cure that hurt more than the wound. And Esther found, suddenly, that all she wanted was to go to bed.

'Take me back,' Esther asked the shadows.

'*No—!*' Miriam snarled, reaching for her. But she was too late. Esther had already disappeared, the grimoire still in her arms.

Esther slipped inside the townhouse enshrouded in darkness, invisible and intangible. It was too late to ask the servants for a bath, so she looked down at herself, at her mud-stained gown, bedraggled and waterlogged, and paid a sliver of soul for the chance to be clean. The shadows draped over her: the fabric of her dress brightened; her hair dried. When she lifted her wrist to her nose, she even smelt faintly of lilies.

The salt was on her windowsill, just as Miriam had said. It was invisible, but Esther ran her finger over the surface and felt a minuscule, jagged ridge. The grains didn't shift at her touch. Esther realised they had been glued down, but it would be easy enough to scrape them off with a nail or needle. And it would be just as easy to slide into bed, and leave Miriam's request unfulfilled.

A shape formed in the darkness outside, then hopped closer to the windowsill. It was her Little Shadow, feathers oil-slick dark, head tilted to watch her.

Esther managed a hesitant smile. 'I have you, also,' she told the bird. 'My dear friend. Forgive me for forgetting that.'

The crow ruffled its feathers.

Esther pressed her finger more firmly against the salt. The crow hopped closer, tapped the glass of the window gently with its beak. She watched it, considering the darkness of its eyes, and the familiar glint of intelligence within them.

She knew that darkness. She had known it her entire life.

Realisation fell as softly as a shroud. Esther didn't even feel surprised. She just felt tired: as tired as if she'd never slept at all, as if she'd been awake for centuries.

'Will you kill him, Miriam?' she asked the crow. 'Once I let you in?'

The crow didn't reply. It stood on the windowsill with its wings half outstretched, as if preparing for flight.

'I did not give you the grimoire,' Esther said. 'I know, if you come in, you will take it from me. And I am afraid.'

On the wall to her left, shadows fluttered and trembled—were they nervous or excited? Had they warned her of this, once, and she had ignored that warning? Their demands were futile, either way.

Perhaps Esther's resistance had been, also.

'You once said I deserved to be loved. Will—will you love me?' She pressed her palm against the frigid glass. 'I do not know what you are, really, or *who* you are—but I think I need that now. I can't pretend, anymore, that I want anything else.'

The crow bowed its head.

Esther made a furrow in the salt with her thumb.

The crow shifted, bled into the night, seeping, gone liquid—the shadows swarmed through the glass of the window, through that tiny crack in the salt, a steady stream that pooled at Esther's feet before growing tall and opaque and material. Then Miriam was there, and she caught Esther's wrist with her hand.

'I'll love you,' she said. 'Of *course* I will, darling.' And then her mouth was on hers.

The kiss was brief and violent, teeth and tongue, and Esther's eyes fluttered closed. As Miriam pulled away, her fingers pressed into the hollow of Esther's back. Her smile was triumphant.

'I will make you mine,' Miriam said, and Esther felt shadows rising to wrap themselves, cool and inquisitive, around her wrists and ankles. They tugged her towards the bed as Miriam stood watching, still smiling—and Esther didn't resist as she was pressed down into the mattress, as the cool hands of the darkness ran like water across her chest and thighs. She gasped something—she wasn't certain herself what she was saying, perhaps Miriam's name—and Miriam came to stand beside the bed, stooping over her, pressing a finger to her lips.

'Hush,' she said. 'I know what you need.'

The shadows parted as Miriam, with gentle reverence, pulled away Esther's dress. The corset beneath was the work of seconds, fingers working deftly, and then Esther was left in her white chemise. The shame of her arousal was evident in her laboured breathing, the cherry-dark rounds of her nipples stiff and visible through the fabric. Miriam ran a finger over her breast, chuckling when Esther whimpered.

'A little death,' Miriam said. 'That is what I've heard some people call it. Will you die for me today, my love?'

Her fingers skimmed the top of Esther's thighs. 'Do I have a choice?' Esther asked, half gasping.

'Certainly. *This*, I want willingly. I want to ruin you, Esther, and I want you to beg me for it.'

'I won't beg.'

Miriam lifted her hand away. 'No?'

Esther could have snarled in frustration; she bit her lip to stop herself from doing so. 'You demean me—'

'Demean?' Miriam laughed sharply, and she ran her nails down Esther's side, through her chemise. It felt painfully good, and Esther arched over the mattress, swallowing a wail. 'Darling, I will *worship* you. Ask me to do so, and I shall.'

Esther felt her resistance slipping.

'Please,' she bit out, trying to push herself into Miriam's hand.

Miriam's lip twitched; her hand didn't move. 'Pardon?'

'Please,' Esther said, craning her head to look at her. 'Touch me. I need you to.'

Miriam said, 'As you wish,' and then her hand pushed up Esther's chemise, and somehow her fingers were everywhere, between her legs and pinching her nipples, and her mouth was on her neck and she smelt like river and iron and it was so good that it was unbearable. Esther's eyes closed. She thought, *I shall die, I might simply die from this.* The movement of Miriam's touch, her fingers rocking back and forth, not enough but almost enough—Esther knew nothing but skin and warmth and pleasure. She was on the edge of a cliff, and she wanted, so desperately, to step forward and fall, fall into the water, disappear beneath it and drown.

And then, briefly, in the darkness behind her eyelids, Esther was suddenly somewhere else. She was someone else, in another place, another time: she was running through the serpentine corridors of an echoing building, a shadow following behind her, the great windows rattling from the storm—

Her pleasure peaked, and all else was forgotten. When she came, it was brutal and demanding, her back arching, a curse on her lips. Miriam worked her through it without hesitation, fingers still moving, whispering encouragements in her ear. When, finally, Esther batted her hands away and opened her eyes, she realised that—for some reason—she had been crying.

Miriam rose over her and kissed her tears away.

'My love,' she said. 'Your dissolution is the loveliest thing I have ever seen.'

Dissolution. That was a good word for it, what Esther felt. She was unmade, undone. Miriam had broken her into pieces and left them scattered over the bed.

They stared at each other, Miriam's face hovering over hers.

Miriam said, 'I think I *must* love you, Esther Harding. There must be no other word for what this is.'

'Love is supposed to be a kind thing, a beautiful thing. That is what the world has always told me.'

'The world lied,' Miriam said.

'Yes,' Esther replied. 'It did.'

16

Miriam watched Esther sleep, her face drenched in moonlight. Their only company was the shadows seething pleasure-drunk at the foot of the bed, the only sound in the room the soft rhythm of Esther's breathing. Miriam didn't sleep herself, but sometimes she approximated it with eyes closed and mind emptied, for hours or even years at a time—still, she would never do so when she was with Esther. It was too important to watch her as she dreamed, so that she could wake her if necessary, and ensure the past didn't pry open the present.

On occasion, Miriam had read mortal poetry, had seen mortal art, had witnessed plays and festivals and learnt of the ruin a beautiful woman could inflict. She had thought herself, naturally, above such concerns. To Miriam, beauty was as fleeting as the landfall of a grain of sand, swept onto the beach and then pulled back by the tide.

But Miriam looked at Esther now, her hair splayed upon the pillow like tongues of flame, her lips parted and eyes fluttering with the whispers of her sleeping mind—and Miriam understood the fear of those men, who had looked at Helen and seen war approaching, who encountered loveliness and fell upon it like a sword. And perhaps, in that moment, a modicum of her contempt for humanity burnt away.

Esther sighed in her sleep. A single drop of soul, golden and glistening, fell from her closed eyelid and slipped down her cheek. Whatever she was dreaming of, it was vivid enough to inflame her magic. Miriam reached out to touch her, then withdrew. Esther was not distressed enough to be remembering something important.

The grimoire was on the bedside table. Miriam stood from the bed, fluid and silent, and took it up to read. It was illuminating, as much as the writing of a madman could be so; the line between Christopher Harding's genius and his delusion was very thin. But the rituals outlined there, the images of the angels with their dozen eyes, undeniably brought Miriam some concern. In the correct hands, the hands of someone with true power—such ravings could become reality. The thought of Esther accessing such magic was startling. If she remembered her previous life, she could draw upon those twin souls to… well. Miriam wasn't certain what, exactly, but the grimoire's rambling descriptions of soul transference and siphoning were certainly worrisome.

The most sensible thing for Miriam to do would be to kill Thomas Harding; kill him, and then return to the shadows, at least until the deal was up. That would minimise the likelihood of her reminding Esther of something and undoing the careful equilibrium they had created for themselves.

But Miriam didn't want to return to the shadows. Glancing at Esther now, she felt a new sort of hunger, one that couldn't be sated with blood or power or sex. Miriam finally understood why people might trade their soul for someone else—and she *hated* that understanding, adored it, wanted to carve it out of herself and cradle it in her arms.

There was one problem, at least, that Miriam was certain she could solve. So—once she was certain that Esther was no longer dreaming—she left the room, and she went to find Thomas Harding.

As much as she would have loved to see Esther kill him herself, the fact was, she clearly didn't have the stomach for it. And so, the task now fell to Miriam, to finally end this nonsense before Thomas became another Martingale and dug his spade into his cousin's neck. *Really*, she mused, as she wandered the townhouse's halls, luxuriating in the dark, *really, how ludicrous it is that such a meagre morsel of a man should cause so much trouble; that he should make a witch as powerful as Esther feel fear.*

This place, this house, was nothing more than a jewellery box for the delusional. It was all padded velvet wallpaper and grotesque baroque paintings, vases of stale flowers drooping their heads over dust-coated rugs. Harding Hall, with its grand windows and vast forests, had been a far more suitable stage for Miriam's work. *This* was a setting for a farce, not a grand tragedy. There was, perhaps, something ominous in the townhouse's low ceilings, in the cramped huddle of its corridors, like a fist closing around you—but what was a fist to the reaper, when the scythe was in her hands?

Miriam went room by room, stepping through each door as a shadow. The study, the main bedroom, the dining room, all empty; in a cramped room on the second floor, Esther's brother snored while sprawled supine on a bedspread stitched with faded copper roses. A room dedicated to a pianoforte still held the vague scent of blood. Curious, Miriam opened the lid of the instrument to find a dead rat with a sigil carved into its stomach, staring in frozen terror at the brass strings. Thomas's work, she supposed. Or perhaps Esther's, in search of ending the curse? Either way, it was a pantomime—style without substance. The rat had died for nothing.

She found him, finally, in a room lit dimly by a single candelabra, the candles balancing uncertainly on a bed. Beside it was a coffin, and beside the coffin was Thomas. His elbows were resting on the coffin's lid, his head in his hands. There was a gun on the coffin, too, an ivory duelling pistol. When Miriam entered, still made of shadows, she was as silent as a whisper. But when she became material, and took an audible step forward, Thomas didn't react. He was too overcome with whatever internal argument he was having, fingers twisting in his hair as if he meant to tear it out.

'You should do it,' Miriam said, gesturing to the gun.

Thomas started, nearly falling off the bed. The movement of the mattress made the candelabra shudder. It nearly tipped over before righting itself.

'Who are you?' he asked, his face wan in the guttering light of the flame.

'Your reckoning,' Miriam replied, and she allowed her pretence of humanity to slip away, as a snake might shed its skin; shadows bled and dripped from her eyes, her mouth, the tips of her fingers.

Thomas, to his credit, neither screamed nor fainted. Instead, he reached for the gun. He stood with the trembling muzzle aimed directly at Miriam's chest. 'Stay back.'

Miriam smiled. She laid a hand on the coffin, considering. 'Who is it within, I wonder?'

His expression morphed into fury. 'Leave her alone.'

'I have no interest in a box of bones, Master Harding, never fear.'

'Did—' The pistol trembled in his hand. 'Did Esther send you, somehow? To stop me?'

'To *stop* you? Oh, sweetheart.' Miriam stroked the wood of the coffin. 'You still think *you* are the villain of this piece? The shadow hiding in the dark? You aren't, I'm afraid. Esther Harding has her share of nightmares chasing her. Compared to me, you are nothing but a pleasant dream.'

Thomas fired the gun.

The bullet embedded itself in Miriam's chest. She'd never been shot before, and it felt strange—a dull, heavy blow, uncomfortable but not painful. Miriam shifted slightly with the hit, but she made no sound in response, and she remained standing.

The door behind them slammed open. In came Esther, chemise unlaced, feet bare, her eyes wild with fear. As she entered the room, the candles blazed with the strength of her panic, power resonating in the air.

The muzzle of the gun was still smoking. 'What have you done?' Esther breathed, looking at Thomas.

Thomas didn't respond. He was staring at Miriam's chest, where the bullet had torn a hole through her shirt, creating a neat crater in her skin. She wasn't bleeding, but shadows were leaking out of the hole and pooling on the floor below. Miriam poked the hole experimentally, then felt something rattle in her lungs. She coughed.

'He shot you,' Esther said. 'Miriam, oh, *God*.' She came to her, tugging desperately at her arm to inspect the wound. Miriam coughed again, twice, three times. She felt something cold and small rise into her throat and fill her mouth. She spat it out into the palm of her hand.

It was the bullet. It glittered in the candlelight like a jewel.

'Monster,' Thomas hissed, dropping the gun. He raised his hands to his chest. *Go on, do it*, Miriam thought, and then felt a thrill of satisfaction when he crossed himself. They *always* did that, eventually.

Miriam grinned and tried to take another step forward. Esther caught her by the sleeve.

'Don't,' Esther said.

Miriam sneered at her. 'You *asked* me, you know, whether I would kill him—'

'You didn't reply!'

'Was my silence not enough? When you broke that line of salt, you understood what the consequences would be.'

'The salt,' Thomas moaned, and he fell to the floor.

'You care so much for his life?' Miriam demanded, gesturing to him. 'This pitiful creature?'

'I care for mine!' Esther snarled. 'I care for my own life, and my mastery of it. This isn't your concern, Miriam. He is *my* cousin, *my* problem—the consequences of *my* curse. He is no longer a threat to me. And if he dies, it will be my decision, not yours.'

There was a coldness in her eyes, a resentment that Miriam hadn't seen in centuries. Miriam paused, beating her frustration into submission. The exertions of the evening, the passion and fury that Esther was feeling—this was the sort of strain that could cause old memories to resurface. The balance of Esther's psyche was tenuous as it was. Miriam couldn't risk breaking that spider-silk thread.

'Darling,' Miriam said, slowly. She reached out and took Esther's hand, cradling it in her own. 'If *you* wish to kill him, then…'

'I don't want to kill him, for God's sake, Miriam.'

'Forgive me. I only wished to keep you safe.'

Miriam pulled her closer. Esther resisted, just for a moment, but then begrudgingly leaned into the touch, allowing Miriam to hold her in her arms.

'You said you loved me,' Esther said, looking up at her. 'As much as something like you can love.'

'I did.'

'Did you mean it?'

'Yes.'

Her expression was flint, sharp and brittle. 'Then *let him go.*'

Miriam wavered. She could hear Thomas whimpering on the floor. It would be so easy to end it now; so easy to step forward and snap his neck.

'Let him go,' Esther repeated, her face softening now, voice a low murmur, as she looked up at Miriam through her lashes in a transparent attempt at manipulation. Was that not cruel? If Miriam hadn't seen her as she had only hours ago, squirming on the bed in her ecstasy, it might not have mattered. But she'd seen it now, and she wanted to see it again. Miriam wanted to taste Esther in every way that was possible.

If she killed him, Esther would never forgive her for it. They had barely half a year until the deal was complete, and, at the very least, they could spend that time together—why not? Esther had yet to remember her past life. Perhaps, if Miriam was careful, she never would.

Miriam said, 'If I allow you this, my dear, I expect to be repaid.'

'I know. I am yours entirely, Miriam, if only you spare him.'

Miriam hummed in satisfaction, bowing down to brush her mouth over Esther's neck.

'Entirely,' she agreed.

She looked over Esther's shoulder at Thomas, who was curled on the rug, shoulders shaking. If his life was to be spared—well. There were other ways to punish him.

Go, she told the shadows, *take what is left*—and, like feasting maggots, the darkness swarmed toward the coffin on the bed. Esther flinched in her arms, then pressed her face against Miriam's chest so she wouldn't see. That was a shame; it was quite the performance. The wood of the coffin began to rot and crumble, the scent of putrescence filling the air. Thomas cried out, stood up, and reached toward the bed—but there was nothing he could do. What was left of his wife's body within began to spill out onto the sheets as the coffin itself disappeared, and the shadows took that, too. They squirmed over the corpse, eating away at the decayed and mummified flesh, until all that remained was a pile of bones lying on the stained coverlet.

Thomas began to sob. Miriam ignored him. She stroked a loving hand over Esther's head. Then she scooped her into her arms, and she carried her away.

The Season was almost over, and Esther felt as if it had lasted for centuries.

Thomas had locked himself in his rooms. Esther couldn't blame him. Meanwhile, Isaac was as he always was—he came to breakfast the morning after Thomas had shot Miriam, and asked, 'Did some furniture fall over last night? I heard a rather loud bang.'

'I didn't hear anything,' Esther said. Isaac gave her a narrow-eyed stare, reaching across the table for the teapot. He was only ever half as naïve as he first appeared.

'You know,' he replied, 'you have an awful habit of trying to shoulder all the burden yourself. You could share it with me, sometimes, if you wanted.'

'I wish I could,' she said. And when he pressed her, she refused to respond.

She couldn't stop thinking about poor Lily, consumed by shadows. She couldn't stop thinking about Thomas, the soft sobs he'd made as the coffin had crumbled to dust. And she couldn't stop thinking about Miriam afterwards, once they'd returned to Esther's room—her head between Esther's thighs, smiling as if she were Paris with Helen in his bed.

There was only one event remaining that the Hardings were expected to attend: the Carroway Ball next week, the highlight of the Season, a party so pre-eminent in importance that missing it was akin to social suicide. Still, Esther was little inclined to go. She'd woken up that morning, and Miriam had been gone. She might've wondered if the events of the previous night had been a dream, except she still had love bites sucked into her thighs, finger-shaped bruises pressed into her lower back. Whatever Miriam was, she still seemed to understand Esther and what she needed, in the same way a clockmaker knows a watch. She had somehow been able to take her apart and fit her back together; to give her pleasure of a sort that, even now, even despite her fear and her horror, made Esther squirm in her chair to think of.

She excused herself from breakfast. In her lime-coloured room, she tried to distract herself by considering her gown for the ball. With the madness of the Season, she hadn't remembered to visit the tailors, and so she was left with a relic from last year. It was fine enough, she supposed, cream with lace to match, albeit a little stained—at a dance last year, another woman had 'accidentally' tipped her wine onto the hem.

Esther held up the dress and looked into the mirror, giving a moue of displeasure. She pressed her fingers against the stain on the dress, closing her eyes. She wanted it white, wanted to *believe* that it was. So, as her power gathered, she conjured images of the colour in her head: blank paper, summer clouds, royal icing on a wedding cake; then snow falling in a forest, limning the leaves with ice, the pale clouds of breath on a winter's day. She pictured herself walking through that forest, the chill on her skin, her skirts heavy as they trailed the ground.

Then the flakes of snow weren't cold anymore; they were warm: ash from a fire, not snow after all. In her mind's eye, Esther looked up to see a building burning, the flames fraying the night sky, the heat making the air dry and caustic. A woman was screaming. Esther's throat ached.

She couldn't breathe. She was dying.

Esther gasped and opened her eyes.

The gown was white now, a pristine ivory, but the lace that trimmed it was the scarlet of fresh blood. And the woman holding the dress in the reflection wasn't her; or—it *was* her, but not quite. Her hair was longer, loose to her shoulders, and her face was twisted into a sneer. Around her throat there was a necklace of black-bruised flesh, as if someone had tried to slit the skin with an inked quill.

'Do not trust her,' the reflection said to Esther. 'And remain vigilant. "Wars begin when you wish them to, but they do not end as you please."'

It was a quote from Machiavelli: one Esther had learnt herself as a girl, when she'd torn through her father's library.

'Who are you?' Esther said.

The reflection shook her head. 'She has begun the war,' she told her, 'but we shall be the ones to finish it.'

Esther reached out to touch the mirror, astonished, but she found only her reflection. Her fingers pressed against the glass. When she pulled away, the only evidence of the encounter were the five smudges her prints had left.

17

The day after her confrontation with Thomas Harding, Miriam flew for hours to the coast—to white cliffs, and the wailing of the wind. She disliked the sea: it reminded her of the day of her birth. Besides, the further out to sea you went, the fewer shadows there were, and the more her power weakened. For someone like Esther, who was made of light, that was no issue. But Miriam needed darkness to do her work, even during the day.

Still, she went there. Miriam had already spent the morning trying to destroy the grimoire. But whatever magic the Harding family had imbued the object with—whatever had preserved it so perfectly in the centuries since its creation—had resisted all of her attempts. The book hadn't burnt; when she'd tried to feed it to the shadows, they'd spat it back out. So, then, she would drown it.

Miriam alighted on a half-dead bush springing from the side of a cliff, blinking the mist of seawater from her eyes, wincing at the burning of the salt. Above her, the moon was in crescent, as it had been the night Harding Hall had burnt. She dropped the grimoire, watching it spin and plummet towards the waves. It landed with a splash and disappeared.

There was little hope for Esther now. The pact would soon be complete. And when her soul was gone, then Miriam could, at least, hold that lovely corpse and bear it to her tomb. She would gild her like a catacomb saint, make relics of her hair and teeth and bones. And to each of those she tormented and consumed, she would speak of Harding, the girl who lived two lives: Miriam would ensure that her love was remembered. That way, Esther's death would be less an ending than a transformation. It would be a form of immortality, even. She would never be forgotten.

Miriam flung herself off the bush and wheeled into the open sky, intending to fly north back to London. Then she noticed a tiny, floating speck atop the waves.

Cawing in anger, she dove down towards the sea, where the grimoire was bobbing gently on the water. As she neared the water, she felt a pressure growing, as if the air was thickening and would soon become impassable. It was the salt; the burning began immediately, and she twisted in the air, writhing, shrieking, vision half blinded by pain. Desperate, clumsy, she took the thing in both talons—hissing as salt touched her skin—and she rose once more, heaving the book away from the coast.

Miriam considered what to do. If she laid the grimoire to rest in the place of its creation, perhaps it would stop haunting her. Cybil had once dug it a grave, after all, and the book ought to obey the family it served. Flying north, her route took her over both forest and field, England shrouded in darkness. She passed over a small village, a squat stone church's spire poking out between hills as an arrowhead through flesh. It remained so familiar, so unchanged. She could see it still, as if it were yesterday: the dogs and the horses, Henry Martingale baying for blood. On the horizon, there were still the mounds where the villagers had danced, and there was the forest where she had first met Cybil, that wild-faced girl with mud on her cheeks and fury in her eyes.

She flew towards Harding Hall—or, at least, what remained of it: a centuries-old foundation still black with char, overgrown with grass. Miriam wondered why they'd never rebuilt. Perhaps people still considered the site cursed, associated it with witchcraft. It was a monument to Cybil's power. She'd wounded this place, and the scar she'd left would outlive them all.

In the woods, Miriam alighted and shifted to her human form. Memory brought her to the correct place. A wizened oak, Gordian-knot roots. Miriam knelt and began to dig. The soil was soft and damp, pleasantly alive in the manner of just-rained-on earth. Worms wriggled against her hands, and seedlings trailed green stalks across her fingers. Eventually, her nails struck something coarse and dry.

She pulled the sack out of its grave.

Inside, the other books were pristine. The gold tooled into their leather covers still shone, pages still pale and flat, and the careful calligraphy within had hardly faded. A linen bag had been all that separated them from the elements for two centuries, and yet they looked the same as when she and Cybil had buried them. Cybil's determination to save them had imbued itself into their pages, and now these books were as immortal as the grimoire was.

She put the grimoire in the sack, and returned the sack to the hole. She kicked dirt and leaves over it until it was impossible to tell the site had been disturbed.

Miriam called the darkness and took to the skies. To the east, the skeleton of Harding Hall mouldered on its hill, and the sun—barely born—began to hook its fingers over the horizon.

Esther didn't know if Miriam was coming to the ball. She hadn't seen her for days, since the night she had taken her to bed—and that stung, as ridiculous as it was. *You shouldn't deal with the devil at all*, Esther told herself, *let alone ask her to dance*. But she'd spent every morning, every night, waiting for her crow to return.

She did not return. The day of the ball, Thomas remained locked in his rooms; Esther was hardly inclined to try to convince him to go. Instead, she spent the afternoon in the elaborate ritual of preparation a woman was expected to undertake for a Society event. A bath, first of all: two of them, one steaming hot, to draw the blood, and one cold as ice, to polish the skin. Afterwards, she shone like a pearl, and the bruises Miriam had left on her looked darker, as if reasserting their claim.

Esther's perfume was lily of the valley, her silk shoes embroidered with the same flowers, white on white. Her hair was curled into minuscule ringlets, as fine as wisteria blossoms. A few of these curls were left dangling to frame her face, but most were piled in a Grecian knot on her head, set with pins glimmering with misshapen opals.

The maid—who was talented; Thomas kept good staff—took out the gown for Esther to inspect, her usual mask of indifference marred by a moue of distaste. The scarlet lace edging the cream silk was gauche, Esther knew. But there was something almost lovely about it, now that she looked at it again. It was like fresh blood on snow.

'Lace it tightly,' she told the maid. She felt the boning wrap closer around her, ribbons pulling through eyelets with a snakelike hiss. For a moment, she recalled the feeling of suffocation that had come when she'd transformed the dress with magic: the curious feeling of ashes in her throat, her lungs. The pain in her neck—the phantom presence of some curious violence she had not experienced, and yet which felt familiar.

Esther closed her eyes, breathing deeply against the iron grip of her stays.

When she looked at herself in the mirror, she was relieved to see her own face looking back.

Esther and Isaac travelled to Carroway House in one of Thomas's carriages. They did not bother to ask for permission. Esther doubted he'd even noticed their leaving.

'Patience and courage,' she told Isaac in the carriage, and he sighed. 'At *all* times, Isaac. Edward Carroway could find you a good position at his company, if you comport yourself well.'

'I'll comport myself how I bloody like,' he replied; then he wilted a little at the acidity of Esther's expression. 'Sorry. It's just—I don't particularly want to be an accountant.'

'What *do* you want to be, then?'

'I don't know.'

'Then you ought to be an accountant until you figure it out,' Esther said. 'I won't always be here, you know. You can't rely on Thomas's charity forever.'

Isaac frowned. 'Don't speak like that.'

'Speak like what?'

'As if you're about to die. It is—unsettling.' Isaac sighed again, and rubbed at his face with his hand. The movement sent a lock of dark hair tumbling over his forehead. He had been attempting to grow sideburns for years now, but they never quite took; there was an aspirational peach fuzz of growth dusting either side of his cheekbones.

He was a child, still. Only a child. How much of his growing had Esther ignored, in her quest for freedom? How many moments unseen, how many more doomed to be so?

Esther imagined reaching out, taking his hand. She did not. She turned to look out the window. The carriage was trundling up the driveway now, and lanterns dotted the path guiding them to Carroway House: a titanic confection of Doric columns, white brick, and marble floors. There were musicians outside, too, greeting the guests with lighthearted music that belied the sheer, raucous intensity of the crowd. Many were already drunk, hooting like animals as they stumbled inside.

When Esther and Isaac exited the carriage, they were accosted by the gazes of those lingering outside the entrance. No one bothered pretending they weren't staring at them. Esther felt the accusation in those eyes, the hostility, and she felt a flush rising on her neck. They were only invited, really, because they were in Thomas's care; and now Thomas hadn't even come with them.

'Come,' she muttered to Isaac. He glared at the other guests as she hauled him through the doorway.

The ballroom was a crush of people, guests spilling out into corridors, the air sweltering from the press of bodies and the hundreds of candles lighting the room. The ceiling was already darkening with soot. The cacophonous murmur of the crowd was deafening. Esther raised her fan and covered half her face so that her eyes could peer across the top. As she and Isaac walked across the room, Esther could feel heads turning to follow them. Her fan fluttered nervously in her grip. She ought to have worn a normal dress; she ought to have demanded Thomas join them; she ought not to have come at all—but she hadn't done any of those things, and it was too late to do so now. Esther's only option was to pretend the attention didn't chafe.

A quartet started a rousing dance. In response, a man in the crowd shouted something in consternation, and elsewhere there was the sound of a glass smashing.

'Where should I leave you?' Isaac asked her. At events like these, women were expected to settle in one spot until they were asked to dance, like weeds waiting to be pulled. He gestured towards a group of ladies giggling in the corner, some of whom Esther knew, but she shook her head.

'Over there,' she said, pointing. He deposited her by a window, where she could stand in the moonlight and stare out into the gardens—it made Esther feel less crowded, although not much.

'Call if you need me,' Isaac said.

'I will. Are you going to find Henry Carroway?'

'Of course not. I'm going to stand in the corridor and smoke.'

'Isaac,' she said severely.

'I— Very well. After the cigar.'

She rolled her eyes and made a dismissive gesture. He fled the ballroom, leaving her at the mercy of the crowd.

Leaning against the window, Esther fanned herself slowly, chewing the inside of her lip. Perhaps, if she remained silent and still, people would assume she was simply part of the furniture and leave her alone; she had intended to use this event to ingratiate herself with someone, *anyone*, but now her courage failed her.

Eventually she was spotted by Alexander Montagu, the eldest brother of the unfortunate Lily. He had squared his shoulders and was approaching her with the grim-faced determination of a gladiator entering the ring.

'Mr Montagu,' Esther said, warningly, as he stopped in front of her.

His bow was perfunctory. 'Miss Harding. My brother-in-law hasn't accompanied you, I see.'

'No, he hasn't.'

'I suppose if he had, he would have had to explain himself,' Montague said, lip curling into a sneer.

'Explain himself?'

'My sister is only a few months cold. Has he no shame?'

Esther saw the vitriol behind the cold mask of his expression. 'What are you implying, sir? My cousin's charity, I assure you, was motivated only by our family connection.'

'Is that what we call it now? *Charity?*'

He was assuming she was Thomas's mistress. Esther would have been well within her rights to slap him, but her horror was far more powerful than her anger. She felt the tips of her fingers prickle with power.

'You ought to leave, Mr Montagu, while my patience holds,' Esther said.

Montagu's eye twitched, and he took a step closer to her.

'You shame yourself, sir,' came the low, dark voice of Miriam Richter as she emerged from the crowd. She stepped between Esther and Montagu, the tails of her red velvet jacket sweeping behind her in a wide arc. She was in white trousers and boots, curls worn loose around her shoulders. Her lips were curved into a dangerous smile. She could have hardly been more out of place if she'd tried.

Montagu gaped at her. Uncaring, Miriam continued. 'Leave, or I'll demand satisfaction for your rudeness.'

'Who are you?'

'To you? A bullet in the throat and a shallow grave. Shall we duel here, or find somewhere more private?'

'This is absurd,' Montagu muttered, but—mystifyingly—he made no comment on Miriam's gender or dress. Instead, he was sufficiently intimidated that he shook his head and turned away, stalking back into the crowd.

'Miriam,' Esther said, baffled.

Miriam took her hand and kissed it. 'Good evening, my dear. I apologise for my lateness. Were you waiting for me?'

'No.'

Miriam smiled at her indulgently. 'You make such a pretty liar, Esther.'

'You shouldn't be here.'

'I don't see why not.'

'Why—because—I can't believe they allowed you inside, wearing that!'

'They see what I want them to see.'

'And what is that?' Esther asked.

'A gentleman.'

Esther looked at the crowd. There were a few wayward glances, some scandalised mutterings in the wake of the argument with Montagu, but none of the silent horror she would've expected in reaction to Miriam's appearance.

'I haven't seen you in days,' Esther said.

'Did you miss me?'

She didn't know how to reply. Lying felt pointless, but honesty felt too much like surrender.

'Why did you come?' she asked instead.

'I thought we ought to dance.'

Esther smiled wryly. 'Dancing with the devil; how far I have fallen.'

Miriam offered her a hand. 'No devils here, darling. No loneliness, no fear. Just us.'

A phantom voice rose suddenly in Esther's mind, as clear as if the words had been spoken beside her—Miriam's voice, although Miriam's lips did not move—

A place without loneliness, without fear. Without the weight of your guilt upon your shoulders. I could bring you there.

It did not feel like magic. It felt like a memory.

The shock made Esther pause, trembling, as Miriam waited expectantly for her to take her hand.

'You promised me, Esther,' Miriam murmured, low and warning, when she didn't move. 'You promised me that you would be mine.'

'I know,' Esther replied. 'I am.'

And she placed her palm in hers.

The first dance was a cotillion, which required a ludicrous amount of spinning. Esther was whirled from partner to partner at great speed, and she could only ever speak with Miriam in breathless snatches before she was pulled away again.

'You look lovely,' Miriam said to her, as they linked arms to form a line.

'I ruined this dress.'

'I don't see how.'

'Blood on snow,' Esther said. 'That is what it reminds me of. A winter someplace long ago.'

Miriam paused—only for a moment, but perceptibly enough. Then she said, in what felt like reproach, 'I want to make this night beautiful, Esther. Something to celebrate.'

'You want to play with your doll in your dollhouse, you mean. See her dressed up all pretty and make her dance.'

Miriam tipped her head back and laughed. 'You are not a doll, my love. If you were, I would have grown bored with you much more quickly.'

Esther opened her mouth to reply, but then she was spinning away again, almost tumbling into the arms of an unsuspecting gentleman. She'd never been very good at dancing, and she tripped over the feet of Alexander Montagu, who glared pointedly at her before he turned away. For a moment, Esther was entirely lost in the crowd of dancers; there were too many people present. Their movements sent the candles surrounding them into ecstasy, casting shivering shadows across the wallpaper, billowing and receding. It almost looked like the walls themselves were alight, as if the whole space might catch fire and trap the guests in an inferno. Entranced, Esther paused to watch the flicker of a nearby flame. The wax of the candle was dripping in a heartbeat rhythm onto the table beneath it.

A hand took hers. 'Esther?' Miriam said, as she pulled her into another twirl. 'What's the matter?'

Esther shook her head. 'I— Nothing. I was distracted.'

Miriam's grip on her hand tightened. 'You are distracted quite often, it seems.'

'I've been seeing strange things,' Esther said. 'As always. I met someone else in the mirror. Myself, but not myself.'

Miriam froze in the middle of the dance floor. 'Someone else?'

'*Miriam*,' Esther said urgently, tugging her back into movement. 'You'll trip everyone up.'

'Who was it you saw, Esther?'

Before she could even consider her reply, someone else was speaking for her through her own mouth, pulling her strings like a puppeteer—her voice the same, but the cold fury in it unfamiliar. 'Who do you think, Mistress Richter?'

Miriam hissed a breath. Meanwhile, the violins sounded a flourish, and Esther was pulled away. Spinning in a wide line at the edge of the dance floor, she saw the faceless, leering figures of the audience watching the dancers; she saw the candle flames roaring, reaching eagerly towards the ceiling; and then she swore she could hear the beat of a tambourine between the strings, and smell the scent of grass.

It was terrifying, but Esther felt a curious sense of relief—as if something long missing had finally slipped into place.

Arms closed around her. 'We ought to stop,' Miriam said into her ear. 'You're flushed.'

'I feel dizzy.'

'We've been spinning too much. Let's fetch you a drink.'

Miriam pulled her away from the dancers to find a server with a tray of glasses. Esther downed a measure of claret in two gulps, and then they retreated to a corner of the room, half obscured by a candelabra.

'Better?' Miriam asked.

Esther shook her head. 'It is becoming worse. These visions, these moments of confusion—they grow worse and worse.'

Miriam didn't reply. She watched her silently, expression unreadable.

'I've always had nightmares,' Esther continued. 'Even when I was a child. I used to dream that my room was on fire; I would wake up to find that I had gotten out of bed, and that I was stomping on the floor, as if to stop the flames.'

'Esther...'

She shook her head. 'Why do I feel as if I've known you all my life? Why are you so *familiar* to me?' Her eyes met Miriam's. 'Sometimes, I despise you so much—I want you so much—that it feels as if you and I are the same person. That it feels as if you are responsible for all the pain I've ever felt.'

Miriam said, 'You cannot trust these visions, Esther. They aren't reality.'

Esther shook her head. 'You are lying to me. You are always lying to me, I think. When you told me you loved me, was that a lie, also?'

'No,' Miriam replied. 'Love is a sort of magic, my dear. It comes slowly or quickly, cruelly or kindly; but exchange is all it requires. It may not be the sort of love you want. But I have given you part of myself, just as you have given me part of you.'

Esther's breath stuttered. 'I know,' she said. 'I know.'

At that moment, Thomas Harding emerged from the crowd, darted forward, and seized Esther's arm.

Esther gasped his name, nearly slipping on the marble floor of the ballroom in her fright. He must have come in a hurry, as he was in disarray, cravat badly tied, erupting in a spider-limb sprawl from his neck. His pupils were minuscule; he had the bitter scent of laudanum on his lips, and as he leaned towards Esther, she could smell it clinging to the air.

He said, 'Where is it?'

Esther resisted the urge to flinch away. Most of the crowd remained on the dance floor or watching the dancers from the walls; but Thomas was making a scene, and they would soon be noticed. 'Where is what?'

'The *grimoire*. The salt—the salt might be gone, but perhaps, perhaps...'

He was delirious. 'Thomas,' Esther said, slowly, 'there is no need for—'

Miriam took a step forward. 'I have it.'

Esther expected him to react with fear, but Thomas was too far gone. He turned his face to her, snarl deepening, revealing the pink-white line of his upper gums. '*You.*'

'Release her,' Miriam said.

His fingers tightened around Esther's arm. 'Why should I? Kill me, demon, if you'd like. I have nothing more to lose.'

Esther saw heads turning towards them, as the dancers sped up their movements—the music was coming to a crescendo, and soon their conversation would be far more audible. Panicking, she called to the shadows. A sharp pain, and then they were her servants once more; they slipped into the skin of her arm, where they burnt so hot that the fabric of her sleeve began to smoke. Thomas flinched away, hissing in pain.

'Stop it, both of you,' Esther snapped. 'We're surrounded by people. We will be noticed.'

Miriam's eyes were so dark they reflected the candles surrounding them, a thousand flames whimpering in the shadows. 'We should not have let him live.'

'Ignore him,' Esther said, desperately. 'He is merely an—an *insect*, Miriam. He isn't worth the bother.'

'I have had enough of your *mercy*, darling. It is a weakness of yours, and one that must be excised.' Miriam rolled her neck, and a dark smile stretched over her face. 'I shall hand you his heart before this night is finished. A fitting gift.'

'I'd really rather you didn't,' Esther replied, as Thomas took another step away, his eyes wide and unfocused. He crashed into the candelabra, and—although it didn't fall—it sent the candle flames billowing, the fire growing taller, plumes of smoke rising to the ceiling—

Then it all fell apart.

She looked into the flames reflexively; they swallowed her whole. The fire was growing, the fire was catching, the fire was a memory and the memory was ashes filling her throat, bitter and hot. She was choking on them. Esther thought, *The Hall is burning, Harding Hall is burning*, and she panicked, tearing herself away from Thomas and Miriam like stitches pulled from a wound, stumbling back into a table of drinks. Gasping, she pressed her palms against the tablecloth, gloves slipping halfway down her arms, chest heaving.

The glasses of claret beneath her outstretched arms smelt cloying, oversweet, and it made her stomach turn. There were bowls of food here, too: cups of trifle oozing blood-red compote, sliced calf's tongue accordioned along its platter, and gnarled, walnut-like oysters piled in a silver bowl. The servant beside the table mistook her horrified stare for interest, and he raised an oyster towards her in offering.

'Fresh in season, miss,' he said. Without waiting for her reply, he took an oyster knife from his belt: a stubby thing with a blade the size of Esther's thumb, its handle twice as long, a filigreed ivory the same shade as Esther's dress. As he began to lever the oyster open, Esther felt a presence at her shoulder.

'Esther?' Miriam murmured. 'Are you with me still?'

Esther didn't respond. She was watching the servant struggling with the oyster, which was evidently harder to crack than he'd first presumed. Hands slipping against the knife's handle, he made a little grunt of frustration. Esther saw the glint of the blade, felt terror well in her throat, and reached forward to snatch the knife from his hands. The oyster flew from his grip, skidding across the floor.

'*Madam*,' said the servant, horrified.

Esther looked down at the knife, and then up into Miriam's face. 'What is happening to me? You know, don't you?'

'Esther, you must sit down—'

'Enough!' Esther snarled. She felt a presence rise within her, a second voice, both the same and discordant with her own. Heat built in her hands. 'I will *not* forget again!'

'Esther,' Miriam said, more urgently. But Esther wasn't listening; there was a fury in her, ancient and terrible, and flames were beginning to dance along her palms. 'Esther, stop, you will raze this place to ashes—'

Esther reached toward her, burning, *burning*—

'Cybil!' Miriam cried. '*Stop.*'

Cybil. The word tore Esther apart, remade her, all in an instant. The flame in her hand flickered and died.

'Cybil,' Esther echoed. She took a stumbling step back, repeating, 'Cybil.' Then her foot came down upon the discarded oyster, and she slipped.

Miriam leapt to catch her, but someone else had already been standing behind her. Esther felt arms loop around her back. She looked up to see Thomas's upside-down face peering at her, grinning with a rabid intensity. He said, 'Lily,' poppy-bitter breath washing over her face.

Esther's back was bowed over his arms, her feet still on the floor. Blood rushed to her head; she felt dizzy. The back of her skull was pressed against his stomach. He was stooped over her, cradling her as if he intended to pull her into his arms. His hands were pressed into her waist, and they were smoking with heat—Esther could smell the terrible stench of charred flesh, but he did not seem to notice or care that she was burning him.

Esther tried to pull away, but Thomas's grip was iron. She looked up at him, and his face changed. Looming over her, there was now another man: hairline receding and features aging, a black hat on his head. And Esther knew with a sudden cold certainty that if she didn't escape this person, she would die.

Her right arm was limp beside her. The oyster knife was in her hand.

She raised the knife and stabbed Thomas in the stomach.

For a moment, nothing happened. He only stared at her, and she stared at him, while the string quartet continued to play the country dance. It was a short knife, sharp, and Esther could hardly tell whether it had met its mark. Then she felt something warm soaking her hand. Thomas said, 'Oh,' very faintly, and he dropped her.

Esther landed heavily on the floor. She scrambled away from Thomas, leaving bloody palm prints on the marble. He stood half bowed, arm twisted over his abdomen, the ivory handle of the knife protruding from his waistcoat.

Miriam said, reverently, 'I knew it would be beautiful.'

Thomas screamed. The crowd around them immediately fell silent. The quartet faltered and then stopped playing. The dancers paused. Hundreds of people had stuttered and stilled, Carroway House trapped in amber.

Someone cried, 'Esther!' as he elbowed his way through the crowd. It was Isaac. He lunged toward her and pulled her up to standing. Then he looked at Thomas, who was staring down, silent and stricken, at the blood saturating his waistcoat. 'Oh, Lord. You've really done it now.'

'I know,' Esther replied.

And then there was chaos.

18

Someone in the crowd screamed, and then there was a great deal of screaming, as if everyone had been awaiting permission to become hysterical. A woman yelled, 'Assault!' and another, 'A doctor, a doctor!' Esther felt a hand drop to her shoulder—some enterprising young man who had thought to apprehend her—and she elbowed him in the stomach, sending him sprawling to the floor.

'Run,' Miriam said, turning to the crowd. Esther required no further instruction. She vaulted across the table, sending a dozen trifles smashing to the floor. Isaac yelled in alarm and tried to chase after her, but he slipped in the puddles of cream and fell flailing to the ground. Esther glanced desperately toward the terrace—there was a large crowd gathered there, all of whom had stopped to stare inside, expressions almost comically shocked.

So, then, to the entrance hallway. Esther dove for the door, dodging would-be apprehenders. Behind her she heard a great crash and a cacophony of glass breaking; she looked over her shoulder to see that an entire chandelier had fallen from the ceiling, scattering the dancers to the corners of the room. Miriam, clearly the culprit, still had her hand raised in supplication to the shadows. Isaac remained on the floor, clutching his ankle and groaning.

Miriam caught Esther's eyes, smiling. Then every candle in the room went out, and all went pitch-black.

Esther found the handle of the door through feel alone. She spilled out into the corridor, gasping for breath. It was dark here, also;

everywhere was dark, all light smothered by Miriam's shadows. She could hear shrieking and clattering as confused guests attempted to navigate.

Esther paused, disoriented. The past was pressing against her mind, bleeding into it like ink into fabric. She was Esther, she was Cybil, she was at Carroway House and Harding Hall. *The roof*, she thought, deliriously. *My mother is on the roof.* And so, when her foot met the base of a set of stairs, she ascended, imagining balustrades and blustery night air.

The first floor was as dark as everywhere else, but at least the yelling of the people downstairs was quieter. Esther wandered aimlessly until she saw a glass door leading to a terrace. The moon illuminated the space dimly, just enough to see by. She opened the door with a shaking hand, ignoring how her fingers were singeing the wooden knob, and spilled out into the open air.

The night was clear and idyllic. The terrace was high up; directly below, the cold marble of the ground-floor patio reflected the sky in a hazy pattern of pinprick lights. Beyond that was the flat green of the courtyard, the gates at its edge closed shut. The iron railing surrounding it was at least twice Esther's height.

Esther stumbled over to the terrace railing and leaned against it, catching her breath. For a moment, clarity returned—and with it came panic. She had no idea what to do. When she was found, she'd likely be sent to the madhouse. What other than insanity would drive a woman to stab her cousin at a Society ball? She'd ruined her reputation entirely, not to mention Isaac's. And your reputation was your entire existence in this place. Esther had, in essence, killed herself. She'd killed her brother, too, or at least ruined his future. She'd failed to do anything to lift the curse—spent years casting petty rituals and praying for deliverance—and now here was the price of her failure.

But for some reason, none of it seemed to matter, not really. Esther could still feel the word *Cybil* in her mouth, lingering there; and she could feel Cybil the person too, wandering the edges of her mind. She knew, somehow, that she was Cybil, but she remained unsure *who* Cybil was. It was paradoxical and disorienting. She imagined that if she returned inside, every guest at the ball would be a paper doll, propped up against the wall. Only Miriam would actually be real, and she'd be laughing at her, saying, *Oh, Esther, you believed me! You truly believed this ridiculous place was genuine!* And then she'd awaken from this dream—to find herself in Harding Hall, risen from its ashes—

The door to the terrace opened. Esther turned, expecting Miriam, but it was Thomas Harding, the oyster knife held in one trembling fist, his other hand still pressed to his belly. He was pale as a piano key. As he approached her, his steps faltered, his face twisting with pain.

'*Why?*' he whispered.

Esther wanted to increase the distance between them, but the railing was at her back. She curled both hands around it in case he attempted to pull her closer. 'You frightened me.'

'So you *stabbed* me?'

'It isn't as if— You wanted me to *die*, Thomas. For Lily, and her soul.'

'I offered you an opportunity for atonement,' he replied, 'and you refused to take it. I should have expected that. I was a fool for expecting compassion from a witch.'

They regarded each other warily.

'You ought to see a doctor,' she told him.

'It is only a shallow wound.'

'You're bleeding.'

He chuckled and snapped his bloody hand towards her. She turned her head. Droplets sprayed across her cheek.

'You disgust me,' she said.

'As you do me,' he replied. '*First Daughter.* It wasn't enough to curse us all; you had to steal all our blessings, too. I was supposed to be born first, you know that? But little Esther came early. If it weren't for you, I'd have the power to fix all of this—to bring Lily back, to continue Christopher Harding's legacy. But I can't. You've ruined it.'

Esther swallowed. 'I didn't choose to be this way. I didn't choose to be cursed.'

'Does that matter?'

It didn't. Esther knew that, and she bowed her head.

207

'You know, my father had a fascinating theory.' Thomas's eyes glittered dangerously, and he turned the knife in his hand, taking a step closer. 'We have our rituals, and our alchemy, but in the end, magic is *belief*—that is all. You must *believe* in something deeply to trade your soul for it. And for generations we have believed, Esther, that the First Daughter is a monster. Perhaps that is why you are the way you are.'

'I— Don't be absurd. You are saying the curse is not real?'

'Of course it is real,' he said. 'It does not matter *why* you are the way you are. It only matters what you have done.'

'I don't understand.'

'Of course you don't.'

There was such contempt in his voice—Esther felt bile rise in her throat. 'Get away from me.'

'A woman with magic,' he continued, ignoring her. 'The seed of Eve. Curse or no, the corruption is inherent. Don't you see, Esther? Power like yours… it is too dangerous to leave unchecked.'

Thomas looked at the knife in his hand.

'We should have left you to the wolves,' he said.

There was such an intense familiarity to these words: *Seed of Eve, left to the wolves. Witch, woman, daughter, danger.* As recognisable as scripture, lingering as a bloodstain.

'Seed of Eve,' she murmured to herself. In response, the shadows at her feet trembled, as if in ecstasy. She stretched out her hand to them, and they rose, curling around her fingers. She heard Thomas gasp sharply; she did not care. A curious, cold sort of calm had fallen over her. A fury so long buried deep, so burning in its intensity, that it had gone from flames to ice.

'Seed of Eve,' she repeated, and her voice was two voices, her words an echo of themselves. 'Eve. Is it truly her fault, Thomas? Is it truly mine? Look at this world we live in, its wickedness, its cruelty. When Eve ate the apple, God despaired. Perhaps He did so because she realised not only *her* sins, but His.'

Thomas took a step back.

'What are you?' he asked. '*Who* are you?'

Who am I?

With that question, Cybil finally returned to her: the skin regrowing, a thousand memories finding purchase in the fissures of her soul. Every beautiful moment of Esther's life, scant as they were, seemed to be snuffed out like a candle flame; every moment of conviction and optimism, of hope and ambition, dripping like wax to the floor. Esther felt herself become a lie, felt the truth disembowel her and then fill the empty spaces left behind. She was a shadow of herself. She was as much dead as alive. Cybil was Esther, Esther was Cybil, Thomas was Henry Martingale and Peter Oswyn and every man who'd ever decided she belonged to him.

Two centuries, and she was back where she began.

Esther lunged for the knife.

Thomas tried to spin out of the way, but she was fast enough that she found purchase on the handle. They stumbled together, each of them trying to wrestle the blade from the other's grip. The tiles beneath them were slippery smooth, and they skidded sideways. The knife flailed between them in a pendulum's swing, silver flashing in the starlight. Thomas tried to swipe it across Esther's arm; she snarled like a wildcat, her magic surged, and the knife glowed white-hot. Thomas dropped it, hissing in pain. Esther caught it before it could hit the floor. Her fingers burnt—she didn't care. She took the blade and slammed it into the base of Thomas's throat.

He fell against her. They both hit the floor.

Thomas gurgled and choked. Rolling away, sprawling on her back, Esther turned her head to watch him. The oyster knife was embedded into the base of his windpipe; he was suffocating. Esther knew exactly how much pain he was feeling, and that, at least, was some comfort. Perhaps a blade was kinder than a spade. She hoped it wasn't.

She scooted towards him, leaned over him like a parody of a lover. Once, Esther had pitied Thomas; but with Cybil returned to her, he seemed to matter so little. He'd called her a monster. Perhaps it was time, finally, for her to believe him.

The darkness around them was whispering, but its whispers were screams. They were ecstatic, gluttonous, feeding on the leaking light of Esther's soul.

'Thomas,' she whispered.

His gaze turned towards her, but it seemed he couldn't see her. His lids fluttered open and closed with sporadic, desperate movements.

'Burn,' she told him, and the shadows did her bidding: as she pulled the knife out of his throat, his body erupted into flames.

Miriam found her, finally, on a terrace on the second floor.

Thomas's corpse lay half propped against the railing, wreathed in fire that seemed to give off no heat, merely an unearthly, golden light. Esther stood between him and Miriam. She was radiant, the shadows lifting her an inch above the ground, blood coating her fingers.

'You know,' Miriam said.

Esther grinned, baring her teeth, more in fury than amusement. Blood splattered the front of her white dress like a scattering of rose petals, and the oyster knife—still smiling in its grim curve—was dripping gore onto the pastel-toned tiles of the veranda.

'I know,' she said.

'Cybil—'

'Esther. I am Esther now, remember? You just couldn't leave me alone, even after all this time. And now—this is all your fault.'

'My fault?'

'Yes.'

'I only wanted the best for you, my love, all this time.' Miriam took a step closer. As she spoke, she lowered her voice, made it the same lull she had used when they were in bed together, when it seemed that Esther was nearing sleep. 'Once there was a girl, brave and terrified, with fire in her veins and fury in her heart; and no one loved her, because she was too strange to love; no one wanted her, because she took all the wanting in the world for herself; but still, I wanted her, and still, I loved her, and I gave her another lifetime rather than lose her to the darkness.'

Esther shook her head. 'No.'

'No?'

'You can't lie to me anymore. You didn't save me, Miriam. You brought me to ruin. I remember you. The clearing—the orchard—the deal we made—'

Miriam raised her hands placatingly. 'Darling, listen to me—'

'You *lied*,' Esther snarled, and her voice sounded like a thousand voices speaking in chorus; the air between them shimmered with heat. 'You lied to me. You told me I would have a chance to break the curse.'

'You never specified you wanted to keep your memories.'

'You *lied*!' Esther cried. 'I know that now, Miriam—I finally understand. It took Thomas's ravings to make me realise. Because it *is* odd, isn't it? You told me yourself, all those years ago: magic is an exchange, not a gamble. There are no *contingencies*. I was dead; you held all the cards. Still, I asked you for a chance—I asked for an opportunity to break the curse—and you gave it to me. Why?'

'I loved you,' Miriam said.

'No, you didn't. You love me *now*, perhaps, in whatever twisted way you can—but not then. No—you agreed because of something else.'

Miriam cocked her head, playing dumb. 'And what might that be?'

Esther laughed, a cruel laugh, jagged as broken glass. The shadows, seething around her like leeches, began to carve slits into her skin, golden soul-light leaking out; she didn't seem to notice, even as they began to feed. 'You knew I would never break the curse. Didn't you?'

Miriam bared her teeth in both a grin and a snarl. 'How would I know that?'

'Because,' Esther said, 'there *is* no curse. There never was.'

Miriam didn't reply.

Esther bowed her head, light shimmering around her. 'Magic is desire. You told me that, once. You want something, and you pay the darkness to give it to you. But these shadows aren't simply servants. They are *parasites*.' A tear trailed down her cheek. She wiped it away with a frustrated gesture, looking at Miriam with wet eyes. 'I have been so alone,' she said, broken. 'For two lives now, I have believed I *had* to be, because the curse would hurt anyone who came near. And the shadows, those willing shadows—they made my belief reality. They saw my fear and they kept everyone away. A self-fulfilling prophecy.'

Miriam made a flippant gesture. 'Many of the deaths you saw were simply accidents,' she said. 'Or caused by their own folly—your mother, for example; or your nursemaid in this life who drowned. You saw the magic that followed you, you heard the fear of those around you, and you blamed them, blamed yourself. In your moments of anger, perhaps, the shadows tried to please you; but most darkness, darling, is nothing compared to that which lies in men's hearts.'

Esther let out a sob, and she floated gently back to the ground.

'You are not alone, Esther,' Miriam murmured. 'Many women with souls like yours have felt the same. Many have believed they were cursed, even when they were not. Hatred rots all it touches, victim and perpetrator alike.'

Esther took a ragged breath. 'Even if it wasn't all my fault—I am responsible for some. As Cybil, I killed the boy with the branch, even if I did not realise it. I burnt the Hall, and now I have murdered Thomas. I am a *monster*.'

'And so?' Miriam returned. 'Why do you still aspire to humanity? What has it ever given you, apart from regret?'

Esther looked down at the knife, at the light dripping down her palms. Downstairs in the ballroom, people were still shrieking; there was a shatter as something toppled over, and then a dim, golden glow filtered through a downstairs window, as someone finally managed to light a candle. Tears overspilled Esther's cheeks, made beads upon her chin. Esther's anger had always been beautiful, but Miriam realised that her grief was even lovelier.

'Nothing,' she said, hollowly. 'It has given me nothing.'

Miriam offered her a hand. 'Let me take you away from here. I can keep you safe.'

'For the few months I have remaining, you mean? Before you *eat* my *soul*? No.' Esther dropped the oyster knife, and it clattered to the marble. 'I'd rather die than spend another moment with you.'

'What are you implying?'

'Twenty-three years, that was our deal. I have not lived them yet.'

Miriam felt her corporeality slip, for just a moment. Her eyes forgot their shape and melted into darkness, dripping down her cheeks and pooling in the hollows of her collarbones. The ends of her fingers blurred, trailing amorphous shadows like smoke. Esther didn't even flinch to see the transformation. There was no fear in her eyes, only disdain.

Esther said, 'Another life. That is what would happen, isn't it? If I died here and now, I would be reborn again.'

'You *cannot*,' Miriam snarled. 'We made a deal.'

'We made a deal that was impossible from the start. That is your fault, Miriam: your design. And perhaps I can't break a curse that doesn't exist, but perhaps I can find a way to escape our pact. I have a stronger soul now than I did as Cybil. My third self will be stronger still.'

Miriam felt the shadows beneath her trembling, trying to pull away from the force of her fury—she pulled them back to her with a clawed hand. 'You have seen the best of me, darling,' Miriam said. 'Don't make me show you the worst. If you love me—'

'I love you,' she said, 'and I hate you, more than I have ever hated anyone. I see it now: you must love someone to truly hate them. They must give you something before they can take it away.'

Miriam shrieked in fury. 'A new life, that was the deal. I have given you that, and my heart besides—have I not?'

'You have,' Esther agreed. 'But I do not want your heart, Miriam. Not anymore.'

Trembling, Esther turned towards the railing of the balcony, and she took a step forward.

'My mother died this way, once,' she said. 'I won't belong to you, in this life or the next. And when I die, I shall die smiling—knowing I denied you the chance to kill me.'

And in that moment, brief and burning, Miriam was almost human. She felt, concurrently, all of the vast palette of emotions she had experienced in the past few weeks: anger and desire and sorrow and regret, lust and despair, joy and grief. She could try to take Esther now, keep her alive, bind her with shadows, force her to live the rest of the year a captive—but what guarantee did Miriam have that she was capable of it? Of the two of them, Miriam was no longer certain who was the more powerful. This *thing* she had created, this radiant creature, with twin souls, determined to die; whatever Esther was now, she was no longer the woman Miriam loved. And all Miriam wanted at this moment was for that woman to return. She could not think of anything else. She was blinded by fury.

Miriam reached down. She picked up the oyster knife.

'I told you,' she said. 'If you must die, darling, it will be on *my* terms, not yours.'

She didn't give Esther time to reply. Miriam lunged forward and drew the blade across Esther's throat in an unflinching arc, arm sweeping as a conductor's towards the sky. Esther didn't cry out in pain—she couldn't—and she didn't try to step away; didn't lift her arms to try to block the blow; didn't fall to her knees in surrender. She blinked at Miriam with her wide, autumn-leaf eyes, uncomprehending of her own blood as it spurted between them. And then, slowly, she smiled.

For a moment, time didn't pass. The world was silent, and Esther was dying, and Miriam was glad, at least, that she was the one who had killed her; but this was not what she had wanted. Esther had chosen this ending, not her. Miriam had surrendered to her, surrendered to her own fury. Now Esther's soul was denied to her once more.

Esther fell into her, gurgling and gasping. The light dancing on her skin faded. Miriam gathered her in an embrace, holding her as she choked. She felt something wet on her cheek, and she raised a hand to wipe it away, presuming it was more of Esther's blood; it was a tear. She stared at it in fascination. She'd never cried before.

Weakly, hands clawed at her back. Miriam pressed a kiss to Esther's hair. 'Enjoy it,' she whispered. 'This is the last victory I will ever give you.'

Esther moaned in pain. The light of her soul flickered as it tried to fade, but the magic of the deal kept it bound. Soon it would tear free, and Miriam would have to wait until another First Daughter came.

'I love you,' Miriam said.

Esther didn't reply. She gasped, twitched, and was still.

Miriam lowered her body gently to the ground, tucking a lock of blood-encrusted hair behind Esther's ear. She pressed her lips against her throat, but there was no pulse, no response, no living person on the terrace at all: only Miriam Richter, a silent shadow, Esther's blood still warm on her cheek.

Intermission

He said, 'You've been following me for a decade now. I don't know what you are, or *who* you are, but it's starting to feel jolly rude you haven't introduced yourself.'

Miriam cocked her head, and hopped one-footed on the branch of the acacia. Isaac had begun to suspect her years ago, and he'd said similar things out loud before; she'd never humoured him with a response. But on this day, she was almost tempted.

It had been ten years exactly since Esther Harding's death, and Isaac's grief had led him to a harbour, a ship, a ceaseless journey through the Mediterranean. He'd been documenting his travels in letters he'd then published in England, to great sensation: *The Nouveau Odysseus*, the collection was called.

Miriam wasn't certain why she was following him, but follow him she had, from the crystalline bays of Cyprus to the green capped mountains of Sicily—and now here, the Eyalet of Tripolitania, still recovering from war and drought. In his wanderings, it often seemed as if Isaac was looking for something specific, but when Miriam looked into his soul, all she found was uncertainty.

He didn't know what would make him happy. Neither did she— not that she particularly cared, either way.

Isaac sighed, shifted on the felled log he was using as a seat. 'Talking to a crow,' he muttered, and he scrubbed at his forehead with the heel of his hand.

The desert was at their backs; to the north loomed the fertile plateau that stood between them and the sea, crowned with a wreath of farms and lush vegetation. This was a place of extremes, heat and sand and a sea that glittered white with salt. He clearly liked it here—so did Miriam—but soon they would leave.

Isaac took a swig from his canteen, then poured a measure onto the dirt beneath his feet.

'Esther,' he said, 'it's been a long time. I like to think that, if you were here, you'd say you've missed me; but you'd probably just tell me to wash the dust off my face.'

He took another drink.

'I think you did love me, in your own way. You weren't much one for sentimentality, but you did.' Isaac kicked at the ground with his boot, then stood up. 'I am sorry for what happened.'

Miriam had never understood why humans apologised for things they did not do. She watched him walk away, to the path that led back to the port, and she launched into the sky to follow him. An eagle swooped in her direction, perhaps sensing a meal—but as it neared, it recognised her as predator, not prey, and it turned to flee.

The breeze shifted behind her, ruffling her feathers. There was something different, suddenly, in the quality of the air—a change in pressure—and by instinct, Miriam turned her head to look back. The horizon was billowing, bubbling, as if the desert itself was water set to boil. Plumes of dust were rising in the distance, gaining speed, approaching as a wave approaches the shore.

She cawed as loud as she could. Isaac paused in his walking to look towards her, and in so doing turned around to see the storm.

'Oh,' he said. 'Bugger.'

Isaac began to run. Miriam followed, although she knew it'd be little use—the port was too far away, the sand moving too quickly. His only chance would be to find shelter. But there was little shelter here, only a few jagged rocks and the stooped branches of the acacia trees. He curled behind one of these rocks, breathing heavily, face wan with fear. His dark hair was slick with sweat and red-brown with dust. Miriam settled on the rock to watch him.

There was a possibility he could die here. She wasn't sure of it—humans were so fragile, it was difficult to tell what could and couldn't kill them—but surely something like this would, at the very least, be detrimental to his health.

He looked up at her and flapped his hand, as if to shoo her away. 'Go,' he said. 'Leave, you half-wit bird. Fly away.'

Miriam had no obligation to help him. Humans died all the time like this, victims to their own hubris, to the fickle hand of fate. It wasn't Miriam's job to save him. They hadn't even made a deal.

But those eyes that looked up at her now, those curious, leaf-shaped eyes; those were Esther's eyes, Cybil's eyes. Darker, yes, but there was still something of his sister there, as there was in the upturned button shape of his nose, the wry humour in his expression as he surveyed the storm. That was why, perhaps, Miriam had followed him all these years. A diversion, a memento. She was not one for sentimentality, either, but—time, in its inexorable march, made fools of all.

The wind howled. In the distance, the sound of the dust was nearer a hiss than a roar—a thousand whispers in tandem. Isaac laced his fingers together in his lap and bowed his head, closing his eyes, muttering softly to himself.

It felt as if all of Tripolitania was holding its breath.

As the dust came, Miriam flung herself forward, pulling the shadows around them. They became as intangible as mist, she and Isaac Harding both; it was only when he opened his eyes that he realised anything had happened at all.

'You,' he said, astonished. Miriam realised that, thoughtlessly, she had shifted into the shape he recognised.

'Hello,' she replied.

Around them, all was coloured a violent red: the light of the sun diffused by the dust, bathing them in scarlet. It was as close to Hell as Miriam would ever come, and that almost made her smile.

'I should've known it was you,' Isaac said. 'What *are* you, exactly?'

'Does it matter?'

'I suppose not. Why are you saving me?'

'I'm not certain,' Miriam replied—but that was a lie, and Isaac could tell.

'Esther,' he said.

'Esther,' Miriam agreed.

'Did you kill her?' he asked. 'Everyone thinks it was Thomas, but I've always wondered otherwise.'

'I loved her.'

'That doesn't answer my question.'

She stared at him, and he stared at her. The dust whispered around them, susurrous against the dry grass of the plain. There were few shadows in this place, the light filtered as it was, and it was taking some effort to keep them intangible; Miriam was already feeling drained.

'Yes,' she said. 'I killed her.'

Isaac twitched at that, a vein in his jaw jumping, but he said nothing in response.

'Life and death are twins, not enemies. Never one without the other.' Miriam took a languid step sideways, reaching out her hand to the dust. Some particles detached from the rest, floating toward her: as they increased in density, they created a figure of a woman, dancing on her open palm like a music-box ballerina. 'Your sister...'

'My sister had her entire future ahead of her, and you took it from her.'

Miriam sighed. 'Her future remains ahead—the future always is, regardless of who is to see it. But Esther wanted this, Master Harding; this was her victory, not mine.'

Isaac turned away from her. Addressing the dust swirling around them, tone flat, he said, 'If it were possible, I would kill you, Miriam Richter.'

'If it were possible, I'd let you.'

'You hate yourself that much?'

'No,' she replied. 'But eternity is a punishment, not a gift.'

It was the first time she'd admitted as much, to herself or to anyone else; it should have felt significant, but it didn't. She'd always known it was so, from the very moment of her birth. That was why she had been so angry to see her creators, huddled around their ritual circle, with their rictus grins.

What have you done? she'd asked them: it was the first thing she'd ever said. *Why have you done this to me?*

Of course, she hadn't given them enough time to respond. There was such satisfaction, such grim irony, in causing the ending of others. An ending would always be denied to her, after all.

Isaac began to walk away, into the storm. Miriam followed him. 'I can't keep you like this unless I'm near,' she said.

'I don't *care*,' he snarled. 'I refuse to make you my saviour.'

Miriam bared her teeth. 'I could have left you to the dust, you know. I didn't need to help you.'

'And yet you did. Because of *Esther*. Because you killed her, and now you are *desperate* for her to forgive you for it. But let me tell you something, Miriam Richter.' He turned to her, eyes flashing, and his expression had so much of his sister in it that Miriam felt something inside her chest twinge. 'Give her a thousand lifetimes, a thousand apologies: it won't matter. Esther will never forgive you. She'll see you reduced to *ashes* before she forgives you.'

Miriam sighed. 'Then ashes I shall be,' she said. 'As will you, Isaac Harding.'

She released her grip on the shadows, and then laughed sharply as Isaac cried out and dropped to the ground. Ignoring the sting of the dust on her skin, she walked away—and walked, and walked, until his figure was gone, and the dust was cleared, and she could finally take to the skies.

I hope he was buried, she told herself.

But later, when she saw a coughing figure struggling down the road to Tripoli, she paused for a moment to watch him; and she stretched the shadows of the trees further forward, to give him a little more shade.

Part III

The Atlantic

19

Rosamund Harding was born on Christmas Eve, 1908, under inauspicious stars. Not that anyone could see the stars, regardless: it had been a cruel winter that year, with snow flurries and howling blizzards, and the night sky over England had for months been devoid of light.

Little Rosamund's intellect advanced with uncommon speed. The doctors, disquieted, told her parents it was a gift, of course, but to be monitored—she said her first word at eight months old, and by three years of age she was reading silently to herself, running chubby fingers over the page with an expression of silent pondering. Mr and Mrs Harding noticed other oddities, too. She was fair and redheaded, little resembling either of them or her younger siblings, and objects, from nursery cots to pieces of much-hated sprouts, had a strange habit of igniting spontaneously around her. She never laughed, rarely cried, and by age ten was referring to both her parents by their first names, cold and detached, as though they were strangers.

Once, at an afternoon tea, twelve-year-old Rosamund's napkin had lit on fire. One of her father's visiting Eton friends had jokingly said, 'Didn't you once mention a curse of some sort, Alfred? Some old family superstition?'

Her father, Alfred, slightly built, fair haired, the spitting image of two dead men—although he didn't know that, of course—had made a dismissive gesture. 'Premodern twaddle. You know, I bloody wish the supposed witchcraft in our family had been real. Maybe she'd do something interesting for once.'

Rosamund had excused herself. And then, in the corridor, she'd laughed, and laughed, and laughed.

Cybil's brother had died; Esther's brother had lived. Rosamund had no brothers at all, and that was a blessing. Family, to her, was nothing more than dead weight. By the time she'd reached her teenaged years, she had figured out how to bend her parents' wills away from suspicion, how to whisper in their minds and say, *Don't look at me, don't think of me, I am nothing to you.* She had no interest in them, or in the six sisters who succeeded her, who all were more beautiful and charming than she—bug-eyed, flame-haired Rosamund, the Harding savant, who was whispered about in the halls of her boarding school with hushed disquiet. She had no friends there, unsurprisingly, but she didn't care. This wasn't *her* life, after all.

This was borrowed time.

The dreams had begun when she was eleven, and by sixteen she had recalled enough of her prior lives to reconstruct, piece by piece, Cybil and Esther in their entirety. Rosamund had a notebook where she'd written everything down, scribbling eyes in the margins, drawing tiny crows between the spaces in the letters. She remembered, but their lives weren't *hers*, at least not yet—they were moving pictures she'd watched on the screen of her mind, plot summaries to which she'd gradually added detail: a dark forest, a bleeding throat; a cracked oyster and the smell of burning flesh.

And she remembered the woman, too.

Rosamund was no artist, not really, but reproducing the face she saw in her dreams was her dearest project. She was gifted a set of drawing pencils for her eleventh birthday. For a year, she'd laboured at the wall concealed behind her headboard: pushing the bed aside each morning, adding a tiny stroke at the lashes, at the chin, until the woman's features emerged in full, grooves of shadow against white plaster.

Eleven-year-old Rosamund looked at the drawing, pencil gripped in trembling fingers. Heavy brows, a pair of moles at chin and cheek, a mane of dark hair. She thought, for the first time—*Miriam.*

Miriam. For the next few years, the name echoed in the caverns of Rosamund's mind, ineffable, inextricable, a question without an answer. Miriam cast herself over Rosamund's psyche like a stained-glass window looming over her, offering Heaven in one hand, Hell in the other. By her adulthood, Rosamund had yet to see her, as a crow or otherwise; maybe Miriam was more of a coward than in her scattered memories, or maybe Miriam was now indifferent. Rosamund didn't know which option was worse. But she knew that Miriam would come for her eventually, and Rosamund knew that when she did, her soul was forfeit.

Unless, of course, she could do something to keep it.

Her gifts to herself, on her eighteenth birthday, were a train ticket, a spade, and a pair of secondhand trench boots that must have once belonged to a soldier with uncommonly small feet. In Suffolk, she had stayed in what had once been the crumbling foundations of Harding Hall: now a quaint bed-and-breakfast with an attached golf course. She had slept badly, trembling beneath flower-printed sheets, listening to the wind rattle the glass. That morning, she'd been served a soft-boiled egg and soldiers, which she'd eaten with little enthusiasm, sprinkling too much salt over the yolk and drowning the bread in butter. She'd toasted the soldiers for longer, too, with the tip of her finger, just to remind herself she could—ignoring the sting of pain as the shadows took their due.

She loved the pain as much as she hated it. It was an old friend, a comfort. A memory and a promise.

It was raining: that light, misty sort of rain that was almost pleasant, and impossible to avoid. As Rosamund trudged further into the woods, her hair stuck to her cheeks with damp; she wasn't sure why she'd bothered to curl it. She was wearing her usual makeup—powder, dark eyeliner, red lipstick—and she could feel, as she walked, that it was all sliding down her face like paint beneath turpentine. She tried not to care.

The forest looked the same as it had in her dreams, eternal and indifferent, trees stooping to watch her as she passed. It was the dead of winter, of course, but it hadn't snowed this year. There were piles of icy sludge slumping over roots, dripping icicles adorning each twisted

225

branch. The colours were so monotone that the whole scene could've been one of the photographs her little sister took with her Brownie camera. Rosamund's breath plumed before her, shoulders hunched beneath her stole, spade heavy in her hands.

In the distance rose an impressive, wizened oak, a knot at the centre of its trunk like an unblinking eye. Rosamund stopped at the oak and tried to dig, but the spade struck the frozen earth with a clang.

Sighing, she dropped the spade and fell to her knees, reaching out her palms towards the soil. She remembered the soldiers that morning, toasting beneath her fingers. She remembered Esther setting Thomas alight. She remembered Harding Hall, devoured by flames.

The familiar pain came as the shadows sipped from her soul. In exchange, heat now radiated from her palms and softened the earth, melting the ice until the soil was sodden and as pliable as flesh. Then she dug, tossing tufts of dirt over her shoulder, until she was panting with exertion and the linen sack was revealed. It contained what Rosamund had expected: books, about a dozen of them, less waterlogged than she'd feared, pages still pale and fresh. What she hadn't expected was the identity of one of the volumes, which she'd presumed destroyed by Miriam a century ago. Black leather, an embossed cover—the three-headed hawk with its open beaks. Past, present, future.

'Jackpot,' she murmured.

Rosamund had been hoping to find a book of *some* use—something that would help her hone her magic, in Miriam's absence—but the grimoire was everything she needed and more. She raised it from the sack, hands trembling, and opened it to the first page, where there was a drawing of a many-eyed angel staring back at her. A droplet landed at the centre of its wings, a single tear. Rosamund quickly blotted it away with her sleeve. She had often wondered, of course, if she was simply mad; if her memories were delusions and her magic false. Here, it seemed, was undeniable proof otherwise.

She turned the page to find dense handwriting. It looked like a foreign alphabet, indecipherable, with sweeping letters and strange, tiny marginalia written in spiral patterns. Her memories hadn't blessed her with a continued knowledge of Elizabethan palaeography. She'd expected as much.

Rosamund tucked the book into her coat and reburied the others. Who knew what would happen? Best to keep the rest of the stash safe, in case another life found her digging by this tree with another spade, another set of hands. Besides, she had what she needed now. The key was hers: all she had to do was turn it.

That night, she reapplied her lipstick and her eyeliner. Then, by candlelight—Rosamund preferred it, despite the electric lamp the bed-and-breakfast had provided—she began to decipher the grimoire.

She had beside her a pen, a notebook, and a compendium on Elizabethan secretary hand. Still, it was a slow process. She suspected that Christopher Harding's handwriting had been difficult to read, even for his contemporaries. Rosamund had to be selective about what she started with. Thankfully, Christopher had a habit of entitling his pages, to give some indication as to their topic. She began with these titles. Several caught her eye: 'On a Lineage of Seraphim'; 'On the Transference and Reversal of Souls'—that section was well thumbed, no doubt thanks to Thomas; 'On the Transformation of the Body'; 'On Concealment'; 'On the Summoning of Demons'.

She turned to the page on demons and began to work. After half an hour, she had produced a tiny scrap in modern English in her notebook. *To weakene a dymon*, it read. *Within the lighte of daye, but beneathe clouds so no shadow is cast, surrounde the creature or those possessed wythyn a circle of salte, or water that runs...*

A circle of salt. It seemed so simple, so *easy*—the Miriam in her mind, malignant and almighty, would never be contained by something so banal. But then it was obvious, wasn't it?

Salt had prevented her from entering the townhouse, all those years ago. If she were surrounded by it, she wouldn't be able to go anywhere.

Magic was exchange. Rosamund knew that. The rituals in this grimoire were pageantry—but Rosamund hypothesised that they were also the basis by which Miriam had been created. She was a shadow given form: something *summoned*, something *made*. If her makers had believed these things would weaken her, it was likely that they would.

Still, weakening was only one step in a more complicated dance. More would have to be done to ensure Rosamund's survival. Miriam would start looking for her eventually, and Rosamund didn't want to be found until she was ready. She turned to the section on conceal-ment, pen in hand. Exhaustion made her eyes water. She looked at yet another long paragraph of unreadable gibberish, and for a moment, Rosamund felt despair. What was the point of all this? Once the deal was up, it wouldn't matter how hidden she was. Her soul would be Miriam's.

Rosamund paused to consider this, recalling a promise she'd made two lifetimes ago.

'My soul will be yours,' she said to herself.

Then she looked to the mirror beside the bed. In her reflection, two other versions of herself stood beside her, their throats bloodied and bruised, their hands on her shoulders. They were smiling, and behind them, the shadows danced on the wall: necks stretching to the ceiling, flickering as the candles burnt themselves out.

Rosamund had the grimoire translated in full by the beginning of spring.

She spent her remaining time in school excelling in her classes and avoiding any interactions with the other girls. And each night, she made a deal with herself: she called the darkness and bore the pain as she carved off slices of her soul for its plate. She would not fear her own power—not this time. If Miriam had ruled the darkness with terror, Rosamund would rule it with love. She whispered to the night with affection and loyalty, fed her light to the shadows so they trem-bled with joy. *Don't tell her where I am*, she told the shadows. *Make me a ghost, a whisper. You fear her, but she cannot give you what I can. I am a kinder mistress than she will ever be.*

Over holidays, when she had to stay with her family in their Holland Park house, she wandered the hallways only half tangible, sending whispers into her family's minds so they would forget she was there. She did whatever she wanted, whenever she wanted; her siblings and her parents knew she existed, of course, but they recalled her presence with the gentle confusion of someone trying to remember a dream. 'Oh, Rosamund,' her eldest sister had once said, walking in on her in the library. 'Where've you been all week?'

To which Rosamund had replied, 'Here, with all of you,' her voice laced with darkness—and to her sister's mind, to *all* their minds, that was now the truth.

Rosamund graduated the next year with an offer to read history at Newnham College. She liked Cambridge well enough, liked the libraries in particular, the dry-paper hush of them; she enjoyed shadow-skating on the Cam during the summer, gliding her fingers through the tall grass along the banks.

Rosamund didn't much like the people at college—just as, she found, she didn't much like the people anywhere, after two deaths and five centuries. It was ironic, in a way. There was no longer the whispered stigma of a curse to impose isolation, but Rosamund was still as isolated as ever. *Once the deal is done*, she told herself, *then I can do whatever I want.* But it rang hollow. Something in her had broken, at some point; maybe in Cybil's life, maybe in Esther's. Either way, Rosamund didn't feel capable of fixing it.

The ladies at the college discussed dictators and the Depression with the earnest and affected air of those insulated by privilege but determined not to be. They spoke softly of the duty their blue blood and education had given them, the elected custodians of the greater good: *Oh, think of it, think of how lucky we are.* Rosamund despised them for it, but she also admired them for caring at all. She wanted to care, too, because that would mean that this was her life and she was living it, that the world and all its cruelties were hers to bear; that she wasn't simply an echo of an echo of a woman who had died in a time when bringing up Wall Street and fascism would have you burnt at the stake for being possessed.

But she still tried, she really did. She *tried* to be alive, to act as Rosamund Harding would have—as if Rosamund Harding was all she was.

For a while, Rosamund dallied with a poet named Astride who wrote her sonnets without punctuation and wept at her beauty; it lasted two months before she gave up. Astride had wanted sweetness and light and tearstained romance, but real love wasn't pretty, and it wasn't sad. Love was fury; love had blood and bones and entrails. Her former lives whispered as much to her, whenever she almost believed otherwise.

That was why Rosamund could both hate Miriam and love her still, after all this time. For she loved her desperately, anguishing over her, longing for her, even as she despised her.

And so, in the end, she gave up on Astride and all the others. She pretended to herself that she was still cursed, that it wasn't her fault she was alone. Rosamund lay in her bed the night before her final exams, touching herself as she pictured the woman who'd killed her, and thought: *So much for redemption.*

Rosamund's dissertation was on the early work of Machiavelli, and she graduated with distinction. Her tutor called her work accomplished, but oddly cynical in tone. 'If you choose to pursue academia further,' he told her, 'you may need to take a… softer approach.'

She had no intention, of course, of pursuing academia. Her ambitions were rather more far-reaching; if things went her way, she'd be able to go anywhere she wanted, see all the parts of the world her previous lives hadn't had access to. So, she took an apartment in London, where she lived off her parents' money and prepared herself for the end of the deal.

On her twenty-second birthday, Rosamund went with one of her sisters to a party in Pimlico. The hosts were bohemians, a couple in matching caftans who took one look at Rosamund with her perfectly curled hair and her jewelled-buckle shoes and labelled her a 'finishing-school princess'. She wanted to ask them, later, as they talked about the dismantlement of the zeitgeist and the revolutionary spirit, whether they had ever set a man on fire just for the pleasure of seeing him burn. But she refrained. Smiling grimly at her sidecar, she stood in the corner of the room, wondering why she'd agreed to come in the first place—why she was still putting on this mask, after all this time.

Rosamund wandered upstairs in search of somewhere quiet, where she could slip into the shadows and leave. She found one room that appeared unoccupied, but when she opened the door, she found two naked men on the bed in a rather compromising position.

She said, 'Excuse me,' mildly, and closed the door again. Rosamund wondered that she was still capable of shock—the mundanity of a human love affair was hardly enough to warrant it.

A moment later, one of the men burst out into the corridor. He was still buttoning his shirt. 'Listen,' he said, in a broad Boston accent, 'I don't know what you saw, but…'

The man was a giant, several heads taller than Rosamund, with acre-wide shoulders and hands the size of tennis racquets. He had dark hair and dark eyes, and when their gazes met, he flashed her a megawatt smile that could pop a lightbulb.

'But?' Rosamund prompted.

'Well—y'know. I'd appreciate it if you didn't mention it.'

There was no threat in the words, or even desperation; he was so innately confident in his own charm that he felt no need for either. Those gleaming teeth, the cut-glass jaw—there was power there. He was not afraid of Rosamund. Maybe he was incapable of fear at all. How refreshing.

'Mention what?' Rosamund asked, and the smile flashed again.

'Attagirl.' The man stuck out one of his enormous hands. 'I'm Walter. Call me Walt.'

'Rosamund.'

'Wow, that's a five-dollar name if I ever heard one. Rosie for short?'

'No,' she said, and he laughed: a laugh like cannon fire, booming through the corridor.

'You're gorgeous,' he said.

'Thank you.'

'Listen—I'm finished with this party, I think. Want to go grab a drink somewhere else?'

Rosamund refused, as reflexively as breathing: an instinct born of centuries, really, to deny and push away, to isolate and hide. 'I can't.'

He slung an arm around her shoulder. Rosamund considered shrugging him off, but it seemed like a lost cause. 'Yes, you can,' he said. 'I don't bite, I promise. And I don't know doodly squat about this town, so I could sure use a local to show me around.'

He wasn't going to take no for an answer; that much was clear. On his head be it.

She said, 'Fine. One drink.'

'One drink,' he agreed. 'And then, I promise—you'll never see me again.'

It wasn't one drink. It was several, that night and the next, and then several more across the month, until Rosamund and Walter were definitively *friends*—because Rosamund liked him, for all his bluster and his bombast, and liking someone was such a novelty that it felt worth the effort.

Building a relationship with Walt made it feel like she was planning for the future, like she hadn't given up on escaping the deal. One afternoon, they went to Claridge's for lunch, where Walt ate three entrées and ordered dessert immediately after.

'Pa's getting antsy,' he told her, through a mouthful of peaches and ice cream. 'This whole vacation was supposed to be a couple of weeks.'

'How long have you been here now?'

'Three months.'

Rosamund snorted and took a prim bite of her own ice cream, leaving a soft rim of red lipstick halfway down the spoon. She was wearing a scarlet dress to match, with a fringe so long it made a sound like a waterfall as she moved. 'He's still sending you money?'

'He's hoping I'll pick up a British girl and bring her back with me. He loves you people, you know that? The whole upper-class fox-hunting set, I mean. No offense.'

'None taken.'

'I think *he* thinks that's how we'll really cement our fortune. Marrying a duchess, or something. I dunno.' He took a sip of his coffee, nose wrinkling. He grabbed three sugars from the bowl and dropped them inside.

Rosamund looked at his cup with disgust. '*Three*, Walt? You're an animal.'

'Thanks, doll,' he replied with a wink. 'You know, you're his dream daughter-in-law—my pa, I mean. He'd be over the moon if we got hitched.'

'A shame you're not looking for a wife.'

He chuckled. 'Yeah. Real shame. You're just torn up about it, aren't you?' He took another bite, and then, with his mouth half full, continued. 'You know what's so great about you, Rosie?'

'What?' she replied, swirling her spoon around the bowl.

'The lack of expectation. As in, I could stand up right now, go over, and lay one on that waiter, and you'd just shrug your shoulders and keep eating your ice cream.'

Rosamund looked down at her bowl. 'It's good ice cream.'

Walter's smile widened. 'What about you?'

'What about me?'

'No secret torch for some English fella?'

'I'm a lesbian, Walt.'

He blinked. 'Oh. Then—*hey*. Wait a moment.'

'What?'

'I've just had the *niftiest* idea.'

They were married a week later at the Register Office. Walt wore a blue shirt with a red bow tie. Rosamund wore a white pantsuit with a seal-fur collar.

Rosamund had agreed to Walter's proposal with only one caveat: they would return to the States in time to see Walter's father that Christmas. She'd been planning to sail that year for her birthday, anyway, and this seemed like a good excuse to do it. But a winter crossing meant choppy seas, a likelihood of storms—Walt complained constantly in the weeks before their departure.

'Let's just wait until spring,' he said, as she was packing her suitcase. 'No need to hotfoot it out of here. Don't you want to spend your birthday on land? Why've we got to celebrate on an ocean liner?'

Rosamund took a book from her purse and carefully transferred it to the case. 'I like the ocean,' she said, and she pressed her fingers into the book's cover; the embossed hawk seemed to shiver beneath her touch.

'What's so swell about a bunch of water?'

She closed the case and turned to look at him, smiling with the sort of satisfaction only centuries could provide.

'It's not the water, Walt,' she said. 'It's the salt.'

20

The RMS *Monumental*, an engorged, tomb-like construction of steel and avarice, set sail on the twenty-second of December 1931. Its outer shell was imperial purple, its guts velveteen and hardwood; but the veneer of luxury couldn't mask the sheer manufactured *mass* of the thing. The *Monumental* wasn't elegant. It had been soldered and hammered into shape, plates and nails and engines. Moving like a metal elephant, it groaned and trumpeted as it cast off. The ship didn't float—it stomped across the ocean floor, a leviathan with a boat-shaped head.

It was nice enough weather, considering the season. Passengers waved with white handkerchiefs to relatives on the docks as the *Monumental* made its interminable slip into the Atlantic. Miriam Richter, who had no relatives, leaned against the railing and pretended to sip an old-fashioned. The breeze ruffled her black curls and pulled threateningly at the lace flower pinned to her suit jacket. She watched the docks of Southampton grow smaller, then disappear.

Tiring of her drink, she tossed the glass out into the water. A pair of young women on deck turned to gawp at her, clutching their hats to prevent their theft by the wind.

'Well, I never,' one of them squawked. 'You can't do *that*.'

Miriam raised a brow at her. 'Why not?'

'You ought to take it back to the bar!'

'I have somewhere to be. I'm sure they have more glasses.'

The ladies traded scandalised looks. 'Look here,' the taller one said, 'I don't know where you're from, but in New York, you'll be expected to act civilised.'

'Don't worry,' Miriam replied. 'I don't intend on visiting anytime soon.'

Then she tipped her hat to the two women, and she strode into the bowels of the *Monumental*.

Miriam was nearly out of time. Twenty-two years, eleven months and twenty-six days this version of Harding had been alive: she knew that much. She had felt the power that was released when her soul had returned, a meteor strike of heat, a brand pressed upon the earth. Miriam had been in the midst of amusing herself with a platoon of soldiers in Bengal, whom she'd lured into the jungle and beset with tiger-shaped shadows. She hadn't even been hungry; it was simply something to do. But the moment she felt that burning brightness, she'd lost all interest in games.

At first, Miriam had purposefully kept her distance. Triggering Harding's memories too early would be disastrous—what had happened with Esther was proof enough of that. With three souls, three lifetimes of experience, this version of her would be exceptionally powerful. The fewer risks Miriam took, the better. Still, by the time Harding was in her twenties, Miriam's resolve had already started to crack. Surely, she could come to her as a crow once more, and see what sort of life her love was living? Surely, that would be enough to assuage this ache inside her, this itch of longing?

And so, she had reached out to the shadows, ordering them to bring her to Harding once more.

The shadows hadn't replied.

How Harding had remained hidden from the darkness, Miriam didn't know. She'd sometimes wondered if she'd died again, through sickness or an accident; but Miriam would have realised if that were the case, surely. She would have *felt* it. They were so aligned, now, magnets brought together—whether a push or pull, she still couldn't tell—but the force was there. The force *should* have been there. When Miriam wanted to find someone, she found them.

And yet, until the *Monumental*, Harding had been nothing. An absence, a ghost, a whisper. A memory made unreal. Miriam didn't panic—it wasn't in her nature—but she did grow angry. Never before had the subject of a deal gone missing, and she wasn't certain what would happen if she couldn't find her. Maybe Harding's soul would detach itself from her body and find Miriam on its own initiative, leaving only a shell behind. What a Pyrrhic victory that would be: to be served that light on a platter, without the glory of the hunt. It wouldn't be worthy of the love they'd shared. When Harding was to die, it would be in Miriam's arms, just as she had two times before. That was only right.

And so, every day, Miriam had searched for her. She had asked shadows in the winding midnight alleys of Quebec and Cairo and Shanghai, enquired with those cast by the harsh sun across temple ruins in Delphi—even the darkest corners of the darkest caverns in the diamond mines of Kimberley. Harding wasn't likely to be in any of these places, of course, but Miriam asked regardless.

Her frustration had made her reckless. And in England, the place she was most likely to find her, each day of searching led to bloody hands and gnashing teeth, as others paid the price for Harding's insolence. Miriam tore through deals, pushing her powers to the limit, until she was so engorged with souls, so sensitive to their light, that all she could hear was the shadows screaming at her, all she could see was the furious blaze of millions of people converging in the streets of London like schools of fish, colliding, shimmering, scattering—

Miriam had never been *sane*, of course, but surely this was some form of going mad.

And then, that morning, something had changed.

She had appeared in Suffolk as dawn broke. The Hall was gone. The village was now a town, the town had motorcars lining the streets, and Miriam stood in front of the old church. It had been rebuilt with white plaster, a war memorial with a long list of martyrs facing it from across the road. An electric lamp stood on the corner of the pavement, illuminating an advertising board that read, *Celebrate the Season with Tilly's Christmas Gift Boxes! Price three shillings from all leading grocers.* In the distance, Miriam could see the Saxon mounds the villagers had once danced around, the low hills presiding over the scene in their eternal silence, immutable and unaffected.

She had closed her eyes and remembered that night, the night they met: the dirt and the darkness, the wind and Cybil streaked with mud. But in Miriam's fantasies it wasn't just Cybil. It was Esther, too, both of them an amalgam. Miriam imagined Harding as she was, as she would be—and if she could have, Miriam would have merged the image with the third version of her, too, the one hiding someplace out there that Miriam couldn't find. She pictured her with the shorter hairstyle the women of this era favoured, eyebrows drawn into delicate arches, fingernails lacquered ruby red. Her voice would be the same—it always was, that petal-wilting tone, high to low.

Miriam, she heard her say. *It's you.*

Miriam. Come find me.

She had started from her reverie, eyes flying open. *That* voice— that wasn't her imagination. It was real.

Miriam. Don't you want me still?

'Yes,' Miriam hissed. '*Yes*—' And then she was calling the shadows to her, almost crowing in her excitement. The darkness seethed forward with such enthusiasm, it swallowed the light of the streetlamp, and the bulb burst with a pop.

'Take me to her,' she'd told them—and then she'd found herself here, on the RMS *Monumental*, iron grating ringing beneath her feet.

Miriam had paused when she'd realised she was on a ship. She'd avoided ships, of course, because of the ocean—the salt, the lack of shadows, the reminder of her birth. She was *surrounded* by salt, in a way: a circle as vast as the Atlantic itself.

Why sail when she could simply step from one landmass to another? This was a novelty, and novelty was a rare thing to her, maybe even precious—but that didn't make it any less risky. She'd thought of the way salt stung her skin, the way it burnt and ached. It was the only thing that had ever given her pain. Apart from Harding, of course.

Miriam knew how difficult it was to fly over salt water. She had never tried to travel by shadows, either, in the middle of an ocean. Staying here was a risk. It was a risk she would be a fool to take.

And then she thought of Harding smiling, eyes molten gold, soul light dripping down her cheeks—and it didn't matter, after all. Miriam was decided.

She wouldn't lose her again.

Miriam had summoned herself a drink to celebrate. She hadn't drunk it, but she'd pantomimed, simply to amuse herself, perhaps in a show of flippancy: she was not so much in a rush to see Harding, after all, that she couldn't have a little fun. But all she had thought of, as she had rolled the glass in her hands, was Harding and how achingly near she was—so the drink had gone overboard, and it was time to get to work. The engines were bellowing, the walls thrumming with their power. A push, a pull, a force undeniable: she was here. After twenty-two years of darkness, Miriam had found her.

She's here, Miriam thought, and her pace increased.

She's finally here.

Meanwhile, in the bedroom of a first-class cabin, Rosamund was flinging evening dresses through the air. Hovering nervously at the door was the startled-looking maid who'd been assigned to help her unpack, calf-eyed and shifting from foot to foot.

'Can I do something for you, ma'am?' the maid asked uncertainly. But Rosamund was too agitated to even look at her. She tossed away a peach-coloured feather boa, and it soared towards the dressing table.

'No!' she said, voice high with nervous excitement. 'No, I'm perfectly fine.'

Where was it? She knew she'd packed it—she *knew* she had— and yet now, with her desperate fingers slipping on silks and velvets and strands of pearls, it suddenly seemed possible she hadn't. And if she hadn't, then everything she'd been planning for the past few years might—

Rosamund felt leather and paper beneath her hands, deep in the confines of her trunk, and she sighed in relief.

'Well, all right,' said the maid, wringing her hands. 'Let me know if you need anything, Mrs Jennings.'

'Of course,' Rosamund said. 'Thank you.'

The maid took that as her cue to leave. She backed away, the door shut, and Rosamund was finally alone.

She flung herself on the bed and stared at the ceiling of her first-class cabin. It was a ridiculous extravagance for an ocean liner. There was gold paint on the cornicing, an embossed image of Venus in her shell peering down at the Turkish rug. Everything about the room, in fact, was extravagant: mint-coloured wallpaper, mahogany furnishings, a tulip-shaped Tiffany lamp. The attached bathroom had a lion-footed tub and a mirror inlaid with mother-of-pearl.

Rosamund felt like a porcelain doll in a display cabinet, surrounded by lovely and pointless things. When she'd powdered her face on their arrival, lips tinted scarlet, silk dressing gown slipping down her shoulders—she felt like she hardly recognised herself. It wasn't as if she'd grown up in difficult circumstances, but this was different. This was bigger. Perhaps it was because she knew it was soon going to end.

She took a cigarette from the monogrammed case on the dresser and put it between her lips, bidding the shadows to light it. A dark hand reached up and pressed its finger lovingly against the tip. Smoke curled upwards; Rosamund inhaled deeply and sighed.

A high-pitched yip resounded from beside the dresser. Rosamund sat up at the noise. A black Pekingese that looked like a wad of cotton rolled in soot was pacing around the carpet, barking without apparent reason. At her attention, he wheezed and spun three times, before walking directly into the wall.

'Caviar, hush,' said Rosamund, frowning. The dog backed up, then walked into the wall again. She grimaced. 'Well, never mind. I imagine it must be difficult, having a brain the size of a Brazil nut.'

She blew a strand of ginger hair away from her face, sending another plume of smoke into the air. There was a familiar mixture of excitement and terror roiling in her stomach. Three days until New York. Three days until her twenty-third birthday.

Three days—it would have to be long enough.

Caviar yapped a second time. He was Walt's dog, and Rosamund had never felt much affection for him. But Walt insisted on hauling him around everywhere they went, and so here Caviar was, on his second transatlantic voyage that year. The Pekingese was four years old, and he had travelled more than she had—a woman living her third life in five centuries. That felt faintly ridiculous.

She checked her watch: it was nearly time for dinner. Rosamund stood up from the bed and stripped down, chewing her lip thoughtfully. She had an array of dresses to choose from, each more ridiculous than the last, lacy and sequined and plunging. In her nervousness, she'd packed thoughtlessly, prioritising style over substance. Now she'd have to wear evening gowns to breakfast.

Rosamund tossed a fur shawl to the floor. Caviar barked at it, frightened. Then he jumped up onto the mattress, into the open travelling case.

'Not that one,' Rosamund said sharply. 'There's something precious in there. Down.'

Caviar whined, but he exited the case. Satisfied, Rosamund went back to sorting through clothes, humming to herself. Eventually the humming devolved into singing. *'But as far as I'm concerned,'* she warbled, out of tune, *'it's a lovely day...'*

The door to the cabin slammed open. Walt strode in and bellowed back to her, in a far more capable singing voice than her own, *'Isn't this a lovely day to get caught in the raa-aa-aain—!'*

His dark hair was slicked back, dinner jacket slung over one arm. She had watched him shave that morning, but there was already a thin layer of stubble on his chin—and the tie she'd so painstakingly tied was askew. Rosamund prepared herself to comment acerbically on this, but then Walt threw his jacket onto the bed, picked her up, and swung her around by her waist.

The dog yipped and hid, quivering beneath the dressing table. Rosamund shrieked and slapped Walt's arm, to little effect.

'Evening, Rosie-Posie,' he said, returning to his normal volume, which was still far too loud. Everything he said sounded like it was coming through a loudspeaker. 'You aren't dressed? Dinner's soon.'

'I can't decide,' she replied, gesturing to the dresses strewn across the bed.

'The green one.'

'Ugh, no. It's a dinner, not a garden party.'

'Oh, pardon me, Your Highness. Silver?'

Rosamund hummed in thought and lifted up the silver gown. It was covered in crystal beads, glittering in the pink-red sunlight shining through the window of the cabin. 'Isn't it a bit much for the first evening?'

'Who cares? You'll knock 'em dead.'

'Hm. Possibly. Zip me up?'

He helped secure her in the dress. The back plunged almost to her hips, and he whistled. 'You look good,' he said. 'Maybe we don't need the lavender in this marriage, after all.'

Rosamund felt a pang of affection for him, which was swiftly followed by guilt. How many lies she'd told him; how little he knew. 'Let's get a drink.'

Then she threaded her arm through his, and he led her out of the cabin.

The first-class bar was an extraordinary room that smelt as much of money as it did the food: chandeliers shimmered with the movement of the water beneath them, and there were ruby velvet tablecloths, and waiters with napkins on their arms and impeccably waxed moustaches. They ordered champagne and caviar. Although Walter had grown up rich, he was the son of a self-made man—that had instilled in him both a wide-eyed appreciation for nice things and a determined entitlement to them. He spread the caviar in great gobs of burst-black juice, once even breaking the cracker in half with the force of his spoon. Meanwhile, Rosamund watched him over the bubbles of her drink, chewing the inside of her cheek.

They talked inanely about music and movies, while the sunset winked at them through the porthole. Walt liked his jazz hot and his pictures racy; Rosamund preferred classical and had a soft spot for romances, although she'd never let that slip. She didn't much want to think about romances now, though. She felt faintly queasy. She'd never sailed before, and she had expected it to be different than this somehow—either more movement or less. Not this strange, half-living shifting of the floor beneath her feet.

'Do you think you'll like America?' Walter asked her.

She winced, taking a hurried sip of her champagne to hide it. 'Of course. Why wouldn't I?'

'True enough. You wanted to get away from England, right? This is definitely away.'

'Yes.'

'It's just—sometimes I worry you're getting cold feet.'

Rosamund huffed. 'I *married* you, Walt. What more commitment do you want?'

He shrugged in acknowledgement of this. 'I already phoned Pa and explained it all,' he said. 'He was so happy about it—fell for it hook, line, and sinker. It'd be awkward to show up empty-handed.'

Hook, line, and sinker. Walt spoke constantly in aphorisms and metaphors, words punctuated by flailing gestures and restless movements. He was wonderfully expressive. The day before the wedding, he'd taken Rosamund to a Catholic Mass, and he'd chewed the wafer with such a pained grimace, it seemed like it had actually turned to flesh in his mouth. Rosamund had hidden her laughter with a cough. Walt often made her laugh. He felt so real, so *human*: a nice change.

'I won't change my mind,' she told him. 'I made a vow, and I meant it. Till death do us part.'

Walt grimaced. 'I hate that bit. Makes it feel like a deal with the devil.'

She had to laugh at that. 'Yes, it does,' she agreed, and they toasted to that with their champagne glasses, as behind them the sun made its death spiral into the Atlantic.

Once they were finished with their caviar, they went to stand by the bar. Walter conversed with some other businessmen, while Rosamund leaned against him and watched the room warily, champagne still fizzing in her gut.

It's fine, she told herself. *It's what you wanted. It's all going well.*

Walt ordered them more drinks: a mai tai for him, and a scotch for Rosamund. As she took her first sip, he elbowed her gently in the side. 'That woman is staring at you.'

Rosamund nearly dropped her drink. 'What? Where?'

Walt gestured with his chin to a woman standing alone by the bar. She was pretty, a bottle blonde, all curves and so short she was halfway on her tiptoes as she spoke to the bartender. Her features were fair and wholesome, and she had a deep, cherubic cleft in her chin.

'She's pretty,' he said.

Rosamund's shoulders slumped. 'Really?'

'C'mon, have some fun. We've got three days to kill here.'

She considered the woman for a moment longer, then shrugged. 'Watch my purse.'

She walked toward the woman and slid onto the seat beside her, putting her scotch down on the bar.

'Are you waiting for someone?' Rosamund asked her.

The woman, who was now staring at her bust quite transparently, said, 'Well—oh—hello,' in a shrill, transatlantic accent.

'Hello,' Rosamund said.

'Um—am I—waiting for someone?'

'Yes, that's what I asked.'

'Gosh, well, no, I'm not. But I'm travelling alone, so I thought I should make a habit of getting out of the cabin, before I get stuck in there.'

Rosamund smiled at her. The blonde grinned in response; then she became embarrassed, and looked away, flustered. She thrust her hand out to Rosamund. 'Vivien Hale,' she said.

'Rosamund Ha— Jennings,' she replied, shaking the hand. 'You said you're travelling alone?'

'My brother was supposed to come with me, but he's ended up at a sanatorium—doctors said best not to move him. We've got family on both ends; I was in London for a couple of years, and now I'm heading back. My mother's in Brooklyn and...'

She continued in this vein for quite a while, offering enough information to fill several biographies. Rosamund swirled her scotch in its glass and sipped slowly, wondering whether this was really worth it. It wasn't as if Vivian was her *type*, after all. She glanced back to Walt, briefly, but he was talking to a stranger: a handsome man, tall and slender, dark-skinned, with buzzed hair and a thin moustache. It was best not to interrupt.

'... Do you?' Vivien Hale was saying.

'Hm?'

'Have family in the States?'

'No.'

'I should've guessed. With that accent, I bet you're English through and through. Probably some sort of lady or duchess or something, huh?' She tittered. 'Do you know any royalty?'

Rosamund drained the rest of her scotch. When she put down the glass, she saw movement in the corner of her eye. It was only a brief vision—a flutter of dark hair, a sharp profile, disappearing behind the door on the other side of the bar. It made her feel as if she'd been thrown into boiling water.

'Mrs Jennings?' Vivien said. 'Is something wrong?'

She shook her head. 'It's nothing. Listen—it was lovely meeting you, Miss Hale. I'm certain we'll see each other again soon.'

'You're leaving?' Vivien said, bereft.

Rosamund slid off her stool. 'Forgive me. I've made other plans.'

'Oh. Well, maybe—'

But Rosamund wasn't listening. She was already walking across the bar, leaving her behind. It was as if there was a harpoon in her chest, a chain being reeled in. She was powerless, propelled forward by invisible hands, pushing her way between tables, beaded gown dragging at her feet in a constant shower of noise. Behind her, she heard Vivien's voice call for her again. She ignored it. Instead, she reached forward with both hands to push open a door marked EMPLOYEES ONLY, evading the notice of the waitstaff. With her arms still outstretched, as if she were navigating blind, she made her way up the steel steps and towards the open air of the promenade.

Even though the weather in London had been unseasonably warm, it was still a winter night on the Atlantic, and the air was shockingly cold. Rosamund was bare-armed, the salty chill of the wind clawing at her elbows like sandpaper. The sea spray had made the floor slick. The area was only barely lit, in reds and dim yellows from the lights peppering the side of the hull. Shuddering, she stumbled across the decking, trying not to slip.

There was no one else on the promenade, and Rosamund sighed. It wouldn't be the first time she thought she'd seen... *something*, only to later realise it wasn't there. But at least the night was gorgeous, stars piercing the black in tiny, glowing stitches, hemming sea and sky together. Rosamund went to the railing and leaned over it, the wind whipping her face. The darkness stretched in an endless sphere above her.

She heard footsteps. Someone came to stand beside her.

She knew who it was. Of course she did.

'Hello, Miriam,' Rosamund said.

21

One hundred and eighteen years, and Miriam hadn't given any thought to what she would say when she first saw Harding again.

She could reach forward to lay a hand on her arm—this shimmering creature, familiar and strange, with hair cut short and leaf-shaped eyes and a scattering of freckles on her shoulders—and tell her, *I am sorry*. But what meaning would there be in such an apology, when Miriam didn't regret what she'd done? She *was* sorry, she supposed, about killing Esther the way she did—in a petty impulse that had denied Miriam her soul for another century. But now that this Harding was here, standing in front of her, Miriam felt little regret. It would be a privilege to watch her die again.

Miriam could gather her into her arms instead, leave a bruise on that lovely throat, and let hands and mouths speak where voices couldn't. Miriam could say, *I love you*—words she still wasn't certain she understood, but she believed they were true, as much as they could be to something like her. Or perhaps she could pass Harding a new knife, let her re-create what had happened all those years ago, their positions reversed. Miriam couldn't die, but she could make a show of it. She wanted to see violence in those eyes again, just once more. The memory of it could never compare to the reality.

But then Harding smiled and said, 'I've missed you,' and Miriam found she couldn't speak, couldn't smile back, couldn't do anything at all.

Her eyes were gold, true gold—brighter than they once were, surely? She looked at Miriam, lids half closed, lips quirked, and Miriam wanted to hold those eyes in her hands. She would sink the *Monumental* and bury them with it, like coins in a shipwreck. No one else deserved to see those eyes. No one else deserved to be seen by them.

'You're not going to say anything?' Harding asked. 'Not even a hello?'

Miriam let out a breathless, gasping sort of chuckle, a sound more human than should have been possible. 'Hello.'

At the sound of her voice, Harding flushed slightly, turning her head away.

'I'm Rosamund now,' she said. 'In case you didn't know that already.'

'Rosamund,' Miriam echoed, considering the taste of the name, the cadence of it.

'Do you like it? I preferred Esther, I think.' She rolled her nails against the railing, the hairs on the back of her hands standing on end from the cold. 'Cybil, too. This name feels too... honest, somehow. *Rosa mundi*, rose of the world. Quick to bloom, quick to die.'

Miriam was silent. Inside the ship, jazz was playing on a phonograph; the crackling hum of the bass dripped from the portholes like honey.

'I thought you'd be angry,' Miriam said.

Rosamund tipped back her head to laugh. The movement bared her throat to the salt wind of the sea, glazing the skin with water. Miriam swallowed.

'Of course I'm angry,' Rosamund said, once her laughter had subsided. 'You *killed* me, Miriam.'

'Because I—'

'Oh, I *know* why. That doesn't mean I can't be angry about it.'

'I've been looking for you for years.'

'I know.'

'I couldn't find you.'

'I know.'

'I couldn't find you, and you're *mine*,' Miriam snarled, fury breaking its leash. 'You are mine, Rosamund, you are here because I made you so, and you kept me away.'

'I know,' Rosamund said once more.

'Who was that man, at the bar?'

She smiled. 'What? Walter? That's my husband.'

'Your *husband*?'

'Oh, my love,' Rosamund murmured, and she took a step closer to her, laying a palm on her chest. 'You needn't be jealous. You killed me once—*twice*, really, if you count Cybil—and you'll do it again in a few days. I am as much yours as I've ever been. And I am angry, of course, but not overly so. What'd be the use? I've spent years trying to figure out a way to escape you, and now, finally, I've accepted that I can't. We might as well enjoy each other while we're here.'

'Enjoy each other,' Miriam repeated, frowning.

Rosamund cocked her head. When she spoke this time, it was an echo in Miriam's mind, as tender as a whisper, as loud as a scream. *Haven't you missed me?*

Miriam looked at Rosamund properly now, dragging her gaze away from those uncanny eyes. Her soul was radiant in her chest—so bright it no longer seemed to be a single point of light, but rather a glow that was diffused throughout her entire body, making her luminous. What sort of magic such a soul could perform, Miriam could hardly imagine. It would more than match her own capabilities. It'd match anyone's.

'You forgive me,' Miriam said, sceptically.

Rosamund shrugged. 'What else is there to do?'

'Cybil didn't forgive me. Esther didn't forgive me.'

She sighed, crossing her arms. 'I— Look. Do you know what an ant mill is?'

'I'm afraid I don't.'

'Sometimes, ants start walking in a death spiral. They walk round and round in a circle, over and over, until they die of exhaustion.'

Miriam blinked. 'Why do they do that?'

'They're following the trails of the other ants in front of them, and they're following the ones in front, and so on… They don't realise they're going nowhere.'

'Tragic,' Miriam said, without sympathy. 'Your point is?'

'Esther repeated Cybil's mistakes. She allowed herself to trust you, believing she could find salvation; I won't do the same. We both know how this ends. I don't see much point in fighting it.'

'You're ready to die.'

'I've been ready since the moment I remembered you,' Rosamund said. 'I remembered you, Miriam, and I knew that the only death I'd ever want would be the one you'll give me.'

The ship hit a wave, and it lurched, sending Rosamund tumbling backwards. Miriam surged forward to catch her. Then they were touching, pressed against each other. Rosamund's hand was on her chest, eyes bright as they met hers. She smelt like perfume, dark and sweet; there was a small chicken-pox scar on her collarbone that she hadn't had in her previous forms. And for a moment, she was *her* Harding entirely, the one that Miriam had laughed with and betrayed and made love to, who had died so prettily in her arms that Miriam was certain she'd never see anything lovelier.

But it wasn't her Harding. It was Rosamund, and Rosamund was something else, languid and seductive and willing in a way Esther and Cybil had never been. And there was something cold, something restrained glimmering behind her inviting expression—*that*, at least, Miriam recognised.

Miriam released her, suddenly disturbed. Rosamund stepped back, lips pressed thin. She looked back to the stars, curling her fingers around the metal railing. Her wedding ring—a diamond the size of a cherry pit—glinted red in the lights of the deck.

'It's a three-day journey,' Rosamund said. 'Will you be gentle, once it's done?'

'Yes.'

'That's all I can ask for.'

'I didn't want this.'

'Didn't want what?' she asked, eyebrows knitting together. 'My soul?'

'Your surrender,' Miriam said. 'I wanted you to fight, as you used to. I wanted your fury and your violence and your pain. Those are the things that I love about you. You know that as well as I do.'

Rosamund leaned over, pressing a kiss to her cheek. 'I *am* fighting, darling,' she replied. 'Machiavelli once said that the best way to defeat an enemy is to do voluntarily what she plans to make you do by force.'

'You have already won, then,' Miriam said, displeased.

Rosamund smiled. Trailing a hand along the sleeve of Miriam's suit, she said, 'Yes. I suppose I have.'

She turned to leave. Miriam allowed her to without protest, watching her hips swaying, silver beads glittering with the movement of her dress. The ship lurched with another wave, and a beam of red light passed over the deck.

At her feet, the shadows seethed curiously. Miriam kicked them away.

Halfway down the promenade, Rosamund turned to look at her over her shoulder. 'Well?'

'Well?' Miriam echoed.

'Aren't you coming?'

'Coming where?'

'Dinner,' Rosamund said. 'It's been centuries, Miriam. Shouldn't we reacquaint ourselves?'

Rosamund requested the private room adjoining the first-class dining hall; the kitchens were reluctant—it was late, dinner service was nearly over—but she mentioned her husband's name, flashed the diamond on her finger, and they relented.

White tablecloth, gold candles, Miriam in a tuxedo looking for all the world like she was about to pull a cigarette holder from her jacket and blow smoke rings at the chandelier. The pianist in the other room was hacking out 'Who's Sorry Now' with the grim efficiency of a dockworker hauling boxes. The sound filtered through the closed door, muffled and tinny.

It was a set menu: the predinner cocktail was a pale green-gold colour, scented sharply with citrus, each glass tinted blue and painted with a stylised rooster. Rosamund—who was already half drunk on champagne and scotch—took a sip to hide her nerves. Then she put the glass down on the table and bent over to laugh.

Miriam said, smirking, 'Is it that bad?'

Rosamund snorted. 'No, it's just... It's a Corpse Reviver.'

'Hm?'

'The cocktail. It's called a Corpse Reviver.'

'How appropriate,' Miriam drawled. She took a sip, wrinkling her nose, and put the glass back down.

'Do you *like* food?'

'Not particularly,' Miriam said. 'But I still have the urge to eat, even if it does little for me.'

'Why?'

'Because I am always hungry,' she replied.

The appetizer came then: oysters on the half shell, served on a bed of chipped ice, gilded at their sharp edges with flecks of gold leaf. Rosamund took one between two fingers, trying not to think of how the waiter must have cracked them open, of smiling knives and bleeding skin. She tipped it down her throat, a swallow of lemon acidity and bitter sea salt. She could feel Miriam's eyes following the bob of her throat.

'You aren't going to try one?' Rosamund asked her. 'Too salty?'

Miriam pushed her plate towards her. The ship hit a wave, making the candle between them flicker. 'Watching you is more than enough.'

Well, then. It wasn't as if Rosamund needed to watch her figure. She had Miriam's oysters, too, licking the brine from her fingers afterwards. The silence between them had grown so weighty that Rosamund wondered if it would plummet like an anchor through the floorboards beneath them, stopping the *Monumental* in its tracks.

The waiters took away their plates. Once they were gone, Miriam said, 'This new age has made you more... brazen.'

'It wasn't the new age, Miriam. It was you.'

'Me?'

Rosamund smirked. 'Everything you did to me, as Esther... Well. There's only so far you can bend someone before they snap.'

'Is that what you've done, darling? You've snapped?'

'I've shattered,' she said. 'And I'm better this way. I have sharp edges now. You can't pick me up without getting cut.'

The waiter came in with the next dish: turtle soup, the liquid deep red with tomato and spices, chunks of pale meat sliced thin yet still gilded with fat. Rosamund ate slowly, closing her lips around the spoon with a languidness so obscene that Miriam laughed outright.

After the soup, the fish course was a red snapper smothered in hollandaise, its enormous golden eye clouded by death. Then the entrée: a whole roast pigeon stuffed with foie gras and truffle, laid on a bed of chestnuts and drizzled with cognac sauce.

Rosamund took a bite of the pigeon. It was exceptionally rich, coating her tongue with salt and oil and the earthy scent of the truffles. She wondered at how, in every lifetime, she had been so exceptionally privileged—maybe if she'd made more of an effort to help people below her station, the world might've been less cruel to her. But it was too late for such thoughts now. She was eating truffles, wearing diamonds, and preparing to die.

'Do you miss your past lives?' Miriam asked her.

'Do you?'

Miriam drummed her fingers on the table. Shadows spurted violently beneath them, as if the tablecloth had open veins.

'Of course,' she said.

'Will you miss *me*—Rosamund—when *I'm* gone?'

Her lips twitched. In amusement? Regret? 'Yes. I believe so.'

'But it is a sacrifice you're willing to make,' Rosamund replied, with false flippancy. 'Like the pigeon on my plate—I might pity the creature, if I saw it living, but that wouldn't stop me from having it for dinner.'

'You don't love the pigeon, Rosamund.'

'As you love me?'

'Yes.'

'It's odd,' Rosamund said darkly. 'I think that somehow makes it worse.'

They remained in silence until dessert. It was devil's food cake, to add insult to injury, served warm with a scattering of raspberries. This, Miriam ate, as if to spite her.

Rosamund hated sweet things; she didn't even try the cake. She put her fork down with a clatter. 'I wanted to ask you something.'

'Yes?'

'We both know how *I* was created,' Rosamund said. 'That night on the balcony, with blood and fury. But what about you? Where do *you* come from?'

'With blood and fury,' Miriam echoed. 'I was made before Cybil's era. Centuries before, I think.'

'You *think*?'

'I don't keep time like you do, darling. If I did, I would have driven myself to madness.' Miriam took up her fork between finger and thumb, inspecting the tines in the light of the candle on the table; then she spoke to her reflection in the steel. 'I was a shadow, once— as I am now—but the sort of shadow that is everywhere, the sort that depends on the light to cast it. Then a group of mages offered me unimaginable power—enough of each of their souls to make me something more. I found a new form. I was freed from the tyranny of the dark.'

'So, you were created by a deal?'

Dark eyes; a darker smile. 'I suppose so. I don't know the particulars—I never will—but they wanted a servant to do their bidding. At the moment I was made, they had paid the price to bring me there, but not to bend me to their will. That was foolish of them. I killed them before they could tie me to their service.'

'You *murdered* your creators?'

Miriam grinned, dropping her fork with a clatter. 'Does that upset you? If we owe our makers favours, Rosamund, then you owe me infinitely.'

Rosamund looked away. 'I don't think of you as my creator.'

'Your destroyer, then.'

'My reckoning.'

'Are you afraid to die, Rosamund? To truly die, without resurrection?'

It seemed pointless to lie. 'Of course I am.'

Miriam put her elbow on the table, extending her palm to the sky. In her empty hand, the shadows swirled, then a shape materialised: an oyster knife, chillingly familiar in its silver gleam.

'Then end it now instead.' Miriam extended her arm, offering the knife to her. 'Wouldn't that be the solution? End it again, before I take your soul, and find another life to live. Perhaps the next one will bring you the meaning you crave.'

Rosamund stared mutely at the knife. The ship rocked gently beneath her feet. In the next room, the pianist trilled the highest notes; there was a muffled round of applause.

After a few moments, Miriam closed her hand around the blade. She dropped her arm, expressionless, even as black blood began to drip from her palm and onto the tablecloth.

'But you won't,' Miriam said. 'You will never end it yourself. Why would you? We both know it won't make a difference. You could have as many souls as stars, my love, and all those lives would be as unhappy as the first.'

Rosamund forced herself to give Miriam a bland smile.

'I know,' she said. 'That's why I am surrendering to you. Did you forget that, Miriam? Our war is over. You don't need to convince me anymore.'

Miriam scowled. She poked the oyster knife into her cake, leaving it there, handle pointing to the ceiling. 'It doesn't feel like a surrender.'

'What does it feel like, then?'

'Like a tragedy on a stage,' Miriam said. 'You and I, wearing our masks again, playing pretend.'

Rosamund felt it, then, more keenly than she had in years: the weight of the mask, somehow heavier for the imminence of its fall. She watched Miriam's eyes fall to her lips, her neck, the glint of the fork in her palm. The *Monumental* rocked and groaned with the anger of the sea beneath it, the piano silent in the other room. And around them the darkness, their constant companion, was quiet and still—as if the night itself was holding its breath.

22

When Rosamund returned to her cabin, there were two men in the bed. She sighed, left her husband and his lover to their sleep, and went to run the bath.

She shed her clothes, plunged into the water, and stretched out with one foot hooked over the brassy metal of the tap. It was hot enough her skin flushed pink, clouds of lavender-scented steam wafting towards the tiled ceiling. She picked up her book—an Oxford World's Classics edition of Isaac Harding's *The Nouveau Odysseus*, well thumbed and well loved—but she couldn't concentrate. She tossed it onto the counter, then reached with a languid left hand towards the shadows cast by the edge of the bath.

The pain was an old friend now; Rosamund had carved off so many pieces of her soul it felt instinctive, like picking at a hangnail. She sometimes wondered if each piece lost did something to her— made her colder, made her sharper, made her less attached to life itself—but she couldn't tell. Whether that was the darkness's fault, or the trauma of her past lives, it was a sacrifice she was willing to make.

In response to her offering, the shadows surged upwards, eager and pliable, draping over her fingers like silk. Rosamund recalled a trick from the grimoire: she concentrated, made her request, and the shadows formed a tiny ship, rocking gently between her fingers as if moving on waves. She played with it a little while, smiling. Then she twitched her thumb too violently. The shadow-ship jolted, and—simultaneously—the entirety of the *Monumental* lurched, sending water slopping out of the bath.

'Whoops,' she murmured.

Chagrined, Rosamund re-formed the shadows into a different shape: a crow, wings half risen in flight. It cocked its featureless head at her.

She remembered the last time she'd seen that crow, the night Miriam had come into the townhouse—the shadows holding her down, Miriam's hand between her legs. *I will make you mine.*

Rosamund felt a pang of arousal, followed by anger. She hadn't expected to still find Miriam as attractive as she did, had thought that resentment would burn away whatever affection remained. But, if anything, that resentment had stoked the flames, had made Rosamund want to rip her apart and taste her and fuck her and *destroy* them both—

The ship lurched again.

Rosamund breathed deeply, closing her eyes, allowing the shadows to dissipate. She couldn't let her anger rule her. She had a plan, and she intended to follow it through. What Miriam had told her at dinner—it didn't matter. It was Rosamund who had control now.

'*Greensleeves, farewell, adieu,*' she sang, reaching for the loofah. '*To God I pray to prosper thee, for I am still thy lover true…*'

The loofah burst into flame in her hands. She let the ashes slip through her fingers.

'*So come once again and love me.*'

Miriam was suspicious—of course she was.

It was all too easy, too simple. Cybil and Esther had been puzzles, challenges, prizes to be won; Rosamund was none of those things. She had offered herself up on a platter, dismissed their history with a sigh and a smile. It was nauseating, undignified, cruel. It was everything that Miriam had wanted and everything she despised.

She watched Rosamund and her husband at breakfast the next day, concealed by shadows in a dark corner of the restaurant. Walter Jennings was sawing through a beefsteak and a pair of sunshine-coloured eggs, the arms of his suit straining against his impressive biceps, gold wedding band sparkling in the light coming through the portholes. Rosamund looked tired, dark circles under her eyes, but she still glowed within the confines of her cherry-toned dress. Its V-neck was cut so deep that you could see the base of her ribcage, the swell of her breasts as she breathed. Miriam decided she liked this era, liked the way Harding wore it, short-haired and scarlet-mouthed. She wanted to bite into her like a peach.

Walter said something; Rosamund laughed softly, covering her mouth with her hand. She had such lovely wrists, so slender—it would be devastatingly easy for Miriam to snap them. Even Walter, with his tree-trunk limbs, would be no match for her strength.

He gesticulated wildly. Rosamund laughed more.

Twitching with jealousy, Miriam called to the shadows.

They slipped across the rug, between table legs and gilt chairs, until they reached the Jennings' table. Then they crawled—slowly, to avoid detection—towards Walter's plate, sinking into his beefsteak.

Walter went to cut another bite. As soon as his knife met flesh, a great spurt of blood fountained upwards, as if from a cut artery; it spattered across the front of his suit and along the table. Rosamund wasn't spared, blood misting her face and collarbones. Walter swore, crying out, stumbling out of his chair. Rosamund remained where she was, the only hint of shock a slight flinch and a grimace.

The blood began to pool on the plate, the pristine white tablecloth, the cream-coloured carpets. There was a general groan of horror across the first-class restaurant. Some servers, uncertain how to help, fluttered closer and then veered back again as the blood spread towards them.

'What in God's name—' Walter snarled, turning to an unsuspecting waiter. 'What the hell kind of steak is this?'

Rosamund sighed and stood up. She used the heel of her hand to swipe blood off her jaw, then said, 'Excuse me.' She turned to look directly at Miriam—that made Miriam smile; of course she'd known she was there—and then she left the restaurant. Her husband was too busy arguing with the staff to notice or care.

Miriam followed Rosamund out into the corridor, still shrouded in shadows. Rosamund must have known she was behind her, but she didn't react. She just kept walking, blood running in rivulets down her shoulder and into the plunging back of her dress. They walked through numerous empty corridors, down a set of stairs. All that time, Rosamund said nothing at all.

Eventually, Miriam tired of the game. Materialising, she said, 'Where are we going?'

Rosamund stopped. They were in a narrow corridor full of cabins. Above them, a crystal chandelier swayed gently with the movement of the ship. There was still blood beaded on her collarbone. Miriam considered pressing her against the wall and licking it away, but she didn't want to distract Rosamund from her anger. The fury in her expression was too exquisite, too wonderfully familiar, to be obscured. *There she is*, Miriam thought. *Just as I remembered her.*

'Leave him alone,' Rosamund said.

'Who?' Miriam asked, in faux innocence, allowing a glimmer of a smile to pass over her lips.

'Walter. He hasn't got anything to do with this—with *us.*'

'I rather think he does, darling,' Miriam purred. 'I am a jealous god. I don't like to share.'

Behind Rosamund, the shadows pushed her forward; she stumbled slightly, then looked over her shoulder as if betrayed. 'You're not *sharing* anything,' she said, a note of resignation in her tone.

'Oh?'

'He's just a friend. The only friend I've ever had, in fact.' Rosamund straightened her back, lifted her chin. 'If you do anything to him, I'll never forgive you. I'll hide myself away again until the deal is done.'

Miriam stepped forward, placing herself in the middle of the corridor, forcing Rosamund to take a step back toward the wall. 'You used to be so much fun,' Miriam said, sighing. 'Remember us, that night in London, when you let me in through the window? When you begged me for it, when you wept with pleasure? Where has that girl gone?'

Rosamund scowled. 'You slit her throat.'

'Oh, yes—so I did. In my defence, she would've killed herself if I hadn't.'

'You couldn't even allow me that,' she said bitterly. 'You had every-thing that mattered—my life, my heart, my soul. Of course you needed my death, too.'

'Don't act as if I never gave you anything, darling.' Miriam took another step forward, forcing Rosamund to press her back against the wall. She reached out, trailed a finger down that lovely throat, catching the final scarlet beads and streaking them across her skin. *Blood on snow.*

Rosamund shivered. Her pupils were wide and dark, her lips half parted. Already, Miriam could see her anger beginning to fade. Rosamund was so weak to her touch; she always had been—without that, without lust, Miriam wondered if she'd ever have signed the deal at all.

'You want me to spare Walter Jennings,' Miriam said.

Mute, Rosamund nodded.

Miriam leaned in and whispered into her ear, 'Then beg me for it.'

Rosamund's breath stuttered; it seemed she still remembered that night in London, after all—the last time Miriam said that to her—despite the century that had passed.

'I...'

'Go on,' Miriam murmured. She skimmed her mouth across her neck, darting out her tongue to taste her skin. Rosamund squirmed. Miriam's lips twitched in triumph. Finally, it felt as it always had: that glorious push and pull, digging in her nails and peeling away Harding's stubbornness, leaving her exposed and raw—

'Go fuck yourself,' Rosamund said, and she disappeared.

Utterly astonished, Miriam took a step back, staring at the blank space on the wall. The corridor was silent, except for the soft, mock-ing tinkle of the chandelier above her head. It had been so sudden, so abrupt, that for a moment, Miriam couldn't believe it had happened. Then she snarled and kicked the wainscoting so hard that it cracked.

Rosamund must have called the shadows to her, made herself ephemeral, and stepped back into the wall. It was an easy-enough trick—Miriam had taught it to Esther herself—but it was the sheer *gall* of it that was so infuriating. What happened to *I missed you*? What happened to *We might as well enjoy each other*?

The chandelier tinkled again. Miriam reached up and pulled it down, sending it crashing to the floor in a thousand shards of glass.

Rosamund had lost her temper; she'd be the first to admit that. And it was likely her husband who would pay the price.

She spent the rest of the morning uneasy, alert to every unexpected noise and shift at the corner of her eye, expecting Miriam to find her again. By the afternoon she was very irritable. Walter, trying to cheer her up, suggested they walk the promenade. There wasn't much else to do, so she agreed.

It looked different in the day, so much more mundane without the dark blurring the edges of the railings, or the ephemeral glow of the hull lights splashing the floor with colour. It was chilly, so Rosamund clutched her mink stole around her as they walked.

Walter said, 'I got an apology from the chef. Because of breakfast. They think it must have been a problem with the cut.'

'How about that.'

'You could have stayed,' he continued, a wounded edge to his tone. 'You just upped and walked away.'

'What else could I have done?'

'I don't know, consoled me about my ruined suit? It's just—it's not like this is a traditional marriage, but it'd be nice if I felt like my wife could support me, sometimes.'

Rosamund scowled. 'Women always have to be *soft* and *supportive* and *sweet*. Why is that?'

'Well, there's nothing wrong with sweet, is there?'

'Sweet things get eaten, Walt,' Rosamund replied. 'Better to be bitter, so they spit you out.'

Defeated, Walter sighed. 'It's your birthday tomorrow. Would it kill you to take things a little less seriously?'

'Probably.'

He rolled his eyes, and they continued to promenade without conversation. They stopped only when they spotted someone they recognised: the man Walt had slept with last night was leaning against a starboard railing, smoking a cigar.

'Jean!' Walt called, and he went over to speak to him. They quickly fell into conversation, laughing together, and Rosamund leaned against the wall to watch them. She hadn't actually *met* Jean—she'd fallen asleep in the bath, and when she'd woken up, he'd already been gone—but Walter had chattered on about him all morning. Clearly, their night together had been a success.

A breeze passed over her, and something flew into her hair. She pulled it away. It was a scarlet petal.

Rosamund whipped around, searching the crowd. At the far end of the promenade, she could see a crow on the railing, watching her intently.

Is this supposed to be a threat? Rosamund said to her. Miriam didn't reply. She just kept staring, blinking two dark eyes, one after the other.

The sound of Walt's laughter rippled across the deck. Rosamund swallowed, imagining that laughter ended—a knife in his throat, a spade to the windpipe—and her stomach lurched.

Now was not the time for pride. This was the last day before her birthday, after all. If she wanted to keep her husband alive—if she wanted everything to go according to plan—she needed Miriam to give her this day without violence, without revenge.

I'm sorry, she said to Miriam. *I didn't mean it.*

The crow cocked its head, considering. Then it flew away.

Walter returned, Jean in tow. 'Rosie,' he said, 'this is Jean. He's on his way to Haiti. He's got a second-class cabin, but I told him I could take him this evening to the first-class bar, for tiki night.'

'Yes, lovely to meet you,' Rosamund said.

In a soft, francophone accent, Jean replied, 'And you, madame.'

Walter frowned at her. 'What's wrong?'

'Nothing,' she replied, through gritted teeth. 'It's nothing.'

Walter shrugged and looked uneasily up to the sky. 'Wow, where'd the sun go? These clouds came in fast.'

'Let's go inside,' Rosamund said.

'I think Jean and I wanted another smoke—'

'Fine,' she snapped, 'enjoy it,' and she marched away before they could protest.

Inside the ship, the bar was being decorated in anticipation for the festivities; staff were draping gaudy laurels of fake hibiscus from the ceiling in soldier-like rows. The flowers were made with cheap fabric, and their petals were tattered at the edges, as if torn rather than cut. As Rosamund passed beneath them, one fell from its moorings and landed squarely on her head. Rosamund snatched it out of her hair and crushed it in her fist. She carried it like that, wadded up in her palm, until she reached the cabin. Then she threw it on the bed, where it combusted and reduced itself immediately to ashes—startling Caviar, who had been asleep on the pillow.

She was tired, that was all. She was tired, and anxious, and the trip was making her seasick. That was why she had this feeling in her stomach, this awful, unshakeable, nauseating *need*. She wanted to go to Miriam, curl her arms around her waist, and beg her to forgive her; or to lie down with her and find a way to make the ruse real, to unburden herself of the anger that had defined her ever since she'd regained her memories. Rosamund wanted to be whole, wanted to be herself. She was sick of being a shadow of her past lives. She was the third act in a story she had never agreed to be part of, and all she could think of was escape.

Caviar yapped. She groaned into the pillow. She'd have to find a way to get Miriam back on her side; this would all be so much easier to pull off if she wasn't being viewed with suspicion. One moment of anger, and now she might've ruined everything.

Sweetness, then, just as Walt had said—that was the key. Miriam wanted Rosamund resistant enough to feel like a conquest, but still pliant enough to use; she could give her that. There were less than forty-eight hours until the deal was up. Until then, Rosamund could be as sweet as Miriam needed, sweeter than Esther had ever been.

Like a fish on a line, Rosamund thought. *Why don't you come a little nearer, darling, and just bite, bite, bite.*

Rosamund called to Miriam that afternoon, her thoughts feather-light, coaxing: *Forgive me, my love. Come find me again.*

Miriam, still angry, nonetheless followed the call with a petulant, reluctant sort of excitement—the excitement only increased when she realised that Rosamund was behind a door labelled TURKISH BATHS. These baths apparently required a ticket, but none of the attendants were much inclined to protest when Miriam strode inside. A young woman offered her a massage—she declined—and another offered her a bathrobe. She declined that, also. Instead, she strode through each muggy, pink-tiled room entirely naked, searching for Rosamund. Some pools were hot, some were cold. There was a sauna and a steam room. Miriam found it extraordinary that this was feasible on a ship, when humans had been slopping their shit into the sea with buckets less than a century ago; that was the gift of mortality, she supposed. The possibility of change.

Miriam found her, eventually, in the hot room. It was a large pool, although shallow, and Rosamund was alone inside, wading at the far end. The steam was thick enough to make the air semiopaque, and it fell around them like a blanket, her figure only faintly visible.

Miriam had entered silently enough that Rosamund didn't react. Her eyes were closed, and she had bent her knees against the tiles, descending into the pool until she was submerged up to her cheekbones. Her hair floated around her in a rust-coloured halo, darkened by the water.

After several minutes of silence, Rosamund, eyes still closed, said, 'It's rude to stare.'

'I'm not certain you should be lecturing me on rudeness, my dear, after that display this morning.'

Rosamund's eyes opened. Her lips quirked. 'I suppose not. You know, the humidity's made your hair frizz.'

Miriam lifted a hand to her hair, patting it curiously.

Rosamund swallowed. 'It's so—*human*, somehow.'

'Do you prefer me that way? Affecting humanity?'

'That's a pointless question. I've seen you for what you are now, and neither of us can pretend otherwise.'

Before Miriam could reply, Rosamund spun around and sank into the water. She made a lazy lap around the edges of the pool. She was naked, and Miriam watched her move with a familiar hunger.

She halted in front of Miriam. 'I did apologise.'

'I'm not certain you meant it.'

'Does it matter if I did? I concede, Miriam.' Rosamund stretched out her arms, bared her throat in invitation. 'The battle is won.'

'The battle, not the war.'

Rosamund shrugged. 'My soul is yours, either way. That's enough, surely.'

Miriam stepped closer to the water. 'I used to think so.'

'But not now?'

'I'm not certain.' Miriam's lips twitched. 'I think you're *hiding* something from me. How novel.'

Rosamund turned away, swam a little further into the pool; Miriam wondered for a moment if she had upset her, but when Rosamund turned back, her expression was perfectly calm.

'Maybe,' she said, '*you* should be afraid of *me*.'

Miriam slipped into the pool. When she stood, she was only semi-submerged, the water lapping at her ribcage. Rosamund watched her, then leaned back against the tiles, exposing her breasts.

Lust curled in Miriam's core. She took a step forwards, her movements slowed by the water. 'I don't feel particularly frightened,' she said.

'That's because you want me—and that's *why* you should be afraid.'

'Oh?'

'I may not be cursed, but there's a reason why all those men wanted to leave me to the wolves.'

'I am not a man.'

'That's true,' Rosamund said. 'But I still have power over you, Miriam Richter. I'm the only person who ever will.'

Miriam finally broached the space between them, sinking into the water so their faces were level. She cupped Rosamund's cheek. Her thumb skimmed across her lips. It was the same face as Cybil's, as Esther's: the same mouth, the same upturned nose.

Why did it feel so different?

Rosamund shivered, despite the warmness of the room. Miriam smiled. 'This won't save you,' she said.

Rosamund smiled back. 'I know that. I don't want to be saved. Not anymore.'

'No?'

'No.' She arched her back, bringing her face towards her. 'I want to be *destroyed*.'

Miriam kissed her. Rosamund moaned, pushed into her, warm and willing. Miriam raised her up, carrying her to the edge of the pool, sitting her on the tiles so that her feet were dangling into the water. Then she stood between her legs and kissed her more, until they were both gasping, all breath and dizzying heat—Rosamund's hand slipping down Miriam's chest, past her stomach, her fingers sinking into soft curls and wet skin.

Miriam felt a sudden conviction that if she had a heart, it would be beating fast enough to feel—that if she breathed, her breath would now be gasps. The warmth of the air around them made it feel as if she were alive, as if she were as flushed as Rosamund was, blood instead of shadows running through her veins. The pleasure of Rosamund's touch was too much, so unbearably powerful in sensation that it was painful. Miriam pushed her hand away.

'Shall I stop?' Rosamund asked, her fingertips pressing into Miriam's side.

Instead of replying, Miriam sank down halfway into the water, so that her head was level with the edge of the pool. Then she gripped Rosamund's knees and spread them apart, trailing kisses up the insides of her thighs. When she tasted her, salt and sweet—her tongue inside her, gentle and searching—Rosamund gasped, tipping her head back. She twisted her fingers in Miriam's hair, hooking her legs over her shoulders. She was so lovely, so willing; it was just as it had been before, just as it always should be. *Mine*, Miriam thought, deliriously, *always mine, she always will be, always has been—finally, finally, mine.*

The air was heavy with steam, the ship rocking beneath them. Rosamund whimpered and begged, but Miriam refused to speed up. There was no urgency to it, no demand. She wanted it to last forever. She wanted to keep Rosamund at the cliff's edge: to allow her to stumble, but never to fall. The longer she had her there, the longer she would be hers entirely, with no thoughts except the pleasure she brought her. Time wouldn't pass; the deal would never come to fruition. She could have her forever.

But Harding denied her, as always. Miriam was a fool to think she wouldn't. Eventually Rosamund cried out, legs convulsing around Miriam's shoulders; then she died again, a little death, a perfect one, as Miriam's hands twisted around her ankles like a pair of chains.

23

'We are losing ourselves,' Esther said, and Cybil and Rosamund said it, too. They were in the many-mirrored corridors of Rosamund's dreaming mind, in which all of them were reflected, and all of them had the same voice.

'It's part of the plan,' Rosamund replied.

'Has time so eroded us?' Cybil asked. 'That two days of her attention might undo our victory?'

Rosamund said, 'Nothing is being undone.'

Cybil said, '*All* is being undone.'

Esther said, 'We love her. We believed we could forget that, but we can't.'

They were silent.

Rosamund pressed her hand to the mirrors, one on her left, one on her right; Cybil, in her golden gown, her drooping-petal ruff, raised her hand simultaneously to meet hers. On the other side, Esther did the same. She was in the green gown she had worn that night in the Dark Walk, pearls still stranded around her throat. Her long, loose hair somehow felt like a mockery of Rosamund's chin-length bob. Rosamund painstakingly curled it every morning, burning her fingers on the iron, holding it in place with chemicals that made her eyes water. She had lived this long, and for what? To prim and pluck herself as she always had, a goose for the table, and hope that Miriam wanted her still?

'We wanted revenge,' Rosamund said. 'To give her hope, so that we could break her as she broke us.'

Esther crossed her arms, raised her head imperiously. A wound on her neck appeared, a weeping line of blood, and she ignored it as it began to swell around the pearls and then drip down onto her dress. 'We *will* break her—we can be sure of that.'

Cybil said, 'The more we delay, the more our resolve wavers. We are weaker than we believed.'

Rosamund replied, 'One day. Surely, we can withstand one day.'

'We must,' Cybil agreed.

'Circle of salt,' Esther said.

'Our soul is hers,' Cybil said.

'The pact complete,' Rosamund said, as the dream fell apart.

The aftermath of tiki night, Rosamund observed, was much like the aftermath of a battle: red leis were strewn across tables like streaks of gore; the tang of pineapple and rum hung on the air, as pervasive as the scent of blood; and the dining area had that off-putting silence of a place suddenly emptied, abrupt absence clear in the tipped-over chairs and the creak of half-fallen lighting fixtures.

As she walked through the restaurant, the mess was being cleaned up and replaced with festive garlands and silver tinsel: it was Christmas Eve, after all. Rosamund had been born around six in the evening— they would dock at seven, only an hour after the twenty-third anniversary of Rosamund's birth. She had little time to prepare.

Walt had tried to eat with her that morning, arranging a birthday breakfast in a private room. She'd had to reject the offer, feigning sickness. Rosamund had other things to do. She had the grimoire in her purse, as well as a precautionary tin of iodised cooking salt, a letter opener, and a tiny bottle of henbane oil that she'd prepared herself the previous spring. It'd have to do. She had selected, for the ritual, a place she knew would be abandoned, and which offered a good vantage point over the rest of the ship: the observation lounge, a plush mahogany-and-emerald room filled with floor-to-ceiling bookshelves. One wall was dedicated to large windows overlooking the Atlantic; the other, a mural depicting the journey of the *Monumental* in stylised waves and ribbons of coastline, England on one side, America on the other. A hand-size mechanical boat had been placed on a rail in front of the mural. It was bobbing gently left to right, from one painted country to another.

It would take only a matter of moments. Rosamund and the shadows were old bedfellows. They were so accustomed to feeding from her that even in this moment of stillness, they began to swarm at her feet in expectation of a meal. Usually, Rosamund gave them only motes of her soul—just enough to achieve what she needed. This time, the deal she made would have a far greater cost.

It was a calculated risk, as calculated as it could be, given the circumstances. Rosamund needed to give the darkness enough of herself that she could surpass Miriam entirely; Miriam, who had collected souls for centuries, who threw them to her fellow shadows like feeding *breadcrumbs* to *ducks*. It was extraordinary, the flippancy with which she wielded such power. But that had always been Miriam's greatest strength, and her greatest weakness: her ruthless vanity. She believed she was unsurpassable. Rosamund would take advantage of that.

Rosamund shut her eyes, felt heat prickle along her hands. The shadows around her whispered questioningly.

I have lived three lives, she told them. *I have lived three lives, and in all three, someone thought I was a monster. Sometimes, I have thought I was a monster. So, then, make me that way. Whatever it costs—make me everything that all those men feared.*

She saw Peter Oswyn in her mind's eye, his horror as she set Harding House ablaze; the fear and fury in Henry Martingale's face as he brought the spade down on her throat; the wrenching sobs of Thomas Harding as the casket on the bed crumbled into dust, his muffled screams as he burnt to ashes. *Every thought they had, everything every Harding patriarch had ever feared, as they laid their First Daughters down in the forest—make me that. Their belief my reality. That is all magic is. Make me a monster. Make me* more *than Miriam— make me darker than shadows.*

A searing heat began at the base of her feet and began to unfurl slowly, burning, relentless, until the pain was intense enough that her throat was closing and tears were building behind her closed lids. Still, she didn't open her eyes. *Darker*, she repeated, *darker, darker*, and in that repetition, her voice in her mind began to ring like a bell: a chime that, with each tone, made the heat hotter, her skin seeming to welt and smoulder. She could smell burning flesh, could feel the flames licking her palms. She stood on a pyre she had built herself, begging for absolution, even as she began to consume herself whole.

Darker, came a voice—many voices, speaking in tandem—and Rosamund began to shudder as she felt a thousand blades slice openings in her flesh, up and down her arms, peeling skin away to sip from her soul. She allowed it, tamping her teeth down on her tongue to prevent herself from screaming, tasting the iron of blood—

The door to the room rattled. Her eyes opened. She'd blocked the door with a chair, but it held only for a moment. The chair was sent flying as Rosamund banished the shadows, tucking the grimoire into the inner pocket of her jacket. The dozens of tiny, glowing fissures on her skin faded and disappeared as quickly as they had come, knitting together like stitched wounds.

Miriam walked inside. She looked at Rosamund, who was still trembling from the lingering pain of the ritual.

'Making deals, my dear?' she asked.

Rosamund's heart pounded. Miriam's eyes were half lidded, her lips twitching—she had seen that expression before. She had seen it as Esther, moments before the knife had met her throat.

Behind them, the waves of the Atlantic roiled.

Miriam walked slowly toward Rosamund, trailing a hand across the back of one of the chairs. 'I *knew* you hadn't given up,' she said. 'It isn't in your nature, darling, to surrender willingly.'

'Much good it has done me,' Rosamund replied, affecting bitterness.

'It didn't work? The darkness didn't take pity on you?' She cocked her head. 'Your soul seems—different. Fainter.'

'I gave it all I could. It wasn't enough.'

It was almost true. In the aftermath of the ritual, Rosamund felt *emptier*, somehow, as if the world had lost some of its colour. Perhaps, if Miriam hadn't interrupted, the darkness might have destroyed her before it could give her the power she craved.

Miriam swooped forward, taking Rosamund's chin between her fingers. She examined her face with narrowed eyes—searching for some hint of a lie.

Rosamund glared at her, defiant. Some of the tears that had welled during the pain of the ritual spilled over and dripped down her cheeks. There couldn't have been a better moment for it; the suspicion fell from Miriam's face. Instead, she now looked as if she wanted to sip those tears like fine wine. The way she brushed them away from Rosamund's cheeks was worshipful, and the way she kissed her even more so—it was as gentle a kiss as they had ever shared.

'You are beautiful, in your desperation,' Miriam murmured. 'Like a dying star.'

Rosamund blinked; more tears spilled. She realised then, that the crying wasn't a ruse, and she pulled herself out of Miriam's grasp, bowing her head to hide herself.

'You needn't be ashamed,' Miriam said.

'Of course I'm ashamed,' Rosamund returned, wishing she was still lying, wishing Miriam would leave her alone, wishing she would stay with her forever. 'You think I want to live like this? Playing a lover scorned? You've been my greatest obsession, my greatest regret, ever since I could remember what you did to me. Rosamund Harding is your echo, Miriam Richter. My entire life is an aftermath.'

Miriam eyed her curiously. 'Maybe Esther was blessed to live in ignorance.'

'Maybe she was. I wish, sometimes, that I didn't remember either.' Rosamund took a step back from Miriam. 'But that's the thing—even if I didn't remember, it wouldn't matter. I'm like water twice boiled, Miriam. *Almost* right, but something will always be a little off.'

Miriam frowned. Then she stepped forward and hugged her.

Rosamund froze in her arms. Next to them, the mechanical boat continued to move blithely from side to side, gears turning.

'Three lives, and I am still as alone as the first,' Rosamund said.

'You aren't alone,' Miriam replied, and Rosamund made a broken noise, sagging against her.

'I know,' she whispered. 'But I will be, soon enough.'

Rosamund pulled away. She looked up at Miriam's face—that terribly familiar face, the only constant in centuries of loneliness and shame—and she wondered whether, in a fourth lifetime, she might've learnt to forgive her. She would never know.

'Let's go to bed,' she said. 'For the last time.'

'For the last time,' Miriam agreed—and there was something in her voice that almost sounded like regret.

It was four in the afternoon, and the sun was already setting. Ice limned the porthole, and the sky—the same deep blue of the ocean beneath it—was clear of all clouds. The last, fading light refracted through that ice, making a prism of colour on Rosamund's cheek. She had fallen asleep after their exertions. Her red hair, spread wildly across the pillow, crowned her with a halo of flame.

The first-class cabin the Jennings were travelling in was just as opulent as Thomas's townhouse, as the vaulted ceilings of Harding Hall. Luxury had surrounded Harding for all her lives, and yet— ill-starred as she was—those lives had been unhappy ones. Miriam knew she was largely to blame for that. Each rebirth was supposed to provide a new opportunity, but they only seemed to compound the problems of the last.

Maybe Miriam was providing some recompense, then, in her inevitable end.

There was movement in the corner of the room. A mass of shadows, amorphous in shape, was watching her from the wall. As she observed them, they shrank a little toward the floor.

She is mine, she told them—and instead of cowering further, they rose up towards the ceiling, defiant, in the shape of a crow far larger than Miriam had ever been.

Hissing in anger, Miriam slid from the bed, careful not to jog Rosamund. *You dare resist me?* she asked the darkness. *I, who feed you from my own hand?*

The shadow-crow spread its wings, feathers squirming as if each were its own insectile creature crawling along the wall.

Where was this defiance coming from? This boldness, this discontent? It was as if the shadows' loyalty had shifted, somehow—as if their fear of Miriam no longer moved them.

Frowning, Miriam glanced to the bed, and then back to the darkness.

She recalled, just a few hours ago, how tears had run down Rosamund's face in the wake of her failed ritual. Was it truly *failed*, after all? This new Harding may have been different in some ways—in her scarlet smile and the sea changes of her moods, the gold gleam of her soul reflecting in her eyes—but she was still a Harding. She remained, fundamentally, the woman who had set the Hall alight, who had burnt Thomas's corpse to ashes. The woman who had killed herself rather than have Miriam take her soul—and yet who now refused the same fate when offered the knife.

Miriam bent over the bed, considering. Rosamund was having a dream—her eyelids were fluttering, and soul-light was gathering in the hollows of her collarbones. Miriam pressed her finger to this light, and when she pulled back, a faint glimmer remained, lingering, on her own skin.

Miriam presented her finger to the shadows on the wall.

You want this, she asked them. *Don't you?*

The darkness trembled.

Our deal is soon complete. You love her—I can tell. I love her, also. But she is mine. For centuries, she has been.

Miriam stretched her hand outwards. The shadows swarmed forward—at the last moment, she pulled back, placing her finger upon her own lips, flicking out her tongue for a taste. There was nothing there, of course—she could not truly consume Rosamund's soul unless a deal was completed—but the theatre made the shadows writhe as if in pain.

If she betrays me, Miriam said, *if you betray me, you will have none of her soul to feed upon. I will complete our deal and keep her light to myself, buried within me, for the rest of my existence. If you are loyal, it will be different. Do you understand?*

The shadows hesitated, flickering—Miriam wondered if this was truly the first moment, in her centuries of life, that the darkness would refuse her.

But it did not. Slowly, it slipped from the wall to the floor, gathering around the jacket Miriam had pulled from Rosamund's shoulders as they'd entered. Miriam went to pick it up and noticed a heaviness in the lining. Something was concealed there.

It was the grimoire.

A bookmark in the shape of a filigreed leaf had been pressed between its pages. Miriam opened it to the correct page.

To weakene a dymon, it read. *Within the lighte of daye, but beneathe clouds so no shadow is cast, surrounde the creature or those possessed wythyn a circle of salte, or water that runs…*

Circle of salt. Water that runs.

Outside, the Atlantic rumbled with the beginnings of a storm.

Miriam dropped the book to the floor. It fell with the decisive heaviness of a guillotine blade, the leather striking the wood with a dark thump. *You have already won,* Miriam had said to her, when they'd met two days ago—and Rosamund had replied, *Yes, I suppose I have.* Her sudden reappearance on the *Monumental*; the strange ritual Miriam had caught her in; and now the grimoire, somehow risen from its grave. She should have suspected earlier. Miriam had known the risks when she came on the ship, but then Rosamund had batted her lashes and—like a lovelorn idiot—Miriam had chosen to trust in her surrender. In return, she had been betrayed.

On the bed, Rosamund stirred. Miriam looked at her. Asleep, her face was naïve and placid, mouth slack and head lolling on the pillow. She was beautiful. Her eyelids fluttered with dreams.

It was unlikely that this plan of hers would *work*, of course. Miriam could simply try to fly to shore; they were close enough. It would be incredibly painful, but it may still be possible, if she waited until the land was visible.

But she didn't want to leave. Miriam was furious. Miriam wanted *justice*.

There was a letter opener on the dressing table, and a collection of hairpins with sharp ends. The curtains of the porthole had long pulls, rope as thick as Rosamund's wrists. The bath was deep enough to drown in. Miriam didn't need any of it, regardless. Her own hands had snapped enough necks.

She approached the bed.

Rosamund sighed and turned in her sleep. Her throat was exposed, as was the pulse beneath it.

Miriam's fingers met Rosamund's neck, so gently she didn't even stir. She was warm. Her skin was soft. It would be so easy. So simple.

But she couldn't do it.

She left the room.

Miriam went to the promenade. It was a cold day, blisteringly so—she could infer this from the lack of people outside, and the way that the single person present was bundled in a coat and scarf. She didn't feel the cold—she never had—but sometimes rage felt to Miriam as she imagined ice felt to a human, the freeze-and-burn contradiction of it, the way it sat in her stomach and made her limbs go tense and shaky.

Salt, water, clouds.

Perhaps Miriam *had* known, all along. She'd said it to Rosamund herself in the baths—*I think you're hiding something from me.* But she had ignored her own doubts, remained in wilful ignorance, just because of her fondness for a woman who was destined to die. She wouldn't make the same mistake again.

Miriam walked to the railing, curling her hands around the iron bars. She squeezed until the metal groaned and began to buckle. There were few shadows here, midday with the sun directly ahead, nothing to cast darkness except the ship itself—still, what few were present began to flinch away, anticipating her anger.

The other person on the promenade approached her, holding something glinting in their hands. Miriam turned violently, expecting to defend herself. But it was just a cigarette case, monogrammed with a gold *W.J.*

'Want a smoke?' asked Walter Jennings.

'*What?*' Miriam ground out, voice like an iron nail scraping glass, and it was testament to either his bravery or his foolhardiness that Walter stood his ground.

'A smoke,' he repeated. 'No offence, miss, but you kind of look like you could use it.'

Miriam's fury flared. She took a step toward him, teeth bared. 'What *is* it about you, Walter Jennings,' she snarled, 'that draws her affection? It can't be your intellect—or attraction. Is it companionship, then? I offered her that, many times, and she always rejected me, in the end.'

He took a step back from her, startled. 'I—well—wait. Are you talking about Rosie?'

'Rosie,' Miriam echoed derisively, and she surged forward to wrap a hand around his elbow. 'Once she was feared, you know. Once her family's name was spoken with terror and reverence. But then the Hall burnt, and they became *domesticated*. I won't let the same thing happen to me. Cybil was right.'

He blinked at her. 'Who's Cybil?'

Miriam ignored the question. 'It's the frog and the scorpion, just as she said. Some things are monsters by nature. I've been playacting humanity for her, but it's time I stopped.'

'Let me go,' Walter said, and his voice was wavering, his eyes wide. He'd realised that Miriam was more than she seemed, but it was too late.

'Is this what you wanted, Rosamund?' Miriam said to the shadows, bidding them to pass the message on: and her voice was a cacophony, discordant, shrieking like the gulls that flew above them, roaring like the waves of the Atlantic, groaning like the iron of the *Monumental*'s hull. 'You wanted retribution, didn't you? You wanted me to be the demon, dragging you to hell. You wanted to hurt *me* the way I've hurt *you*. I'm sure you'd appreciate something new to avenge.'

'Don't—' Walter said.

'Then here it is,' Miriam said, and she threw him over the side of the ship.

It took only an instant. Her strength was such that Walt plummeted toward the water like a cannonball. The Atlantic rose to meet him, and he disappeared beneath the waves. He didn't even have time to scream—and besides, if he had screamed, the wailing of the wind would have drowned it out. Miriam could have been merciful, and sent the darkness after him, to grant him a quick death. She didn't. She would let him drown.

Miriam stretched out her arms and bid the shadows to her. They came without complaint, seething around her shoulders, draping themselves across her hands.

'Come find me, darling,' she said. 'It's been so long since we last danced.'

24

You wanted retribution—

You wanted me to be the demon, dragging you to hell—

Rosamund was in her silk dressing gown—shell-pink, bias-cut, feather-edged—barefoot, disoriented, her tiny bottle of henbane oil clutched in one fist. She stumbled out of her cabin and into the corridor. She could hear Miriam's voice in her mind, over and over; could feel the press of shadows around her, pulling her forward. Her vision was doubled, the narrow plum-carpeted hallways of the *Monumental* interposed with the dark wood of Thomas's townhouse, the tapestried walls of Harding Hall. On either side of her, she saw mirrors: Cybil's face, Esther's face, reflected back to her, blood dripping from their throats. The air was thick with the scent of wilting roses, the tang of iron.

She knew this was magic, knew this was Miriam's influence, but the onslaught was too strong to resist. Rosamund allowed the shadows to tug her forward. Behind one door, leading to some other cabin, she heard a woman screaming. Rosamund stumbled and stopped, feeling her eyes well with tears.

'Mother?' she said, pressing herself to the door—but the screaming went silent as abruptly as it had begun, and when she tried the handle, the door was locked.

Around the corner, a male figure was watching her. *Isaac*, she thought, and she ran forward, reaching for him. She wanted to tell him she was sorry, she had since the moment she'd remembered him;

sorry for her coldness as Esther, her cruelty to him. She'd spent her life pushing him away because of a curse that didn't exist. He'd needed her, and she hadn't been there for him.

'Isaac, I'm sorry,' she said, rounding the corner. But no one was there.

At the end of this corridor was an iron door, leading to the promenade. A Miriam-shaped shadow stood in front of it, watching her.

Rosamund drew in a ragged breath. She'd started crying at some point—she didn't know when. 'Please,' she pleaded, 'if you love me, stop this.'

The shadow laughed, cruel and cold, and then it disappeared.

There was nowhere to go but forward. Rosamund lurched toward the door. When she opened it, she found herself in an orchard.

The deck of the ship was gone. The ground was soft beneath her feet, damp soil and wet grass. It was raining, but the rain didn't touch her, instead making a halo around her as it dissipated inches from her skin. The air smelt like fermenting apples and rotting leaves. In the distance, there stood the towering lead and brick and glass of a familiar building, and Rosamund almost cried out in shock at seeing it again.

Miriam was standing behind her. She curled an arm around her waist, keeping her in place, and tucked Rosamund's hair behind her ear. 'Welcome home.'

'Why are we here?' Rosamund asked, staring in horror at Harding Hall.

'I found the grimoire, darling. I thought a reminder was in order: what happens to those who refuse me. The shadows obliged. They betrayed you. Fear is stronger than love, in the end.'

Rosamund flinched. Miriam's arm remained in place, unmoving as iron. 'I don't want to be here. I don't want to see this place.'

'Poor thing,' Miriam said. 'Does it hurt to remember? You were always so *raw* as Cybil, you know. You burnt so fiercely. No wonder things caught fire.'

'I was sheltered,' Rosamund said, voice trembling. 'Naïve.'

'Do you blame yourself for what happened?'

'A little. Not much. What happened to Cybil... no one deserves that.'

'Do you blame me?'

Rosamund laughed, choked. 'What do you think?'

Miriam kissed her throat. Rosamund let her do it.

'What did you do, Miriam?' she asked. 'I heard you call to me, just a few minutes ago—you said that you'd give me something new to avenge.'

Miriam spun Rosamund in her arms, so they were face-to-face. 'Do you remember the song you used to sing?' she said, pressing her fingers into Rosamund's cheek. 'When you were Cybil?'

It was clear she wouldn't give an answer to the question, clear that she was furious—Rosamund could see that in the coldness of her smile, feel it in the tightness of her grip. Miriam was capable of killing her, she'd done it once before, and Rosamund knew they were only moments away from the same thing happening again. But she was too unravelled, too confused to take hold of her power and escape the illusion.

Rosamund, trying to hide the tremble in her voice, replied, '"Greensleeves".'

'Yes, that was it. A song of love lost, and love returning.'

'I've never been a good singer.'

Miriam laughed indulgently. 'Not particularly. But I heard you singing, you know, even before we met that night in the clearing. I heard how fiercely you longed for freedom. You needed me then, my dear. You needed me as Esther, too; and still, you need me now.'

Rosamund couldn't reply. She closed her eyes, unable to look at her.

'*Alas, my love, you do me wrong,*' Miriam sang softly, '*to cast me off discourteously.*'

The sound of the rain fell away. It was replaced with the soft hum of dozens of distant voices. String instruments picked up the melody as Miriam's voice faded. Rosamund opened her eyes to find that they were standing on the balcony of Carroway House. The night sky stretched above them, the sounds of the Ton drifting through the building's closed doors. Despite the absence of rain, there was no change in the temperature of the air; it was like being on a movie screen, noises and shapes without presence.

'Trite,' Rosamund said. 'They weren't playing "Greensleeves" at the ball.'

'Forgive me my inaccuracies, darling. I find myself distracted.'

Rosamund glanced at the house and shuddered. 'We should've stayed at Harding Hall.'

'Why?'

'This is the moment I hated you the most,' she said. 'When I knew I could never forgive you.'

Miriam released her, stepping back. Something glinted in her hand: the oyster knife.

Rosamund's eyes widened, her pulse speeding. 'Don't.'

Smiling, Miriam raised the knife, holding the blade between thumb and forefinger. It glinted in the light of the false stars above them. 'We have both killed with this,' she said. 'We are alike, you and I.'

'We are nothing alike.'

'We both know that isn't true.'

'And that is *your fault*!' Rosamund cried. 'It's *all* your fault, Miriam. I was human, once. And now you've made me—made me into this creature, this monster, thinking only of you, your destruction, your love.'

'It was Christopher Harding who made you, darling. Him, your mother, your cousin, yourself—all those who believed in the curse, who taught you to believe in it, who moulded your darkness in their image.'

'That doesn't matter. It was you who forced me to live three lives, to drown in my loneliness three times over. You *killed* me.'

'And you brought me to life!' Miriam shrieked back, voice rending the air with her fury. 'Before you, Rosamund Harding, I had never known love, and I had never known regret. Now you have wounded me with these things, you have made me fallible. I will never forgive you for that, just as you will never forgive me.'

Rosamund closed her eyes once more, balling her fists. She felt the presence of the shadows all around her, dancing themselves into the shape of Carroway House, into the unearthly glow of the stars above them, all at Miriam's command. Rosamund needed to command them instead.

Enough, she told them, offering a piece of her soul, small and bright and burning. *Enough*.

A sharp pain pierced through her core, as savage as any deal she had made so far. The music of the fake ball stuttered, then stopped.

Rosamund opened her eyes. Around them, the horizon and the sky and Carroway House were beginning to drip downwards, like paint beneath turpentine.

Miriam looked alarmed. 'What are you doing?'

'Three lives a witch, Miriam,' Rosamund told her, voice straining with effort. 'Three souls to sell, and centuries of fear to make reality. I didn't waste this life, you know, on dancing and tapestries. You might be the same as you always were, but I've grown stronger. I've made many more deals while you were away.'

Reaching for the shadows, Miriam commanded, 'Come to me.' In her palm, she offered a piece of some ill-gotten soul—the darkness seethed over it eagerly. For a moment, the vision of Carroway House wavered, and then it began to strengthen. The music resumed; the stars roared back to life.

Rosamund gritted her teeth and pushed through the pain, carving another piece from herself, coaxing the shadows back to her.

The music stopped again.

'Enough of this,' Miriam said. 'What—'

'I'll only ask once more. What did you *do*, Miriam, before you called me here? Why did you say I'd have something new to avenge?'

Miriam paused, then grinned at her.

'Avenge him,' she said. 'Why not? It hardly matters now. See if your anger will give this new life meaning, in the hours you have left.'

'Who?' Rosamund replied, and then she realised.

'I fed him to the Atlantic,' Miriam said. 'He went quietly, too. I didn't give him enough time to scream.'

Rosamund should have expected it. Because she *was* cursed, after all—that curse stood in front of her, smiling grimly, satisfied that she had taken her due.

That didn't make it hurt any less. That didn't make her throat loosen or her tears dry; and it didn't douse the burning coal of anger that tumbled into the base of her belly, that set her alight from the inside out.

'I'll *kill* you,' Rosamund snarled.

'Oh, sweetheart. If you strike a match, you shouldn't be surprised when it catches fire. But you can try, if you'd like.'

Miriam offered her the oyster knife. Rosamund took it from her. And, for a moment, she had the urge to slit her *own* throat; to deny Miriam one more time. Another life, another soul—why limit herself? Why not stay this way forever, live ceaseless lives of mortal drudgery, watching those who loved her be destroyed? Too many memories, too many broken hearts, and any woman would become incapable of feeling. Someday, eventually, Rosamund would stop caring about what Miriam Richter had done to her, and she would finally be at peace.

But she felt the phantom flames of the ritual she'd performed, still licking at her heels; she could feel the fear of all those who'd hated her writhing beneath her skin. Rosamund would use that fear like kindling, set herself alight with it. She had a plan. She would see it through.

Stepping forward, she pulled Miriam in for a kiss. As her teeth sank into her bottom lip, she plunged the oyster knife into Miriam's chest.

Miriam allowed the kiss to continue for a moment longer, then pulled away. She glanced down at the knife embedded in her skin and smirked. 'Did that make you feel better?'

'No,' Rosamund said. 'But this will.'

Then she tore off a piece of her soul that was so great, so funda-mental, that she screamed and shattered at the pain, unmade, red-hot as a poker in the fire—but it was enough. Of course it was enough. It was more than anything she had ever given before, and more than anything Miriam could ever give. The shadows bowed to her entirely; they fell over her, grateful, loving, and Rosamund disappeared.

She had always been lonely.

Rosamund had *made* herself lonely, across centuries, across life-times. She had made herself lonely because of the curse, but the curse hadn't been real; and that wouldn't have mattered, anyway. All of her relationships had been brief and fragile. There had only ever been one person who didn't abandon her—and that person wasn't a person at all.

Shadows are fickle, and they leave at the hint of light. But they return, always. They are the only thing that will never leave you. There was no Harding without Richter: she had accepted that the first time she died. Without Miriam, she would have lived an entire life as Cybil, miserable and isolated. She would have made that cavern-ous Hall a coffin to bury herself in. She would have never known the power she could wield.

Sometimes, Rosamund was relieved to be spared such a fate.

Sometimes, she wanted it so badly she could barely breathe.

Once, she had thought that to be human meant to love and be loved. Her curse, real or no, had prevented those things, and so prevented her humanity in turn. But now Rosamund knew that *feeling* wasn't human, not inherently—Miriam had proven that. Although that swirling darkness in Miriam's heart had once seemed an emptiness, a void, three lifetimes had shown otherwise. Miriam wasn't human, but she grieved, she exulted, she angered. She *had* a soul, just as Rosamund did. A soul of a different kind, maybe, but a soul still.

To be human: it was an impossible dream, and one Rosamund had finally had to discard. She had lived three lives, none of them happy. Like a gambler down on their luck, she was sometimes tempted to throw the dice again, to end this life and start a new one; hoping beyond hope that this time she'd find something in her own mortality that would make it all worthwhile. But Rosamund knew her life as a human was a losing game. If she wanted to be free, truly free, to love as she wished—to *burn* as she wished, to look at the world with defi-ance, not surrender—she needed to change the rules.

My soul will be yours, Cybil had once said.

All magic was exchange, after all.

25

There was a storm brewing over the Atlantic.

One hour until sunset, and all the passengers of the RMS *Monumental* had been sequestered in their cabins in anticipation of the rough weather. The sky had gone grey, a half darkness falling like an uncertain nightfall. The wind wasn't howling, not yet, but it was in the dangerous moment of susurrus that heralded a tempest: the windowpanes trembled in their moorings, the chandeliers quaking a soft, occasional chime. The silence that had fallen meant that Miriam could hear each of her footsteps against the carpeting with absolute clarity: the plush, almost flesh-like squish of her dress shoes as she crept between empty tables and up abandoned staircases. In the bar, a phonograph had been left to play a soft piano piece, the jolting of the ship punctuating the music with an occasional harsh crackle. The water in the Turkish baths quivered with the groaning of the hull. In the observation lounge, the tiny mechanical ship was blissful and untroubled in its journey, cogs turning, the sky of the mural unflaggingly blue. Miriam paused to observe it for a moment, then pulled the tiny ship out of its mechanism entirely, tossing it over her shoulder.

Their deal was almost up, and Miriam couldn't find Rosamund at all. She'd disappeared in an instant as brief as a blink. Miriam was sure she wasn't dead—she couldn't be; Miriam would *know*—and so she must have travelled somewhere, stepping through the darkness as Miriam herself often did. A final moment of stubborn defiance, a final display of power. Miriam admired it as much as it made her furious.

She turned to the shadows. *Bring her to me*, she told them, but they faded only partially before returning without result: they couldn't decide which master they served. And the wind, that *infernal* wind, kept battering the side of the ship like fists on a drum, mocking her failure.

Miriam was starting to believe that Rosamund had left the ship entirely. Maybe she had transported herself back to England, or straight to New York. It was no use, of course—the deal would complete either way, Rosamund's soul tearing free from her body, flying like a shooting star across the Atlantic so that Miriam could consume it. But the thought of such an outcome gave Miriam no pleasure. She wanted to hold Rosamund in her arms as her light left her, to give her empty shell the mercy of a death. Why would Rosamund deny her that? Was she truly so petty as to remain a walking corpse?

Miriam returned to the Jennings' cabin. It was empty, of course; as was the promenade, the metal grille beneath her like a spiderweb of steel. The only one caught there was her. To her left, the sea roiled, water made ink dark by the clouds.

Frustrated, convinced that Rosamund was gone, Miriam stepped forward, intending to emerge at the port of Southampton.

Her foot came down on metal. The *Monumental* groaned with the force of it, and when she lifted her shoe, she'd stepped so hard that she'd dented the steel.

Miriam tried again. Nothing happened.

Mystified, she turned to the ocean, frowning. The ship juddered over a wave, misting her with spray. She licked her lips.

Salt.

Miriam threw her head back and laughed. *Circle of salt, water that runs.* She'd known this was a possibility, hadn't she? Rosamund had believed the water would contain her, and she was right. Unless she attempted the painful flight to shore, Miriam was stuck until the ship made port. Rosamund would turn twenty-three before then, of course—and the deal would be complete—but Miriam had to admire her gumption.

The *Monumental* rocked. In the distance came a thunderous boom, the howl of thunder as it snapped at lightning's heels.
Miriam raised her head to watch the storm, and then noticed—far
above her—the iron monolith of the crow's nest, teetering dangerously with the swaying of the ship. A figure stood in the window,
watching her.

Miriam grinned and grew wings.

She took flight. As she ascended, the wind buffeted her, the storm
picking up speed. Miriam landed on the sill of the window, digging
her talons into the metal. Rosamund was leaning against the wall on
the opposite side, watching her with an inscrutable expression. She
was still dressed in nothing but her feather-edged silk dressing gown.
Her cheeks were flushed red with cold. On the back of her hands,
eye-shaped slits glowed so brightly with soul-light, it was as if she was
studded with stars.

The crow's nest was nothing but a steel box, all four sides half open
to make space for the windows, which were all broken. Shards of
glass littered the floor in front of them. Miriam didn't know whether
the storm or Rosamund had done that.

'Hello, Little Shadow,' Rosamund said. 'You took your time.'

Miriam became a woman again and crawled inside. 'I've been
looking for you.'

'I know.'

'Circle of salt,' Miriam said. 'Very clever.'

'Thank you.'

'Where do you intend this to lead, my dear?'

Rosamund shook her head. 'You killed Walter,' she said, ignoring
the question.

'My love for you is violent, Rosamund,' Miriam told her, with
straining patience—was this truly such a revelation? 'My love for you
is furious and hungry. If it were otherwise, we wouldn't be here now.
You would be a skeleton under Suffolk dirt.'

'Your love for me is a lightning rod,' Rosamund returned. 'I am
sick of the storm.'

Miriam swept her arm out, gesturing to the sky. 'Then why have
you done this?'

'Clouds without shadow: no light, no darkness.'

'Just us,' Miriam said.

'Just us,' Rosamund agreed.

'You can't kill me.'

'I don't intend to.'

'The pact is soon complete.' Miriam stepped closer to her; Rosamund stood her ground. 'You can feel it, can't you? The way your soul sings for me. It will leave you soon.'

Rosamund said, with grim resignation, 'I know.'

Lightning flashed again. The thunder, this time, was so loud it took hold of the crow's nest and shook it like a petulant child.

Miriam smiled. 'This reminds me of the fete. Do you remember?'

'Yes. Why did you always call for storms, even though they weaken the darkness?'

'I told you the first time we met: storms suit you, my dear. You are always most beautiful with a little fear in your face.'

Rosamund's lip curled in fury, gold eyes sparking like embers. Her fingers twitched, and the *Monumental* suddenly pitched upwards at an acute angle. It hit a wave prow first, a wall of water slamming down on the deck like a hammer hitting a nail.

Miriam felt a moment of unease. 'Temper, darling.'

'You've underestimated me,' Rosamund said, and there was triumph in her voice now: a promise Miriam could not decipher.

'Maybe so.'

'My entire life, I've been alone.' She breached the space between them, and then—to Miriam's shock—she wound her arms around her neck. The look Rosamund gave her then was as fond as it was furious, as loving as it was hateful. It was Cybil in the orchard, Esther beneath her on the bed, it was every storm they'd ever stood in and every kiss they'd ever shared. 'Until *you* came. You're the only one who's ever understood me, I think.'

Miriam pressed a hand to Rosamund's neck, feeling the heartbeat she had ended and begun; wondering what it would be to hear silence instead. 'And you me.'

'I'm grateful that I met you,' Rosamund said. 'My blessing, my curse. I love you, Miriam. I always will.'

'Me, too,' Miriam echoed, confused, unable to resist as Rosamund pulled her in for a kiss. It was sweet, soft, the sort of kiss that promised something they'd never had: something without transaction, without deadline. And when Rosamund pulled away, her expression was entirely without hostility, mouth curved slightly, eyes half lidded.

'I love you,' Rosamund said. 'That's why this must end.'

Then she lunged sideways and threw herself out of the crow's nest.

Miriam screamed. Miriam had never screamed before: the sound was unlike anything she had ever heard, like someone was ripping the air apart, a vacuum of noise simultaneously silent and cacophonous. And then, as the scream itself died—replaced by another crack of thunder—she saw a bird fly down towards the promenade.

Miriam, enraged, leapt after her.

A hawk sliced through the air, golden-eyed, glowing with light. A crow followed it. Above them, the clouds swirled with the wind, lightning arcing toward the ship. The wind was roaring, buffeting them with such force that it took all of Miriam's concentration just to stay airborne; it felt as if the shadows that formed her feathers would be torn away from her. All she could focus on was the brightness in front of her, the meteoric glow of Rosamund as she carved a path across the storm-grey sky.

She didn't know how Rosamund was maintaining this form. The power it would take was immense; the amount of soul she was feeding the darkness beyond anything she'd ever attempted before. The pain must have been unimaginable, but Rosamund didn't seem much affected, her flight as elegant as if she had been born to the air, dancing between gusts of wind and furious fistfuls of rain. She swooped around the mast in a tight circle, and Miriam trailed behind her. Rosamund plummeted down toward the deck—for a moment, Miriam wondered if she had remembered she *wasn't* a bird, after all—but then she went insubstantial, falling through the iron grating. When Miriam did the same, she found herself following Rosamund's flitting form through the coal-hot hollow of the ship's underbelly. Men shovelled fuel into furnaces, slick with sweat: they didn't notice the shadows and sparks that darted between them, as Miriam snapped at Rosamund with talon and beak, dodging plumes of steam and the heavy swing of metal mallets. The sound of the workers was extraordinary—yelling and hammering and the roar of flames—but Miriam could still hear, between it all, the fluttering of Rosamund's wings.

They passed from one side of the ship to the other, through steel beams and solid walls, until they were once again up in the open air, in the rolls of thunder and the stark white flashes of the lightning. Rosamund went faster, higher, and Miriam did the same, until the wind was almost too strong to counter, and the *Monumental* was only a speck beneath them, surrounded by the cracked-glass edges of storm-swollen waves.

Then Rosamund plunged down again, passing Miriam by mere inches. And as Miriam followed, glorying in the chase, she realised she never wanted this to end. If she caught Rosamund, maybe she would kill her. Why not? Why not keep the deal indefinitely, see how often Harding could be reborn? That way, Miriam would never lose her. They could stay like this forever: Harding and Richter, shadows and storm, pulling each other towards their own destruction.

They fell together, wings tucked into their bodies. The wind wailed, partly frozen rain tearing through feathers and talons. The light around Rosamund shifted and warped, until she had changed into a woman again, her hair rippling around her head like a crown of flames, her skin luminous. Miriam did the same, swallowing her own beak, folding her wings into her torso, growing arms so that she could reach out a hand for her. Rosamund took it, pulling her closer as they plunged.

Miriam looked down, and saw they were heading toward the water.

'Shadows don't sink,' she said into Rosamund's ear.

'No, they don't,' Rosamund agreed. 'But maybe they can drown.'

They hit the Atlantic, breaking the surface with enough force it would have shattered the bones of anyone else—but they were *just* immaterial enough that they sank without true impact. Rosamund's hand slipped out of hers, and the sea sucked her downwards, leaving Miriam floating unmoored in the half-frozen water.

The darkness here was entire, so deep and impenetrable that even Miriam could see nothing. Salt stung her eyes and clawed at her skin, the shadows inside her writhing in revulsion. Miriam revelled in the pain, rare as it was to her. How far had they sunk? When she looked up, she could see a faint glimmer of grey—the fading light of the sky—but to her sides and below, there was only a void.

She reached out with her mind. *Rosamund?*

I'm here.

When Miriam tried to see her, there was nothing. She focused more, tried to find the light of her soul. Still, there was only darkness.

Miriam spun in the water. *Where are you?*

What's the difference between love and hatred? Rosamund asked, her voice echoing, everywhere and nowhere.

There isn't one.

They can coexist, yes, Rosamund said. *I know that without doubt. But there's a difference.*

And what is that?

There were hands on hers then, a mouth against her neck. *Love takes. It makes you* want, *makes you* need, *empties you out until there is nothing left but the love itself.*

And hatred?

Hatred is a gift, Miriam. It gives you the strength you need to survive.

Then Rosamund was pulling her up, up out of the water, up toward the sky. And they were birds again, flying without aim or reason, spinning in a dance around the ship as it continued to cleave the waves. There was ice in the air, frozen salt tossed up from the sea: never before had Miriam flown for so long, so fast, nor had she needed to expend so much power just to stay aloft. The shadows were reluctant, drawn to Rosamund's light even as they answered Miriam's orders. And it was only as Rosamund started flying higher again, preparing for another fall, that Miriam finally realised what was happening. Rosamund was trying to tire her out.

Miriam *was* tired, now she thought of it. She could feel the strain of commanding the shadows in her limbs, her hollow chest. She had consumed several souls before coming onto the ship, but that had been days ago, of course, and now she had expended so much magic in the chase—her reserves had their limits. She and Rosamund were competing: to see which of them could keep themselves flying for the longest, immaterial for the longest, before they ran out of power to feed the darkness. Once, Miriam would've been confident in her victory. But Rosamund had three souls within her, three souls greater even when separated than any others Miriam had ever seen. Despite the price Rosamund had already paid, she still burnt so fiercely that Miriam wondered if this was a fight she would lose.

But she couldn't bring herself to end the chase, not when there was something so brutally joyous about it, the wind and the water and Rosamund flying before her. She thought of the girl in the forest with mud on her face, and wondered what she would say to see her ascension. Miriam hoped that Harding understood just how far she'd come. She hoped that she was proud.

So, Miriam flew until she felt the shadows start to give way. She flew until she was entirely material again, until she fell to the deck of the ship on her knees, vision swimming. Rosamund alighted beside her, a woman now as much as Miriam was; Miriam craned her head to look up at her.

'You win,' Miriam said. 'Much joy should it give you. The pact is still nearly complete.'

Rosamund smiled tightly. 'Yes, it is,' she replied. She offered Miriam a hand, helping her stand.

'You fly well,' Miriam told her, vision swimming.

'As do you.' Rosamund stepped closer, cupped her cheek with her palm. 'Will you miss me, once I'm gone?'

'Of course. I've told you I will.'

'But you won't spare me.'

'I can't,' Miriam said. There was a gnawing inside her belly: the pact begging its due. She was hungry. She had waited centuries for this.

Rosamund's palm slid downward, towards Miriam's chest. She rested her fingers in the hollow of her throat, pressing the heel of her hand into her sternum. 'Whoever made you, they made you empty. That's why you aren't human; why you're a shadow.'

'Yes.'

'But you *do* have a soul, Miriam,' Rosamund said, with the gentle tone of someone instructing a child. 'Everyone does. You wouldn't love me if you didn't. You wouldn't feel anything at all.'

'No,' Miriam said, automatically. She had made her assumptions, when she was born, and to reconsider them *now* seemed ludicrous. What need did she have of something so human? 'I am a shadow, I am soulless; that is how my creators made me.'

Rosamund shook her head. 'I don't think so. I think you have a soul made of darkness, instead of light. That's why you are so hungry for light in the first place: you need it to cast the shadow your soul is made of.'

Souls were a weakness, the distinction between prey and predator—something to be reaped, to be consumed. There was something revolting, something unnatural, about the idea that she could have one of her own. 'No,' she said again, even as the idea took root, insidious and somehow *feasible*, despite it all. 'No, it can't be. It—it can't.'

'Just because you believe you're a monster doesn't make you one.'

'Why does it matter?'

'It matters,' Rosamund said, 'because it's what will save me.'

Miriam's eyes narrowed. She tried to take a step back—she couldn't. When she looked down, she saw a thin line of sea salt surrounding her feet. 'How...'

'The wind drew it for me, while we were flying. This is *my* storm, Miriam, not yours.'

'What—what are you doing?'

'It's a ritual,' Rosamund said. 'One that poor Thomas Harding wanted to attempt, all those years ago, before you reduced his wife to dust. I needed to empower myself for it—I had to give so much of myself away—but it should work. It has to work.'

Miriam said, both incredulous and pleading, 'You can't undo the pact. It's impossible.'

'I don't intend to,' Rosamund replied. And then she began to glow.

A strange, tearing sensation started in Miriam's chest. She tried to flinch away, but all her power was spent. She could no longer become immaterial, no longer step into the darkness.

'Rosamund,' Miriam gasped. 'I don't understand. What are you doing?'

'Don't worry, Miriam. I made a promise, centuries ago: one I mean to keep. My soul will be yours.'

A searing light surrounded them, so bright it was blinding, that Miriam's vision was made white as snow. She felt pain, *real* pain, a pain so intense she couldn't speak, couldn't scream. Distantly, she could hear the wind roaring, the crack of thunder.

'And yours will be mine,' Rosamund said.

Then—as the shadows within her fell away—Miriam understood. The grimoire had said that salt and water would weaken a demon; the grimoire had given instructions on the swapping of souls. She should have known. *She should have known.*

It was too late now.

Mortality came to her as a revelation of fire: she felt all the world set itself alight, felt her own life burn from her and then reform, molten. She was falling apart and then she was together again, but the alignment of herself, her heart and bones and blood and darkness, was different and awful and *wrong*. If this was what it was to be born, Miriam wondered that people could ever be frightened of death. Nothing could be worse than this, the knowledge that you were at the mercy of your own flesh.

Her skin prickled. For the first time, she felt the cold. She felt the ship rock beneath her, and her stomach lurch in turn. She felt the thin layer of salt on her hands, the dampness of her clothes, the weight of them. Her legs trembled. There was a tightness in her chest, and after a moment, she gasped a breath: the relief was immediate. She needed to breathe. Miriam had never *needed* to breathe before.

As her vision cleared, she looked at Rosamund.

But she was no longer Rosamund, nor Esther, nor Cybil: she was something else. Her eyes were black and empty, the eyes that studded her arms shimmering with darkness instead of light. When she smiled, the shadows curled themselves possessively around her shoulders.

'What have you done?' said Miriam.

'You know what I've done,' said Harding. 'I swapped them: light for darkness. My soul is yours, and the pact is fulfilled.'

Miriam looked down at her chest, at the light there, blazing still. 'No.'

'A witch's soul, at least.' Harding smiled. 'You haven't lost everything.'

'And *you*—'

'I'll use my immortality well; better than you have, at least. After three lifetimes of suffering, I'll appreciate it far more than you ever did.'

'*No*,' Miriam repeated.

Harding said, '*Yes*, my love. And you know something? Fear suits you, too.'

The storm had stopped. The ship creaked beneath them, thunder silenced, clouds above starting to clear.

Miriam said—too stunned to be angry—'You can't do this to me.'

'I can, and I have.'

'You've *destroyed* me.'

'Don't think of it as a destruction. Think of it as—a remaking. A rebirth.' Harding laughed, tipping her head back. Her voice echoed, skipped over the water like a stone across the pond; it was the most beautiful thing Miriam had ever heard, the most horrifying. 'The same as you gave me, twice before. You should be grateful.'

The icy wind raked itself over Miriam, and she shuddered.

Harding stepped forward and took Miriam's elbow, steering her toward the railing of the deck, facing the prow. Miriam was too numb with shock to resist.

Harding pointed out into the distance. 'There,' she said. 'Do you see it?'

Miriam *did* see it: like stars brought to earth, a collection of tiny lights, scattered by an unseen hand across the horizon. It was the sort of thing she had seen many times, civilisation at a distance—she soared above all things, stepped away from all things, with such ease; it was difficult to be impressed.

But she could not soar above it now. This was humanity, the thousands, the hundreds of thousands, the *millions*. Miriam was not exceptional anymore. She saw the lights of the town and she imagined herself walking among them, peering up at the highest floors of the highest towers, knowing she could not reach them. And perhaps there was something wonderful about that: the impossibility of it all. Something mundane was now as magical to her as any pact, any shadow, any soul.

'New York,' Harding said. 'We've arrived. Three hundred and thirty-two years ago, we made a deal. Do you think it was worth it, even now? To have lost your immortality?'

Miriam considered this—for only a moment. Her teeth chattered. She was so *cold*.

It was horrifying. It was extraordinary.

She said, 'Yes. It was.'

Harding paused at that. For the first time since her transformation, she looked uncertain.

'Enjoy it, then,' she said. 'Your humanity.'

Then the shadows began to seethe around her, and she started to fade from view.

'Wait!' Miriam cried, trying to take hold of the darkness, to pull it back to her—it slipped from her hands, intangible. 'Wait, *please*—'

It was too late. Harding was gone.

Miriam gasped once more, pressing herself over the railing. She was still shaking from the cold, too shocked to cry—she'd never wanted to cry before, but she wanted to now—and all she could think of was Harding's face, Harding's black eyes, the way she had cupped her cheek, had told her she loved her.

'I can't do this,' she said to the shadows, and they trembled as if in sympathy.

'I can't do this,' she said again, voice louder—a realisation, and somehow a glorious one. It turned out weakness was *beautiful*, somehow, that uncertainty was exciting to her in a way that nothing had ever been before. Miriam couldn't do it: she had no idea who she was, what she was. She brought her fingers to her lips, tasted the salt of them, felt the warmth of her tongue and the coldness of her skin. She laughed, panicked and joyous and desperate. 'I can't do this without you, Harding. Don't leave me here. If I must be human to atone, then that is what I'll do. I'll—I'll *welcome* it, even. But I can't do this alone. Don't make me do this alone.'

The Atlantic replied with nothing but shrieking gulls.

'Please,' Miriam said. 'Please.' And then she *did* cry, crying and laughing at the same time, at the cruelty and the perfection of it all. The tears were hot as they streamed down her face, and when she curled her hand around the railing, the metal was unforgiving and immovable.

She stood there until the sun had entirely set, and only then did she accept that no reply was coming.

But when she turned around, Harding was watching her.

She offered Miriam a palm.

Miriam stepped forward, placed her hand in hers. 'You came back.'

'I did. I realised I wanted to. And why shouldn't I have what I want?' Rosamund pulled her closer and raised herself up on the balls of her feet, pressing a kiss to the corner of Miriam's mouth. 'It's lonely, isn't it, Miriam? Being human. But you don't need to be alone—not anymore. I'll stay with you, if you want.'

'Really?'

'Of course. There's one way to ensure it.'

Miriam looked into her eyes. They were dark, darker than shadows, and just as difficult to escape. She could drown in that dark and never see the light again. How many people had looked into Miriam's eyes and seen the same? How many of them had carved their names into Miriam's skin? That soul, now Harding's, had swallowed so many others. And in Harding's face, Miriam could see the face of every person she had ever consumed: the starving and the broken, the desperate and the tearstained. Now she realised that some part of her had wanted to be human, just like them. Since the very moment of her creation, Miriam had playacted as a person, had loved and regretted and hungered for something better. No one had ever forced her to be a woman. She had chosen to be.

Frog or scorpion, the outcome was the same.

Miriam smiled. Harding smiled back.

'Let's make a deal,' she said.

ACKNOWLEDGEMENTS

This was a difficult and wonderful book to write, and I was incredibly fortunate to work with incredible people every step of the way. First and foremost, I must thank my extraordinary agent, Catherine Cho, whose formidable dedication to this manuscript and finding its home was genuinely awe-inspiring—I'll be forever grateful. And my talented editors on both sides of the pond, Vicky Leech Mateos and Ariana Sinclair: What a privilege it is to work with you both.

Thanks also to my team at Bloomsbury: Áine Feeney, Charlotte Webb, Fabrice Wilmann, Abi Walton, Beth Maher, and Ben Chisnall. And to Carmen Balit, for her wonderful work on the spectacular UK and US covers.

And to those at Morrow: DJ DeSmyter, Tess Day, Dale Rohrbaugh, Elina Cohen, Leah Stanisic-Carlson, and my brilliant copyeditor Kathleen Cook.

At Paper Literary, thanks so much to Melissa Pimentel for her advice and insight, and to the amazing foreign-rights team for championing this novel abroad, in particular Elisa Beretta at the Italian Literary Agency for bringing this book to an Italian audience.

To the amazing authors who've inspired me and made me feel so welcome in the publishing community—there are so many of you! Kat Delacorte, Esmie Jikiemi-Pearson, S. T. Gibson, Rosie Talbot, Sarah Underwood, Ania Poranek, Bea Fitzgerald, and all others who've been so kind and supportive.

To Tara Gilbert and Jesse Shuman, who helped me find my feet in the industry and have taught me so much—I'll always be grateful! Thank you always for the support and inspiration you've both offered me.

To my dear friends to whom this book is dedicated—Evangeline Barata, Hannah Whitfield, and Susannah Esiri-Bloom—I adore you all. You've been so wonderful reading drafts of all my books, listening to me kvetch, supporting me through thick and thin. I'm so lucky to have such brilliant women in my life. And to my other wonderful friends who've been so supportive of my writing career and read my work, including but not limited to Yasmin, Jacob, Margarida, Sophie, Ellen, Grace, and Becky. Thank you all so much!

To the readers of my previous novels, who sent me messages of thanks or encouragement, who took the time to post reviews or make edits or share with others... I am utterly indebted to you all, always. You're what makes this worth doing.

To my wonderful family: Estela Cabacungan; Belinda Rasmussen; my grandmother Danielle; my uncle Jonathan; Aunt Alex; my fantastic cousins Arthur, Darius, Louise, and Malte; Mana; and my grandpa Jim. To my father, Kim, your support has always meant the world to me. To my brother, Jonas—I'm so glad I got to watch you grow up into the incredible person you are. You are and always will be much cooler than I am.

To my mother, Caroline, who taught me to love stories, whose imagination and empathy have made me who I am today. I can't believe how lucky I am to have been raised by you.

And to Omar, of course. If I had three lives, I'd love you in all of them.

A NOTE ON THE AUTHOR

NATASHA SIEGEL is a writer of historical fiction, fantasy and romance. She was born and raised in London, where she grew up in a Danish-Jewish family surrounded by stories.

She studied English and History at the University of York, and she has an MA in Early Modern Studies from University College London.

She lives in North West London with her partner and spends her spare time chasing after the family dog, a rescue lurcher named Cleo.